Maradick at Forty
A Transition

by

Hugh Walpole

Double 9
BOOKS

Maradick at Forty
A Transition
by Hugh Walpole

Copyright © 2024

All Rights reserved.

ISBN: 978-93-63055-31-5

Published by

DOUBLE 9 BOOKS

2/13-B, Ansari Road
Daryaganj, New Delhi – 110002
info@double9books.com
www.double9books.com
Tel. 011-40042856

ABOUT THE AUTHOR

English writer Hugh Seymour Walpole, lived from 13 March 1884 to 1 June 1941. Following the publication of The Wooden Horse in 1909, Walpole wrote a lot, finishing at least one book year. The eldest of the Rev. Somerset Walpole's three children, Walpole was born in Auckland, New Zealand. Mildred Helen, née Barham, was his wife (1854-1925). His first piece was published in 1905; he began studying history at Emmanuel College in Cambridge in 1903. He accepted a position as a lay missioner with the Mersey Mission to Seamen in Liverpool upon his graduation from Cambridge in 1906. He obtained employment in 1908 as a French instructor at Epsom College and a book critic for The Standard. Walpole was a passionate music fan, so when he heard a new tenor at the Proms in 1920, he was quite moved and went in search of him. Lauritz Melchior became one of his closest friends, and Walpole contributed significantly to the singer's burgeoning career. Diabetes was detrimental to his health. In May 1941, after participating in a protracted march and giving a speech at the start of Keswick's fundraising "War Weapons Week," he overexerted himself and passed away at Brackenburn from a heart attack at the age of 57. He is interred at Keswick's St. John's graveyard.

CONTENTS

PART I
THE ROOM OF THE MINSTRELS

CHAPTER I
THE PLACE 9

CHAPTER II
IN WHICH OUR HERO AND THE PLACE MEET
ONCE AGAIN 11

CHAPTER III
IN WHICH THE ADMONITUS LOCORUM
BEGINS TO HAVE FUN WITH TWO ENTIRELY
RESPECTABLE MEMBERS OF SOCIETY 22

CHAPTER IV
IN WHICH THE AFORESAID ADMONITUS LEADS
THE AFORESAID MEMBERS OF SOCIETY A DANCE 41

CHAPTER V
MARADICK MAKES A PROMISE AND
MEETS AN ITINERANT OPTIMIST 61

CHAPTER VI
SUPPER WITH JANET MORELLI 79

CHAPTER VII
MARADICK LEARNS THAT "GETTING A VIEW"
MAY HAVE ITS DANGERS AS WELL AS ITS REWARDS ... 96

CHAPTER VIII
THEY ALL EAT CHICKEN IN THE GORSE
AND FLY BEFORE THE STORM 105

PART II
PUNCH

CHAPTER IX

MORELLI BREAKS SOME CROCKERY
AND PLAYS A LITTLE MUSIC....................... 127

CHAPTER X

IN WHICH EVERYONE FEELS THE AFTER
EFFECT OF THE PICNIC.................... 149

CHAPTER XI

OF LOVE—AND THEREFORE TO BE SKIPPED
BY ALL THOSE WHO ARE TIRED OF THE SUBJECT.............. 164

CHAPTER XII

OUR MIDDLE-AGED HERO IS BURDENED
BY RESPONSIBILITY BUT BOLDLY UNDERTAKES
THE ADVENTURE 175

CHAPTER XIII

MORE OF THE ITINERANT OPTIMIST; ALICE
DU CANE ASKS MARADICK A FAVOUR.................. 196

CHAPTER XIV

MARADICK IN A NEW RÔLE—HE AFTERWARDS
SEES TONY'S FACE IN A MIRROR.................... 213

CHAPTER XV

WHY IT IS TO BE THE TWENTY-SEVENTH,
AND WHAT THE CONNEXION WAS BETWEEN
JANET'S BEING FRIGHTENED AND TOBY'S
JOINING THE GREAT MAJORITY.................. 227

PART III
THE TOWER

CHAPTER XVI

MRS. LESTER, TOO, WOULD LIKE IT TO BE
THE TWENTY-SEVENTH BUT MARADICK IS
AFRAID OF THE DEVIL.................... 246

CHAPTER XVII

MORNING AND AFTERNOON OF THE TWENTY-
SEVENTH—TONY, MARADICK, JANET, AND
MISS MINNS HAVE A RIDE AFTER THE WEDDING 260

CHAPTER XVIII

AFTERNOON AND EVENING OF THE TWENTY-
SEVENTH—MARADICK GOES TO CHURCH
AND AFTERWARDS PAYS A VISIT TO MORELLI......................... 280

CHAPTER XIX

NIGHT OF THE TWENTY-SEVENTH—
MARADICK AND MRS. LESTER.. 295

CHAPTER XX

MARADICK TELLS THE FAMILY, HAS
BREAKFAST WITH HIS WIFE, AND SAYS
GOOD-BYE TO SOME FRIENDS 307

CHAPTER XXI

SIX LETTERS.. 322

CHAPTER XXII

THE PLACE 328

PART I
THE ROOM OF THE MINSTRELS

CHAPTER I
THE PLACE

The grey twilight gives to the long, pale stretches of sand the sense of something strangely unreal. As far as the eye can reach, it curves out into the mist, the last vanishing garments, as it were, of some fleeing ghost. The sea comes, smoothly, quite silently, over the breast of it; there is a trembling whisper as it catches the highest stretch of sand and drags it for a moment down the slope, then, with a little sigh, creeps back again a defeated lover.

The sky is grey, with an orange light hovering on its outer edges, the last signal of the setting sun. A very faint mist is creeping gradually over the sea, so faint that the silver circle of the rising moon shines quite clearly through the shadows; but it changes the pale yellow of the ghostly sand into a dark grey land without form and void, seeming for a moment to be one with sea and sky, and then rising again, out of obscurity, into definite substance.

There is silence here in the creek, save for the rustling and whisper of the sea, but round the bend of the rocks the noises of the town come full upon the ear.

The town is built up from the sand on the side of the hill, and rises, tier upon tier, until it finds its pinnacle in the church tower and the roofs of the "Man at Arms."

Now, in the dusk, the lights shine, row upon row, out over the sand. From the market comes the sound of a fair—harsh, discordant tunes softened by the distance.

The church clock strikes eight, and a bell rings stridently somewhere in the depths of the town.

There is a distant rumble, a roar, a flash of light, and a train glides into the station.

But the sea pays no heed, and, round the bend of the creek, the sand gleams white beneath the moon, and the mist rises from the heart of the waves.

CHAPTER II
IN WHICH OUR HERO AND THE PLACE MEET ONCE AGAIN

The Maradicks had reserved four seats by the 10.45, and so really there was no reason for arriving at Paddington a few minutes after ten. But, as it happened, it was quite fortunate, because there were so many people travelling that the porters seemed to have little scruple as to whether you'd reserved something or not, and just went about pulling pink labels off and sticking pink labels on in a way that was really grossly immoral. But Mrs. Maradick, having discovered that her own pink ticket was all right—"James Maradick, Esq.: Four seats by the 10.45. Travelling to Treliss"—could afford to be complacent about other people, and even a little triumphant over the quite amusing misfortunes of a party of six who seemed to have no chance whatever of securing a seat.

Mrs. Maradick always shut her mouth very tight indeed when going off for a holiday. She entered the station with the air of one who had a very sharp battle to fight and wasn't going to be beaten under any circumstances. She selected a porter with the confidence of a very old general who could tell a man at a glance, and she marshalled him up and down the platform with a completeness and a magnificent strategy that left him at last breathless and confused, with scarcely energy enough to show indignation at the threepence with which she rewarded his services. But to-day things were finished sooner than usual, and by half-past ten, with a quarter of an hour to spare, she was able to pay attention to her friends.

Quite a number of them had come to see her off—Mrs. Martin Fraser, Louie Denis, Mrs. Mackintosh, Maggie Crowder, and those silly girls, the Dorringtons; and actually Tom Craddock—very short, very fat, very breathless—a little bit of a bounder, perhaps, but a man who served her husband with a quite pathetic devotion. Yes, of course, *he'd* come to say good-bye to James, so he didn't count in quite the same way, but still it was nice of him.

"Oh! the papers! James, I *must* have papers! Oh! thank you, Mr. Craddock. What? Oh, I think, perhaps, the *Lady's Pictorial* and the *Queen*—

and oh! if you wouldn't mind, the *Daily Mail* and the *Mirror*, and—oh! James has the *Mail*, so perhaps the *Express* would be better—and yes, just something for the girls—what do you say, Annie dear? The *Girl's Realm?* Yes, please, the *Girl's Realm*, Mr. Craddock, and the *Girl's Own Paper* for Isabel. Rather a lot, isn't it, Louie, but it's *such* a long journey—hours and hours—and the girls get so restless."

The ladies gathered in a little phalanx round the carriage window. They always felt this departure of Emmy Maradick's; every year it was the same. Epsom wasn't a bit the same place whilst she was away, and they really couldn't see why she should go away at all. Epsom was at its very nicest in August, and that was the month of the year when she could be most useful. Everyone gave their tennis-parties then; and there were those charming little summer dances, and there was no garden in Epsom like the Maradicks'! Besides, they liked her for herself. Things always seemed to go so well when she was there, she had such a—what was the word?—a French phrase—*savoire-vivre* or *savoir-faire*—yes, it really was a pity.

"We shall miss you, dear." This from Mrs. Mackintosh.

"That's sweet of you, Katie darling. And I shall miss all of you, ever so much. And a hotel's never the same thing, is it? And the garden's just beginning to look lovely. You'll go in, once or twice, won't you, Louie, and see that things are all right? Of course they ought to be; but you never can tell, with quite a new gardener, too. I think he's steady enough—at least, he had excellent testimonials, and James heard from Mr. Templeton, where he was before, you know, that he was quite a reliable man; but you know what it is when one's away, how everything seems to go——Oh! no, it's all right, Mr. Craddock, I don't think it's going just yet. Sit down, Annie dear, and don't lean against the door."

The ladies then passed before the door, one after another, delivered their little messages, and lined up on the other side. Thus Mrs. Mackintosh—

"Well, dear, I *do* hope you have the rippingest time. I'm sure you deserve it after that old bazaar—all the worry——"

And Mrs. Martin Fraser—

"Mind, a postcard, dear—when you get there—just a line. We shall all so want to know."

And Louie Denis—

"Darling, don't forget the sketch you promised. I shall have a frame all ready—waiting."

And Maggie Crowder—

"I hope it will be fine, dear—such a nuisance if it's wet; and then there's our tennis dance next week, it won't be a bit the same thing if——"

Lastly the Dorrington girls together—

"Dear Mrs. Maradick—good-bye—ripping—awfully sorry——" the rest lost in nervous laughter.

And then began that last dreadful minute when you do so wish in spite of yourself that the train would go. You have said your last words, you have given your last embrace, and you stare passionately down the platform hoping for that final whistle and the splendid waving of a green flag.

At last it came. The ladies surged forward in a body and waved their handkerchiefs. Mrs. Maradick leaned for a moment out of the window and waved hers. Tom Craddock shouted something hoarsely about James that no one could hear, and Epsom was finally bereft of its glory.

Mrs. Maradick collected her bags with her rugs, and then considered her girls. They were seated quietly, each in a corner, their faces bent studiously over their magazines. They were very much alike, with straight flaxen hair and pink and white complexions, light blue cotton frocks, and dark green waistbands.

Yes, they were nice girls—they were dear girls. Then she thought of her husband. James Maradick had stood in the background during the farewells. He had, indeed, been busy up to the very last moment, but he was a reserved and silent man, and he really hadn't anything very much to say. He was well over six feet, and broad in proportion. He was clean shaven, with features very strongly marked, and a high forehead from which the hair, closely cut and a little grey at the temples, was brushed back and parted on the right side. His eyes were grey and, at times, wonderfully expressive. Epsom said that he was a dreadful man for looking you through. He wore a suit of dark brown excellently cut. He was sitting now opposite his wife and looking out of the window. He was thinking of Tom Craddock.

"James dear, where is my book? You know—that novel you gave me—'Sir Somebody or other's heir' or something. I just like to know where everything is before I settle down. It was really awfully nice of Louie Denis coming all that way to say good-bye—and of the others too. I wonder Jack Hearne wasn't there. He could have seen Louie back, and it would have been a good chance; but perhaps he didn't know she was coming. It was nice of Mr. Craddock coming up, though of course he came to see you."

She paused for a denial, but he didn't say anything, so she went on— "But, poor fellow, he's getting dreadfully fat. I wonder whether he couldn't take something for it—baths or something—though of course exercise is the thing——"

Maradick looked up. "Yes, poor old Tom. He's a good chap. But he's getting on—we're all getting on. I shall be stout soon—not as young as we were——"

"Nonsense, James. I'm sure you haven't altered a bit since you were twenty. Mr. Craddock was always stout."

She leaned back and put her hand to her forehead. "This train does shake most dreadfully. I'm going to have one of those horrible headaches again. I can feel it coming. Just look for my smelling-salts, will you? I think they are in that little black handbag."

He, wise through much experience, soon found what she wanted, settled cushions at her back, drew the blind down the window to keep the sun from her eyes, and then sank back into his seat again and watched the country flash past.

How many holidays had there been before exactly like this one? He could not count them. There had always been people to see them off—people who had said the same things, made the same jokes, smiled and laughed in the same way. There had always been the same hurried breakfast, the agitated drive, the crowded station, the counting of boxes. There had not, of course, been always the girls; there had been a nurse, and they had travelled in another carriage because the noise troubled his wife. His wife! He looked at her now as she lay back against her cushions with her eyes closed. She had changed very little during all those married years; she was still the same dainty, pretty little woman—something delicate and fragile—whom he had loved so passionately fifteen years before. He thought of those years before he had met her. They had been exciting, adventurous years. Whenever he went out, were it only to pay a call, there had been always the thought that now, perhaps, at last, he was to meet that wonderful Fate that was waiting somewhere for him. He had often thought that he had met it. He remembered Miss Suckling, a pretty girl, a parson's daughter, and then Lucy Armes with her wonderful dark hair and glorious eyes, and then little Rose Craven—yes, he had loved her pretty badly, only some one else had stepped in and carried her off.

And then at last his Fate had come; there had been a delirious courting, a glorious proposal, a rapturous engagement, and a wonderful wedding. It was all so swift and so exciting that he had not had time to think about it at all. The world had seemed a very wonderful, glowing place then, and he had wondered why people thought that rapture faded and gave place to other feelings—mistrust and criticism and then estrangement. He remembered the wonderful letters that he had written, and the sealing of them with great blots of red sealing-wax—every night he had written. On looking back, it seemed that he had done most of the wooing; she had been very charming and dainty and delightful, but she had taken things very quietly and soberly.

And now? He looked at her again, and then out of the window. Nothing had happened, of course. He could look to no definite act or event and point to it as the dividing line. He had discovered very quickly that she had nothing to give him, that there was no question, nor indeed could ever be, of partnership or companionship. That, of course, had been at first. He had put it down to his own stupidity, his ignorance, his blindness; but he had tried her on every side, he had yielded her every allowance, and there was nothing there, simply nothing at all.

Then he had discovered another thing. She had not married him for himself, nor indeed, to do her justice, for his position or anything material that he could give her, but simply that she might have children. He did not know how he had discovered this, but he had known it by the end of the first year of their life together, and then, as their girls had grown, he had seen it increasingly plainly. Any other man would have done equally well— some men might have done better—and so he had done his duty.

Then, when he saw what had happened and that there was an end to his dreams, he had set his teeth and given his soul for the making of money. Whether it had been a fair exchange he did not know, but he had succeeded. They had plenty—plenty for the present, plenty for the future. He need not do another day's work all his life unless he wished, and he was only forty.

He smiled grimly as he looked out of the window. He did not whine or complain. There were doubtless thousands and thousands of other people in the same case—only, what a muddle! what a silly, hideous muddle.

He was forty, and in perfect health. He looked at his wife again. She was happy enough; she had her house and her friends and her girls! She did not want anything at all. And they would go on, of course, to the end of things like that. For years now it had been the same thing. He had played the game, and she had never guessed that he wanted anything; she had probably never thought about him at all.

He was forty, and life was over—its adventures, its emotions, its surprises, its vices, its great romance; he was a bird in a cage, and he had put himself inside and locked the door. He looked at his girls; they aroused no emotion whatever, he did not care for them at all. That was wrong, of course, but it was quite true; and then it was equally true that they didn't care for him. His head began to nod, and at last he was asleep. He was dreaming of the station and poor Tom Craddock—he grew fatter and fatter—he filled the carriage—everyone had to squeeze against the wall to get out of his way—Tom, Tom—this won't do, really—have some consideration. . . .

There was perfect silence in the carriage. The girls had not spoken a word since the journey began. The shining landscape flew past them; things darted up at the window; cows and trees and hedges and telegraph wires leapt wildly up and down for no apparent reason whatever. At last an official arrived and commanded them to take their places for lunch, and there was instant confusion. Mrs. Maradick sailed into the dining-car followed closely by her girls; Maradick brought up the rear.

Her sleep had refreshed her, and she was bright and amusing. "Now, James, look your brightest. Well, Annie darling, and was the *Girl's Realm* amusing? Yes? I'm so glad, and what was the thing that you liked best?"

Annie spoke softly and deliberately. "There was a story, mother, about a girl's adventures in America that I liked rather, also an article on 'How to learn the Violin' was very good." She folded her hands on her lap and looked straight in front of her.

But Mrs. Maradick was deep in the menu. "It's always roast mutton or boiled lamb," she exclaimed; "I never knew anything so monotonous—and cheese *or* sweet"—she dived into her soup with relish.

"It's really not so bad," she cried a little later. "And they do have the things hot, which is so important. Think, girls, we're half-way already. We'll be in splendid time for dinner. I wonder who'll be there this year. There were those nice Jacksons last year—you remember—that Miss Jackson with the fuzzy hair and the short skirt—quite nice people, they were. I don't think you took to them much, James."

"No, I didn't care very much about them," he replied grimly.

"No—such a pity. We so often like different people. And then there were the Dalrymples—quite nice—and Lucy Dalrymple was such a good friend for the girls; you remember Lucy, don't you, dears?"

And so it was to be the same thing again—the same monotonous round that it had been before. He had liked Treliss at first. It had been quaint, romantic, interesting, and he had loved the sea. And then the hotel with its quaint name, "The Man at Arms," and its picturesque Elizabethan architecture. If he could be there alone, just for a day!

They went back to their carriage, and found that the two extra seats, tenanted hitherto by a man and his wife who were negligible from every point of view, were now occupied by two very young people. A further glance classified them as "honeymooners," and Mrs. Maradick found them no longer interesting. She sank into her novel, and there was absolute stillness save for the soft whirr of the wheels beneath them and the rush of the air outside the windows.

The couple opposite him were very quiet—sometimes there was a whisper or a laugh as their eyes met. He knew that look in the eyes and that clasp of the hand. He knew that they were, both of them, outside the train, flying through space, without thought of time or any confining boundaries. What fools they were; he would like to tell them so. He would like to show them that he had been like that once, fifteen years before. He had thought that there would never be an end to it, and it had lasted barely a year.

And so they passed into Cornwall. Every year at that moment there came the same strange thrill, the same emotion as of something ancient and immutable crossing the very modern and changing texture of his own life.

Mrs. Maradick put down her novel and looked about her.

"It will soon be Truro," she said; "and then there'll be all that troublesome changing at Trewth. It's really too absurd that one should have that all the time. Dear Louie! I wonder what she's doing now—gone to look at the garden, I expect, like the dear girl she is. I hope they will give us the same rooms again this year. You wrote for them, didn't you?"

"Yes, dear."

"Because you know last year they tried to put those stupid Jones's in, and if I hadn't made quite a row about it they'd have turned us into the east wing with that great dreary sweep of sea and not a glimpse of the town in front."

He remembered that he had rather envied those rooms in front; there had been a magnificent view of the sea, and a little corner with an old greystone pier and red fishing-boats.

Mrs. Maradick turned her attention to the girls.

"Now, dears, come and talk." They moved towards her, and sat one on each side, expectant. "I had your reports, dears, just before I left home, and they were both most satisfactory. Miss Maynard says about your French, Isabel, that you show some ability and great diligence. Which was Miss Maynard, dear, at the prize-giving? That nice-looking girl with that rather smart frock? I remember noticing her at the time."

"No, mother, that was Miss Lane; Miss Maynard had pince-nez."

"Oh, yes; and beat time to the songs, I remember. As for the arithmetic— —"

He watched them, and knew that he had been forgotten altogether. Were other people's children like that? He knew some little girls who climbed on to their father's knee, and pulled his moustache and clutched his hand; but then, it must be largely his own fault, because he knew that if his girls had tried to do that he would have prevented them. He should not have known what to say!

There was a wonderful glow over the land as they came into Trewth. Already he felt the breath of the sea and the salt sting in the air; down the long platform the winds came laughing and screaming round the boxes and the bundles and the absurd mortals who clung to their hats and cloaks and neatly bound hair.

"Come, girls." Mrs. Maradick collared her porter and shouted "Treliss!" into his ear. "Don't forget anything, James. Have you my green bag and the little brown holdall? and—oh, yes—my black bag there on the seat." She hurried down the platform.

It was always at this moment that a general review took place, and you discovered whether there was going to be anyone you knew at Treliss. Everyone was waiting for the other train to come in, so that you had a splendid time for inspection. Mrs. Maradick was an adept at the difficult art of knowing all about people in half a minute without looking anywhere near them.

"No, the Dalrymples aren't there. I dare say they've come already. What a wind! Really, it's most annoying having to wait. James, have you got all the boxes there? Twelve altogether, counting that portmanteau of yours— —"

She was looking very pretty indeed, her colour heightened by the wind, her hair blowing in little golden whisps about her cheek, the light green of her dress, and the little jingle of gold bracelets, and the pearl necklace at her throat.

They walked up and down the platform silently until the train came in. They never talked when they were together because there was nothing to say. When other people were there they kept it up because they had to play a game, but when they were alone it really wasn't worth while. He wondered sometimes whether she realised that he was there at all. He would have liked to make her angry; he had tried once, but it was no good, she only smiled and stared through him as though he had been a brick wall.

They got into the train and sped on that fairy-journey to Treliss. It was always the most magical thing in the world. The trains helped to add to the romance of it—strange lumbering, stumbling carriages with a ridiculous little engine that shrieked for no reason and puffed and snorted in order to increase its own importance. They often stopped suddenly while something was put right; and they would lie there, for several minutes, in the heart of the golden sand with the blue sea smiling below. He was often tempted to get out and strike across the green dunes, and so down into the heart of the little town with its red roofs and shining spires. He caught the gleam of the wet sand, and he saw the red-brown outline of the rocks as they rounded the curve.

That platform was crowded, and he had some difficulty in securing a cab; but they were settled at last, and turned the corner down the cobbled street.

Mrs. Maradick lay back quite exhausted. "We'd never have got that cab if I hadn't held on to that man's arm," she said breathlessly. "It was positively the last, and we should have had to wait at that station hours before we got another. I call it regular bad management. It's the most important train in the day and they ought to have had plenty of things to meet it."

Treliss has not, as yet, been spoiled by the demands of modern civilisation. "Touristy" it is in August, and the "Man at Arms" is one of the most popular hotels in the West of England; but it has managed to keep undefiled its delightfully narrow streets, its splendidly insufficient shops, its defective lighting, and a quite triumphant lack of competition. Its main street runs steeply up the hill, having its origin in the wet, gleaming sands of the little bay and its triumphant conclusion in the splendid portals and shining terraces of the "Man at Arms." The street is of cobbles, and the houses still hang over it with crooked doorposts and bending gables, so that the Middle Ages stalks by your side as you go, and you expect some darkly cloaked figure to point menacingly with bony fingers up the dark alleys and twisting corners. There are shops of a kind along the way, but no one has ever taken them seriously. "You can buy nothing in Treliss" is the constant cry of all visitors; and it is generally followed by the assertion that you have to pay double West End prices all the same.

The ancient four-wheeler containing the Maradicks bumped slowly up the hill, and at every moment it seemed as though the avalanche of boxes on the top must come down with a rush and a roar and scatter their contents over the cobbles.

Mrs. Maradick said nothing, her mind was fixed on the forthcoming interview with her hotel manager. She would have to fight for those rooms, she knew, but she would win her victory and give no quarter. The charm of the place had caught Maradick once more in its arms. In the dust and heat of the London year he had thought that he had lost it altogether; but now, with a glimpse of the curving bay and the cobbled street, with that scent of spray and onions and mignonette and fishing-nets (it was compounded of all those things) in his nostrils, his heart was beating excitedly, and he was humming a little tune that he had heard the year before. What was the tune? He had forgotten it; he had never thought of it in London, but now it was with him again. He had heard a sailor sing it in an inn on the quay. He had stood outside in the dusk and listened. He remembered the last line:—

And there's gold in the creek and the sands of the sea,
So ho! for the smuggler's cargo!

It meant nothing, of course—a kind of "Pirates of Penzance" absurdity— but the little tune was beating in his brain.

Half-way up the hill there is the market-place, standing on a raised plateau as it were, with the town-hall as its central glory.

They drove through with difficulty, because there was a fair that filled the market and overflowed into the crooked streets up and down the hill. They only caught a passing glimpse as they bumped and stumbled through: a merry-go-round and rows of booths and shouting crowds of men and girls, and a strange toothless old woman in a peaked hat seated on a barrel and selling sweets.

"How they can allow it I don't know!" Mrs. Maradick leant back from the window. "One might as well—Whitechapel, you know, and all that sort of thing."

The last turn of the road to the hotel was very steep indeed, and the weight of the boxes seemed to accumulate with every step; the horses strained and tugged, and for a moment they hesitated and half slid backward, then with a hoarse shout from the driver, a gigantic straining of limb and muscle, they were through the hotel gates. For the hotel stands in its own grounds, and, as you approach it up a drive of larch and birch, its privacy is startling and unusual.

One hundred years before it had been the manor of the estate, the feudal castle of a feudal town, ruling, like some Italian despot, the country at its feet. Then its masters had fallen at the feet of the Juggernaut of modern civilisation and improvement, and their tyranny had passed into the hands of others. For some years the house had lain desolate and threatened to fall into utter ruin and decay; its gardens had been transformed into a wilderness, and its rooms had gathered dust and mildew into their quarters.

Then in 1850 or thereabouts young Mr. Bannister of Manchester had seen his chance. Treliss, at that time, was an obscure and minute village of no fame whatever; but it had fishing, colour and bathing, so Mr. Bannister seized his opportunity.

He had large resources at his back and a very original brain at his service, so he set to work and was immediately successful. He had no intention of turning it into a modern watering-place—there was enough of that (speaking now of 1860) to be done elsewhere—he had Pendragon and Port Looth in his mind. No, he would let it keep its character—indeed, he would force it to keep its character. For some years there were other things to do and his plans were still in embryo; then in 1870 (no longer young Mr. Bannister, but stout and prosperous Mr. Bannister) he took the house in hand.

He interfered in no way with its original character. There were a great many alterations, of course, but, through it all, it retained that seventeenth-century charm and spaciousness—that air of surprise and unexpected corners, the sudden visions of hidden gardens bordered by close-clipped box and the broad depths of wide stone staircases and dark oak panelling—a charm that was to be found in no other hotel in England, a delicious survival that gave you seventeenth-century England without any of its discomforts and drawbacks, sanitary or otherwise.

For now, in 1908, it had all the very latest improvements. There were lifts, and the very best methods of ventilation; the electric light was of a delicious softness, and carpets and chairs were so luxurious that it was difficult to force oneself outside. But then, when you were outside, you wondered how you could ever stay in; for there were lawns with the most wonderful views of the sea and tennis and croquet and badminton and— and now the Maradicks were at the door.

There were several people scattered about the grounds who watched them with curiosity; but it was nearly dressing-time, and already the shadows were lengthening over the lawns and the yews flung long fantastic shapes over the roses and pinks. There was a little breeze in the tops of the trees, and very faintly, like some distant solemn music, came the roll of the sea.

The doors closed on the Maradicks.

.

CHAPTER III
IN WHICH THE ADMONITUS LOCORUM
BEGINS TO HAVE FUN WITH TWO ENTIRELY
RESPECTABLE MEMBERS OF SOCIETY

The hall of the "Man at Arms" was ever a place of mystery. The high roof seemed to pass into infinite space, and on every side there appeared passages and dark oaken doors that led, one fancied, into the very heart of secrecy.

At the other end, opposite to the great doors, was the wide stone staircase leading to other floors, and down the passages to right and left deep-set windows let in shafts of light.

Mrs. Maradick greeted Mr. Bannister cordially, but with reserve. He was a little stout man like a top, scrupulously neat and always correct. He liked to convey to his guests the spirit of the place—that they were received from no mercenary point of view, but rather with the greeting of a friend. Of course, there would ultimately be a bill—it was only the horrid necessity of these, our grasping times—but let it be forgotten and put aside until the final leave-taking. He would have preferred, if possible, to send bills afterwards by post, directed by another hand; but that gave opportunity to unscrupulous adventurers. He would have liked to have entertained the whole world, at any rate the whole social world, free of charge; as it was—well, the bills were heavy. He was always disappointed when his guests failed to grasp this point of view; sometimes they were blustering and domineering, sometimes they were obsequious and timorous—either manner was disagreeable.

About Mrs. Maradick he was never quite sure. He was afraid that she scarcely grasped the whole situation; there was no doubt that she found it impossible to eliminate the bill altogether.

"And our rooms?"

Mrs. Maradick looked up at him. She was smiling, but it was a smile that threatened to disappear.

"I think you will be completely satisfied, Mrs. Maradick. A most delightful suite on the second floor with a view of the sea— —"

"Ah—but our rooms. My husband wrote, I think. We had the same last year—I— —"

"I'm afraid that there's been a little difficulty. We had had previous orders. I would have written to explain had I not been sure that the rooms that we had allotted you would be completely satisfactory."

"Now, Mr. Bannister, that is too bad of you." The smile had gone and her eyes flashed. There was to be a battle as she had foreseen. "We had the same trouble last year, I think— —"

"I am extremely sorry, Mrs. Maradick." He watched her a little anxiously. This was one of the occasions on which he was not certain of her. Would she remember the true ethics of the situation? He hoped for her sake that she would. "I am really very sorry, but I am afraid in this case that there is nothing to be done. Sir Richard and Lady Gale ordered the rooms so long ago as last Christmas. It is of some importance to him, I believe, owing to reasons of health. They laid some stress on it."

"Lady Gale?"

"Yes." Mr. Bannister smiled again. "Really, Mrs. Maradick, I think that you would be perfectly satisfied with your rooms if you would come up for a moment."

"Is Lady Gale here?" Mrs. Maradick was considering.

"Yes. They arrived last night."

"Well," this slowly and with hesitation, "let us go and see them, James. One never knows, after all."

Maradick was relieved. He always waited in the background during these interviews—there were many throughout the year. But this was delightfully over. Had it been the Jones's! Well, he had no doubt that it would have been a prolonged struggle; after all, there *was* a difference.

Mrs. Maradick hurried to the lift, her girls in close attendance, and Mr. Bannister at her side. Maradick was about to follow, when he felt a touch on his elbow and turned round. At his side stood a young man with dark curly hair and a snub nose; not snub enough to mind, but just enough to give you the impression that "everything turned up"—the corners of his mouth and the tips of his ears.

He seemed very young indeed, and had that very clean, clear skin that is the best thing in a decent young man; at least, that is more or less how Maradick summed him up. He was in evening dress, and it suited him.

"I say, I'm most awfully sorry."

He was smiling, so Maradick smiled too.

"I beg your pardon," he said.

"About the rooms, you know. It is my people—my name is Gale—who have them. I'm afraid it was most annoying, and I'm sure my mother will be extremely sorry." He blushed and stammered.

"Oh, please——" Maradick felt quite embarrassed. "It really doesn't matter at all. My wife liked those rooms—we were there last year—and she's naturally asked about them; but these others will suit us splendidly."

"No, but your being there last year seems almost as though you had a right, doesn't it? It is true about my father, it makes rather a difference to him, and they are ripping rooms."

"Yes, of course," Maradick laughed again, "we shall be perfectly comfortable."

There was a moment's pause. There was nothing more to say: then suddenly, simultaneously—"It's very decent . . ." and at that they laughed again. Then Maradick hurried up the stairs.

The boy stayed where he was, the smile lingering at the corners of his mouth. Although it was half-past seven the daylight streamed into the hall. People were passing to and fro, and every now and again glanced at him and caught his infectious smile.

"By Jove, a pretty woman, but a bit of a Tartar," he said, thinking of Mrs. Maradick; then he turned round and walked up the stairs, down a passage to the right, and in a moment young Gale had opened their sitting-room door. The rooms under discussion were certainly very delightful and the view was charming, down over the town and out to the sea beyond. There were glimpses of the crooked streets and twisted gables, and, at last, the little stone pier and a crowd of herring-boats sheltering under its protection.

In the sitting-room was Lady Gale, waiting to go down to dinner. At this time she was about fifty years of age, but she was straight and tall as she had been at twenty. In her young days as Miss Laurence, daughter of Sir Douglas Laurence, the famous Egyptologist, she had been a beauty, and she was magnificent now with a mass of snow-white hair that, piled high on her head, seemed a crown worthily bestowed on her as one of the best and gentlest women of her generation; but perhaps it was her eyes that made you conscious at once of being in the presence of some one whose judgment was unswerving with a tenderness of compassion that made her the confidante of all the failures and wastrels of her day. "Lady Gale will tell you that you are wrong," some one once said of her; "but she will tell you so that her condemnation is better than another person's praise."

At her side stood a man of about thirty, strikingly resembling her in many ways, but lacking in animation and intelligence. You felt that his carefully controlled moustache was the most precious thing about him, and that the cut of his clothes was of more importance than the cut of his character.

"Well, Tony?" Lady Gale greeted him as he closed the door behind him. "Getting impatient? Father isn't ready. I told him that we'd wait for him; and Alice hasn't appeared — —"

"No, not a bit." He came over to her and put his hand on her shoulder. "I'm not hungry, as a matter of fact, too big a tea. Besides, where's Alice?"

"Coming. She told us not to wait, but I suppose we'd better."

"Oh, I say! Mother! I've discovered the most awfully decent fellow downstairs, really; I hope that we shall get to know him. He looks a most thundering good sort."

The red light from the setting sun had caught the church spire and the roofs of the market-place; the town seemed on fire; the noise of the fair came discordantly up to them.

"Another of your awfully decent chaps!" This from his brother. "My dear Tony, you discover a new one every week. Only I wish you wouldn't thrust them on to us. What about the charming painter who borrowed your links and never returned them, and that delightful author-fellow who was so beastly clever that he had to fly the country — —?"

"Oh, chuck it, Rupert. Of course one makes mistakes. I learnt a lot from Allison, and I know he always meant to send the links back and forgot; anyhow he's quite welcome to them. But this chap's all right—he is really— he looks jolly decent— —"

"Yes; but, Tony," said his mother, laughing, "I agree with Rupert there. Make your odd acquaintances if you like, but don't bring them down on to us; for instance, that horrid little fat man you liked so much at one time, the poet— —"

"Oh, Trelawny. He's all right now. He's going to do great things one day."

"And meanwhile borrows money that he never intends to repay. No, Tony, these sudden acquaintances are generally a mistake, take my word for it. How long have you known this man downstairs?"

"Only a minute. He's just arrived with his wife and two little girls."

"And you know him already?"

"Well, you see his wife wanted these rooms—said she ordered them or something—and then went for old Bannister about it, and he, naturally enough, said that we'd got them; and then he stuck it on about their rooms and said that they were much the nicest rooms in the place, and then she went off fairly quiet."

"Well, where did the man come in?"

"He didn't at all, and, from the look of her, I shouldn't think that he ever does. But I went up and said I was jolly sorry, and all that sort of thing——"

"Well, I'm——!" from Rupert. "Really, Tony! And what on earth was there to apologise for! If we are going to start saying pretty things to everyone in the hotel who wants these rooms we've got our work cut out."

"Oh! I didn't say pretty things; I don't know why I really said anything at all. The spirit moved me, I suppose. I'm going to be friends with that man. I shall like him."

"How do you know?"

"By three infallible signs. He looks you straight in the eyes, he's got a first-class laugh, and he doesn't say much."

"Characteristics of most of the scoundrels in the kingdom," Rupert said, yawning. "By Jove! I wish father and Alice would hurry up."

A girl came in at that moment; Tony danced round her and then caught her hand and led her to his mother.

"Your Majesty! I have the honour of presenting her Grace the Duchess of——"

But the girl broke from him. "Don't, Tony, please, you're upsetting things. Please, Lady Gale, can't we go down? I'm so hungry that no ordinary dinner will ever satisfy me."

"Don't you pretend, Alice," cried Tony, laughing. "It's the dress, the whole dress, and nothing but the dress. That we may astonish this our town of Treliss is our earnest and most humble desire." He stopped. "It is high time, you know, mother; nearly half-past eight."

"I know, but it's your father. You might go and see if he's nearly ready, Tony."

As he moved across the room her eyes followed him with a devotion that was the most beautiful thing in the world. Then she turned to the girl.

Miss Alice Du Cane was looking very lovely indeed. Her dress was something wonderful in pink, and that was all that the ordinary observer would have discovered about it; very beautiful and soft, tumbling into all manner of lines and curves and shades as she walked. Quite one of the beauties of the season, Miss Alice Du Cane, and one of the loveliest visions that your dining-halls are likely to behold, Mr. Bannister! She was dark and tall and her smile was delightful—just a little too obviously considered, perhaps, but nevertheless delightful!

"Yes, dear, you look very nice." Lady Gale smiled at her. "I only wish that all young ladies nowadays would be content to dress as simply; but, of course, they haven't all got your natural advantages!"

Then the door opened once more and Sir Richard Gale appeared, followed closely by Tony. He was a man of magnificent presence and wonderful preservation, and he was probably the most completely selfish egoist in the kingdom; on these two facts he had built his reputation. The first gave him many admirers and the second gave him many enemies, and a splendid social distinction was the result.

He was remarkably handsome, in a military-cum-Embassy manner; that is, his moustache, his walk, and the swing of his shoulders were all that they should be. He walked across the room most beautifully, but, perhaps, just a little too carefully, so that he gave the onlooker the impression of something rather precariously kept together—it was the only clue to his age.

He spent his life in devising means of enabling his wife to give sign and evidence to the world of her affection. He was entirely capricious and unreliable, and took violent dislikes to very many different kinds of people. He had always been a very silent man, and now his conversation was limited to monosyllables; he disliked garrulous persons, but expected conversation to be maintained.

The only thing that he said now was "Dinner!" but everyone knew what he meant, and an advance was made: Lady Gale and her husband, Miss Du Cane between Rupert and Tony, accompanied by laughter and a good deal of wild jesting on the part of the last named.

The going in to dinner at home was always a most solemn affair, even when no one save the family were present. Sir Richard was seen at his best in the minutes during which the procession lasted, and it symbolised the dignity and solemnity befitting his place and family. The Gales go in to dinner! and then, Sir Richard Gale goes in to dinner!—it was the moment of the day.

And now how greatly was the symbolism increased. Here we are in the heart of the democracy, sitting down with our fellow-creatures, some of whom are most certainly commoners, sitting down without even a raised platform; not at the same table, it is true, but nevertheless on the same floor, beneath the same ceiling! It was indeed a wonderful and truly British ceremony.

He generally contrived to be a little late, but to-day they were very late indeed, and his shoulders were raised just a little higher and his head was just a little loftier than usual.

The room was full, and many heads were raised as they entered. They were a fine family, no doubt—Sir Richard, Lady Gale, Rupert—all distinguished and people at whom one looked twice, and then Alice was lovely. It was only Tony, perhaps, who might have been anybody; just a nice clean-looking boy people were inclined to call him, but they always liked him. Their table was at the other end of the room, and the procession was slow. Tony always hated it—"making a beastly monkey-show of oneself and the family"—but his father took his time.

The room was charming, with just a little touch of something unusual. Mr. Bannister liked flowers, but he was wise in his use of them; and every table had just that hint of colour, red and blue and gold, that was needed, without any unnecessary profusion.

There were a great many people—the season was at its height—and the Maradicks, although late, were fortunate to have secured a table by the windows. The girls were tired and were going to have supper in bed—a little fish, some chicken and some shape—Mrs. Maradick had given careful directions.

Through the windows came the scents of the garden and a tiny breeze that smelt of the sea. There were wonderful colours on the lawn outside. The moon was rising, a full moon like a stiff plate of old gold, and its light flung shadows and strange twisted shapes over the grass. The trees stood, tall and dark, a mysterious barrier that fluttered and trembled in the little wind and was filled with the whispers of a thousand voices. Beyond that again was the light pale quivering blue of the night-sky, in which flashed and wheeled and sparkled the stars.

Mr. and Mrs. Maradick were playing the game very thoroughly to-night; you could not have found a more devoted couple in the room. She looked charming in her fragile, kittenish manner, something fluffy and white and apparently simple, with a slender chain of gold at her throat and a small spray of diamonds in her hair. She was excited, too, by the place and the people and the whole change. This was, oh! most certainly! better than Epsom, and Mrs. Martin Fraser and Louie had faded into a very distant past. This was her métier!—this, with its lights and its fashion! Why didn't they live in London, really in London? She must persuade James next year. It would be better for the girls, too, now that they were growing up; and they might even find somewhere with a garden. She chattered continuously and watched for the effect on her neighbours. She had noticed one man whisper, and several people had looked across.

"It is so wonderful that I'm not more tired after all that bolting and jolting, and you know I felt that headache coming all the time. . . only just kept it at bay. But really, now, I'm quite hungry; it's strange. I never could eat anything in Epsom. What is there?"

The waiter handed her the card. She looked up at him with a smile. "Oh! no consommé! thank you. Yes, Filet de sole and Poularde braisée—oh! and Grouse à la broche—of course—just in time, James, to-day's only the fifteenth. Cerises Beatrice—Friandises—oh! delightful! the very thing."

"Bannister knows what to give us," he said, turning to her.

She settled back in her seat with a little purr of pleasure. "I hope the girls had what they wanted. Little dears! I'm afraid they were dreadfully tired."

He watched her curiously. There had been so many evenings like this—evenings when those around him would have counted him a lucky fellow; and yet he knew that he might have been a brick wall and she would have talked in the same way. He judged her by her eyes—eyes that looked through him, past him, quite coldly, with no expression and no emotion. She simply did not realise that he was there, and he suddenly felt cold and miserable and very lonely. Oh! if only these people round him knew, if they could only see as he saw. But perhaps they were, many of them, in the same position. He watched them curiously. Men and women laughing and chatting with that intimate note that seemed to mean so much and might, as he knew well, mean so little. Everybody seemed very happy; perhaps they were. Oh! he was an old, middle-aged marplot, a kill-joy, a skeleton at the feast.

"Isn't it jolly, dear?" he said, laughing across the table; "this grouse is perfection."

"Tell me," she said, with that little wave of her wrist towards him that he knew so well—"tell me where the Gales are. I don't suppose you know, though, but we might guess."

"I do know," he answered, laughing; "young Gale came and spoke to me just before I came up to dress. He seemed a nice young fellow. He came up and said something about the rooms—he had heard you speaking to Bannister. They came in just now; a fine-looking elderly man, a lady with beautiful white hair, a pretty girl in pink."

"Oh! of course! I noticed them! Oh, yes! one could tell they were somebody." She glanced round the room. "Yes, there they are, by the wall at the back; quite a lovely girl!" She looked at them curiously. "Oh, you spoke to young Gale, did you? He looks quite a nice boy. I hope they have liked the rooms, and, after all, ours aren't bad, are they? Really, I'm not sure that in some ways——"

She rattled on, praising the grouse, the bread sauce, the vegetables. She speculated on people and made little jokes about them, and he threw the ball back again, gaily, merrily, light-heartedly.

"You know I don't think Louie really cares about him. I often hoped for her sake, poor girl, that she did, because there's no denying that she's getting on; and it isn't as if she's got looks or money, and it's a wonder that he's stuck to her as he has. I've always said that Louie was a marrying woman and she'd make him a good wife, there's no doubt of that."

Her little eyes were glittering like diamonds and her cheeks were hot. People were arriving at the fruit stage, and conversation, which had murmured over the soup and hummed over the meat, seemed to Maradick to shriek over the grapes and pears. How absurd it all was, and what was the matter with him? His head was aching, and the silver and flowers danced before his eyes. The great lines of the silver birch were purple over the lawn and the full moon was level with the windows. It must have been the journey, and he had certainly worked very hard these last months in town; but he had never known his nerves like they were to-night, indeed he had often wondered whether he had any nerves at all. Now they were all on the jump; just as though, you know, you were on one of those roundabouts, the horses jumping up and down and round, and the lights and the other people jumping too. There was a ridiculous man at a table close to them with a bald head, and the electric light caught it and turned it into a fiery ball. Such a bald head! It shone like the sun, and he couldn't take his eyes away from it: and still his wife went on talking, talking, talking—that same little laugh, that gesticulating with the fingers, that glance round to see whether people had noticed. In some of those first years he had tried to make her angry, had contradicted and laughed derisively, but it had had no effect. She simply hadn't considered him. But she *must* consider him! It was absurd; they were husband and wife. He had said—what had he said that first day in church? He couldn't remember, but he knew that she ought to consider him, that she oughtn't to look past him like that just as though he wasn't there. He pulled himself together with a great effort and finished the champagne in his glass: the waiter filled it again; then he leant back in his chair and began to peel an apple, but his fingers were trembling.

"That woman over there," said Mrs. Maradick, addressing a table to her right and then glancing quickly to her left, "is awfully like Mrs. Newton Bassett—the same sort of hair, and she's got the eyes. Captain Bassett's coming home in the autumn, I believe, which will be rather a blow for Muriel Bassett if all they say is true. He's been out in Central Africa or somewhere, hasn't he? Years older than her, they say, and as ugly as—Oh, well! people do talk, but young Forrest has been in there an awful lot lately, and he's as nice a young fellow as you'd want to meet."

He couldn't stand it much longer, so he put the apple down on his plate and finished the champagne.

"If I went out to Central Africa," he said slowly, "I wonder whether——"

"These pears are delicious," she answered, still looking at the table to her left.

"If I went out to Central Africa——" he said again.

She leant forward and played with the silver in front of her.

"Look here, I want you to listen." He leant forward towards her so that he might escape the man with the bald head. "If I went out to Central Africa, you—well, you wouldn't much mind, would you? Things would be very much the same. It's rather comforting to think that you wouldn't very much mind."

Maradick's hands were shaking, but he spoke quite calmly, and he did not raise his voice because he did not want the man with the bald head to hear.

"You wouldn't mind, would you? Why don't you say?" Then suddenly something seemed to turn in his brain, like a little wheel, and it hurt. "It's been going on like this for years, and how long do you think I'm going to stand it? You don't care at all. I'm just like a chair, a table, anything. I say it's got to change—I'll turn you out—won't have anything more to do with you—you're not a wife at all—a man expects——" He did not know what he was saying, and he did not really very much care. He could not be eloquent or dramatic about it like people were in books, because he wasn't much of a talker, and there was that little wheel in his head, and all these people talking. It had all happened in the very briefest of moments. He hardly realised at the time at all, but afterwards the impression that he had of it was of his fingers grating on the table-cloth; they dug into the wood of the table.

For only a moment his fingers seemed, of their own accord, to rise from the table and stretch out towards her throat. Sheer animal passion held him, passion born of her placidity and indifference. Then suddenly he caught her eyes; she was looking at him, staring at him, her face was very white, and he had never seen anyone look so frightened. And then all his rage left him and he sat back in his chair again, shaking from head to foot. There were all those years between them and he had never said a word until now! Then he felt horribly ashamed of himself; he had been intolerably rude, to a lady. He wasn't quite certain of what he had said.

"I beg your pardon," he said slowly, "I have been very rude. I didn't quite know what I was saying."

For a moment they were silent. The chatter went on, and the waiter was standing a little way away; he had not heard anything.

"I am rather tired," said Mrs. Maradick; "I think I'll go up, if you don't mind."

He rose and offered her his arm, and they went out together. She did not look at him, and neither of them spoke.

Tony Gale was absurdly excited that evening, and even his father's presence scarcely restrained him. Sir Richard never said very much, but he generally looked a great deal; to-night he enjoyed his dinner. Lady Gale watched Tony a little anxiously. She had always been the wisest of mothers in that she had never spoken before her time; the whole duty of parents lies in the inviting of their children's confidence by never asking for it, and she had never asked. Then she had met Miss Alice Du Cane and had liked her, and it had struck her that here was the very girl for Tony. Tony liked her and she liked Tony. In every way it seemed a thing to be desired, and this invitation to accompany them to Cornwall was a natural move in the right direction. They were both, of course, very young; but then people did begin very young nowadays, and Tony had been "down" from Oxford a year and ought to know what he was about. Alice was a charming girl, and the possessor of much sound common-sense; indeed, there was just the question whether she hadn't got a little too much. The Du Canes were excellently connected; on the mother's side there were the Forestiers of Portland Hall down in Devon, and the Craddocks of Newton Chase—oh!

that was all right. And then Tony had a fortune of his own, so that he was altogether independent, and one couldn't be quite sure of what he would do, so that it was a satisfaction to think that he really cared for somebody that so excellently did! It promised to be a satisfactory affair all round, and even Sir Richard, a past master in the art of finding intricate objections to desirable plans, had nothing to say. Of course, it was a matter that needed looking at from every point of view. Of the Du Canes, there were not many. Colonel Du Cane had died some years before, and Lady Du Cane, a melancholy, faded lady who passed her time in such wildly exciting health-resorts as Baden-Baden and Marienbad, had left her daughter to the care of her aunt, Miss Perryn. There *were* other Du Canes, a brother at Eton and a sister in France, but they were too young to matter; and then there was lots of money, so really Alice had nothing to complain of.

But Lady Gale was still old-fashioned enough to mind a little about mutual affection. Did they really care for each other? Of course it was so difficult to tell about Tony because he cared about everyone, and was perpetually enthusiastic about the most absurdly ordinary people. His geese were all swans, there was no question; but then, as he always retorted, that was better than thinking that your swans, when you did meet them, were all geese. Still, it did make it difficult to tell. When, for instance, he rated a man he had met in the hall of the hotel for the first time, and for one minute precisely, on exactly the same scale as he rated friends of a lifetime, what were you to think? Then Alice, too, was difficult.

She was completely self-possessed and never at a loss, and Lady Gale liked people who made mistakes. You always knew exactly what Alice would say or think about any subject under discussion. She had the absolutely sane and level-headed point of view that is so annoying to persons of impulsive judgment. Not that Lady Gale was impulsive; but she was wise enough to know that some of the best people were, and she distrusted old heads on young shoulders. Miss Du Cane had read enough to comment sensibly and with authority on the literature of the day. She let you express your opinion and then agreed or differed with the hinting of standards long ago formed and unflinchingly sustained, and some laughing assertion of her own ignorance that left you convinced of her wisdom. She always asserted that she was shallow, and shallowness was therefore the last fault of which she was ever accused.

She cared for Tony, there was no doubt of that; but then, so did everybody. Lady Gale's only doubt was lest she was a little too matter-of-fact about it all; but, after all, girls were very different nowadays, and the display of any emotion was the unpardonable sin.

"Grouse! Hurray!" Tony displayed the menu. "The first of the year. I'm jolly glad I didn't go up with Menzies to Scotland; it's much better here, and I'm off shooting this year——"

"That's only because you always like the place you're in better than any other possible place, Tony," said Alice. "And I wish I had the virtue. Oh! those dreary months with mother at Baden! They're hanging over me still."

"Well, I expect they gave your mother a great deal of pleasure, my dear," said Lady Gale, "and that after all is something, even nowadays."

"No, they didn't, that's the worst of it. She didn't want me a bit. There was old Lady Pomfret and Mrs. Rainer, and oh! lots of others; bridge, morning, noon, and night, and I used to wander about and mope."

"You ought to have been writing letters to Tony and me all the time," said Rupert, laughing. "You'll never get such a chance again."

"Well, I did, didn't I, Tony? Speak up for me, there's a brick!"

"Well, I don't know," said Tony. "They were jolly short, and there didn't seem to be much moping about it."

"That was to cheer you up. You didn't want me to make you think that I was depressed, did you?"

Sir Richard had finished his grouse and could turn his attention to other things. He complained of the brilliancy of the lights, and some of them were turned out.

"Where's your man, Tony?" said Rupert. "Let's see him."

"Over there by the window—a man and a woman at a table by themselves—a big man, clean shaven. There, you can see him now, behind that long waiter—a pretty woman in white, laughing."

"Oh, well! He's better than some," Rupert grudgingly admitted. "Not so bad—strong, muscular, silent hero type—it's a pretty woman." He fastened his eye-glass, an attention that he always paid to anyone who really deserved it.

"Yes, I like him," said Lady Gale; "what did you say his name was?"

"I didn't quite catch it; Marabin, or Mara—no, I don't know—Mara—something. But I say, what are we going to do to-night? We must do something. I was never so excited in my life, and I don't a bit know why."

"Oh, that will pass," said Rupert; "we know your moods, Tony. You must take him out into the garden, Alice, and quiet him down. Oh! look, they're going, those Marabins or whatever their names are. She carries herself well, that woman."

Dinner always lasted a long time, because Sir Richard enjoyed his food and had got a theory about biting each mouthful to which he entirely attributed his healthy old age; it entailed lengthy meals.

They were almost the last people in the room when at length they rose to go, and it was growing late.

"It's so sensible of them not to pull blinds down," said Tony, "the moon helps digestion." Sir Richard, as was his custom, went slowly and majestically up to his room, the others into the garden.

"Take Alice to see the view from the terraces, Rupert," said Lady Gale. "Tony and I will walk about here a little."

She put her arm through her son's, and they passed up and down the walks in front of the hotel. The vision of the town in the distance was black, the gardens were cold and white under the moon.

"Oh! it is beautiful." Lady Gale drew a deep breath. "And when I'm in a place like this, and it's England, I'm perpetually wondering why so many people hurry away abroad somewhere as soon as they've a minute to spare. Why, there's nothing as lovely as this anywhere!"

Tony laughed. "There's magic in it," he said. "I hadn't set foot in the place for quarter of an hour before I knew that it was quite different from all the other places I'd ever been in. I wasn't joking just now at dinner. I meant it quite seriously. I feel as if I were just in for some enormous adventure—as if something important were most certainly going to happen."

"Something important's always happening, especially at your time of life; which reminds me, Tony dear, that I want to talk to you seriously."

He looked up in her face. "What's up, mother?"

"Nothing's up, and perhaps you will think me a silly interfering old woman; but you know mothers are queer things, Tony, and you can't say that I've bothered you very much in days past."

"No." He suddenly put his arm round her neck, pulled her head towards his and kissed her. "It's all right. There's nobody here to see, and it wouldn't matter a bit if there were. No, you're the very sweetest and best mother that mortal man ever had, and you're cursed with an ungrateful, undutiful scapegrace of a son, more's the pity."

"Ah," she said, shaking her head, "that's just what I mean. Your mother is a beautiful and delightful joke like everything and everybody else. It's time, Tony, that you were developing. You're twenty-four, and you seem to me to be exactly where you were at eighteen. Now I don't want to hurry or worry you, but the perpetual joke won't do any longer. It isn't that I myself want you to be anything different, because I don't. I only want you to be happy; but life's hard, and I don't think you can meet it by playing with it."

He said nothing, but he gave her arm a little squeeze.

"Then you know," she went on, "you have absolutely no sense of proportion. Everybody and everything are on exactly the same scale. You don't seem to me to have any standard by which you estimate things. Everybody is nice and delightful. I don't believe you ever disliked anybody, and it has always been a wonder to all of us that you haven't lost more from suffering so many fools gladly. I always used to think that as soon as you fell in love with somebody—really and properly fell in love with some nice girl—that that seriousness would come, and so I didn't mind. I don't want to hurry you in that direction, dear, but I would like to see you settled. Really, Tony, you know, you haven't changed at all, you're exactly the same; so much the same that I've wondered a little once or twice whether you really care for anybody."

"Poor old mother, and my flightiness has worried you, has it? I am most awfully sorry. But God made the fools as well as the wits, and He didn't ask the fools which lot they wanted to belong to."

"No, but, Tony, you aren't a fool, that's just it. You've got the brain of the family somewhere, only you seem to be ashamed of it and afraid that people should know you'd got it, and your mother would rather they did know. And then, dear, there is such a thing as family pride. It isn't snobbery, although it looks like it; it only means, don't be too indiscriminate. Don't have just anybody for a friend. It doesn't matter about their birth, but it does matter about their opinions and surroundings. Some of them have been— well, scarcely clean, dear. I'm sure that Mr. Templar wasn't a nice man, although I dare say he was very clever; and that man to-night, for instance: I dare say he's an excellent man in every way, but you owe it to the family to find out just a little about him first; you can't tell just in a minute——"

He stopped her for a minute and looked up at her quite seriously. "I'll be difficult to change, mother, I'm afraid. How you and father ever produced such a vagabond I don't know, but vagabond I am, and vagabond I'll remain in spite of Oxford and the Bond Street tailor. But never you grieve, mother dear, I'll promise to tell you everything—don't you worry."

"Yes. But what about settling?"

"Oh, settling!" he answered gravely. "Vagabonds oughtn't to marry at all."

"But you're happy about everything? You're satisfied with things as they are?"

"Of course!" he cried. "Just think what kind of a beast I'd be if I wasn't. Of course, it's splendid. And now, mother, the jaw's over and I'm the very best of sons, and it's a glorious night, and we'll be as happy as the day is long."

They knelt on the seat at the south end and looked down into the crooked streets; the moon had found its way there now, and they could almost read the names on the shops.

Suddenly Lady Gale put her hand against his cheek. "Tony, dear, I care for you more than anything in the world. You know it. And, Tony, always do what you feel is the straight thing and I shall know it is right for you, and I shall trust you; but, Tony, don't marry anybody unless you are quite certain that it is the only person. Don't let anything else influence you. Marriage with the wrong person is——" Her voice shook for a moment. "Promise me, Tony."

"I promise," he answered solemnly, and she took his arm and they walked back down the path.

Rupert and Alice were waiting for them and they all went in together. Lady Gale and Rupert said good night. Rupert was always tired very early in the evening unless there was bridge or a dance, but Alice and Tony sat in the sitting-room by the open window watching the moonlight on the sea and listening to the muffled thunder of the waves. Far out into the darkness flashed the Porth Allen Lighthouse.

For a little while they were silent, then Tony suddenly said:

"I say, am I awfully young?"

She looked up. "Young?"

"Yes. The mater has been talking to me to-night. She says that it is time that I grew up, that I haven't grown a bit since I was eighteen, and that it must be very annoying for everybody. Have you felt it, too?"

"Well, of course I know what she means. It's absurd, but I always feel years older than you, although by age I'm younger. But oh! it's difficult to explain; one always wants to rag with you. I'm always at my silliest when you're there, and I *hate* being at my silliest."

"I know you do, that's your worst fault. But really, this is rather dreadful. I must proceed to grow up. But tell me honestly, am I a fool?"

"No, of course you're not, you're awfully clever. But that's what we all think about you—you could do so many things and you're not doing anything."

He sat on the window-sill, swinging his legs.

"There was once," he began, "the King of Fools, and he had a most splendid and widely attended Court; and one day the Wisest Man in Christendom came to see and be seen, and he talked all the wisest things that he had ever learnt, and the fools listened with all their ears and thought that they had never heard such folly, and after a time they shouted derisively, not knowing that he was the Wisest Man, 'Why, he is the biggest fool of them all!'"

"The moral being?"

"Behold, the Wisest Man!" cried Tony, pointing dramatically at his breast. "There, my dear Alice, you have the matter in a nutshell."

"Thanks for the compliment," said Alice, laughing, "only it is scarcely convincing. Seriously, Tony, Lady Gale is right. Don't be one of the rotters like young Seins or Rocky Culler or Dick Staines, who spend their whole day in walking Bond Street and letting their heads wag. Not, of course, that you'd ever be that sort, but it would be rather decent if you did something."

"Well, I do," he cried.

"What?" she said.

"I can shoot a gun, I can ride a horse, I can serve corkers from the back line at tennis, and score thirty at moderate cricket; I can read French, German, Italian. I can play bridge—well, fairly—I can speak the truth, eat meringues all day with no evil consequences, stick to a pal, and walk for ever and ever, Amen. Oh, but you make me vain!"

She laughed. "None of those things are enough," she said. "You know quite well what I mean. You must take a profession; why not Parliament, the Bar, writing?—you could write beautifully if you wanted to. Oh, Tony!"

"I have one," he said.

"Now! What?"

"The finest profession in the world—Odysseus, Jason, Cœur-de-Lion, St. Francis of Assisi, Wilhelm Meister, Lavengro. By the beard of Ahasuerus I am a wanderer!"

He struck an attitude and laughed, but there was a light in his eyes and his cheeks were flushed.

Then he added:

"Oh! what rot! There's nobody so boring as somebody on his hobby. I'm sorry, Alice, but you led me on; it's your own fault."

"Do you know," she said, "that is the first time, Tony, that I've ever heard you speak seriously about anything, and really you don't do it half badly. But, at the same time, are you quite sure that you're right . . . now? What I mean is that things have changed so. I've heard people talk like that before, but it has generally meant that they were unemployed or something and ended up by asking for sixpence. It seems to me that there's such a lot to be done now, and such a little time to do it in, that we haven't time to go round looking for adventure; it isn't quite right that we should if we're able-bodied and can work."

"Why, how serious we are all of a sudden," he cried. "One would think you ran a girls club."

"I do go down to Southwark a lot," she answered. "And we're badly in need of subscriptions. I'd meant to ask you before."

"Who's the unemployed now?" he said, laughing. "I thought it would end in that."

"Well, I must go to bed," she said, getting up from the window-sill. "It's late and cold, and I'm sure we've had a most inspiring talk on both sides. Good night, old boy."

"Ta-ta," said Tony.

But after she had gone he sat by the window, thinking. Was it true that he was a bit of a loafer? Had he really been taking things too easily? Until these last two days he had never considered himself or his position at all. He had always been radiantly happy; self-questioning had been morbid and unnecessary. It was all very well for pessimists and people who wrote to the *Times*, but, with Pope, he hummed, "Whatever is, is best," and thought no more about it.

But this place seemed to have changed all that. What was there about the place, he wondered? He had felt curiously excited from the first moment of his coming there, but he could give no reason for it. It was a sleepy little place, pretty and charming, of course, but that was all. But he had known no rest or peace; something must be going to happen. And then, too, there was Alice. He knew perfectly well why she had been asked to join them, and he knew that she knew. Before they had come down he had liked the idea. She was one of the best and true as steel. He had almost decided, after all, it was time that they settled down. And then, on coming here, everything had been different. Alice, his father, his mother, Rupert had changed; something was wrong. He did not, could not worry it out, only it was terribly hot, it was a beautiful night outside, and he wouldn't be able to sleep for hours.

He passed quietly down the stairs and out into the garden. He walked down to the south end. It was most wonderful—the moon, the stars, the whirling light at sea, and, quite plainly, the noise of the fair.

He leant over the wall and looked down. He was suddenly conscious that some one else was there; a big man, in evening dress, smoking a cigar. Something about him, the enormous arms or the close-cropped hair, was familiar.

"Good evening," said Tony.

It was Maradick. He looked up, and Tony at once wished that he hadn't said anything. It was the face of a man who had been deep in his own thoughts and had been brought back with a shock, but he smiled.

"Good evening. It's wonderfully beautiful, isn't it?"

"I'm Gale," said Tony apologetically, "I'm sorry if I interrupted you."

"Oh no," Maradick answered. "One can think at any time, and I wanted company. I suppose the rest of the hotel is in bed—rather a crime on a night like this." Then he suddenly held up a warning finger. "Listen!" he said.

Quite distinctly, and high above the noise of the fair, came the voice of a man singing in the streets below. He sang two verses, and then it died away.

"It was a tune I heard last year," Maradick said apologetically. "I liked it and had connected it with this place. I——" Then suddenly they heard it again.

They were both silent and listened together.

CHAPTER IV
IN WHICH THE AFORESAID ADMONITUS LEADS THE AFORESAID MEMBERS OF SOCIETY A DANCE

The two men stood there silently for some minutes; the voice died away and the noise of the fair was softer and less discordant; past them fluttered two white moths, the whirr of their wings, the heavy, clumsy blundering against Tony's coat, and then again the silence.

"I heard it last year, that song," Maradick repeated; he puffed at his cigar, and it gleamed for a moment as some great red star flung into the sky a rival to the myriads above and around it. "It's funny how things like that stick in your brain—they are more important in a way than the bigger things."

"Perhaps they are the bigger things," said Tony.

"Perhaps," said Maradick.

He fell into silence again. He did not really want to talk, and he wondered why this young fellow was so persistent. He was never a talking man at any time, and to-night at any rate he would prefer to be left alone. But after all, the young fellow couldn't know that, and he had offered to go. He could not think connectedly about anything; he could only remember that he had been rude to his wife at dinner. No gentleman would have said the things that he had said. He did not remember what he had said, but it had been very rude; it was as though he had struck his wife in the face.

"I say," he said, "it's time chaps of your age were in bed. Don't believe in staying up late." He spoke gruffly, and looked over the wall on to the whirling lights of the merry-go-round in the market-place.

"You said, you know," said Tony, "that you wanted company; but, of course——" He moved from the wall.

"Oh! stay if you like. Young chaps never will go to bed. If they only knew what they were laying in store for themselves they'd be a bit more careful. When you get to be an old buffer as I am——"

"Old!" Tony laughed. "Why, you're not old."

"Aren't I? Turned forty, anyhow."

"Why, you're one of the strongest-looking men I've ever seen." Tony's voice was a note of intense admiration.

Maradick laughed grimly. "It isn't your physical strength that counts, it's the point of view—the way you look at things and the way people look at you."

The desire to talk grew with him; he didn't want to think, he couldn't sleep—why not talk?

"But forty anyhow," said Tony, "isn't old. Nobody thinks you're old at forty."

"Oh, don't they? Wait till you are, you'll know."

"Well, Balzac——"

"Oh, damn your books! what do they know about it? Everyone takes things from books nowadays instead of getting it first hand. People stick themselves indoors and read a novel or two and think they know life—such rot!"

Tony laughed. "I say," he said, "you don't think like that always, I know—it's only just for an argument."

Maradick suddenly twisted round and faced Tony. He put his hand on his shoulder.

"I say, kid," he said, "go to bed. It doesn't do a chap of your age any good to talk to a pessimistic old buffer like myself. I'll only growl and you won't be the better for it. Go to bed!"

Tony looked up at him without moving.

"I think I'll stay. I expect you've got the pip, and it always does a chap good, if he's got the pip, to talk to somebody."

"Have you been here before?" asked Tony.

"Oh yes! last year. I shan't come again."

"Why not?"

"It unsettles you. It doesn't do to be unsettled when you get to my time of life."

"How do you mean—unsettles?"

Maradick considered. How exactly did he mean—unsettles? There was no doubt that it did, though.

"Oh, I'm not much good at explaining, but when you've lived a certain time you've got into a sort of groove—bound to, I suppose. I've got my work, just like another man. Every morning breakfast the same time, same rush to the station, same train, same morning paper, same office, same office-boy, same people; back in the evening, same people again, same little dinner, same little nap—oh, it's like anyone else. One gets into the way of thinking that that's life, bounded by the Epsom golf course and the office in town. All the rest one has put aside, and after a time one thinks that it isn't there. And then a man comes down here and, I don't know what it is, the place or having nothing to do upsets you and things are all different." Then, after a moment, "I suppose that's what a holiday's meant for."

He had been trying to put his feelings into words, but he knew that he had not said at all what he had really felt. It was not the change of life, the lazy hours and the pleasant people; besides, as far as that went, he might at any moment, if he pleased, change things permanently. He had made enough, he need not go back to the City at all; but he knew it was not that. It was something that he had felt in the train, then in the sight of the town, some vague discontent leading to that outbreak at dinner. He was not a reading man or he might have considered the Admonitus Locorum. He had never read of it nor had he knowledge of such a spirit; but it *was*, it must be, the place.

"Yes," said Tony, "of course I've never settled down to anything, yet, you know; and so I can't quite see as you do about the monotony. My people have been very decent; I've been able to wander about and do as I liked, and last year I was in Germany and had a splendid time. Simply had a *rucksack* and walked. And I can't imagine settling down anywhere; and even if I had somewhere—Epsom or anywhere—there would be the same looking for adventure, looking out for things, you know."

"Adventures in Epsom!"

"Why not? I expect it's full of it."

"Ah, that's because you're young! I was like that once, peering round and calling five o'clock tea a romance. I've learnt better."

Tony turned round. "It's so absurd of you, you know, to talk as if you were eighty. You speak as if everything was over, and you're only beginning."

Maradick laughed. "Well, that's pretty good cheek from a fellow half your age! Why, what do you know about life, I'd like to know?"

"Oh, not much. As a matter of fact, it's rather funny your talking like that, because my people have been talking to me to-night about that very thing—settling down, I mean. They say that my roving has lasted long enough, and that I shall soon be turning into a waster if I don't do something. Also that it's about time that I began to grow up. I don't know," he added apologetically, "why I'm telling you this, it can't interest you, but they want me to do just the thing that you've been complaining about."

"Oh no, I haven't been complaining," said Maradick hastily. "All I'm saying is, if you do get settled down don't go anywhere or do anything that will unsettle you again. It's so damned hard getting back. But what's the use of my giving you advice and talking, you young chaps never listen!"

"They sound as if they were enjoying themselves down there," said Tony a little wistfully. The excitement was still in his blood and a wild idea flew into his brain. Why not? But no, it was absurd, he had only known the man quarter of an hour. The lights of the merry-go-round tossed like a thing possessed; whirl and flash, then motionless, and silence again. The murmured hum of voices came to their ears. After all, why not?

"I say," Tony touched Maradick's arm, "why shouldn't we stroll down there, down to the town? It might be amusing. It would be a splendid night for a walk, and it's only twenty to eleven. We'd be back by twelve."

"Down there? Now!" Maradick laughed. But he had a strange yearning for company. He couldn't go back into the hotel, not yet, and he would only lose himself in his own thoughts that led him nowhere if he stayed here alone. A few days ago he would have mocked at the idea of wandering down with a boy he didn't know to see a round-about and some drunken villagers; but things were different, some new impulse was at work within him. Besides, he rather liked the boy. It was a long while since anyone had claimed his companionship like that; indeed a few days ago he would have repelled anyone who attempted it with no uncertain hand.

Maradick considered it.

"Oh, I say, do!" said Tony, his hand still on Maradick's arm, and delighted to find that his proposal was being seriously considered. "After all, it's only a stroll, and we'll come back as soon as you wish. We can get coats from the hotel; it might be rather amusing, you know."

He was feeling better already. It was, of course, absurd that he should go out on a mad game like that at such an hour, but—why not be absurd? He hadn't done anything ridiculous for fifteen years, nothing at all, so it was high time he began.

"It *will* be a rag!" said Tony.

They went in to get their coats. Two dark conspirators, they plunged down the little crooked path that was the quickest way to the town. On every side of them pressed the smell of the flowers, stronger and sweeter than in the daylight, and their very vagueness of outline gave them mystery and charm. The high peaks of the trees, outlined against the sky, assumed strange and eerie shapes—the masts of a ship, the high pinnacle of some cathedral, scythes and swords cutting the air; and above them that wonderful night sky of the summer, something that had in its light of the palest saffron promise of an early dawn, a wonderful suggestion of myriad colours seen dimly through the curtain of dark blue.

> "By night we lingered on the lawn,
> For underfoot the herb was dry;
> And genial warmth, and o'er the sky
> The silvery haze of summer drawn:

> "And bats went round in fragrant skies,
> And wheeled or lit the filmy shapes
> That haunt the dusk, with ermine capes
> And woolly breasts and beaded eyes:"

quoted Tony. "Tennyson, and jolly good at that."

"Don't know it," said Maradick rather gruffly. "Bad for your business. Besides, what do those chaps know about life? Shut themselves up in their rooms and made rhymes over the fire. What could they know?"

"Oh, some of them," said Tony, "knew a good bit. But I'm sorry I quoted. It's a shocking habit, and generally indulged in to show superiority to your friends. But the sky is just like that to-night. Drawn lightly across as though it hid all sorts of things on the other side."

Maradick made no answer, and they walked on in silence. They reached the end of the hotel garden, and passed through the little white gate into a narrow path that skirted the town wall and brought you abruptly out into the market-place by the church. It passed along a high bank that towered over the river Ess on its way to the sea. It was rather a proud little river as little rivers go, babbling and chattering in its early, higher reaches, with the young gaiety suited to country vicarages and the paper ships of village children; and then, solemn and tranquil, and even, perhaps, a little important, as it neared the town and gave shelter to brown-sailed herring-boats, and then, finally, agitated, excited, tumultuous as it tumbled into its guardian, the sea.

To-night it passed contentedly under the walls of the town, singing a very sleepy little song on its way, and playing games with the moonlight and the stars. Here the noise of the fair was hidden and everything was very still and peaceful. The footsteps of the two men were loud and clear. The night air had straightened Maradick's brain and he was more at peace with the world, but there was, nevertheless, a certain feeling of uneasiness, natural and indeed inevitable in a man who, after an ordered and regulated existence of many years, does something that is unusual and a little ridiculous. He had arrived, as was, indeed, the case with so many persons of middle age, at that deliberate exclusion of three sides of life in order to grasp fully the fourth side. By persistent practice he had taught himself to believe that the other three sides did not exist. He told himself that he was not adaptable, that he had made his bed and must lie on it, that the moon was for dreamers; and now suddenly, in the space of a day, the blind was drawn from the window before which he had sat for fifteen years, and behold! there were the stars!

Then Tony began again. It had been said of him that his worst fault was his readiness to respond, that he did not know what it was to be on his guard, and he treated Maradick now with a confidence and frankness that was curiously intimate considering the length of their acquaintance. At length he spoke of Alice Du Cane. "I know my people want it, and she's an awful good sort, really sporting, and the kind of girl you'd trust to the end of your days. A girl you'd be absolutely safe with."

"Do you care about her?" said Maradick.

"Of course. We've known each other for years. We're not very sentimental about it, but then for my part I distrust all that profoundly. It isn't what you want nowadays; good solid esteem is the only thing to build on."

Tony spoke with an air of deep experience. Maradick, with the thought of his own failure in his mind, wondered whether, after all, that were not the right way of looking at it. It had not been his way, fifteen years before; he had been the true impetuous lover, and now he reaped his harvest. Oh! these considering and careful young men and girls of the new generation were learning their lesson, and yet, in spite of it all, marriage turned out as many failures as ever. But this remark of the boy's had been little in agreement with the rest of him; he had been romantic, impetuous, and very, very young, and this serious and rather cynical doctrine of "good solid esteem" was out of keeping with the rest of him.

"I wonder if you mean that," he said, looking sharply at Tony.

"Of course. I've thought a great deal about marriage, in our set especially. One sees fellows marrying every day, either because they're told to, or because they're told not to, and both ways are bad. Of course I've fancied I was in love once or twice, but it's always passed off. Supposing I'd married one of those girls, what would have come of it? Disaster, naturally. So now I'm wiser."

"Don't you be too sure. It's that wisdom that's so dangerous. The Fates, or whatever they are, always choose the cocksure moment for upsetting the certainty. I shouldn't wonder if you change your views before you're much older. You're not the sort of chap, if you'll pardon my saying so, to do those things so philosophically. And then, there's something in the air of this place — — "

Tony didn't reply. He was wondering whether, after all, he was quite so cocksure. He had been telling himself for the last month that it was best, from every point of view, that he should marry Miss Du Cane; his people, his future, his certainty of the safety of it, all urged him, and yet—and yet . . . His mother's words came back to him. "Tony, don't marry anybody unless you are quite certain that it is the only person. Don't let anything else influence you. Marriage with the wrong person is . . ."

And then, in a moment, the fair was upon them. It had just struck eleven and the excitement seemed at its height. The market-place was very French in its neatness, and a certain gathering together of all the life, spiritual and corporate, of the town; the church, Norman, and of some historical interest, filled the right side of the square. Close at its side, and squeezed between its grey walls and the solemn dignity of the Town Hall, was a tall rectangular tower crowded with little slits of windows and curious iron bars that jutted out into the air like pointing fingers.

There was something rather pathetically dignified about it; it protested against its modern neglect and desertion. You felt that it had, in an earlier day, known brave times. Now the ground floor was used by a fruiterer; apples and plums, cherries and pears were bought and sold, and the Count's Tower was Harding's shop.

There were several other houses in the Square that told the same tale, houses with fantastic bow-windows and little pepper-pot doors, tiny balconies and quaintly carved figures that stared at you from hidden corners; houses that were once the height of fashion now hid themselves timidly from the real magnificence of the Town Hall. Their day was over, and perhaps their very life was threatened. The Town Hall, with its dinners and its balls and its speeches, need fear no rivalry.

But to-night the Town Hall was pushed aside and counted for nothing at all. It was the one occasion of the year on which it was of no importance, and the old, despised tower was far more in keeping with the hour and the scene.

Down the centre of the Square were rows of booths lighted by gas-jets that flamed and flared in the night-air with the hiss of many serpents. These filled the middle line of the market. To the right was the round-about; its circle of lights wheeling madly round and round gave it the vitality of a living thing—some huge Leviathan on wheels bawling discordantly the latest triumph of the Halls, and then, excited by its voice, whirling ever swifter and swifter as though it would hurl itself into the air and go rioting gaily through the market, and then suddenly dropping, dead, exhausted, melancholy at the ceasing of its song:—

Put me amongst the—girls!
Those wi-th the curly curls!

and then a sudden vision of dark figures leaping up and down into the light and out of it again, the wild waving of an arm, and the red, green and yellow of the horses as they swirled up and down and round to the tune.

In another corner, standing on a plank laid upon two barrels, his arms raised fantastically above his head, was a preacher. Around him was gathered a small circle of persons with books, and faintly, through the noise of the merry-go-round and the cries of those that bought and sold, came the shrill, wavering scream of a hymn:—

So like little candles
We shall shine,
You in your small corner
And I in mine.

Down the central alley passed crowds of men and women, sailors and their sweethearts, for the most part; and strangely foreign looking a great many of them were—brown and swarthy, with black curling hair and dark, flashing eyes.

There were many country people wearing their Sunday clothes with an uneasiness that had also something of admitted virtue and pride about it. Their ill-fitting and absurdly self-conscious garments hung about them and confined their movements; they watched the scene around them almost furtively, and with a certain subdued terror. It was the day, the night of the year to them; it had been looked forward to and counted and solemnised with the dignity of a much-be-thumbed calendar, and through the long dreary days of winter, when snow and the blinding mist hemmed in solitary farms with desolation, it had been anticipated and foreseen with eager intensity. Now that it was here and was so soon to stand, a lonely pillar in the utterly uneventful waste-land of the year, they looked at it timorously, fearfully, and yet with eager excitement. These lights, this noise, this crowd, how wonderful to look back upon it all afterwards, and how perilous it all was! They moved carefully through the line of booths, wondering at the splendour and magnificence of them, buying a little once or twice, and then repenting of what they had done. Another hour and it would be over; already they shuddered at the blackness of to-morrow.

With the townspeople, the fishermen and sailors from Penzance, it was an old affair; something amusing and calculated to improve materially matters financial and matters amatory, but by no means a thing to wonder at. The last night of the three days fair was, however, of real importance. According to ancient superstition, a procession was formed by all the citizens of the town, and this marched, headed by flaming torches and an ancient drum, round the walls. This had been done, so went the legend, ever since the days of the Celts, when naked invaders had marched with wild cries and derisive gestures round and round the town, concluding with a general massacre and a laying low of the walls. The town had soon sprung to life again, and the ceremony had become an anniversary and the anniversary a fair. The last dying screams of those ancient peoples were turned, now, into the shrieking of a merry-go-round and the sale of toffy and the chattering of many old women; and there were but few in the place who remembered what those origins had been.

Excitement was in the air, and the Square seemed to grow more crowded at every moment. The flaring of the gas flung gigantic shadows on the walls, and the light was on the town so that its sides shone as though with fire. The noise was deafening—the screaming of the roundabout, the shouts of the riders, the cries and laughter of the crowd made a confused babel of sound, and in the distance could be heard the beating of the drum. It was the hour of the final ceremony.

"I wonder," said Maradick, "what the people in those houses think of it. Sleep must be a difficulty under the circumstances."

"I should think," said Tony, laughing, "that they are all out here. I expect that most of the town is here by this time." And, indeed, there was an enormous crowd. The preacher was in danger of being pushed off his plank; the people surged round dancing, singing, shouting, and his little circle had been caught in the multitude and had been swallowed up. Very few of the people seemed to be listening to him; but he talked on, waving the book in his hand, standing out sharply against the shining tower at his back.

Words came to them: "To-morrow it will be too late. I tell you, my friends, that it is now and now only that . . . And the door was shut . . . We cannot choose . . ."

But the drum was in the Square. Standing on the steps of the Town Hall, clothed in his official red, the Town Clerk, a short, pompous man, saluted the fair. No words could penetrate the confusion, but people began to gather round him shouting and singing. The buying and selling entered into the last frenzied five minutes before finally ceasing altogether. Prices suddenly fell to nothing at all, and wise and cautious spirits who had been waiting for this moment throughout the day crowded round and swept up the most wonderful bargains.

The preacher saw the crowd had no ears for him now, and so, with a last little despairing shake of the arm, he closed his book and jumped off his plank. The round-about gave a last shriek of enthusiasm and then dropped exhausted, with the happy sense that it had added to the gaiety of the nations and had brought many coppers into the pockets of its master.

The crowd surged towards the little red beadle with the drum, and Maradick and Tony surged with it. It was beyond question a very lively crowd, and it threatened to be livelier with every beat of the drum. The sound was intoxicating beyond a doubt, and when you had already paid a visit to the "Red Lion" and enjoyed a merry glass with your best friend, of course you entered into the spirit of things more heartily than ever.

And then, too, this dance round the town was the moment of the year. It was the one occasion on which no questions were asked and no surprise ever shown. Decorum and propriety, both excellent things, were for once flung aside; for unless they were discarded the spirit of the dance was not enjoyed. It was deeply symbolic; a glorious quarter of an hour into which you might fling all the inaction of the year—disappointment, revenge, jealousy, hate went, like soiled and useless rags, into the seething pot, and were danced away for ever. You expressed, too, all your joy and gratitude for a delightful year and a most merry fair, and you drank in, as it were, wine, encouragement and hope for the year to come. There had been bad seasons and disappointing friends, and the sad knowledge that you weren't as strong as you had once been; but into the pot with it all! Dance it away into limbo! and, on the back of that merry drum, sits a spirit that will put new heart into you and will send your toes twinkling down the street.

And then, best of all, it was a Dance of Hearts. It was the great moment at which certainty came to you, and, as you followed that drum down the curving street, you knew that the most wonderful thing in the world had come to you, and that you would never be quite the same person again;

perhaps she had danced with you down the street, perhaps she had watched you and listened to the drum and known that there was no question any more. I do not know how many marriages in Treliss that drum had been answerable for, but it knew its business.

The crowd began to form into some kind of order with a great deal of pushing and laughter and noise. There were whistles and little flags and tin horns. It was considered to bring good luck in the succeeding year, and so every kind of person was struggling for a place. If you had not danced then your prospects for the next twelve months were poor indeed, and your neighbours marked you down as some one doomed to misfortune. Very old women were there, their skirts gathered tightly about them, their mouths firm set and their eyes on the drum. Old men were pushed aside by younger ones and took it quietly and with submission, contenting themselves with the thought of the years when they had done their share of the fighting and had had a place with the best. Towards the front most of the young men were gathered. The crowd wound round the market, serpent-wise, coiling round and over the booths and stalls, twisting past the grey tower, and down finally into grey depths where the pepper-pot houses bent and twisted under the red flare of the lights.

Maradick and Tony were wedged tightly between flank and rear; as things were it was difficult enough to keep one's feet. At Maradick's side was an old woman, stout, with her bonnet whisked distractingly back from her forehead, her grey hairs waving behind her, her hands pressed tightly over a basket that she clasped to her waist.

"Eh sirs . . . eh sirs!" pantingly, breathlessly she gasped forth, and then her hand was hurriedly pressed to her forehead; with that up flew the lid of the basket and the scraggy lean neck of a hen poked miserably into the air and screeched frantically. "Down, Janet; but the likes of this . . . never did I see." But nevertheless something triumphant in it all; at least she kept her place.

Already feet were beating to the tune of the drum; a measured stamp, stamp on the cobbles spoke of an itching to be off, a longing for the great moment. Waves of excitement surged through the crowd. For a moment it seemed as though everyone would be carried away, feet would lose their hold of the pavement and the multitude would tumble furiously down the hill; but no, the wave surged to the little red drum and then surged back again. The drum was not ready; everyone was not there. "Patience" — you could hear it speak, stolidly, resolutely, in its beats — "Patience, the time is coming if you will only be patient. You must trust me for the great moment."

Maradick was crushed against the old lady with the basket; for an instant, a movement in the crowd flung him forward and he caught at the basket to steady himself. Really, it was too ridiculous! His hat had fallen to the back of his head, he was hot and perspiring, and he wanted to fling off his overcoat, but his hands were pressed to his sides. Mechanically his feet were keeping time with the drum, and suddenly he laughed. An old man in front of him was crushed sideways between two stalwart youths, and every now and again he struggled to escape, making pathetic little movements with his hands and then sinking back again, resigned. His old, wrinkled face, with a crooked nose and an expression of timid anxiety, seemed to Maradick infinitely diverting. "By Jove," he cried, "look at that fellow!" But Tony was excited beyond measure.

He was crushed against Maradick, his cap balancing ridiculously on the back of his head; his mouth was smiling and his feet were beating time. "Isn't it a rag? I say, isn't it? Such fun! Oh, I beg your pardon, I'm afraid that I stepped on you. But there is a crowd, isn't there? It's really awfully hard to help it. Oh! let me pick it up for you—a cucumber, you said? Oh, there it is, rolled right away under that man there." "Oh thank you, if you wouldn't mind!" "No, it's none the worse, missis. I say, Maradick, aren't they decent; the people, I mean?"

And then suddenly they were off. The red coat of the town-crier waved in the wind and the drum moved.

For a moment a curious silence fell on the crowd. Before, there had been Babel—a very ocean of voices mingled with cries and horns and the blaring of penny whistles—you could scarcely hear yourself speak. But now there was silence. The drum beat came clearly through the air—one, two, one, two—and then, with a shout the silence was broken and the procession moved.

There was a sudden linking of arms down the line and Tony put his through Maradick's. With feet in line they passed down the square, bending forward, then back; at one moment the old woman's basket jumped suddenly into Maradick's stomach, then he was pushed from behind. He felt that his cap was wobbling and he took it off, and, holding it tightly to his chest, passed on bareheaded.

At the turning of the corner the pace became faster. The beat of the drum, heard faintly through the noise of the crowd, was now "two, three, two, three." "Come along, come along, it's time to move, I'm tired of standing still!"

A delirium seemed to seize the front lines, and it passed like a flame down the ranks. Faster, faster. For heaven's sake, faster! People were singing, a strange tune that seemed to have no words but only a crescendo of sound, a murmur that rose to a hum and then to a scream, and then sank again back into the wind and the beat of the drum.

They had left the market-place and were struggling, pressing, down the narrow street that led to the bay. Some one in front broke into a kind of dance-step. One, two, three, then forward bending almost double, your head down, then one, two, three, and your body back again, a leg in air, your head flung behind. It was the dance, the dance!

The spirit was upon them, the drum had given the word, and the whole company danced down the hill, over the cobbles. One, two, three, bend, one, two, three, back, leg in air! "Oh, but I can't!" Maradick was panting. He could not stop, for they were pressing close behind him. The old woman had lost all sense of decorum. She waved her basket in the air, and from its depths came the scream of the hen. Tony's arm was tight through his, and Tony was dancing. One, two, three, and everyone bent together. One, two, three, legs were in the air. Faces were flushed with excitement, hands were clenched, and the tune rose and fell. For an instant Maradick resisted. He must get out of it; he tried to draw his arm away. It was held in a vice and Tony was too excited to listen, and then propriety, years, tradition went hustling to the winds and he was dancing as the others. He shouted wildly, he waved his cap in the air; then he caught the tune and shouted it with the others.

A strange hallucination came upon him that he was some one else, that he, as Maradick, did not exist. Epsom was a lie and the office in town a delusion. The years seemed to step off his back, like Pilgrim's pack, and so, shouting and singing, he danced down the street.

They reached the bottom of the hill and turned the corner along the path that led by the bay. The sea lay motionless at their feet, the path of the moon stretching to the horizon.

The tune was wilder and wilder; the dance had done its work, and enough marriages were in the making to fill the church for a year of Sundays. There was no surprise at the presence of Tony and Maradick. This was an occasion in which no one was responsible for their actions, and if gentlemen chose to join, well, there was nothing very much to wonder at.

To Tony it seemed the moment of his life. This was what he had been born to do, to dance madly round the town. It seemed to signify comradeship, good fellowship, the true equality. It was the old Greek spirit come to life again; that spirit of which he had spoken to Alice—something that Homer had known and something that Whitman had preached. And so up the hill! madly capering, gesticulating, shouting. Some one is down, but no one stops. He is left to pick himself up and come limping after. Mr. Trefusis the butcher had been for a twelvemonth at war with Mr. Curtis the stationer, now they are arm in arm, both absurdly stout; the collar of Mr. Curtis is burst at the neck, but they are friends once more. Mrs. Graham, laundress, had insulted Miss Penny, dressmaker, four months ago, and they had not spoken since; now, with bonnets awry and buttons bursting down the back, it is a case of "Mary" and "Agnes" once again.

Oh! the drum knew its work.

And then it was suddenly over. The top of the hill completed the circle and the market was reached again. The drum beat a frantic tattoo on the steps of the Town Hall, the crowd surged madly round the square, and then suddenly the screams died away, a last feeble beat was heard, and there was silence. People leaned breathlessly against any support that might be there and thought suddenly of the disorder of their dress. Everyone was perhaps a little sheepish, and some had the air of those who had suddenly awaked from sleep.

Maradick came speedily to his senses. He did not know what he had been doing, but it had all been very foolish. He straightened his tie, put on his cap, wiped his forehead, and drew his arm from Tony's. He was very thankful that there was no one there who knew him. What would his clerks have said had they seen him? Fancy the office-boy! And then the Epsom people. Just fancy! Louie, Mrs. Martin Fraser, old Tom Craddock. Maradick, James Maradick dancing wildly down the street with an old woman. It was incredible!

But there was still that strange, half-conscious feeling that it had not been Maradick at all, or, at any rate, some strange, curious Maradick whose existence until to-night had never been expected. It was not the Maradick of Epsom and the City. And then the Admonitus Locorum, perched gaily on his shoulder, laughed hilariously and winked at the Tower.

Tony was excited as he had never been before, and was talking eagerly to an old deaf man who had managed to keep up with the company but was sadly exhausted by the doing of it.

"My last," sighed the old man between gasps for breath. "Don't 'ee tell me, young feller, I shan't see another."

"Nonsense," Tony waved his arms in the air, "why, you're quite young still. You're a fisherman, aren't you? How splendid. I'd give anything to be a fisherman. I'll come down and watch you sometimes and you must come up and have tea."

At this point Maradick intervened.

"I say, let's get out of this, it's so hot. Come away from the crowd." He pulled Tony by the arm.

"All right." Tony shook the old man by the hand. "Good-bye, I'll come and watch you fish one morning. By Jove, it is hot! but what fun! Where shall we go?"

"I propose bed," said Maradick, rather grimly. He felt suddenly out of sympathy with the whole thing. It was as though some outside power had slipped the real Maradick, the Maradick of business and disillusioned forty, back into his proper place again. The crowd became something common and even disgusting. He glanced round to assure himself that no one who mattered had been witness of his antics as he called them; he felt a little annoyed with Tony for leading him into it. It all arose, after all, from that first indiscreet departure from the hotel. He now felt that an immediate return to his rooms was the only secure method of retreat. The dance stood before him as some horrible indiscretion indulged in by some irresponsible and unauthorised part of him. How could he! The ludicrous skinny neck of the shrieking hen pointed the moral of the whole affair. He felt that he had, most horribly, let himself down.

"Yes, bed," he said. "We've fooled enough." But for Tony the evening was by no means over. The dance had been merely the symbol of a new order of things. It was the physical expression of something that he had been feeling so strangely, so beautifully, during these last few days. He had called it by so many names—Sincerity, Simplicity, Beauty, the Classical Spirit, the Heroic Age—but none of these names had served, for it was made up of all these things, and, nevertheless, was none of them alone. He had wondered at this new impulse, almost, indeed, new knowledge; and yet scarcely new, because he felt as if he had known it all, the impulse and the vitality and the simplicity of it, some long time before.

And now that dance had made things clearer for him. It was something that he had done in other places, with other persons, many hundreds, nay, thousands of years ago; he had found his place in the golden chain that encircled the world. And so, of course, he did not wish to go back. He would never go back; he would never go to sleep again, and so he told Maradick.

"Well, I shall go," said Maradick, and he led the way out of the crowd. Then Tony felt that he had been rude. After all, he had persuaded Maradick to come, and it was rather discourteous now to allow him to return alone.

"Perhaps," he said regretfully, "it would be better. But it is such a splendid night, and one doesn't get the chance of a game like that very often."

"No," said Maradick, "perhaps it's as well. I don't know what led me; and now I'm hot, dusty, beastly!"

"I say a drink," said Tony. They had passed out of the market-place and were turning up the corner of the crooked street to their right. A little inn, the "Red Guard," still showed light in its windows. The door flung open and two men came out, and, with them, the noise of other voices. Late though the hour was, trade was still being driven; it was the night of the year and all rules might be broken with impunity.

Maradick and Tony entered.

The doorway was low and the passage through which they passed thick with smoke and heavy with the smell of beer. The floor was rough and uneven, and the hissing gas, mistily hanging in obscure distance, was utterly insufficient. They groped their way, and at last, guided by voices, found the door of the taproom. This was very full indeed, and the air might have been cut with a knife. Somewhere in the smoky haze there was a song that gained, now and again, at chorus point, a ready assistance from the room at large.

Tony was delighted. "Why, it's Shelley's Inn!" he cried. "Oh! you know! where he had the bacon," and he quoted: "'. . . A Windsor chair, at a small round beechen table in a little dark room with a well-sanded floor.' It's just as though I'd been here before. What ripping chaps!"

There was a small table in a corner by the door, and they sat down and called for beer. The smoke was so thick that it was almost as though they had the room to themselves. Heads and boots and long sinewy arms appeared through the clouds and vanished again. Every now and again the opening of the door would send the smoke in whirling eddies down the room and the horizon would clear; then, in a moment, there was mist again.

"'What would Miss Warne say?'" quoted Tony. "You know, it's what Elizabeth Westbrook was always saying, the sister of Harriet; but poets bore you, don't they? Only it's a Shelley night somehow. He would have danced like anything. Isn't this beer splendid? We must come here again."

But Maradick was ill at ease. His great overwhelming desire was to get back, speedily, secretly, securely. He hated this smelly, smoky tavern. He had never been to such a place in his life, and he didn't know why he had ever suffered Tony to lead him there. He was rather annoyed with Tony, to tell the truth. His perpetual enthusiasm was a trifle wearisome and he had advanced in his acquaintanceship with a rapidity that Maradick's caution somewhat resented. And then there was a lack of scale that was a little humiliating. Maradick had started that evening with the air of one who confers a favour; now he felt that he was flung, in Tony's brain, into the same basket with the old fisherman, the landlord of the "Red Guard," and the other jovial fellows in the room. They were all "delightful," "charming," "the best company"; there was, he felt resentfully, no discrimination. The whole evening had been, perhaps, a mistake, and for the future he would be more careful.

And then suddenly he noticed that some one was sitting at their little table. It was strange that he had not seen him before, for the table was small and they were near the door. But he had been absorbed in his thoughts and his eyes had been turned away. A little man in brown sat at his side, quite silently, his eyes fixed on the window; he did not seem to have noticed their presence. His age might have been anything between forty and fifty, but he had a prosperous air as of one who had found life a pleasant affair and anything but a problem; a gentleman, Maradick concluded.

And then he suddenly looked up and caught Maradick's gaze. He smiled. It was the most charming smile that Maradick had ever seen, something that lightened not only the face but the whole room, and something incredibly young and engaging. Tony caught the infection of it and smiled too. Maradick had no idea at the time that this meeting was, in any way, to be of importance to him; but he remembered afterwards every detail of it, and especially that beautiful sudden smile, the youth and frankness in it. In other days, when the moment had assumed an almost tragic importance in the light of after events, the picture was, perhaps, the most prominent background that he possessed; the misted, entangled light struck the little dark black table, the sanded floor, the highraftered ceiling: then there were the dark spaces beyond peopled with mysterious shapes and tumultuous with a hundred voices. And finally the quiet little man in brown.

"You have been watching the festival?" he said. There was something a little foreign in the poise and balance of the sentence; the English pronunciation was perfect? but the words were a little too distinct.

Maradick looked at him again. There *was*, perhaps, something foreign about his face—rather sallow, and his hair was of a raven blackness.

"Yes," said Maradick. "It was most interesting. I have never seen anything quite like it before."

"You followed it?" he asked.

"Yes." Maradick hesitated a little.

"Rather!" Tony broke in; "we danced as well. I never had such fun. We're up at the hotel there; we saw the lights and were tempted to come down, but we never expected anything like that. I wish there was another night of it."

He was leaning back in his chair, his greatcoat flung open and his cap tilted at the back of his head. The stranger looked at him with appreciation.

"I'm glad you liked it. It's *the* night for our little town, but it's been kept more or less to ourselves. People don't know about it, which is a good thing. You needn't tell them or it will be ruined."

"Our town." Then the man belonged to the place. And yet he was surely not indigenous.

"It's not new to you?" said Maradick tentatively.

"New! Oh! dear me, no!" the man laughed. "I belong here and have for many years past. At least it has been my background, as it were. You would be surprised at the amount that the place contains."

"Oh, one can see that," said Tony. "It has atmosphere more than any place I ever knew—medieval, and not ashamed of it, which is unusual for England."

"We have been almost untouched," said the other, "by all this modernising that is ruining England. We are exactly as we were five hundred years ago, in spite of the hotel. For the rest, Cornwall is being ruined. Look at Pendragon, Conister, and hundreds of places. But here we have our fair and our dance and our crooked houses, and are not ashamed."

But Maradick had no desire to continue the conversation. He suddenly realised that he was very tired, sleepy—bed was the place, and this place with its chorus of sailors and smoke. . . . He finished his beer and rose.

"I'm afraid that we must be getting back," he said. "It's very late. I had no intention really of remaining as late." He suddenly felt foolish, as though the other two were laughing at him. He felt strangely irritated.

"Of course," he said to Tony, "it's only myself. Don't you hurry; but old bones, you know— —" He tried to carry it off with a laugh.

"Oh! I'm coming," said Tony. "We said we'd be back by twelve, and we've got five minutes. So we'll say good night, sir."

He held out his hand to the man in brown. The stranger took out a card case and handed his card.

"In case you would care to see round the place—there's a good deal that I could show you. I should be very pleased at any time if you are making a lengthy stay; I shall be here for some months now, and am entirely at your service."

He looked at Maradick as he spoke and smiled, but it was obviously Tony for whom the invitation was meant. Maradick felt absurdly out of it.

"Oh, thank you," said Tony, "I should be awfully glad. I think that we shall be here some time; I will certainly come if I may."

They smiled at each other, the stranger bowed, and they were once more in the cooler air.

Under the light of the lamp Tony read the card: —

"Mr. Andreas Morelli,

19 Trevenna Street, Treliss."

"Ah! a foreigner, as I thought," said Tony. "What an awfully nice man. Did you ever see such a smile?"

"Rather a short acquaintance!" said Maradick. "We only spoke to him for a minute, and then he offered his card. One has to be a little careful."

"Oh! you could tell he was all right," said Tony; "look at his eyes. But what fun it's all been. Aren't you glad you came down?"

Maradick couldn't honestly say that he was, but he answered in the affirmative. "Only, you know," he said, laughing, "it's an unusual evening for a man like myself. We run along on wheels and prefer sticking to the rails."

They were climbing the hill. "Why, this is Trevenna Street!" cried Tony, catching sight of the name on one of the houses. "The man lives here."

The street was quaint and picturesque, and on some of the walls there was ancient carving; heads leered at them from over the doors and window-ledges. Then it struck twelve from somewhere in the town, and immediately all the lights went out; the street was in darkness, for, at the moment, the clouds were over the moon.

"We're in the provinces," said Tony, laughing. "We ought to have link-boys."

Suddenly above their heads there was a light. A window was flung up and some one was standing there with a candle. It was a girl; in the candle-light she stood out brilliantly against the black background. She leaned out of the window.

"Is that you, father?" she called.

Then some one spoke from inside the room. There was a petulant "Oh bother! Miss Minns!" and then the window closed.

Maradick had scarcely noticed the affair. He was hurrying up the hill, eager to reach the hotel.

But Tony stood where he was. "By Jove!" he cried. "Did you see her eyes? Wonderful! Why, you never in all your life— —!"

"Candle-light is deceptive," said Maradick.

"She was wonderful! Glorious! Just for a moment like that out of the darkness! But this is indeed a city of miracles!" He looked back; the house was in absolute darkness.

"She doesn't like Miss Minns," he added, "I expect Miss Minns is a beast; I, too, hate Miss Minns."

At last, in the dark, mysterious hall they parted. "Oh! for bed!" said Maradick.

"But what a night!" cried Tony. "By heaven! what a night!"

And the Admonitus Locorum smiled, very knowingly, from the head of the stairs.

CHAPTER V
MARADICK MAKES A PROMISE AND
MEETS AN ITINERANT OPTIMIST

The house was the cleverest in the world. There was nothing in Europe of its kind, and that was because its cleverness lay in the fact that you never thought it clever at all. It could, most amazingly, disappear so utterly and entirely that you never had any thoughts about it at all, and merely accepted it without discussion as a perfect background. And then, suddenly, on a morning or an evening, it would leap out at you and catch you by the throat; and the traveller wondered and was aghast at its most splendid adaptability.

It was, indeed, all things to all men; but it nevertheless managed to bring out the best parts of them. All those strange people that it had seen — painters and musicians, the aristocracy and old maids, millionaires and the tumbled wastrels cast out from a thousand cities — it gathered them all, and they left it, even though they had passed but a night in its company, altered a little. And it achieved this by its adaptability. In its rooms and passages, its gardens and sudden corners, its grey lights and green lawns, there was that same secret waiting for an immediate revelation. Some thought the house a tyranny, and others called it a surprise, and a few felt that it was an impossibility, but no one disregarded it.

For Maradick, in these strange new days into which he was entering, its charm lay in its age. That first view with the dark, widening staircase that passed into hidden lights and mysteries overhead and turned so nobly towards you the rich gleam of its dark brown oak, the hall with its wide fireplace and passages that shone, as all true passages should, like little cups of light and shadow, grey and blue and gold, before vanishing into darkness — this first glimpse had delighted him; it was a hall that was a perfect test of the arriving visitor, and Maradick had felt that he himself had been scarcely quite the right thing. It was almost as though he ought to have apologised for the colourless money-making existence that had hitherto been his; he had felt this vaguely and had been a little uncomfortable. But there were things higher up that were better still. There were rooms that had, most wisely, been untouched, and their dark, mysterious panelling, the wistful scent of dried flowers and the wax of dying candles; the suggestion—so that he held his breath sometimes to listen whether it were really so—of rustling brocades and the tiny click of shining heels on the polished floor, was of a quite unequalled magic for him. Of course there was imagination in it, and in the last few days these things had grown and extended their influence over him, but there must have been something there before, he argued, to impress so matter-of-fact and solid a gentleman.

There was one room that drew him with especial force, so that sometimes, before going to bed, he would enter with his candle raised high above his head, and watch the shadow on the floor and the high gloom of the carved ceiling. It contained a little minstrels gallery supported on massive pillars of gleaming oak, and round the bottom of the platform were carved the heads of grinning lions, reminding one of that famous Cremona violin of Herr Prespil's. In the centre of the room was an old table with a green baize cloth, and against the wall, stiffly ranged and dusty from disuse, high-backed quaintly carved chairs, but for the rest no carpet and no pictures on the dark, thick walls.

It was sometimes used for dancing, and at times for a meeting or a sale of work; or perchance, if there were gentlemen musically inclined, for chamber music. But it was empty during half the year, and no one disturbed its dust; it reminded Maradick of that tower in the market-place. They were, both of them, melancholy survivals, but he applauded their bravery in surviving at all, and he had almost a personal feeling for them in that he would have liked them to know that there was, at least, one onlooker who appreciated their being there.

There were rooms and passages in the upper part of the house that were equally delightful and equally solitary. He himself had in his former year at Treliss thought them melancholy and dusty; there had been no charm. But now the room of the minstrels had drawn him frequently to its doors, partly by reason of its power of suggestion—the valuation, for him, of light and sound and colour, in their true and most permanent qualities—partly by the amazing view that its deep-set windows provided. It hung forward, as it were, over the hill, so that the intervening space of garden and tower and wood was lost and there was only the sea. It seemed to creep to the very foot of the walls, and the horizon of it was so distant that it swept into infinite space, meeting the sky without break or any division. The height of the room gave the view colour, so that there were deeper blues and greens in the sea, and in the sky the greys and whites were shot with other colours that the mists of the intervening air had given them.

In these last few days Maradick had watched the view with ever-increasing wonder. The sea had been to him before something that existed for the convenience of human beings—a means of transit, a pleasant place to bathe, sands for the children, and the pier for an amusing walk. Now he felt that these things were an impertinence. It seemed to him that the sea permitted them against its will, and would, one day, burst its restraint and pour in overwhelming fury on to that crowd of nurses and nigger-minstrels and parasols; he almost hoped that it would.

Loneliness was, however, largely responsible for this change of view. There had been no one this time at the hotel to whom he had exactly taken. There had been men last year whom he had liked, excellent fellows. They had come there for the golf and he had seen a good deal of them. There might be some of the same kind now, but for some reason, unanalysed and very mistily grasped, he did not feel drawn towards them.

The Saturday of the end of that week was a terribly hot day, and after lunch he had gone to his room, pulled down his blinds, and slumbered over a novel. The novel was by a man called Lester; he had made his name several years before with "The Seven Travellers," a work that had succeeded in pleasing both critics and public. It was now in its tenth edition. Maradick had been bored by "The Seven Travellers"; it had seemed effete and indefinite. They were, he had thought, always travelling and never getting there, and he had put it down unfinished. The man knew nothing of life at first hand, and the characters were too obviously concerned in their own emotions to arouse any very acute ones in the reader. But this one, "To Paradise," was better. If the afternoon had not been so very hot it might even have kept him awake. The characters were still effete and indefinite, motives were still crudely handled and things were vague and obscure, but there was something in its very formlessness that was singularly pleasing. And it was beautiful, there was no doubt about that; little descriptions of places and people that were charming not only for themselves but also for the suggestions that they raised.

When he woke it was nearly four o'clock. He remembered that he had promised his wife to come down to tea. She had met the Gales the day before and they were coming to tea, and he had to be useful. There were a good many little drawing-rooms in the hotel, so that you could ask more people to tea than your own room would conveniently hold, and nevertheless be, to all intents and purposes, private.

He yawned, stretched his arms above his head, and left his room. Then he remembered that he had left a book in the room with the minstrels gallery that morning. He went upstairs to fetch it. The room itself lay in shadow, but outside, beyond the uncurtained windows, the light was so fierce that it hurt his eyes.

He had never seen anything to approach the colour. Sea and sky were a burning blue, and they were seen through a golden mist that seemed to move like some fluttering, mysterious curtain between earth and heaven. There was perfect stillness. Three little fishing-boats with brown sails, through which the sun glowed with the red light of a ruby, stood out against the staring, dazzling white of the distant cliffs.

He found his book, and stood there for a moment wondering why he liked the place so much. He had never been a man of any imagination, but now, vaguely, he filled the space around him with figures. He could not analyse his thoughts at all, but he knew that it all meant something to him now, something that had not been there a week ago.

He went down to tea.

The drawing-room was lying in shadow; the light and heat were shut out by heavy curtains. His wife was making tea, and as he came in at the door he realised her daintiness and charm very vividly. The shining silver and delicate china suited her, and there were little touches of very light blue about her white dress that were vague enough to seem accidental; you wondered why they had happened to be so exactly in precisely the right places. There were also there Lady and Sir Richard Gale, Alice Du Cane, Mrs. Lawrence, and in the background with a diminutive kitten, Tony.

"Something to eat, Miss Du Cane? What, nothing, really?" He sat down beside her and Tony. She interested him, partly because she was so beautiful and partly because she was perhaps going to marry Tony. She looked very cool now; a little too cool, he thought.

"Well? Do you like this place?" he said.

"I? Oh yes! It's lovely, of course. But I think it would be better if one had a cottage here, quite quietly. Of course the hotel's beautiful and most awfully comfortable, but it's the kind of place where one oughtn't to have to think of more than the place; it's worth it. All the other things—dressing and thinking what you look like, and *table d'hôte*—they all come in between somehow like a wall. One doesn't want anything but the place."

That, he suddenly discovered, was why he liked the little room upstairs, because it was, so simply and clearly, the place. He looked at her gratefully.

"Yes," he said, "that's just what I've been feeling. I missed it last year somehow. It didn't seem fine in quite the same way."

But he saw that she was not really interested. She thought of him, of course, as a kind of middle-aged banker. He expected that she would soon try to talk to him about self and the *table d'hôte* and bridge. He was seriously anxious to show her that there were other things that he cared for.

"You've changed a lot since the other day, Alice," said Tony suddenly. "You told me you didn't like Treliss a bit, and now you think it's lovely."

"I do really," said Alice, laughing. "That was only a mood. How could one help caring? All the same you know I don't think it's altogether good for one, it's too complete a holiday."

"That's very strenuous, Miss Du Cane," said Maradick. "Why shouldn't we have holidays? It helps."

"Ah, yes," said Alice. "But then you work. Here am I doing nothing all the year round but enjoy myself; frankly, I'm getting tired of it. I shall buy a typewriter or something. Oh! if I were only a man!"

She looked at Tony. He laughed.

"She's always doing that, Maradick—pitching into me because I don't do anything; but that's only because she doesn't know in the least what I'm really doing. She doesn't know——"

"Please, Mr. Maradick," she said, turning round to him, "make him start something seriously. Take him into your office. He can add, I expect, or be useful in some way. He's getting as old as Methuselah, and he's never done a day's work in his life."

Although she spoke lightly, he could see that she meant it very seriously. He wondered what it was that she wanted him to do, and also why people seemed to take it for granted that he had influence over Tony; it was as if Fate were driving him into a responsibility that he would much rather avoid. But the difficulty of it all was that he was so much in the dark. These people had not let him into things, and yet they all of them demanded that he should do something. He would have liked to have asked her to tell him frankly what it was that she wanted him to do, and, indeed, why she had appealed to him at all; but there was no opportunity then. At any rate he felt that some of her indifference was gone; she had let him see that there were difficulties somewhere, and that at least was partial confidence.

Mrs. Maradick interrupted: "Miss Du Cane, I wonder if you would come and make a four at bridge. It's too hot to go out, and Sir Richard would like a game. It would be most awfully good of you."

Alice moved over to the card-table. Sir Richard played continually but never improved. He sat down now with the air of one who condescended;

he covered his mistakes with the assurance that it was his partner who was playing abominably, and he explained carefully and politely at the end of the game the things that she ought to have done. Mrs. Maradick and Mrs. Lawrence played with a seriousness and compressed irritation that was worthy of a greater cause.

Tony had slipped out of the room, and Lady Gale crossed over to Maradick by the window.

"How quickly," she said, "we get to know each other in a place like this. We have only been here a week and I am going to be quite confidential already."

"Confidential?" said Maradick.

"Yes, and I hope you won't mind. You mustn't mind, because it's my way. It always has been. If one is going to know people properly then I resent all the wasted time that comes first. Besides, preliminaries aren't necessary with people as old as you and I. We ought to understand by this time. Then we really can't wait."

He looked into her face, and knew that here at least there would be absolute honesty and an explanation of some kind.

"Forgive me, Lady Gale," he said, "but I'm afraid I don't understand. I've been in the dark and perhaps you'll explain. Before I came down here I'd been living to myself almost entirely—a man of my age and occupations generally does—and now suddenly I'm caught into other people's affairs, and it's bewildering."

"Well, it's all very simple," she answered. "Of course it's about Tony. Everyone's interested in Tony. He's just at the interesting age, and he's quite exciting enough to make his people wonder what he'll turn into. It's the chrysalis into the—well, that just depends. And then, of course, I care a great deal more than the rest. Tony has been different to me from the rest. I suppose every mother's like that, but I don't think most of them have been such chums with their sons as I've been with Tony. We were alone in the country together for a long time and there was nobody else. And then the time came that I had prepared for and knew that I must face, the time when he had things that he didn't tell me. Every boy's like that, but I trusted him enough not to want to know, and he often told me just because I didn't ask. Then he cared for all the right things and always ran straight; he never bent his brain to proving that black's white and indeed rather whiter than most whites are, as so many people do. But just lately I've been a little anxious— we have all been—all of us who're watching him. He ought to have settled down to something or some one by this time and one doesn't quite know why he hasn't; and he hasn't been himself for the last six months. Things ought to have come to a head here. I don't know what he's been up to this week, but none of us have seen anything of him, and I can see that his thoughts are elsewhere all the time. It isn't in the least that I doubt him or am unhappy, it is only that I would like some one to be there to give him a hand if he wants one. A woman wouldn't do; it must be a man, and——"

"You think I'm the person," said Maradick.

"Well, he likes you. He's taken to you enormously. That's always been a difficulty, because he takes to people so quickly and doesn't seem to mind very much whom it is; but you are exactly the right man, the man I have wanted him to care for. You would help him, you could help him, and I think you will."

Maradick was silent.

"You mustn't, please, think that I mean you to spy in any way," she continued. "I don't want you to tell me anything. I shall never ask you, and you need never say anything to me about it. It is only that I shall know that there is some one there if he gets into a mess and I shall know that he's all right." She paused again, and then went on gently—

"You mustn't think it funny of me to speak to you like this when I know you so slightly. At my age one judges people quickly, and I don't want to waste time. I'm asking a good deal of you, perhaps; I don't know, but I think it would have happened in any case whether I had spoken or no. And then you will gain something, you know. No one can be with Tony—get to know him and be a friend of his—without gaining. He's a very magical person."

Maradick looked down on the ground. He knew quite well that he would have done whatever Lady Gale had asked him to do. She had seemed to him since he had first seen her something very beautiful and even wonderful, and he felt proud and grateful that she had trusted him like that.

"It's very good of you, Lady Gale," he said; "I will certainly be a friend of Tony's, if that is what you want me to do. He is a delightful fellow, much too delightful, I am afraid, to have anything much to do with a dull, middle-aged duffer like myself. I must wake up and shake some of the dust off."

She smiled. "Thank you; you don't know how grateful I am to you for taking an interest in him. I shall feel ever so much safer."

And then the door opened and Tony came in. He crossed over to her and said eagerly, "Mother, the Lesters are here. Came this afternoon. They're coming up in a minute; isn't it splendid!"

"Oh, I am glad—not too loud, Tony, you'll disturb the bridge. How splendid they're coming; Mildred said something in town about possibly coming down in the car."

"He's the author-fellow, you know," said Tony, turning round to Maradick. "You were reading 'To Paradise' yesterday; I saw you with it. His books are better than himself. But she's simply ripping; the best fun you ever saw in your life."

That Maradick should feel any interest in meeting a novelist was a new experience. He had formerly considered them, as a class, untidy both in morals and dress, and had decidedly preferred City men. But he liked the book.

"Yes. I was reading 'To Paradise this afternoon,' he said. "It's very good. I don't read novels much, and it's very seldom that I read a new one, but there was something unusual——"

Then the door opened and the Lesters came in. She was not pretty exactly, but striking—even, perhaps, he thought afterwards, exciting. He often tried on later days to call back the first impression that he had had of her, but he knew that it had not been indifference. In the shaded half-lights of the room, the grey blue shadows that the curtains flung on to the dark green carpet made her dress of light yellow stand out vividly; it had the color of primroses against the soft, uncertain outlines of the walls and hidden corners. There was a large black hat that hid her face and forehead, but beneath it there shone and sparkled two dark eyes that flung the heightened colour of her cheeks into relief. But the impression that he had was something most brilliantly alive; not alive in quite Tony's way—that was a vitality as natural as the force of streams and torrents and infinite seas; this had something of opposition in it, as though some battle had created it. Her husband, a dark, plain man, a little tired and perhaps a little indifferent, was in the background. He did not seem to count at the moment.

"Oh, Mildred, how delightful!" Lady Gale went forward to her. "Tony's just told me. I had really no idea that you were coming; of course with a car one can do anything and get anywhere, but I thought it would have been abroad!"

"So it ought to have been," said Mrs. Lester. "Fred couldn't get on with the new book, and suddenly at breakfast, in the way he does, you know, said that we must be in Timbuctoo that evening. So we packed. Then we wondered who it was that we wanted to see, and of course it was you; and then we wondered where we wanted to go, and of course it was Treliss, and then when we found that you and Treliss were together of course the thing was done. So here we are, and it's horribly hot. I only looked in to see you for a second because I'm going to have a bath immediately and change my things."

She crossed for a moment to the card-table and spoke to Sir Richard. "No, don't get up, Sir Richard, I wouldn't stop the bridge for the world. Just a shake of the fingers and I'm off. How are you? Fit? I'm as right as a trivet, thanks. Hullo, Alice! I heard you were here! Splendid! I'll be down later."

Her husband had shaken hands with Lady Gale and talked to her for a moment, then they were gone.

"That's just like Mildred," said Lady Gale, laughing. "In for a moment and out again, never still. When she and Tony are together things move, I can tell you. Well, I must go up to my room, any amount of letters to write before dinner. Good-bye, Mr. Maradick, for the moment. Thank you for the chat."

When they were left alone Tony said, "Come out. It's much cooler now. It will be ripping by the sea. You've been in all the afternoon."

"Yes," said Maradick, "I'll come."

He realised, as he left the room, that he and his wife had scarcely met since that first evening. There had always been other people, at meals, outside, after dinner; he knew that he had not been thinking of her very much, but he suddenly wondered whether she had not been a little lonely. These people had not accepted her in quite the same way that they had accepted him, and that was rather surprising, because at Epsom and in town it had always been the other way about. He had been the one whom people had thought a bore; everyone knew that she was delightful. Of course the explanation was that Tony had, as it were, taken him up. All these people were interested in Tony, and had, therefore, included Maradick. He could help a little in the interpretation or rather the development of Tony, and therefore he was of some importance. For a moment there was a feeling of irritation at the position, and then he remembered that it was scarcely likely that anyone was going to be interested in him for himself, and the next best thing was to be liked because of Tony. But it must, of course, be a puzzle to his wife. He had caught, once or twice, a look, something that showed that she was wondering, and that, too, was new; until now she had never thought about him at all.

Tony chattered all the way down to the hall.

"The Lesters are ripping. We've known Milly Lester ever since the beginning of time. She's not much older than me, you know, and we lived next door to each other in Carrington Gardens. Our prams always went out and round the Square together, and we used to say goo-goo to each other.

Then later on I used to make up stories for her. She was always awfully keen on stories and I was rather a nailer at them; then we used to fight, and I slapped her face and she pinched me. Then we went to the panto together, and used to dance with each other at Christmas parties. I was never in love with her, you know: she was just a jolly good sort whom I liked to be with. She's always up to a rag; *he* thinks it's a little too often. He's a solemn sort of beggar and jolly serious, lives more in his books than out of them, which doesn't make for sociability. Rather hard luck on her."

"What was his attraction for her?" asked Maradick.

"Oh, I don't know," said Tony; "she admired his books awfully and made the mistake of thinking that the man was like them. So he is, in a way; it's as if you'd married the books, you know, and there wasn't anything else there except the leather."

They were silent for a little time, and then Tony said, "On a day like this one's afraid—'Timeo Danaos et dona ferentes,' you know—it's all *too* beautiful and wonderful and makes such a splendid background for the adventure that we're on the edge of."

"Adventure?" said Maradick.

"Yes; you haven't forgotten the other night, have you? I've been waiting for you to speak to me about it. And then this afternoon I saw it was all right. My asking you to come out was a kind of test, only I knew you'd say yes. I knew that mother had been talking to you about it. About me and whether you'd help me? Wasn't it?"

"That's between your mother and myself," said Maradick.

"Well, it was, all the same. And you said yes. And it's ripping, it's just what I so especially wanted. They've all been wondering what I'm up to. Of course they could see that something was up; and they're simply longing to know all about it, the others out of curiosity and mother because she cares. It isn't a bit curiosity with her, you know, it's only that she wants to know that I'm safe, and now that she's stuck you, whom she so obviously trusts, as a kind of bodyguard over me she'll be comfortable and won't worry any more. It's simply splendid—that she won't worry and that you said yes."

He paused and stood in the path, looking at Maradick.

"Because, you know," he went on, with that charming, rather crooked little smile that he had, "I do most awfully want you for a friend quite apart from its making mother comfortable. You're just the chap to carry it through; I'm right about it's being settled, aren't I?"

Maradick held out his hand.

"I expect I'm a fool," he said, "at my age to meddle in things that don't concern me, but anyhow, there's my hand on it. I like you. I want waking up a bit and turning round, and you'll do it. So it's a bargain."

They shook hands very solemnly and walked on silently down the path. They struck off to the right instead of turning to the left through the town. They crossed a stile, and were soon threading a narrow, tumbling little path between two walls of waving corn. In between the stems poppies were hiding and overhead a lark was singing. For a moment he came down towards them and his song filled their ears, then he circled up and far above their heads until he hung, a tiny speck, against a sky of marble blue.

"You might tell me." said Maradick, "what the adventure really is. I myself, you know, have quite the vaguest idea, and as I'm so immediately concerned I think I ought to know something about it."

"Why? I told you the other night," said Tony; "and things really haven't gone very much further. I haven't seen her again, nor has Punch, and he has been about the beach such a lot that he'd have been sure to if she'd been down there. But the next step has to be taken with you."

"What is it?" said Maradick a little apprehensively.

"To call on that man who gave us his card the other night. He's got a lot to do with her, I know, and it's the very best of luck that we should have met him as we did."

"I must say I didn't like him for some quite unexplained reason. But why not go and call without me? He doesn't want to see me; it was you he gave the card to."

"No, you must come. I should be afraid to go alone. Besides, he might show you things in Treliss that you'd like to see, although I suppose you've explored it pretty well for yourself by this time. But, by the way, wherever have you been this week? I've never seen you about the place or with people."

"No," said Maradick. "I discovered rather a jolly room up in the top of the house somewhere, a little, old, deserted place with an old-fashioned gallery and a gorgeous view. I grew rather fond of the place and have been there a good deal."

"You must show it me. We ought to have struck the place by now. Oh, there it is, to the right."

They had arrived at the edge of the cliff, and were looking for a path that would take them down to the beach. Below them was a little beach shut in on three sides by cliff. Its sand was very smooth and very golden, and the sea came with the very tiniest ripple to the edge of it and passed away again with a little sigh. Everything was perfectly still. Then suddenly there was a bark of a dog and a man appeared on the lower rocks, sharply outlined against the sky.

"What luck!" cried Tony. "It's Punch. I wanted you to meet him, and he may have a message for me."

The man saw them and stepped down from the rocks on to the beach and came towards them, the dog after him. A little crooked path brought them to him, and Maradick was introduced. It was hard not to smile. The man was small and square; his legs were very short, but his chest was enormous, and his arms and shoulders looked as though they ought to have belonged to a much bigger man. His mouth and ears were very large, his nose and eyes small; he was wearing a peaked velvet cap, a velveteen jacket and velveteen knickerbockers. Maradick, thinking of him afterwards, said of him that he "twinkled;" that was the first impression of him. His legs, his eyes, his nose, his mouth stretched in an enormous smile, had that "dancing" effect; they said, "We are here now and we are jolly pleased to see you, but oh! my word! we may be off at any minute, you know!"

The dog, a white-haired mongrel, somewhat of the pug order, was a little like its master; its face was curiously similar, with a little nose and tiny eyes and an enormous mouth.

"Let me introduce you," said Tony. "Punch, this is a friend of mine, Mr. Maradick. Maradick, this is my friend and counsellor, Punch; and, oh, yes, there's Toby. Let me introduce you, Toby. Mr. Maradick—Toby. Toby—Mr. Maradick!"

The little man held out an enormous hand, the dog gravely extended a paw. Maradick shook both.

"I'm very pleased to meet you," he said. "Tony has told me about you."

"Thank you, sir, I'm sure," the man answered; "I'm very pleased to meet *you*, sir."

There was a pause, and they sat down on the sand with their backs against the rocks.

"Well, Punch," said Tony, "how's the show? I haven't seen you since Thursday."

"Oh, the *show's* all right," he answered. "There's never no fear about that. My public's safe enough as long as there's children and babies, which, nature being what it is, there'll always be. It's a mighty pleasant thing having a public that's always going on, and it ain't as if there was any chance of their tastes changing either. Puppies and babies and kittens like the same things year in and year out, bless their little hearts."

"You have a Punch and Judy show, haven't you?" said Maradick a little stiffly. He was disgusted at his stiffness, but he felt awkward and shy. This wasn't the kind of fellow that he'd ever had anything to do with before; he could have put his hand into his pocket and given him a shilling and been pleasant enough about it, but this equality was embarrassing. Tony obviously didn't feel it like that, but then Tony was young.

"Yes, sir; Punch and Judy shows are getting scarce, what with yer cinematographs and pierrots and things. But there's always customers for 'em and always will be. And it's more than babies like 'em really. Many's the time I've seen old gentlemen and fine ladies stop and watch when they think no one's lookin' at 'em, and the light comes into their eyes and the colour into their cheeks, and then they think that some one sees 'em and they creep away. It's natural to like Punch; it's the banging, knock-me-down kind of humour that's the only genuine sort. And then the moral's tip-top. He's always up again, Punch is, never knows when he's beat, and always smiling."

"Yes," said Maradick, but he knew that he would have been one of those people who would have crept away.

"And there's another thing," said the man; "the babies know right away that it's the thing they want. It's my belief that they're told before they come here that there's Punch waiting for them, otherwise they'd never come at all. If you gave 'em Punch right away there wouldn't be any howling at all; a Punch in every nursery, I say. You'd be surprised, sir, to see the knowin' looks the first time they see Punch, you'd think they'd seen it all their lives. There's nothing new about it; some babies are quite *blasé* over it."

"And then there are the nursemaids," said Tony.

"Yes," said Punch, "they're an easy-goin' class, nursemaids. Give them a Punch and Judy or the military and there's nothing they wouldn't do for you. I've a pretty complete knowledge of nursemaids."

"I suppose you travel about?" said Maradick; "or do you stay more or less in one part of the country?"

"Stay! Lord bless you, sir! I never stay anywhere; I'm up and down all the time. It's easy enough to travel. The show packs up small, and then there's just me and Toby. Winter time I'm in London a good bit. Christmas and a bit after. London loves Punch and always will. You'd think that these music-halls and pantomimes would knock it out, but not a bit of it. They've a real warm feeling for it in London. And they aren't the sort of crowd who stand and watch it and laugh and smack their thighs, and then when the cap comes round start slipping off and pretendin' they've business to get to, not a bit of it. They'd be ashamed not to pay their little bit."

"And then in the summer?" said Maradick.

"Oh! Cumberland for a bit and then Yorkshire, and then down here in Cornwall. All round, you know. There are babies everywhere, and some are better than others. Now the Cumberland babies beat all the rest. Give me a Cumberland baby for a real laugh. They're right enough down here, but they're a bit on their dignity and afraid of doing the wrong thing. But I've got good and bad babies all over the place. I reckon I know more about babies than anyone in the land. And you see I always see them at their best—smiling and crowing—which is good for a man's 'ealth."

The sun was sinking towards the sea, and there was perfect silence save for the very gentle ripple of the waves. It was so still that a small and slightly ruffled sparrow hopped down to the edge of the water and looked about it. Toby saw him, but only lazily flapped an ear. The sparrow watched the dog for a moment apprehensively, then decided that there was no possible danger and resumed its contemplation of the sea.

The waves were so lazy that they could barely drag their way up the sand. They clung to the tiny yellow grains as though they would like to stay and never go back again; then they fell back reluctantly with a little song about their sorrow at having to go.

A great peace was in Maradick's heart. This was the world at its most absolute best. When things were like this there were no problems nor questions at all; Epsom was an impossible myth and money-making game for fools.

Tony broke the silence:

"I say, Punch, have you any message for me?"

"Well, sir, not exactly a message, but I've found out something. Not from the young lady herself, you understand. She hasn't been down again—not when I've been there. But I've found out about her father."

"Her father?" said Tony excitedly; and Toby also sat up at attention as though he were interested.

"Yes; he's the little man in brown you spoke of. Well known about here, it seems. They say he's been here as long as anyone can remember, and always the same. No one knows him—keeps 'imself to 'imself; a bit lonely for the girl."

"That man!" cried Tony. "And he's asked me to call! Why, it's fate!"

He grasped Maradick's arm excitedly.

"He's her father! her father!" he cried. "And he's asked us to call! *Her* father, and we're to call!"

"You're to call!" corrected Maradick. "He never said anything about me; he doesn't want me."

"Oh, of course you're to come. 'Pon my word, Punch, you're a brick. Is there anything else?"

"Well, yes," said Punch slowly. "He came and spoke to me yesterday after the show. Said he liked it and was very pleasant. But I don't like 'im all the same. I agree with that gentleman; there's something queer there, and everyone says so."

"Oh, that's all right," said Tony. "Never mind about the man. He's her father, that's the point. My word, what luck!"

But Punch shook his head dubiously.

"What do they say against him, then?" said Tony. "What reasons have they?"

"Ah! that's just it," said Punch; "they haven't got no reasons. The man 'asn't a 'istory at all, which is always an un'ealthy sign. Nobody knows where 'e comes from nor what 'e's doing 'ere. 'E isn't Cornish, *that's* certain. 'E's got sharp lips and pointed ears. I don't like 'im and Toby doesn't either, and 'e's a knowing dog if ever there was one."

"Well, I'm not to be daunted," said Tony; "the thing's plainly arranged by Providence."

But Maradick, looking at Punch, thought that he knew more than he confessed to. There was silence again, and they watched a gossamer mist, pearl-grey with the blue of the sea and sky shining through, come stealing towards them. The sky-line was red with the light of the sinking sun, and a very faint rose colour touched with gold skimmed the crests of tiny waves that a little breeze had wakened.

The ripples that ran up the beach broke into white foam as they rose.

"Well, I must be getting on, Mr. Tony," said Punch, rising. "I am at Mother Shipton's to-night. Good-bye, sir," he shook hands with Maradick, "I am pleased to 'ave met you."

Tony walked a little way down the beach with him, arm in arm. They stopped, and Punch put his hand on the boy's shoulder and said something that Maradick did not catch; but he was speaking very seriously. Then, with the dog at his heels, he disappeared over the bend of the rocks.

"We'd better be getting along too," said Tony. "Let's go back to the beach. There'll be a glorious view!"

"He seems a nice fellow," said Maradick.

"Oh, Punch! He's simply ripping! He's one of the people whose simplicity seems so easy until you try it, and then it's the hardest thing in the world. I met him in town last winter giving a show somewhere round Leicester Square way, and he was pretty upset because Toby the dog was ill. I don't know what he'd do if that dog were to die. He hasn't got anyone else properly attached to him. Of course, there are lots of people all over the country who are very fond of him, and babies, simply any amount, and children and dogs—anything young—but they don't really belong to him."

But Maradick felt that, honestly, he wasn't very attracted. The man was a vagabond, after all, and would be much better earning his living at some decent trade; a strong, healthy man like that ought to be keeping a wife and family and doing his country some service instead of wandering about the land with a dog; it was picturesque, but improper. But he didn't say anything to Tony about his opinions—also he knew that the man didn't annoy him as he would have done a week ago.

As they turned the bend of the cliffs the tower suddenly rose in front of them like a dark cloud. It stood out sharply, rising to a peak biting into the pale blue sky, and vaguely hinting at buildings and gabled roofs; before it the sand stretched, pale gold.

Tony put his arm through Maradick's.

At first they were not sure; it might be imagination. In the misty and uncertain light figures seemed to rise out of the pale yellow sands and to vanish into the dusky blue of the sea. But at the same moment they realised that there was some one there and that he was waiting for them; they recognised the brown jacket, the cloth cap, the square, prosperous figure. The really curious thing was that Maradick had had his eyes fixed on the sand in front of him, but he had seen no one coming. The figure had suddenly materialised, as it were, out of the yellow evening dusk. It was beyond doubt Mr. Andreas Morelli.

He was the same as he had been a week ago. There was no reason why he should have changed, but Maradick felt as though he had been always, from the beginning, the same. It was not strange that he had not changed since last week, but it was strange that he had not changed, as Maradick felt to be the case, since the very beginning of time; he had always been like that.

He greeted Tony now with that beautiful smile that Maradick had noticed before; it had in it something curiously intimate, as though he were referring to things that they both had known and perhaps done. Tony's greeting was eager and, as usual with him, enthusiastic.

Morelli turned to Maradick and gravely shook hands. "I am very pleased to see you again, sir," he said. "It is a most wonderful evening to be taking a stroll. It has been a wonderful day."

"It has been too good to be true," said Tony; "I don't think one ought ever to go indoors when the weather is like this. Are you coming back to the town, Mr. Morelli, or were you going farther along the beach?"

"I should be very glad to turn back with you, if I may," he said. "I promised to be back by half-past seven and it is nearly that now. You have never fulfilled your promise of coming to see me," he said reproachfully.

"Well," said Tony, "to tell you the truth I was a little shy; so many people are so kind and invite one to come, but it is rather another thing, taking them at their word and invading their houses, you know."

"I can assure you I meant it," said Morelli gravely. "There are various things that would interest you. I have quite a good collection of old armour and a good many odds and ends picked up at different times." Then he added, "There's no time like the present; why not come back and have supper with us now? That is if you don't mind taking pot-luck."

Tony flushed with pleasure. "I think we should be delighted, shouldn't we, Maradick? They're quite used to our not coming back at the hotel."

"Thank you very much," said Maradick. "It's certainly good of you."

He noticed that what Punch had said was true; the ears were pointed and the lips sharp and thin.

The dusk had swept down on them. The lights of the town rose in glittering lines one above the other in front of them; it was early dusk for an August evening, but the dark came quickly at Treliss.

The sea was a trembling shadow lit now and again with the white gleam of a crested wave. On the horizon there still lingered the last pale rose of the setting sun and across the sky trembling bars of faint gold were swiftly vanishing before the oncoming stars.

Morelli talked delightfully. He had been everywhere, it appeared, and spoke intimately of little obscure places in Germany and Italy that Tony had discovered in earlier years. Maradick was silent; they seemed to have forgotten him. .

They entered the town and passed through the market-place. Maradick looked for a moment at the old tower, standing out black and desolate and very lonely.

In the hotel the dusk would be creeping into the little room of the minstrels. There would be no lights there, only the dust and the old chairs and the green table; from the open window you would see the last light of the setting sun, and there would be a scent of flowers, roses and pinks, from the garden below.

They had stopped outside the old dark house with the curious carving. Morelli felt for the key.

"I don't know what my daughter will have prepared," he said apologetically, "I gave her no warning."

CHAPTER VI
SUPPER WITH JANET MORELLI

The little hall was lit by a single lamp that glimmered redly in the background. Small though the hall was, its darkness gave it space and depth. It appeared to be hung with many strange and curious objects—weapons of various kinds, stuffed heads of wild animals, coloured silks and cloths of foreign countries and peoples. The walls themselves were of oak, and from this dark background these things gleamed and shone and twisted under the red light of the lamp in an alarming manner. An old grandfather clock tick-tocked solemnly in the darkness.

Morelli led them up the stairs, with a pause every now and again to point out things of interest.

"The house is, you know," he said almost apologetically, "something of a museum. I have collected a good deal one way and another. Everything has its story."

Maradick thought, as his host said this, that he must know a great many stories, some of them perhaps scarcely creditable ones. The things that he saw had in his eyes a sinister effect. There could be nothing very pleasant about those leering animals and rustling, whispering skins; it gave the house, too, a stuffy, choked-up air, something a little too full, and full, too, of not quite the pleasantest things.

The staircase was charming. A broad window with diamond-shaped panes faced them as they turned the stair and gave a pleasant, cheerful light to the walls and roof. A silver crescent moon with glittering stars attending it shone at the window against an evening sky of the faintest blue; a glow that belonged to the vanished sun, and was so intangible that it had no definite form of colour, hung in the air and passed through the window down the stairs into the dark recesses of the hall. The walls were painted a dark red that had something very cheerful and homely about it.

Suddenly from the landing above them came voices.

"No, Miss Minns, I'm going to wait. I don't care; father said he'd be back. Oh! I hear him."

A figure came to the head of the stairs.

"Father, do hurry up; Miss Minns is so impatient at having to wait, and I said I wouldn't begin till you came, and the potatoes are black, black, black."

Maradick looked up and saw a girl standing at the head of the stairs. In her hand she held a small silver lamp that flung a pale circle of yellow behind and around her; she held it a little above her head in order that she might see who it was that mounted the stairs.

He thought she was the most beautiful girl that he had ever seen; her face was that of a child, and there was still in it a faint look of wonderment and surprise, as though she had very recently broken from some other golden dream and discovered, with a cry, the world.

Her mouth was small, and curved delicately like the petals of a very young rose that turn and open at the first touch of the sun's glow. Her eyes were so blue that there seemed no end at all to the depth, and one gazed into them as into a well on a night of stars; there were signs and visions in them of so many things that a man might gaze for a year of days and still find secrets hidden there. Her hair was dark gold and was piled high in a great crown, and not so tightly that a few curls did not escape and toss about her ears and over her eyes. She wore a gown of very pale blue that fell in a single piece from her shoulders to her feet; her arms to the elbow and her neck were bare, and her dress was bound at the waist by a broad piece of old gold embroidered cloth.

Her colouring was so perfect that it might have seemed insipid were it not for the character in her mouth and eyes and brow. She was smiling now, but in a moment her face could change, the mouth would grow stiff, her eyes would flash; there was character in every part of her.

She was tall and very straight, and her head was poised perfectly. There was dignity and pride there, but humour and tenderness in the eyes and mouth; above all, she was very, very young. That look of surprise, and a little perhaps of one on her guard against a world that she did not quite understand, showed that. There was no fear there, but something a little wild and undisciplined, as though she would fight to the very last for her perfect, unfettered liberty: this was Janet Morelli.

She had thought that her father was alone, but now she realised that some one was with him.

She stepped back and blushed.

"I beg your pardon. I didn't know — —"

"Let me introduce you," said Morelli. "Janet, this is Mr. Maradick and this Mr. Gale. They have come to have supper with us."

She put the lamp down on the little round table behind her and shook hands with them. "How do you do?" she said. "I hope you're not in the least bit hungry, because there's nothing whatever to eat except black potatoes, and they're not nice at all."

She was quite without embarrassment and smiled at Maradick. She put her arm on her father's shoulder for a moment by way of greeting, and then they walked into the room opposite the staircase. This was in strong contrast to the hall, being wide and spacious, with but little furniture. At one end was a bow-window with old-fashioned lozenge-shaped panes; in this a table laid for three had been placed. The walls were painted a very pale blue, and half-way up, all the way round, ran a narrow oaken shelf on which were ranged large blue and white plates of old china, whereon there ran riot a fantastic multitude of mandarins, curiously twisted castles, and trembling bridges spanning furious torrents. There were no pictures, but an open blue-tiled fireplace, the mantelpiece of which was of dark oak most curiously carved. There were some chairs, two little round tables, and a sofa piled high with blue cushions. There were lamps on the tables, but they were dim and the curtains were not drawn, so that through the misty panes the lights of the town were twinkling in furious rivalry with the lights of the dancing stars.

By the table was waiting a little woman in a stiff black dress. There was nothing whatever remarkable about her. There was a little pretentiousness, a little pathos, a little beauty even; it was the figure of some one who had been left a very long time ago, and was at last growing accustomed to the truth of it—there was no longer very much hope or expectation of anything, but simply a kind of fairy-tale wonder as to the possibility of the pumpkin's being after all a golden coach and the rats some most elegant coachmen.

"Miss Minns," said Morelli, "let me introduce you. These are two gentlemen who will have supper with us. Mr. Maradick and Mr. Gale."

"I am very pleased to meet you," said Miss Minns a little gloomily.

There was a servant of the name of Lucy, who laid two more places clumsily and with some noise. Janet had disappeared into the kitchen and Morelli maintained the conversation.

There was, however, a feeling of constraint. Maradick had never known Tony so silent. He stood by the fireplace, awkwardly shifting from one leg to the other, and looking continually at the door. He was evidently in a state of the greatest excitement, and he seemed to pay no attention to anyone in the room. Miss Minns was perfectly silent, and stood there gravely waiting. Morelli talked courteously and intelligently, but Maradick felt that he himself was being used merely as a background to the rest of the play. His first feeling on seeing Janet had been that Tony was indeed justified in all his enthusiasm; his second, that he himself was in for rather a terrible time.

He had not in the least expected her to be so amazingly young. He had, quite without reason or justification, expected her to be older, a great deal older, than Tony, and that chiefly, perhaps, because he couldn't, by any stretch of imagination, believe her to be younger. Tony was so young in every way—in his credibility, his enthusiasm, his impatience, his quite startling simplicity. With this in front of him, Maradick had looked to the lady as an accomplice; she would help, he had thought, to teach Tony discretion.

And now, with that vision of her on the stairs, he saw that she was, so to speak, "younger than ever," as young as anyone possibly could be. That seemed to give the whole business a new turn altogether; it suddenly placed him, James Maradick, a person of unimaginative and sober middle age, in a romantic and difficult position of guardian to a couple of babies, and, moreover, babies charged to the full with excitement and love of hurried adventure. Why, he thought desperately, as he listened politely to Morelli's conversation, had he been made the centre of all this business? What did he or could he know of young people and their love affairs?

"I am afraid," he said politely, "I know nothing whatever about swords."

"Ah," said Morelli heartily, "I must show you some after supper."

Janet entered with chops and potatoes, followed by Lucy with the coffee. Tony went forward to help her. "No, thank you," she said, laughing. "You shan't carry the potatoes because then you'll see how black they are. I hope you don't mind coffee at the beginning like this; and there's only brown bread." She placed the things on the table and helped the chops. Tony looked at his plate and was silent.

It was, at first, a difficult meal, and everyone was very subdued; then suddenly the ice was broken. Maradick had said that he lived in London. Miss Minns sat up a little straighter in her chair, smoothed her cuffs nervously, and said with a good deal of excitement—

"I lived a year in London with my brother Charles. We lived in Little Worsted Street, No. 95, near the Aquarium: a little house with green blinds; perhaps, sir, you know it. I believe it is still standing; I loved London. Charles was a curate at St. Michael's, the grey church at the corner of Merritt Street; Mr. Roper was rector at the time. I remember seeing our late beloved

Queen pass in her carriage. I have a distinct recollection of her black bonnet and gracious bow. I was very much moved."

Maradick had, very fortunately, touched on the only topic that could possibly be said to make Miss Minns loquacious. Everyone became interested and animated.

"Oh! I should so love London!" Janet said, looking through the window at the stars outside. "People! Processions! Omnibuses! Father has told me about it sometimes—Dick Whittington, you know, and the cat. I suppose you're not called Dick?" she said, looking anxiously at Tony.

"No," said Tony, "I'm afraid I'm not. But I will be if you like."

"It is scarcely polite, Janet," said Morelli, "to ask a gentleman his name when you've only known him five minutes."

"I wasn't," she answered. "Only I do want to know a Dick so very badly, and there aren't any down here; but I expect London's full of them."

"It's full of everything," said Tony, "and that's why I like this place so awfully. London chokes you, there's such a lot going on; you have to stop, you know. Here you can go full tilt. May I have another chop, please? They're most awfully good."

Tony was rapidly becoming his usual self. He was still a little nervous, but he was talking nonsense as fluently as ever.

"You really must come up to London though, Miss Morelli. There are pantomimes and circuses and policemen and lots of funny things. And you can do just what you like because there's no one to see."

"Oh! theatres!" She clapped her hands. "I should simply love a theatre. Father took me once here; it was called 'The Murdered Heir,' and it was most frightfully exciting; but that's the only one I've ever seen, and I don't suppose there'll be another here for ages. They have them in Truro, but I've never been to Truro. I'm glad you like the chops, I was afraid they were rather dry."

"They are," said Morelli. "It's only Mr. Gale's politeness that makes him say they're all right. They're dreadfully dry."

"Well, you were late," she answered; "it was your fault."

She was excited. Her eyes were shining, her hands trembled a little, and her cheeks were flushed. Maradick fancied that there was surprise in her glance at her father. Miss Minns also was a little astonished at something. It was possibly unusual for Morelli to invite anyone into the house, and they were wondering why he had done it.

Morelli was a great puzzle. He seemed changed since they had sat down at the table. He seemed, for one thing, considerably younger. Outside the house he had been middle-aged; now the lines in his forehead seemed to disappear, the wrinkles under his eyes were no longer there. He laughed continually.

It was, in fact, becoming very rapidly a merry meal. The chops had vanished and there was cheese and fruit. They were all rather excited, and a wave of what Maradick was inclined to call "spirited childishness" swept over the party. He himself and Miss Minns were most decidedly out of it.

It was significant of the change that Morelli now paid much more attention to Tony. The three of them burst into roars of laughter about nothing; Tony imitated various animals, the drawing of a cork, and a motor-omnibus running into a policeman, with enormous success. Miss Minns made no attempt to join in the merriment; but sat in the shadow gravely silent. Maradick tried and was for a time a miserable failure, but afterwards he too was influenced. Morelli told a story that seemed to him extraordinarily funny. It was about an old bachelor who always lived alone, and some one climbed up a chimney and stuck there. He could not afterwards remember the point of the story, but he knew that it seemed delightfully amusing to him at the time. He began to laugh and then lost all control of himself; he laughed and laughed till the tears ran down his cheeks. He stopped for a moment and then started again; he grew red in the face and purple—he took out his handkerchief and wiped his eyes. "Oh, dear!" he said, gasping, "that's a funny story. I don't know when I've laughed like that before. It's awfully funny." He still shook at the thought of it. It was a very gay meal indeed.

"You have been at the University, I suppose, Mr. Gale?" said Morelli.

"Yes, Oxford," said Tony. "But please don't call me Mr.; nobody calls me Mr., you know. You have to have a house, a wife and a profession if you're Mr. anybody, and I haven't got anything—nothing whatever."

"Oh, I wonder," said Janet, "if you'd mind opening the door for me. We'll clear the table and get it out of the way. Saturday is Lucy's night out, so I'm going to do it."

"Oh, let me help," said Tony, jumping up and nearly knocking the table over in his eagerness. "I'm awfully good at washing things up."

"You won't have to wash anything up," she answered. "We'll leave that for Lucy when she comes back; but if you wouldn't mind helping me to carry the plates and things into the other room I'd be very grateful."

She looked very charming, Maradick thought, as she stood piling the plates on top of one another with most anxious care lest they should break. Several curls had escaped and were falling over her eyes and she raised her hand to push them back; the plates nearly slipped. Maradick, watching her, caught suddenly something that seemed very like terror in her eyes; she was looking across the table at her father. He followed her glance, but Morelli did not seem to have noticed anything. Maradick forgot the incident at the time, but afterwards he wondered whether it had been imagination.

"Do be careful and not drop things," she said, laughing gaily, to Tony. "You seem to have got a great many there; there's plenty of time, you know."

She was delightful to watch, she was so entirely unconscious of any pose or affectation. She passed into the kitchen singing and Tony followed her laden with plates.

"Do you smoke, Mr. Maradick?" said Morelli. "Cigar? Cigarette? Pipe?—Pipe! Good! much the best thing. Come and sit over here."

They drew up their chairs by the window and watched the stars; Miss Minns sat under the lamp sewing.

Maradick was a little ashamed of his merriment at dinner; he really didn't know the man well enough, and a little of his first impression of cautious dislike returned. But Morelli was very entertaining and an excellent talker, and Maradick reproached himself for being unnecessarily suspicious.

"You know," said Morelli, "it's a great thing to have a home like this. I've been a wanderer all my days—been everywhere, you might say—but now I've always got this to come back to, and it's a great thing to feel that it's there. I'm Italian, you know, on my father's side, and hence my name; and so it seems a bit funny, perhaps, settling down here. But one country's the same to me as another, and my wife was English."

He paused for a moment and looked out of the window; then he went on—

"We don't see many people here; when you've got a girl to bring up you've got to be careful, and they don't like me here, that's the truth."

He paused again, as though he expected Maradick to deny it. He had spoken it almost as an interrogation, as though he wanted to know whether Maradick had heard anything, but Maradick was silent. He felt strongly again, as he had felt at the time of their first meeting, that they were hostile to one another. Polite though Morelli was, Maradick knew that it was because of Tony, and not in the least because of himself. Morelli probably felt that he was an unnecessary bore, and resented his being there. It was Tony that he cared about.

"That is a very delightful boy," Morelli said, nodding in the direction of the kitchen. "Have you known him a long while? Quite one of the most delightful people——"

"Oh, no," said Maradick a little stiffly. "We are quite new acquaintances. We have only known each other about a week. Yes, he is an enormously popular person. Everyone seems to like him wherever he goes. He wakes people up."

Morelli laughed.

"Yes, there's wonderful vitality there. I hope he'll keep it. I hope that I shall see something of him while he is here. There isn't much that we can offer you, but you will be doing both my daughter and myself a very real kindness if you will come and see us sometimes."

"Thank you," said Maradick.

"Oh! I promised to show you those swords of mine. Come and see them now. I think there are really some that may interest you."

They got up and left the room. In a moment the door was opened again and Janet and Tony returned.

"Let's sit in front of the window," Janet said, "and talk. Father's showing your friend his swords and things, I expect, and he always takes an enormous time over that, and I want to talk most frightfully."

She sat forward with her hands round her knees and her eyes gazing out of the window at the stars. Tony will always remember her like that; and as he sat and watched her he had to grip the side of his chair to prevent his leaning forward and touching her dress.

"I want to talk too," he answered; "it's an 'experience' evening, you know, one of those times when you suddenly want to exchange confidences with some one, find out what they've been doing and thinking all the time."

"Oh! I know that feeling," she answered eagerly, "but I've never had anyone to exchange them with. Sometimes I've felt it so that I haven't known what to do; but it's been no good, there's been nobody except father and Miss Minns. It's very funny, isn't it? but you're the first person of my own age I've ever met. Of course you're older really, but you're near enough, and I expect we think some of the same things; and oh! it's so exciting!"

She said "person" like a creature of fifty, and he smiled, but then her "exciting" brought his heart to his mouth. She was obviously so delighted to have him, she accepted him so readily without any restrictions at all, and it was wonderful to him. Every girl that he had ever met had played a game either of defence or provocation, but there was perfect simplicity here.

"Let's begin," he said, "and find out whether we've had the same things. But first I must tell you something. This isn't the only time that I've seen you."

"It's not!" she cried.

"No; there was the other day on the beach; you were with your father. I looked at you from behind a rock and then ran away. And the other time was one night about a week ago, quite late, and you leaned out of a window and said something to Miss Minns. There was a lamp, and I saw your face."

"Oh! which night?" she said quite eagerly.

"Well, let me see, I think it was a Thursday night—no, I can't remember—but there was a fair in the town; they danced round the streets. We had been, Maradick and I, and were coming back."

"Oh! I remember perfectly," she said, turning round and looking at him. "But, do you know, that's most curious! I was tremendously excited that night, I don't quite know why. There was no real reason. But I kept saying to Miss Minns that I knew something would happen, and she laughed at me and said, 'What could?' or something, and then I suddenly opened the window and two people were coming up the street. It was quite dark. There was only the lamp!"

She spoke quite dramatically, as though it was something of great importance.

"And fancy, it was you!" she added.

"But, please," she said, "let's begin confidences. They'll be back, and we'll have to stop."

"Oh! mine are ordinary enough," he said, "just like anybody else's. I was born in the country; one of those old rambling country houses with dark passages and little stairs leading to nowhere, and thick walls with a wonderful old garden. Such a garden, with terraces and enormous old trees, and a fountain, and a sun-dial, and peacocks. But I was quite a kid when we left that and came to town. It is funny, though, the early years seem to remain with one after the other things have gone. It has always been a background for me, that high old house with the cooing of pigeons on a hot summer's afternoon, and the cold running of some stream at the bottom of the lawn!"

"Oh! how beautiful," she said. "I have never known anything like that. Father has talked of Italy; a little town, Montiviero, where we once lived, and an old grey tower, and a long, hard white road with trees like pillars. I have often seen it in my dreams. But I myself have never known anything but this. Father has stayed here, partly, I think, because the old grey tower in the market-place here is like the tower at Montiviero. But tell me about London," she went on. "What is it like? What people are there?"

"London," he said, "has grown for me as I have grown to know it. We have always lived in the same house. I was six when I first went there, an old dark place with large solemn rooms and high stone fireplaces. It was in a square, and we used to be taken out on to the grass in the morning to play with other children. London was at first only the square—the dark rooms, my nurse, my father and mother, some other children, and the grass that we played upon. Then suddenly one day the streets sprang upon me—the shops, the carriages, some soldiers. Then it grew rapidly; there were the parks, the lake, the Tower, and, most magical of all, the river. When I was quite a small boy the river fascinated me, and I would escape there when I could; and now, if I lived alone in London, I would take some old dark rooms down in Chelsea and watch the river all day."

"Chelsea!" she said. "I like the sound of that. Is there a very wonderful river, then, where London is?"

"Yes," he answered, "it is dirty and foggy, and the buildings along the banks of it are sometimes old and in pieces. But everyone that has known it will tell you the same. Then I went to a pantomime with my nurse."

"Oh! I know what a pantomime is," she said. "Miss Minns once saw one, but there was a man with a red nose and she didn't like it. Only there were fairies as well, and if I'd been there I should only have seen the fairies."

"Well, this was 'Dick Whittington.' There was a glorious cat. I don't remember about the rest; but I went home in a golden dream and for the next month I thought of nothing else. London became for me a dark place with one glorious circle of light in the midst of it!"

"Oh! It must have been beautiful!" she sighed.

"Then," he went on, "it spread from that, you know, to other things, and I went to school. For a time everything was swallowed up in that, beating other people, coming out top, and getting licked for slacking. London was fun for the holidays, but it wasn't a bit the important thing. I was like that until I was seventeen."

"You were very lucky," Janet said, "to go to school. I asked father once, but he was very angry; and, you know, he is away for months and months sometimes, and then it is most dreadfully lonely. I have never had anyone at all to talk to until you came, and now they'll take you away in a moment, so do hurry up. There simply isn't a minute!"

Miss Minns was heard to say:

"Aren't you cold by the window, Janet? I think you'd better come nearer the table."

"Oh! please don't interrupt, Miss Minns!" She waved her hand. "It's as warm as toast, really. Now please go on, it's a most terribly exciting adventure."

"Well," he said, sinking his voice and speaking in a dramatic whisper, "the next part of the tremendous adventure was books and things. I suddenly, you know, discovered what they were. I'd read things before, of course, but it had always been to fill in time while I was waiting for something else, and now I suddenly saw them differently, in rows and rows and rows, each with a secret in it like a nut, and I cracked them and ate them and had the greatest fun. Then I began to think that I was awfully clever and that I would write great books myself, and I was very solemn and serious. I expect I was simply hateful."

"And did you write anything?" she said in an awed voice.

"Yes," he answered solemnly, "a very long story with heaps of people and lots of chapters. I have it at home. They liked it down in the kitchen, but it never had an end."

"Why not?" Janet asked.

"Because, like the Old Woman in the Shoe, I had so many children that I didn't know what to do. I had so many people that I simply didn't know what to do with them all. And then I grew out of that. I went to Oxford, and then came the last part of the adventure."

"Where is Oxford?" she asked him.

"Oh! It's a university. Men go there after leaving school. It's a place where a man learns a good many useless habits and one or two beautiful ones. Only the beautiful ones want looking for. The thing I found was walking."

He looked at her and laughed for the very joy of being so near to her. In the half light that the lamp flung upon them the gold of her hair was caught and fell like a cloud about her face, the light blue of her dress was the night sky, and her eyes were the stars. Oh! it was a fine adventure, this love! There had been no key to the world before this came, and now the casket was opened and stuffs of great price, jewels and the gold-embroidered cloths of

God's workshop were spread before him. And then a great awe fell upon him. She was so young and so pure that he felt suddenly that all the coarse thoughts and deeds of the world rose in a dark mist between them, and sent him, as the angel with the flaming sword sent Adam, out of so white a country.

But she suddenly leant over and touched his arm. "Oh! do look at Miss Minns!" she said. Miss Minns was falling asleep and struggling valiantly against the temptation. Her hands mechanically clicked the needles and clutched the piece of cloth at which she was working, but her head nodded violently at the table as though it was telling a story and furiously emphasising facts. The shadow on the wall was gigantic, a huge fantastic Miss Minns swinging from side to side on the ceiling and swelling and subsiding like a curtain in the wind. The struggle lasted for a very short time. Soon the clicking of the needles ceased, there was a furious attempt to hold the cloth, and at last it fell with a soft noise to the ground. Miss Minns, with her head on her breast, slept.

"That's better," said Janet, settling herself back in her chair. "Now about the walking!"

"Ah! you're fond of it too," he said. "I can see that. And it's the only thing, you know. It's the only thing that doesn't change and grow monotonous. You get close right down to earth. They talk about their nature and culture and the rest, but they haven't known what life is until they've felt the back of a high brown hill and the breast of a hard white road. That saved me! I was muddled before. I didn't know what things stood for, and I was unhappy. My own set weren't any use at all, they were aiming at nothing. Not that I felt superior, but it was simply that that sort of thing wasn't any good for me. You couldn't see things clearly for the dust that everybody made. So I left the dust and now I'm here."

"And that's all?" she said.

"Absolutely all," he answered. "I'm afraid it's disappointing in incident, but it is at any rate truthful."

"Oh, but it's adventurous," she said, "beside mine. There's nothing for me to tell at all. I've simply lived here with father always. There have been no books, no children, nothing at all except father."

She paused then in rather a curious way. He looked up at her.

"Well?" he said.

"Oh! father's so different—you never know. Sometimes he's just as I am, plays and sings and tells stories. And then, oh! he's such fun. There never was anybody like him. And sometimes he's very quiet and won't say anything, and then he always goes away, perhaps it's only a day or two, and then it's a week or a month even. And sometimes," she paused again for a moment, "he's angry, terribly angry, so that I am awfully frightened."

"What! with you?" Tony asked indignantly.

"No; with no one exactly, but it's dreadful. I go and hide." And then she burst out laughing. "Oh, and once he caught Miss Minns like that, and he pulled her hair and it fell all over her shoulders. Oh! it was so funny. And a lot of it came out altogether; it was false, you know. I think that father is just like a child. He's ever so much younger than I am really. I'm getting dreadfully old, and he's as young as can be. He tells stories—beautiful stories! and then he's cross and he sulks, and sometimes he's out of doors for days together, and all the animals simply love him."

All these facts she brought out, as it were, in a bunch, without any very evident connexion, but he felt that the cord that bound them was there and that he could find it one day. But what surprised him most was her curious aloofness from it all, as if he were a friend, perhaps a chum, sometimes a bother and sometimes a danger, but never a father.

"But tell me about yourself," he said, "what you like and what you do."

"No, there's really nothing. I've just lived here always, that's all. You're the first man I've talked to, except father, and you're fun. I hope that we shall see you sometimes whilst you are staying here," she added, quite frankly.

"Somebody told you to say that," he said, laughing.

"Yes, it's Miss Minns. She teaches me sometimes about what you ought to say, and I'm dreadfully stupid. There are so many of them. There's 'at a wedding' and 'at a funeral' and there's 'the dinner party,' a nice one and a dull one and a funny one, and there's 'at the theatre,' and lots more. Sometimes I remember, but I've never had anyone to practise them on. You're quite the first, so I think I ought to give you them all."

The door opened and Maradick and Morelli came in. The pair at the window did not see them and the two men stood for a moment at the door. Morelli smiled, and Maradick at once felt again that curious unfounded sensation of distrust. The man amazed him. He had talked about his "things," his armour, some tapestry, some pictures, with a knowledge and enthusiasm that made him fascinating. He seemed to have the widest possible grip on every subject; there was nothing that he did not know. And there had been, too, a lightness of touch, a humorous philosophy of men and things for which he had been quite unprepared.

And then again, there would be suddenly that strange distrust; a swift glance from under his eyelids, a suspicious lifting of the voice, as though he were on his guard against some expected discovery. And then, most puzzling of all, there was suddenly a simplicity, a *naïveté*, that belonged to childhood, some anger or pleasure that only a child could feel. Oh! he was a puzzle.

At the sight of those two in the window he felt suddenly a sharp, poignant regret! What an old fool he was to meddle with something that he had passed long, long before. You could not be adaptable at forty, and he would only spoil their game. A death's head at the feast indeed, with his own happy home to think of, his own testimony to fling before them. But the regret was there all the same; regret that he had not known for ever so many years, and a feeling of loneliness that was something altogether new.

He knew now that, during these last few days, Tony had filled his picture, some one that would take him out of himself and make him a little less selfish and even, perhaps, a little younger; but now, what did Tony— Tony in love, Tony with a new heaven and a new earth—want with a stout cynic of forty! It would have been better, after all, if they had never met.

Suddenly Miss Minns awoke, and was extremely upset. Some half-remembered story of gentlemen winning a pair of gloves under some such circumstances flew to her mind; at any rate it was undignified with two new persons in the room.

"I really——" she said. "You were quite a long time. I have been sewing."

At the sound of her voice Tony turned back from the window. He was so happy that he would have clasped Miss Minns round the neck and kissed her, if there had been any provocation. The lamp flung a half-circle of light, leaving the corners in perfect darkness, so that the room was curved like a shell; the shining tiles of the fireplace sparkled under the leaping flame of the fire.

"You have been a very long time," said Janet.

"That's scarcely a compliment to Mr. Gale," said Morelli.

"Oh, but I haven't found it so," she answered quickly. "It has been enormously interesting. We have been discovering things. And now, father, play. Mr. Gale loves music, I know."

That Morelli played was a little surprising. There was no piano in the room, and Maradick wondered what the instrument would be. They all sat down in a circle round the fireplace, and behind them, in the dusk of the room, Morelli produced a flute from his pocket. He had said nothing, and they were all of them suddenly silent.

The incident seemed to Maradick a key—a key to the house, to the man, and, above all, to the situation. This was not a feeling that he could in the least understand. It was only afterwards that he saw that his instinct had been a right one.

But the idea that he had of their all being children together—Tony, Janet, Morelli—was exactly represented by the flute. There was something absolutely irresponsible in the gay little tune piped mysteriously in the darkness, a little tune that had nothing in it at all except a pressing invitation to dance, and Maradick could see Tony's feet going on the floor. It would not be at all impossible, he felt, for them suddenly to form a ring and dance riotously round the room; it was in the air.

He was a person of very slight imagination, but the tune gave him the long hillside, the white sails of the flying clouds, the shrill whistle of wind through a tossing forest of pines, white breakers against a black cliff, anything open and unfettered; and again he came back to that same word— irresponsible. The little tune was repeated again and again, with other little tunes that crept shyly into it for a moment and then out and away. The spell increased as the tune continued.

For Tony it was magical beyond all words. Nothing could have put so wonderful a seal on that wonderful evening as that music. His pulse was beating furiously and his cheeks were burning; he wanted now to fling himself on his knees, there on the floor, and say to her, "I love you! I love you!" like any foolish hero in a play. He moved his chair ever so slightly so that it should be nearer hers, and then suddenly, amazed at his daring, his heart stopped beating; she must have noticed. But she gazed in front of her, her hands folded in her lap, her eyes gravely bent towards the floor.

And this melancholy little tune, coming mysteriously from some unknown distance, seemed to give him permission to do what he would. "Yes, love," it commanded. "Do what is natural. Come out on to the plain where all freedom is and there are winds and the clear sky and everything that is young and alive."

He could almost fancy that Morelli himself was giving him permission, but at a thought so wild he pulled himself up. Of course Morelli didn't know; he was going too fast.

Maradick began to be vaguely irritated and at last annoyed. There was something unpleasant in that monotonous little tune coming out of the darkness from nowhere at all; its note of freedom seemed to become rapidly something lawless and undisciplined. Had he put it into pictures, he would have said that the open plain that he had seen before became suddenly darkened, and, through the gloom, strange animals passed and wild, savage faces menaced him. Afterwards, in the full light of day, such thoughts would seem folly, but now, in the darkened room, anything was possible. He did not believe in apparitions—ghosts were unknown in Epsom—but he was suddenly unpleasantly aware that he would give anything to be able to fling a glance back over his shoulder.

Then suddenly the spell was broken. The tune died away, revived for an instant, and then came to an abrupt end.

Morelli joined the circle.

"Thank you so very much," said Maradick. "That was delightful." But he was aware that, although the little tune had been played again and again, it had already completely passed from his memory. He could not recall it.

"What was the name of it?" he asked.

"It has no name," Morelli answered, smiling. "It's an old tune that has been passed down from one to another. There is something rather quaint in it, and it has many centuries behind it."

Then Tony got up, and to Maradick's intense astonishment said: "I say, Maradick, it's time we were going, it's getting awfully late."

He had been willing to give the boy as long a rope as he pleased, and now—but then he understood. It was the perfect moment that must not be spoiled by any extension. If they waited something might happen. He understood the boy as far as that, at any rate.

Morelli pressed them to stay, but Tony was firm. He went forward and said good night to Miss Minns, then he turned to Janet.

"Good night, Miss Morelli," he said.

"Good night," she answered, smiling. "Please come again and tell me more."

"I will," he said.

Morelli's good-bye was very cordial. "Whenever you like," he said, "drop in at any time, we shall be delighted."

They walked back to the hotel in absolute silence. Tony's eyes were fixed on the hill in front of him.

As they passed under the dark line of trees that led to the hotel he gripped Maradick's hand very hard.

"I say," he said, "help me!"

CHAPTER VII
MARADICK LEARNS THAT "GETTING A VIEW" MAY HAVE ITS DANGERS AS WELL AS ITS REWARDS

Two days after the arrival of the Lesters Lady Gale arranged a picnic; a comprehensive, democratic picnic that was to include everybody. Her motives may be put down, if you will, to sociability, even, and you involve a larger horizon, to philanthropy. "Everybody," of course, was in reality only a few, but it included the Lesters, the Maradicks, and Mrs. Lawrence. It was to be a delightful picnic; they were to drive to the top of Pender Callon, where there was a wonderful view, then they were to have tea, and then drive back in the moonlight.

DEAR MRS. MARADICK (the letter went)—

It would give me such pleasure if you and your husband could come with us for a little Picnic at Pender Callon to-morrow afternoon, weather permitting, of course. The wagonette will come round about two-thirty.

I do hope you will be able to come.

Yours sincerely,

BEATRICE GALE.

Mrs. Maradick considered it a little haughtily. She was sitting in the garden. Suddenly, as she turned the invitation over in her mind, she saw her husband coming towards her.

"Oh!" she said, as he came up to her, "I wanted to talk to you."

He was looking as he always did—big, strong, red and brown. Oh! so healthy and stupid!

She did feel a new interest in him this morning, certainly. His avoiding her so consistently during the week was unlike him, was unusually strong. She even felt suddenly that she would like him to be rude and violent to her again, as he had been that other evening. Great creature! it was certainly his métier to be rude and violent. Perhaps he would be.

She held Lady Gale's invitation towards him.

"A picnic." she said coldly. "To-morrow; do you care to go?"

"Are you going?" he said, looking at her.

"I should think that scarcely matters," she answered scornfully, "judging by the amount of interest you've taken in me and my doings during the last week."

"I know," he said, and he looked down at the ground, "I have been a brute, a cad, all these days, treating you like that. I have come to apologise."

Oh! the fool! She could have struck him with her hand! It was to be the same thing after all, then. The monotonous crawling back to her feet, the old routine of love and submission, the momentary hope of strength and contradiction strangled as soon as born.

She laughed a little. "Oh, you needn't apologise," she said, "and, in any case, it's a little late, isn't it? Not that you need mind about me. I've had a very pleasant week, and so have the girls, even though their father *hasn't* been near them."

But he broke in upon her rapidly. "Oh! I'm ashamed of myself," he said, "you don't know how ashamed. I think the place had something to do with it, and then one was tired and nervy a bit, I suppose; not," he hastily added, "that I want to make excuses, for there really aren't any. I just leave it with you. I was a beast. I promise never to break out again."

How could a man! she thought, looking at him, and then, how blind men were. Why couldn't they see that it wasn't the sugar and honey that women were continually wanting, or, at any rate, the right sort of woman!

She glanced at him angrily. "We'd better leave the thing there," she said. "For heaven's sake spare us any more scenes. You were rude—abominably—I'm glad you've had the grace at last to come and tell me so."

She moved as though she would get up, but he put out his hand and stopped her.

"No, Emmy, please," he said, "let's talk for a moment. I've got things I want to say." He cleared his throat, and stared down the white shining path. Mrs. Lawrence appeared coming towards them, then she saw them together and turned hurriedly back. "I've been thinking, all these days, about the muddle that we've made. My fault very largely, I know, but I have so awfully wanted to put it right again. And I thought if we talked——"

"What's the use of talking?" she broke in hastily; "there's nothing to say; it's all as stale as anything could be. You're so extraordinarily dull when you're in the 'picking up the pieces' mood; not content with behaving like a second-rate bricklayer and then sulking for a week you add to it by a long recital, 'the virtues of an obedient wife'—a little tiresome, don't you think?"

Her nerves were all to pieces, she really wasn't well, and the heat was terrible; the sight of him sitting there with that pathetic, ill-used look on his face, drove her nearly to madness. To think that she was tied for life to so feeble a creature.

"No, please," he said, "I know that I'm tiresome and stupid. But really I've been seeing things differently these last few days. We might get along better. I'll try; I know it's been largely my fault, not seeing things and not trying——"

"Oh!" she broke in furiously, "for God's sake stop it. Isn't it bad enough and tiresome enough for me already without all this stuff! I'm sick of it, sick of it, I tell you. Sick of the whole thing. You spoke your mind the other night, I'll speak mine now. You can take it or leave it." She rose from her chair and stood looking out to sea, her hands clenched at her sides. "Oh! these years! these years! Always the same thing. You've never stuck up to anything, never fought anything, and it's all been so tame. And now you want us to go over the same old ground again, to patch it up and go on as if we hadn't had twenty long dreary years of it and would give a good deal not to have another." She stopped and looked at him, smiling curiously. "Oh! James! My poor dear, you're such a bore. Try not to be so painfully good; you might even be a little amusing!"

She walked slowly away towards the girls. She passed, with them, down the path.

He picked up the broken pieces of his thoughts and tried to put them slowly together. His first thought of her and of the whole situation was that it was hopeless, perfectly hopeless. He had fancied, stupidly, blindly, that his having moved included her moving too, quite without reason, as he now thoroughly saw. She was just where they had both been a week ago, she was even, from his neglect of her during these last days, a little farther back; it was harder than ever for her to see in line. His discovery of this affected him very little. He was very slightly wounded by the things that she had said to him, and her rejection of his advances so finally and completely distressed him scarcely at all. As he sat and watched the colours steal mistily across the sea he knew that he was too happy at all the discoveries that he was making to mind anything else. He was setting out on an adventure, and if she would not come too it could simply not be helped; it did not in the least alter the adventure's excitement.

It was even with a new sense of freedom that he went off, late that afternoon, to the town; he was like a boy just out of school. He had no very vivid intention of going anywhere; but lately the town had grown before him so that he loved to stand and watch it, its life and movement, its colour and romance.

He loved, above all, the market-place with its cobbled stones over which rattled innumerable little carts, its booths, its quaint and delightful chatter, its old grey tower. It was one of the great features of his new view that places mattered, that, indeed, they were symbols of a great and visible importance; stocks and stones seemed to him now to be possessed of such vitality that they almost frightened him, they knew so much and had lived so long a time.

The evening light was over the market-place; the sun, peering through a pillar of cloudless blue, cut sharply between the straight walls of the Town Hall and a neighbouring chimney, flung itself full upon the tower.

It caught the stones and shot them with myriad lights; it played with the fruit on the stall at the tower's foot until the apples were red as rubies and the oranges shone like gold. It bathed it, caressed it, enfolded it, and showed the modern things on every side that old friends were, after all, the best, and that fine feathers did not always make the finest birds.

The rest of the market-place was in shadow, purple in the corners and crevices, the faintest blue in the higher air, a haze of golden-grey in the central square. It was full of people standing, for the most part, discussing the events of the day; in the corner by the tower there was a Punch and Judy show, and Maradick could hear the shrill cries of Mr. Punch rising above the general chatter. Over everything there was a delicious scent of all the best things in the world — ripe orchards, flowering lanes, and the sharp pungent breath of the sea; in the golden haze of the evening everything seemed to be waiting, breathlessly, in spite of the noise of voices, for some great moment.

Maradick had never felt so perfectly in tune with the world.

He passed across to the Punch and Judy show, and stood in a corner by the fruit stall under the tower and watched Mr. Punch. That gentleman was in a very bad temper to-night, and he banged with his stick at everything that he could see; poor Judy was in for a bad time, and sank repeatedly beneath the blows which should have slain an ox. Toby looked on very indifferently until it was his turn, when he bit furiously at Mr. Punch's trousers and showed his teeth, and choked in his frill and behaved like a most ferocious animal. Then there came the policeman, and Mr. Punch was carried, swearing and cursing, off to prison, but in a moment he was back again, as perky as before, and committing murders at the rate of two a minute.

There was a fat baby, held aloft in its mother's arms, who watched the proceedings with the closest attention; it was intensely serious, its thumb in its mouth, its double chin wrinkling with excitement. Then a smile crept out of its ears and across its cheeks; its mouth opened, and suddenly there came a gurgle of laughter. It crowed with delight, its head fell back on its nurse's shoulder and its eyes closed with ecstasy; then, with the coming of Jack Ketch and his horrible gallows, it was solemn once more, and it watched the villain's miserable end with stern approval. There were other babies in the crowd, and bottles had to be swiftly produced in order to stay the cries that came from so sudden an ending. The dying sun danced on Punch's execution; he dangled frantically in mid-air, Toby barked furiously, and down came the curtain.

The old lady at the fruit stall had watched the performance with great excitement. She was remarkable to look at, and had been in the same place behind the same stall for so many years that people had grown to take her as part of the tower. She wore a red peaked hat, a red skirt, a man's coat of black velvet, and black mittens; her enormous chin pointed towards her nose, which was hooked like an eagle; nose and chin so nearly met that it was a miracle how she ever opened her mouth at all. She nodded at Maradick and smiled, whilst her hands clicked her needles together, and a bit of grey stocking grew visibly before his eyes.

"It's a fine show," she said, "a fine show, and very true to human nature." Then suddenly looking past him, she screamed in a voice like the whistle of a train: "A-pples and O-ranges—fine ripe grapes!"

Her voice was so close to his ear that it startled him, but he answered her.

"It is good for the children," he said, shadowing his eyes with his hand, for the sun was beating in his face.

She leaned towards him and waved a skinny finger. "I ought to know," she said, "I've buried ten, but they always loved the Punch . . . and that's many a year back."

How old was she, he wondered? He seemed, in this town, to be continually meeting people who had this quality of youth; Tony, Morelli, Punch, this old woman, they gave one the impression that they would gaily go on for ever.

"People live to a good old age here," he said.

"Ah! it's a wonderful town," she said. "There's nothing like it. . . . Many's the things I've seen, the tower and I."

"The tower!" said Maradick, looking up at its grey solemnity now flushing with the red light of the sun.

"I've been near it since I was a bit of a child," she said, leaning towards him so that her beak of a nose nearly touched his cheek and her red hat towered over him. "We lived by it once, and then I moved under it. We've been friends, good friends, but it wants some considering."

"What wants considering mother?" said a voice, and Maradick turned round; Punch was at his elbow. His show was packed up and leant against the wall; by his side was Toby, evidently pleased with the world in general, for every part of his body was wagging.

"Good evening, sir," said Punch, smiling from ear to ear. "It's a beautiful evening—the sea's like a pome—what wants considering mother? and I think I'll have an apple, if you don't mind—one of your rosiest."

She chose for him an enormous red one, which with one squeeze of the hand he broke into half. Toby cocked an ear and raised his eyes; he was soon munching for his life. "What wants considering mother?" he said again.

"Many things," she answered him shortly, "and it'll be tuppence, please." Her voice rose into a shrill scream—"A-pples and O-ranges and fine ripe grapes." She sat back in her chair and bent over her knitting, she had nothing more to say.

"I've been watching your show," Maradick said, "and enjoyed it more than many a play I've seen in town."

"Yes, it went well to-night," Punch said, "and there was a new baby. It's surprisin' what difference a new baby makes, even Toby notices it."

"A new baby?" asked Maradick.

"Yes. A baby, you know, that 'asn't seen the show before, leastways in this world. You can always tell by the way they take it." Then he added politely, "And I hope you like this town, sir."

"Enormously," Maradick answered. "I think it has some quality, something that makes it utterly different from anywhere else that I know. There is a feeling——"

He looked across the market-place, and, through the cleft between the ebony black of the towering walls, there shone the bluest of evening skies, and across the space floated a pink cushion of a cloud; towards the bend of the green hill on the horizon the sky where the sun was setting was a bed of primroses. "It is a wonderful place."

"Ah, I tell you sir," said Punch, stroking one of Toby's ears, "there's no place like it. . . . I've been in every town in this kingdom, and some of them are good enough. But this!"

He looked at Maradick a moment and then he said, "Forgive my mentioning it, sir, but you've got the feeling of the place; you've caught the spirit, as one might say. We watch, folks down here, you strangers up there at the 'Man at Arms.' For the most part they miss it altogether. They come for the summer with their boxes and their bags, they bathe in the sea, they drive on the hill, and they're gone. Lord love you, why they might have been sleepin'." He spat contemptuously.

"But you think that I have it?" said Maradick.

"You've got it right enough," said Punch. "But then you're a friend of young Mr. Gale's, and so you couldn't help having it; 'e's got it more than anyone I ever knew."

"And what exactly is—It?" asked Maradick.

"Well, sir," said Punch, "it's not exactly easy to put it into words, me bein' no scholar." He looked at the old woman, but she was intent over her knitting. The light of the sun had faded from the tower and left it cold and grey against the primrose sky. "It's a kind of Youth; seeing things, you know, all freshly and with a new colour, always caring about things as if you'd met 'em for the first time. It doesn't come of the asking, and there are places as well as people that 'ave got it. But when a place or a person's got it, it's like a match that they go round lighting other people's candles with." He waved his arm in a comprehensive sweep. "It's all here, you know, sir, and Mr. Gale's got it like that . . . 'e's lit your candle, so to speak, sir, if it isn't familiar, and now you've got to take the consequences."

"The consequences?" said Maradick.

"Oh, it's got its dangers," said Punch, "specially when you take it suddenly; it's like a fever, you know. And when it comes to a gentleman of your age of life and settled habits, well, it needs watchin'. Oh, there's the bad and good of it."

Maradick stared in front of him.

"Well, sir, I must be going," said Punch. "Excuse me, but I always must be talking. Good night, sir."

"Good night," said Maradick. He watched the square, stumpy figure pass, followed by the dog, across the misty twilight of the market-place. Violet shadows lingered and swept like mysterious creeping figures over the square. He said good night to the old woman and struck up the hill to the hotel.

"Consequence? Good and bad of it?" Anyhow, the man hadn't expressed it badly. That was his new view, that strange new lightness of vision as though his pack had suddenly been rolled from off his back. He was suddenly enjoying every minute of his life, his candle had been lighted. For a moment there floated across his mind his talk with his wife that afternoon. Well, it could not be helped. If she would not join him he must have his fun alone.

At the top of the hill he met Mrs. Lester. He had seen something of her during the last two days and liked her. She was amusing and vivacious; she had something of Tony's quality.

"Hullo, Mr. Maradick," she cried, "hurrying back like me to dinner? Isn't it wicked the way that we leave the most beautiful anything for our food?"

"Well, I must confess," he answered, laughing, "that I never thought of dinner at all. I just turned back because things had, as it were, come to an end. The sun set, you know."

"I heard it strike seven," she answered him, "and I said Dinner. Although I was down on the beach watching the most wonderful sea you ever saw, nothing could stop me, and so back I came."

"Have you been down here before?" he asked her. "To stay, I mean."

"Oh yes. Fred likes it as well as anywhere else, and I like it a good deal better than most. He doesn't mind so very much, you know, where he is. He's always living in his books, and so real places don't count." She gave a little sigh. "But they do count with me."

"I'm enjoying it enormously," he said, "it's flinging the years off from me."

"Oh, I know," she answered, "but I'm almost afraid of it for that very reason. It's so very—what shall I say—champagney, that one doesn't know what one will do next. Sometimes one's spirits are so high that one positively longs to be depressed. Why, you'd be amazed at some of the things people, quite ordinary respectable people, do when they are down here."

As they turned in at the gate she stopped and laughed.

"Take care, Mr. Maradick," she said, "I can see that you are caught in the toils; it's very dangerous for us, you know, at our time of life."

And she left him, laughing.

CHAPTER VIII
THEY ALL EAT CHICKEN IN THE GORSE AND FLY BEFORE THE STORM

"It's the most ripping rag," said Tony, as he watched people climb into the wagonette. "Things," he added, "will probably happen." Lady Gale herself, as she watched them arrange themselves, had her doubts; she knew, as very few women in England knew, how to make things go, and no situation had ever been too much for her, but the day was dreadfully hot and there were, as she vaguely put it to herself, "things in the air." What these things were, she could not, as yet, decide; but she hoped that the afternoon would reveal them to her, that it would, indeed, show a good deal that this last week had caused her to wonder about.

The chief reasons for alarm were the Maradicks and Mrs. Lawrence, without them it would have been quite a family party; Alice, Rupert, Tony, and herself. She wondered a little why she had asked the others. She had wanted to invite Maradick, partly because she liked the man for himself and partly for Tony's sake; then, too, he held the key to Tony now. He knew better than any of the others what the boy was doing; he was standing guard.

And so then, of course, she had to ask Mrs. Maradick. She didn't like the little woman, there was no question about that, but you couldn't ask one without the other. And then she had to give her some one with whom to pair off, and so she had asked Mrs. Lawrence; and there you were.

But it wasn't only because of the Maradicks that the air was thundery; the Lesters had quarrelled again. He sat in the wagonette with his lips tightly closed and his eyes staring straight in front of him right through Mrs. Maradick as though she were non-existent. And Mrs. Lester was holding her head very high and her cheeks were flushed. Oh! they would both be difficult.

She relied, in the main, on Tony to pull things through. She had never yet known a party hang fire when he was there; one simply couldn't lose one's temper and sulk with Tony about the place, but then he too had been different during this last week, and for the first time in his life she was not sure of him. And then, again, there was Alice. That was really worrying her very badly. She had come down with them quite obviously to marry Tony; everyone had understood that, including Tony himself. And yet ever since the first evening of arrival things had changed, very subtly, almost imperceptibly, so that it had been very difficult to realise that it was only by looking back that she could see how great the difference had been. It was not only, she could see, that he had altered in himself, but that he had altered also with regard to Alice. He struck her as being even on his guard, as though he were afraid, poor boy, that they would drive him into a position that he could not honourably sustain. Of this she was quite sure, that whereas on his coming down to Treliss he had fully intended to propose to Alice within the fortnight, now, in less than a week after his arrival, he did not intend to propose at all, was determined, indeed, to wriggle as speedily as might be out of the whole situation. Now there could be only one possible explanation of such a change: that he had, namely, found some one else. Who was it? When was it? Maradick knew and she would trust him.

And what surprised her most in the whole affair was her feeling about it all, that she rather liked it. That was most astonishing, because, of course, Tony's marriage with Alice was from every point of view a most suitable and admirable business; it was the very thing. But she had looked on it, in spite of herself, as a kind of chest into which Tony's youth and vitality were inevitably going; a splendid chest with beautiful carving and studded with golden nails, but nevertheless a chest. Alice was so perfectly right for anybody that she was perfectly wrong for Tony; Lady Gale before the world must approve and even further the affair, but Lady Gale the mother of Tony had had her doubts, and perhaps this new something, whatever it might be, was romantic, exciting, young and adventurous. Mr. Maradick knew.

But it is Mrs. Maradick's view of the drive that must be recorded, because it was, in fact, round her that everything revolved. The reason for her prominence was Rupert, and it was he who, quite unconsciously and with no after knowledge of having done anything at all, saved the afternoon.

He was looking very cool and rather handsome; so was Mrs. Maradick. She was indeed by far the coolest of them all in very pale mauve and a bunch of carnations at her breast and a broad grey hat that shaded her eyes. He had admired her from the first, and to-day everyone else seemed hot and flustered in comparison. Neither Alice nor Mrs. Lester were at their best, and Mrs. Lawrence was obviously ill at ease, but Mrs. Maradick leaned back against the cushions and talked to him with the most charming little smile and eyes of the deepest blue. He had expected to find the afternoon boring in the extreme, but now it promised to be amusing, very amusing.

Mrs. Maradick had come out in the spirit of conquest. She would show these people, all of them, what they had missed during these last two weeks. They should compare her husband and herself, and she had no fear of the result; this was her chance, and she meant to seize it. She never looked at him, and they had not, as yet, spoken, but she was acutely conscious of his presence. He was sitting in a grey flannel suit, rather red and hot, next to Mrs. Lester. He would probably try and use the afternoon as the means for another abject apology.

She was irritated, nevertheless, with herself for thinking about him at all; she had never considered him before. Why should she do so now? She glanced quickly across for a moment at him. How she hated that Mrs. Lester! There was a cat for you, if ever there was one!

They had climbed the hill, and now a breeze danced about them; and there were trees, tall and shining birch, above their heads. On their right lay the sea, so intensely blue that it flung into the air a scent as of a wilderness of blue flowers, a scent of all the blue things that the world has ever known. No breeze ruffled it, no sails crossed its surface; it was so motionless that one would have expected, had one flung a pebble, to have seen it crack like ice. Behind them ran the road, a white, twisting serpent, down to the town.

The town itself shone like a jewel in a golden ring of corn; its towers and walls gleamed and flashed and sparkled. The world lay breathless, with the hard glazed appearance that it wears when the sun is very hot. The colour was so intense that the eye rested with relief on a black clump of firs clustered against the horizon. Nothing moved save the carriage; the horses crawled over the brow of the hill.

"Well, that's awfully funny," said Mrs. Maradick, leaning over and smiling at Rupert. "Because I feel just as you do about it. We can't often come up, of course, and the last train to Epsom's so dreadfully late that unless it's something *really* good, you know — —"

"It's dreadfully boring anyhow," said Rupert, "turning out at night and all that sort of rot, and generally the same old play, you know. . . . Give me musical comedy — dancing and stuff."

"Oh! you young men!" said Mrs. Maradick, "we know you're all the same. And I must say I enjoyed '*The Girl and the Cheese*' the other day, positively the only thing I've seen for ages."

From the other side Mrs. Lawrence could be heard making attack on Mr. Lester. "It was really too awfully sweet of you to put it that way, Mr. Lester. It was just what I'd been feeling, but couldn't put into words; and when I came across it in your book I said to myself, 'There, that's just what

I've been feeling all along.' I simply love your book, Mr. Lester. I feel as if it had been written specially for me, you know."

Mr. Lester flushed with annoyance. He hated, beyond everything, that people should talk to him about his books, and now this silly woman! It was such a hot day, and he had quarrelled with his wife.

"But what I've really always so often wanted to ask you," pursued Mrs. Lawrence, "is whether you took Mrs. Abbey in 'To Paradise' from anyone? I think you must have done; and I know some one so exactly like her that I couldn't help wondering—Mrs. Roland Temmett—she lives in Hankin Street, No. 3 I think it is. Do you know her? If you don't you must meet her, because she's the very image, exactly like. You know in that chapter when she goes down to poor Mr. Elliot——"

But this was too much for Mr. Lester.

"I have never met her," he said brusquely, and his lips closed as though he never meant to open them again. Mrs. Lester watched them and was amused. She knew how her husband hated it; she could even sympathise with him, but it would punish him for having been so horrid to her.

She herself was rapidly recovering her temper. It was such a lovely day that it was impossible to be cross for long, and then her husband had often been cross and disagreeable before, it wasn't as though it were anything new. What a dreadful woman that Mrs. Maradick was! Why had Lady Gale invited her? Poor Mr. Maradick! She rather liked him, his size and strength and stolidity, but how dreadful to be tied to such a woman for life! Even worse, she reflected, than to be tied for life to a man such as her own special treasure! Oh! our marriage system.

She turned round to Maradick.

"It's better, thank you," she said.

"What is?" he asked her.

"My temper," she answered. "It was just the Devil when we started. I was positively fuming. You must have noticed——"

"You have been perfectly charming," he said.

"Well, it's very nice of you to say so, but I assure you it was through my clenched teeth. My hubby and I had a tiff before we started, and it was hot, and my maid did everything wrong. Oh! little things! but all enough to upset me. But it's simply impossible to stay cross with a view and a day like this. I don't suppose you know," she said, looking up at him, "what it is to be bad-tempered."

"I?" He laughed. "Don't I? I'm always in a bad temper all the year round. One has to be in business, it impresses people; it's the only kind of authority that the office-boy understands."

"Don't you get awfully tired of it all?" she asked him. "Blotting-paper, I mean, and pens and sealing-wax?"

"No. I never used to think about it. One lived by rule so. There were regular hours at which one did things and always every day the same regular things to do. But now, after this fortnight, it will, I think, be hard. I shall remember things and places, and it will be difficult to settle down."

She looked at him critically. "Yes, you're not the sort of man to whom business would be enough. Some men can go on and never want anything else at all. I know plenty of men like that, but you're not one of them." She paused for a moment and then said suddenly, "But oh, Mr. Maradick, why did you come to Treliss?"

"Why?" he said, vaguely echoing her.

"Yes, of all places in the world. There never was a place more unsettling; whatever you've been before Treliss will make you something different now, and if anything's ever going to happen to you it will happen here. However, have your holiday, Mr. Maradick, have it to the full. I'm going to have mine."

They had arrived. The wagonette had drawn up in front of a little wayside inn, "The Hearty Cow," having for its background a sweeping moor of golden gorse; the little brown house stood like a humble penitent on the outskirts of some royal crowd.

Everyone got down and shovelled rugs and baskets and kettles; everyone protested and laughed and ran back to see if there was anything left behind, and ran on in front to look at the view. At the turn of the brow of the hill Maradick drew a deep breath. He did not think he had ever seen anything so lovely before. On both sides and behind him the gorse flamed; in front of him was the sea stretching, a burning blue, for miles; against the black cliffs in the distance it broke in little waves of hard curling white. They had brought with them a tent that was now spread over their heads to keep off the sun, they crowded round the unpacking of the baskets. Conversation was general.

"Oh, paté de foie gras, chicken, lobster salad, that's right. No, Tony, wait a moment. Don't open them yet, they're jam and things. Oh! there's the champagne. Please, Mr. Lester, would you mind?"

"So I said to him that if he couldn't behave at a dance he'd better not come at all—yes, look at the view, isn't it lovely?—better not come at all; don't you think I was perfectly right, Mr. Gale? Too atrocious, you know, to speak——"

"The bounder! Can't stand fellows that are too familiar, Mrs. Maradick. I knew a chap once——"

"Oh Lord! Look out! It's coming! My word, Lester, you nearly let us have it. It's all right, mother, the situation's saved, but it was a touch and go. I say, what stuff! Look out, Milly, you'll stick your boot into the pie. No, it's all right. It was only my consideration for your dress, Milly, not a bit for the pie; only don't put your foot into it. Hullo, Alice, old girl, where have you been all this time?"

This last was Tony, his face red with his exertions, his collar off and his shirt open at the neck. When he saw Alice, however, he stopped unpacking the baskets and came over to her. "I say," he said, bending down to her, "come for a little stroll while they're unpacking the flesh-pots. There's a view just round the corner that will fairly make you open your eyes."

They went out together. He put his arm through hers. "What is the matter, Miss Alice Du Cane?" he said. Then as she gave no answer, he said, "What's up, old girl?"

"Oh! nothing's up," she said, looking down and digging her parasol into the ground. "Only it's hot and, well, I suppose I'm not quite the thing. I don't think Treliss suits me."

"Oh! I say, I'm so sorry," he said. "I'd noticed these last few days that you were a bit off colour. I'd been wondering about it."

"Oh, it's nothing," she said, driving her parasol into the path still more furiously. "Only—I hate Treliss. I hate it. You're all awfully good to me, of course, but I think I'd better go."

"Go?" he said blankly.

"Yes, up to Scotland or somewhere. I'm not fit company for anyone as I am."

"Oh! I say, I'm sorry." He looked at her in dismay. "You said something before about it, but I thought it was only for the moment. I've been so jolly myself that I've not thought about other people. But why don't you like the place?"

"I don't know, I couldn't tell you. I know it's awfully ungrateful of me to complain when Lady Gale has given me such a good time. . . . I've no explanation at all. . . . It's silly of me."

She stared out to sea, and she knew quite well that the explanation was of the simplest, she was in love with Tony.

When it had come upon her she did not know. She had certainly not been in love with him when she had first come down to Treliss. The idea of marrying him had been entertained agreeably, and had seemed as pleasant a way of settling as any other. One had to be fixed and placed some time, and Tony was a very safe and honourable person to be placed with. There were things that she would have altered, of course; his very vitality led him into a kind of indiscriminate appreciation of men and things that meant change and an inability to stick to things, but she had faced the whole prospect quite readily and with a good deal of tolerance.

Then, within the week, everything had changed. She wondered, hating herself for the thought, whether it had been because he had shown himself less keen; he hadn't sought her out in quite the way that he had once done, he had left her alone for days together. But that could not have been all; there was something else responsible. There was some further change in him, something quite apart from his relation to her, that she had been among the first to recognise. He had always had a delightful youth and vitality that people had been charmed by, but now, during the last week, there had been something more. It was as though he had at last found the thing for which he had so long been looking. There had been something or some one outside all of them, their set, that he had been seeing and watching all the time; she had seen his eyes sparkle and his mouth smile at some thought or vision that they most certainly had not given him. And this new discovery gave him a strength that he had lacked before; he seemed to have in her eyes a new grandeur, and perhaps it was this that made her love him. But no, it was something more, something that she could only very vaguely and mistily put down to the place. It was in the air, and she felt that if she could only get away from Treliss, with its sea and its view and its crooked town, she would get straight again and be rid of all this contemptible emotion.

She had always prided herself on her reserve, on the control of her emotions, on her contempt for animal passion, and now she could have flung her arms round Tony's neck and kissed his eyes, his hair, his mouth. She watched him, his round curly head, his brown neck, the swing of his shoulders, his splendid stride.

"Let's sit down here," he said; "they can't see us now. I'm not going to help 'em any more. They'll call us when they're ready."

She sat down on a rock and faced the sweep of the sea, curved like a purple bow in the hands of some mighty archer. He flung himself down on to his chest and looked up at her, his face propped on his hands.

"I say, Alice, old girl," he said, "this is the first decent talk we've had for days. I suppose it's been my fault. I'm awfully sorry, and I really don't know how the time's gone; there's been a lot to do, somehow, and yet it's hard to say exactly what one's done."

"You've been with Mr. Maradick," she said almost fiercely.

He looked up at her, surprised at her tone. "Why, yes, I suppose I have. He's a good chap, Maradick. I have been about with him a good bit."

"I can't quite see," she said slowly, looking down at the ground, "what the attraction is. He's nice enough, of course; a nice old man, but rather dull."

"Oh, I don't know about old, Alice. He's much younger than you'd think, and he's anything but dull. That's only because you don't know him. He is quiet when other people are there; but he's awfully true and straight. And you know as one gets older, without being priggish about it, one chooses one's friends for that sort of thing, not for superficial things a bit. I used to think it mattered whether they cared about the same ideas and were—well, artistic, you know. But that's all rot; what really matters is whether they'll stick to you and last."

"One thing I always said about you, Tony," she answered, "is that you don't, as you say, stick. It's better, you know, to be off with the old friends before you are on with the new."

"Oh! I say!" He could scarcely speak for astonishment. "Alice! what's the matter? Why, you don't think I've changed about you, do you? I know— these past few days——"

"Oh, please don't apologise, Tony," she said, speaking very quickly. "I'm not making complaints. If you would rather be with Mr. Maradick, do. Make what friends you like; only when one comes down to stay, one expects to see something of you, just at meals, you know."

He had never seen her like this before. Alice, the most self-contained of girls, reserving her emotions for large and abstract causes and movements, and never for a moment revealing any hint of personal likes or dislikes, never, so far as he had seen, showing any pleasure at his presence or complaining of his absence; and now, this!

"Oh! I say!" he cried again, "I'm most awfully sorry. It's only been a few days—I know it was jolly rude. But the place has been so ripping, so beautiful, that I suppose I didn't think about people much. I've been awfully happy, and that makes one selfish, I suppose. But I say," he put a hand on her dress, "please don't be angry with me, Alice, old girl. We've been chums for ages now, and when one's known some one a jolly long time it isn't kind of necessary to go on seeing them every day, one goes on without that, takes it on trust, you know. I knew that you were there and that I was there and that nothing makes any difference."

The touch of his hand made her cheeks flame. "I'm sorry," she said, almost in a whisper, "I don't know why I spoke like that; of course we're chums, only I've been a bit lonely; rotten these last few days, I'm sure I don't know why." She paused for a moment and then went on: "What it really is, is having to change suddenly. Oh, Tony, I'm such a rotter! You know how I talked about what I'd do if I were a man and the way I could help and the way you ought to help, and all the rest of it; well; that's all gone suddenly — I don't know why or when — and there's simply nothing else there. You won't leave me quite alone the rest of the time, Tony, please? It isn't that I want you so awfully much, you know, but there isn't anyone else."

"Oh! we'll have a splendid time," he said. "You must get to know Maradick, Alice. He's splendid. He doesn't talk much, but he's so awfully genuine."

She got up. "You don't describe him very well, Tony; all the same, genuine people are the most awful bores, you never know where you are. Well, forgive my little bit of temper. We ought to get back. They'll be wondering where we are."

But as they strolled back she was very quiet. She had found out what she wanted to know. There *was* some one else. She had watched his face as he looked at the sea; of course that accounted for the change. Who was she? Some fisher-girl in the town, perhaps some girl at a shop. Well, she would be no rival to anyone. She wouldn't fight over Tony's body; she had her pride. It was going to be a hard time for her; it would be better for her to go away, but that would be difficult. People would talk; she had better see it out.

"It's simply too dreadfully hot in the sun," Tony was conscious of Mrs. Lawrence saying as he joined them. He took it as a metaphor that she was sitting with her back to the sea and her eyes fixed upon the chicken. He wanted to scream, "Look at the gorse, you fool!" but instead he took a plate and flung himself down beside Mrs. Maradick.

She nodded at him gaily. "You naughty boy! You left us to unpack; you don't deserve to have anything."

"Indeed, Mrs. Maradick, I stayed until I was in the way. Too many cooks, you know."

He watched everyone, and detected an air of cheerfulness that had certainly not been there before. Perhaps it was the lunch; at any rate he was hungry.

He talked, waving a piece of bread and butter. "You people don't deserve anything. You ought to go and see a view before eating; grace before meat. Alice and I have done our duty and shall now proceed to enjoy our food twice as much as the rest of you."

"Well, I think it's too bad, that gorse," said Mrs. Maradick, with a little pout and a flash of the eye towards Rupert Gale. "It puts all one's colours out." She gave her mauve a self-satisfied pat.

"Oh! Emmy dear! You look perfectly sweet!" ecstatically from Mrs. Lawrence.

Suddenly Mr. Lester spoke, leaning forward and looking at Mrs. Maradick very seriously. "Have you thought, Mrs. Maradick, whether perhaps you don't put the gorse out?"

"Oh! Mr. Lester! How cruel! Poor little me! Now, Mr. Gale, do stand up for me."

Rupert looked at the gorse with a languid air. "It simply don't stand a chance," he said.

"Talking about gorse," began Mrs. Lawrence. She was always telling long stories about whose success she was in great doubt. This doubt she imparted to her audience, with the result that her stories always failed.

This one failed completely, but nobody seemed to mind. The highest spirits prevailed, and everyone was on the best of terms with everyone else. Lady Gale was delighted. She had thought that it would go off all right, but not quite so well as this.

Of course it was largely due to Tony. She watched him as he gathered people in, made them laugh, and brought the best out of them. It was a kind of "Open Sesame" that he whispered to everyone, a secret that he shared with them.

But what Lady Gale didn't recognise was that it was all very much on the surface; nobody really had changed at all. She might have discovered that fact from her own experience had she thought about it. For instance, she didn't care for Mrs. Maradick any more than before; she liked her, indeed, rather less, but she smiled and laughed and said *Dear* Mrs. Maradick." Everyone felt the same. They would have embraced their dearest enemies; it was in the air.

Mrs. Lester even addressed her husband —

"No, Ted dear, no more meringues. You know it's bad for you, and you'll be sorry to-night."

He looked at her rather gloomily, and then turned and watched the gorse. Maradick suddenly leaned over and spoke to his wife.

"Emmy dear, do you remember that day at Cragholt? It was just like this."

"Of course I do," she said, nodding gaily back at him. "There was that funny Captain Bassett. . . . Such a nice man, dear Lady Gale. I wonder if you know him. Captain Godfrey Bassett. . . . Such fun."

"I wonder," said Lady Gale, "if that is one of the Bassetts of Hindhurst. There was a Captain Bassett— —"

Maradick watched the golden curtain of gorse. The scent came to him; bees hummed in the air.

"Well, I like being by the sea, you know. But to be *on* it; I've crossed the Atlantic seven times and been ill every time. There is a stuff called—Oh! I forget—Yansfs. Yes, you can't pronounce it—You-are-now-secure-from-sea-sickness—it wasn't any good as far as I was concerned, but then I think you ought to take it before— —"

This was his wife.

Mrs. Lester suddenly spoke to him. "You are very silent, Mr. Maradick. Take me for a stroll some time, won't you? No, not now. I'm lazy, but later."

She turned away from him before he could reply, and leaned over to her husband. Then he saw that Tony was at his elbow.

"Come down and bathe," the boy said, "now. No, it isn't bad for you, really. That's all tommy-rot. Besides, we mayn't be able to get away later." They left the tent together.

"Is it champagne?" he asked.

"What?" asked Tony.

"All this amiability. I was as gruff as a—as my ordinary self—coming, and then suddenly I could have played a penny whistle; why?"

"Oh! I don't know!" said Tony, flinging his arms about. "I'm much too happy to care. Maradick, I've been seeing her, here in the gorse—wonderful—divine. We will go back to-morrow; yes, we must. Of course you've got to come. As to everybody's good temper, that doesn't mean anything. The spirits of the place have their games, you know, and there we are. Everybody will be awfully cross at tea. And you know it *is* cheek! For us all to go and plant our tent and eat our chicken in the middle of a view like this. And they'll leave paper bags about, and they'll pop ginger-beer. I don't mind betting that the gods play some games before they've done with us."

They climbed down the rocks to a little cove that lay nestling under the brow of the hill. The sand was white, with little sparkles in it where the sun caught the pebbles; everything was coloured with an intensity that hurt the eye. The cove was hemmed in by brown rocks; a little bird hopped along the sand, then rose with a little whirl of pleasure above their heads and disappeared.

They flung off their clothes with an entire disregard of possible observers. A week ago Maradick would have died rather than do such a thing; a bathing-machine and a complete bathing-suit had been absolute essentials, now they really never entered his head. If he had thought of it at all, they would have seemed to him distinctly indecent, a kind of furtive winking of the eye, an eager disavowal of an immorality that was never there at all.

As Maradick felt the water about his body his years fell from him like Pilgrim's pack. He sank down, with his eyes for a moment on the burning sky, and then gazing through depths of green water. As he cleaved it with his arm it parted and curled round his body like an embrace; for a moment he was going down and down and down, little diamond bubbles flying above him, then he was up again, and, for an instant, the dazzling white of the cove, the brown of the rocks, the blue of the sky, encircled him. Then he lay on his back and floated. His body seemed to leave him, and he was something utterly untrammelled and free; there were no Laws, no Creeds, no Arguments, nothing but a wonderful peace and contentment, an absolute union with something that he had been searching for all his life and had never found until now.

"Obey we Mother Earth . . . Mother Earth." He lay, smiling, on her breast. Little waves came and danced beneath him, touching his body with a caress as they passed him; he rose and fell, a very gentle rocking, as of some mother with her child. He could not think, he could remember nothing; he only knew that he had solved a riddle.

Then he struck out to sea. Before him it seemed to spread without end or limit; it was veiled in its farthest distance by a thin purple haze, and out of this curtain the blue white-capped waves danced in quick succession towards him. He struck out and out, and as he felt his body cut through the water a great exultation rose in him that he was still so strong and vigorous. Every part of him, from the crown of his head to the soles of his feet, seemed clean and sound and sane. Oh! Life! with its worries and its dirty little secrets and its petty moralities! and the miserable pessimistic sauntering in a melancholy twilight through perpetual graveyards! Let them swim, let them swim!

He shouted to Tony, "It's great. One could go on for ever!" He dived for a moment downward, and saw the great white curve of his body from his foot to the hip, the hard smooth strength of the flesh.

Then he turned slowly back. The white beach, the brown rocks, and the blue sky held out hands to him.

"All those people," he shouted to Tony, "up there, eating, sleeping, when they might be in this!" Mrs. Lester, he knew, would have liked it. He thought for a moment of his wife, the dresses she would need and the frills. He could see her stepping delicately from the bathing-machine; her little scream as her feet touched the water, "Oh Jim! it's cold!" He laughed as he waded back on to the beach. The pebbles burnt hot under his feet, and the sand clung to his toes; he dug his legs deep into it. The sun curled about his body and wrapped him, as it were, in a robe of its own glorious colour. He could feel it burning on his back.

Tony joined him, panting. "Oh! my word! I've never had such a bathe, never! I could have stayed in for ever! But they'd be coming to look for us, and that wouldn't do. I say, run round with me! I'll beat you five times round."

They raced round the beach. The sun, the wind, and the waves seemed to go with them; the water fell from them as they ran, and at last they flung themselves dry and breathless on to the hot sand.

Whilst they dressed, Tony dealt with the situation more practically and in detail.

"There are going to be a lot of difficulties, I'm afraid," he said, as he stood with his shirt flapping about his legs, and his hands struggling with his collar. "In the first place, there's mother. As I told you, she's not got to know anything about it, because the minute she hears anything officially, of course, she'll have to step in and ask about it, and then there'll be no end of trouble with the governor and everybody. It's not that she disapproves really, you know—your being there makes that all right; but she hasn't got to realise it until it's done. She won't ask anything about it, but of course she can't help wondering."

"Well, I hope it is all right," said Maradick anxiously. "My being a kind of moral danger-signal makes one nervous."

"Oh! she trusts you," said Tony confidently. "That's why it's so perfectly splendid your being there. And then," went on Tony, "they are all of them wondering what we are at. You see, Treliss has that effect on people, or at any rate it's having that kind of effect on us here and now. Everybody is feeling uneasy about something, and they are most of them putting it down to me. Things always do happen when you jumble a lot of people together in a hotel, the gods can't resist a game; and when you complicate it by putting them in Treliss! My word!"

"Well, what's the immediate complication?" asked Maradick. The water had made his hair curl all over his head, and his shirt was open at the neck and his sleeves rolled up over his arms.

"Well, the most immediate one," said Tony slowly, "is Alice, Miss Du Cane. She was talking to me before lunch. It's rather caddish to say anything about it, but I tell you everything, you know. Well, she seemed to think I'd been neglecting her and was quite sick about it. She never is sick about anything, because she's much too solid, and so I don't know what's set her off this time. She suspects a lot."

Maradick said nothing.

"But the funny thing is that they should worry at all. Before, when I've done anything they've always said, 'Oh! Tony again!' and left it at that. Now, when I've done nothing, they all go sniffing round."

"Yes," said Maradick, "that's the really funny thing; that nothing has been done for them to sniff at, yet. I suppose, as a matter of fact, people have got so little to do in a hotel that they worry about nothing just to fill up time."

He stretched his arms and yawned.

"No," said Tony, "it's the place. Whom the gods wish to send mad they first send to Treliss. It's in the air. Ask that old fellow, Morelli."

"Why Morelli?" Maradick asked quickly.

"Well, it's absurd of me," said Tony. "But I don't mind betting that he knows all about it. He's uncanny; he knows all about everything. It's just as if he set us all dancing to his tune like the Pied Piper." He laughed. "Just think! all of us dancing; you and I, mother, father, Alice, Rupert, the Lesters, Mrs. Maradick, Mrs. Lawrence—and Janet!" he added suddenly.

"Janet," he said, catching Maradick's arm and walking up the beach. "Can't you see her dancing? that hair and those eyes! Janet!"

"I'm sleepy," said Maradick unsympathetically. "I shall lie with my head in the gorse and snore."

He was feeling absolutely right in every part of his body; his blood ran in his veins like a flame. He hummed a little tune as he climbed the path.

"Why! that's Morelli's tune," said Tony, "I'd been trying to remember it; the tune he played that night," and then suddenly they saw Mrs. Lester.

She sat on a rock that had been cut into a seat in the side of the hill. She could not see the beach immediately below because the cliff projected in a spreading cloud of gorse, but the sea lay for miles in front of her, and the gold of the hill struck sharp against the blue. She herself sat perched on the stone, the little wind blowing her hair about her face. She was staring out to sea and did not see them until they were right upon her.

Tony shouted "Hullo, Milly," and she turned.

"We have been bathing," he said. "It was the most stupendous bathe that there has ever been." Then he added, "Why are you alone?"

"The rest went to see a church on a hill or something, but I didn't want anything except the view; but Lady Gale is still there, at the tent. She told me to tell you if I saw you to come to her."

"Right you are." He passed singing up the hill. Maradick stood in front of her, his cap in his hand, then she made room for him on her seat and he sat beside her.

"A view like this," she said, "makes one want very much to be good. I don't suppose that you ever want to be anything else."

"There's some difference between wanting and being," he answered sententiously. "Besides, I don't suppose I'm anything real, neither good nor bad, just indifferent like three-fourths of the human race."

He spoke rather bitterly, and she looked at him. "I think you're anything but indifferent," she said, nodding her head. "I think you're delightful. You're just one of the big, strong, silent men of whom novels are full; and I've never met one before. I expect you could pick me up with one finger and hurl me into the sea. Women like that, you know."

"You needn't be afraid that I shall do it," he said, laughing. "I have been bathing and am as weak as a kitten; and that also accounts for my untidiness," he added. He had been carrying his coat over his shoulder, and his shirt was open at the neck and his sleeves rolled up over his arms.

They did not speak again for several minutes. She was looking at the view with wide-open, excited eyes.

Then she turned round and laid her hand upon his arm. "Oh! I don't expect you've needed it as I have done," she said, "all this colour; I'm drinking it in and storing it so that I can fill all the drab days that are coming with it. Drab, dull, stupid days; going about and seeing people you don't want to see, doing things you don't want to do, saying things you don't want to say."

"Why do you?" he said.

"Oh! one has to. One can't expect to be at Treliss for ever. It's really bad for one to come here, because it always makes one discontented and unsettles one. Last year," she smiled at the recollection, "was most unsettling."

"Well," he answered, "I've got to go back to the office, you know. It will do me good to have these days to remember."

She was silent again; then the grasp on his arm tightened and she said—

"Oh! Mr. Maradick, I am so unhappy."

He moved a little away from her. Here were more confidences coming! Why had all the world suddenly taken it into its incautious head to trust him with its secrets? He! Maradick! whom no one had ever dreamt of trusting with anything before?

"No, I don't want to bother you. It won't bother you, will it? Only it is such a rest and a comfort to be able to tell some one." She spoke with a little catch in her voice, but she was thinking of the year before when she had trusted Captain Stanton, "dear old Reggie," with similar confidences; and there had been Freddie Stapylton before that. Well, they had all been very nice about it, and she was sure that this big man with the brown neck and the curly hair would be just as nice.

"No, but you will be a friend of mine, won't you?" she said. "A woman wants a friend, a good, sensible, strong friend to whom she can tell things, and I have nobody. It will be such a comfort if I can talk to you sometimes."

"Please," he said.

Providence seemed to have designed him as a kind of general nursemaid to a lot of irresponsible children.

"Ah! that's good of you." She gave a little sigh and stared out to sea. "Of course, I'm not complaining, other women have had far worse times, I know that; but it is the loneliness that hurts so. If there is only one person who understands it all it will make such a difference."

Mrs. Lester was not at all insincere. She liked Maradick very much, and her having liked Captain Stanton and Mr. Stapylton before him made no difference at all. Those others had been very innocent flirtations and no harm whatever had come of them, and then Treliss was such an exciting place that things always did happen. It must also be remembered that she had that morning quarrelled with her husband.

"You see," she said, "I suppose I was always rather a romantic girl. I loved colour and processions and flowers and the Roman Catholic Church. I used to go into the Brompton Oratory and watch the misty candles and listen to them singing from behind the altars and sniff the incense. And then I read Gautier and Merimée and anything about Spain. And then I went to Italy, and I thought I could never leave it with the dear donkeys and Venice and carnivals, but we had to get back for Ascot. Oh! I suppose it was all very silly and like lots of other girls, but it was all very genuine, Mr. Maradick."

He nodded his head.

"It's so sweet of you to understand," she said. "Well, like most girls, I crowded all these dreams into marriage. That was going to do everything for me. Oh! he was to be such a hero, and I was to be such a wife to him. Dear me! How old it makes one feel when one thinks of those girlish days!"

But Maradick only thought that she looked very young indeed, Tony's age.

"Then I read some of Fred's essays; Mr. Lester, you know. They used to come out in the *Cornhill*, and I thought them simply wonderful. They said all that I had been thinking, and they were full of that colour that I loved so. The more I read them the more I felt that here was my hero, the man whom I could worship all my days. Poor old Fred, fancy my thinking that about him."

Maradick thought of Mr. Lester trailing with bent back and languid eye over the gorse, and wondered too.

"Well, then I met him at a party; one of those literary parties that I used to go to. He was at his best that night and he talked wonderfully. We were introduced, and—well, there it all was. It all happened in a moment. I couldn't in the least tell you how; but I woke one morning and, like Mr. Somebody or other, a poet I think, found myself married."

Here there was a dramatic pause. Maradick didn't know what to say. He felt vaguely that sympathy was needed, but it was difficult to find the right words.

"That changed me," Mrs. Lester went on in a low voice with a thrill in it, "from an innocent warm-hearted girl into a woman—a suffering, experienced woman. Oh! Mr. Maradick, you know what marriage is, the cage that it can be; at least, if you haven't experienced it, and I sincerely hope you haven't, you can imagine what it is. A year of it was enough to show me how cruel life was."

Maradick felt a little uncomfortable. His acquaintance with Mrs. Lester had been a short one, and in a little time he was going back to have tea with Mr. Lester; he had seemed a harmless kind of man.

"I am very sorry——" he began.

"Oh, please," she went on quickly, "don't think that I'm unhappy. I don't curse fate or do anything silly like that. I suppose there are very few persons who find marriage exactly what they expect it to be. I don't complain. But oh! Mr. Maradick, never marry an author. Of course you can't—how silly of me!—but I should like you to understand a little what I have felt about it all."

He tried clumsily to find words.

"All of us," he said, "must discover as we get on that things aren't quite what we thought they would be. And of marriage especially. One's just got to make up one's mind to it. And then I think there's a lot to be grateful for if there's only one person, man or woman, to whom one matters; who, well, sticks to one and——"

"Oh! I know," she sighed reminiscently.

"What I mean is that it doesn't so much matter what that person is, stupid or ugly or anything, if they really care. There isn't so much of that steady affection going about in the world that we can afford to disregard it when it comes. Dear me!" he added with a laugh, "how sentimental I am!"

"I know," she said eagerly. "That's just it; if Fred did care like that, oh dear, how wonderful it would be! But he doesn't. I don't really exist for him at all. He thinks so much about his books and the people in them that real people aren't there. At first I thought that I could help him with his work, read to him and discuss it with him; and I know that there were a lot of grammatical mistakes, but he wouldn't let me do anything. He shut me out. I was no use to him at all."

She clenched her hands and frowned. As a matter of fact she got on with him very well, but they had quarrelled that morning, over nothing at all, of course. And then it made things more exciting if you thought that you hated your husband, and Mr. Maradick was a fine-looking man.

And he thought how young she was and what a dreary stretch of years was before her. He knew what his own married life had been: fifteen years of disillusion and misunderstanding and sullen silence.

"I am so sorry," he said, and he looked at her very sympathetically. "I can understand a little how hard it is. We don't all of us make lucky shots, but then we have just got to grin and bear it; cold sort of comfort, I know, and if it really does comfort you to feel that you have a friend you may count on me."

She liked his sympathy, the dear old strong thing! and at any rate she would pull Fred pretty sharply out of his books for once. Captain Stanton and Mr. Stapylton had had just that effect; she had never known Fred so charming as he was after their final exit.

He looked down at her with a fatherly smile. "We'll be friends," he said.

"It's perfectly sweet of you," she said, her voice trembling a little. "I felt that you would understand. I cannot tell you how it has helped me, this little talk of ours. Now I suppose we ought to be going back or they'll be wondering where we are."

And he stood thanking God for a wonderful world. At last there were people who wanted him, Tony and Mrs. Lester; and at the same time he had begun to see everything with new eyes. It was his view! They talked of life being over at forty; why, it had never begun for him until now!

They walked back to the tent, and he talked to her gravely about helping others and the real meaning of life. "He can," she thought, "be most awfully dull, but he's a dear old thing."

The expedition in search of a church had scarcely been a success, and when one considers the members of it there is little room to wonder. Tony had been right about the gods. They had seen fit to play their games round the tent on the gorse, and the smiles with which they had regarded the luncheon-party speedily changed to a malicious twinkle. Everyone had been too pleasant to be true, and, after the meal was over, the atmosphere became swiftly ominous. For one thing, Tony had departed with Maradick for a bathe, and his absence was felt. Lady Gale had a sudden longing for sleep, and her struggles against this entirely precluded any attempt at keeping her guests pleasantly humoured. Mrs. Maradick was never at her best after a meal, and now all her former irritation returned with redoubled force. She had been far too pleasant and affable to these people; she could not think what had induced her to chatter and laugh like that at lunch, she must be on her dignity. Mr. Lester's remark about her clothes and the gorse also rankled. What impertinence! but there, these writing people always did think that they could say anything to anybody! Novelist, forsooth! everyone was a novelist nowadays. Mrs. Lawrence didn't make things any better by an interminable telling of one of her inconclusive stories. Mrs. Maradick bristled with irritation as she listened. ". . . So there poor Lady Parminter was, you know—dreadfully stout, and could scarcely walk at all—with her black poodle and her maid and no motor and raining cats and dogs. It was somewhere near Sevenoaks, I think; or was it Canterbury? I think perhaps it was Canterbury, because I know Mr. Pomfret said something about a cathedral; although it might have been Sevenoaks, because there was a number in it, and I remember saying at the time . . ."

Mrs. Maradick stiffened with annoyance.

Mr. Lester gloomily faced the sea and Mrs. Lester chatted rather hysterically to Lady Gale, who couldn't hear what she said because she was so sleepy. Mr. Lester hated quarrelling, because it disturbed his work so; he knew that there would be a reconciliation later, but one never knew how long it would be.

It was eventually Rupert who proposed the church. He had found Mrs. Maradick very amusing at lunch, and he thought a stroll with the little woman wouldn't be bad fun. So he interrupted Mrs. Lawrence's story with "I say, there's a rotten old church somewhere kickin' around. What d'you say to runnin' it to earth, what?"

Everyone jumped up with alacrity. Mrs. Lester shook her head. "I shall stay and keep guard over the tent," she said.

"No, Milly dear, you go," said Lady Gale, "I'm much too sleepy to move."

"Well, then, I'll stay to keep guard over you as well," said Mrs. Lester, laughing; "I'm lazy."

So Rupert, Alice Du Cane, Mr. Lester, Mrs. Maradick and Mrs. Lawrence started off. The expedition was a failure. The church wasn't found, and in the search for it the tempers of all concerned were lost. It was terribly hot, the sun beat down upon the gorse and there was very little breeze. The gorse passed and they came to sand dunes, and into these their feet sank heavily, their shoes were clogged with it. Nobody spoke very much. It was too hot and everybody had their own thoughts; Mrs. Lawrence attempted to continue her story, but received no encouragement.

"I vote we give up the church," said Rupert, and they all trudged drearily back again.

Mrs. Maradick was wondering why Mrs. Lester hadn't come with them. It didn't make her wonder any the less when, on their arrival at the tent, she saw Lady Gale and Tony in sole possession. Where was the woman? Where was her husband? She decided that Rupert Gale was a nuisance. He had nothing to say that had any sense in it, and as for Mr. Lester . . .!

Tea was therefore something of a spasmodic meal. Everybody rushed furiously into conversation and then fled hurriedly out again; an air of restraint and false geniality hung over the teacups. Even Tony was quiet, and Lady Gale felt, for once, that the matter was beyond her; everyone was cross.

Then Mrs. Lester and Maradick appeared and there was a moment's pause. They looked very cheerful and contented, which made the rest of the party only the more irritable and discontented. Why were they so happy? What right had they to be so happy? They hadn't got sand in their shoes and a vague search after an impossible church under a blazing sun in their tempers.

Mrs. Lester was anything but embarrassed.

"Oh! there you all are! How nice you all look, and I do hope you've left something! No, don't bother to move, Rupert. There's plenty of room here! Here you are, Mr. Maradick! Here's a place; yes, we've had such a nice stroll, Mr. Maradick and I. It was quite cool down by the beach. . . . Thanks, dear, one lump and cream. Oh! don't trouble, Tony, I can reach it . . . yes, and did you see your church? Oh! what a pity, and you had all that trouble for nothing. . . ."

"There's going to be a storm!" said Mr. Lester gloomily.

A little wind was sighing, up and down, over the gorse. The sun shone as brilliantly as ever, but on the horizon black, heavy clouds were gathering. Then suddenly the little breeze fell and there was perfect stillness. The air was heavy with the scent of the gorse. It was very hot. Then, very faintly, the noise of thunder came across the sea.

"The gods are angry," said Tony.

"Oh! my dear!" said Lady Gale. "And there isn't a cover to the wagonette thing! Whatever shall we do? We shall get soaked to the skin. I never dreamt of its raining."

"Perhaps," said Maradick, "if we started at once we might get in before it broke."

The things were hurriedly packed and everyone hastened over the gorse. They clambered into the wagonette. Across the sky great fleets of black clouds were hurrying and the sound of the thunder was closer at hand. Everything was still, with the immovability of something held by an invisible hand, and the trees seemed to fling black pointing fingers to the black gloomy sky.

For a mile they raced the storm, and then it broke upon them. The thunder crashed and the lightning flared across their path, and then the rain came in sheeted floods. What fun for the gods! They cowered back in their seats and not a word was spoken by anyone; the driver lashed his horses along the shining road.

Whilst they journeyed, each traveller was asking himself or herself a question. These questions must be recorded, because they will all be answered during the course of this history.

Lady Gale's question. Why did everything go wrong?

Mrs. Maradick's question. Why had a malevolent providence invented Mrs. Lester, and, having invented her, what could James see in her?

Mrs. Lester's question. At what hour that evening should she have her reconciliation scene with her husband and for how long could she manage to spin it out?

Alice Du Cane's question. What was Tony keeping back?

Tony's question. Was Janet afraid of thunder?

Maradick's question. What did it all mean?

Mr. Lester's question. What was the use of being alive at all?

Rupert's question. Why take a new suit to a picnic when it always rained?

Mrs. Lawrence's question. Would the horses run away?

The only question that received an immediate answer was Mrs. Lawrence's, because they didn't.

That evening, Maradick went for a moment to the room of the minstrels. The storm was passing. On the horizon there stole a very faint band of gold. Out of the black bank of cloud a star shone, and suddenly there burst from the dark shadows of the fleeing storm a silver crescent moon. The light of it fell on the boards of the floor and then touched faintly the grinning face of the carved lion.

THE PROLOGUE IS CONCLUDED

PART II
PUNCH

CHAPTER IX
MORELLI BREAKS SOME CROCKERY
AND PLAYS A LITTLE MUSIC

Punch was in bed asleep, with the bedclothes drawn up to his ears. It had just struck six, and round the corner of the open window the sun crept, flinging a path of light across the floor. Presently it would reach the bed and strike Punch's nose; Toby, awake and curled up on a mat near the door, watched the light travel across the room and waited for the inevitable moment.

The room was of the simplest. Against the wall leant the Punch and Judy show, on the mantelpiece was a jar that had once held plum jam and now contained an enormous bundle of wild flowers. Two chairs, a bed, a chest of drawers and a washstand completed the furniture. Against the wall was pinned an enormous outline map of England. This Punch had filled in himself, marking roads, inns, houses, even trees; here and there the names of people were written in a tiny hand. This map was his complete history during the last twenty years; nothing of any importance that had happened to him remained unchronicled. Sometimes it would only be a cross or a line, but he remembered what the sign stood for.

The sun struck his nose and rested on his hair, and he awoke. He said "Ugh" and "Ah" very loudly several times, rubbed his eyes with his knuckles, raised his arms above his head and yawned, and then sat up. His eyes rested for a moment lovingly on the map. Parts of it were coloured in chalk, red and yellow and blue, for reasons best known to himself. The sight of it opened unending horizons: sharp white roads curving up through the green and brown into a blue misty distance, the round heaving shoulder of some wind-swept down over which he had tramped as the dusk was falling and the stars came slowly from their hiding-places to watch him, the grey mists rising from some deep valley as the sun rose red and angry—they stretched, those roads and hills and valleys, beyond his room and the sea, for ever and ever. And there were people too, in London, in country towns, in lonely farms and tiny villages; the lines and crosses on the map brought to his mind a thousand histories in which he had played his part.

He looked at Toby. "A swim, old man," he said; "time for a swim—out we get!" Toby unrolled himself, rubbed his nose on his mat twice like an Eastern Mahommedan paying his devotions, and strolled across to the bed. His morning greeting to his master was always the same, he rolled his eyes, licked his lips with satisfaction, and wagged an ear; then he looked for a moment quite solemnly into his master's face with a gaze of the deepest devotion, then finally he leapt upon the bed and curled up at his master's side.

Punch (whose real name, by the way, was David Garrick—I don't know why I didn't say so before—he hadn't the slightest connexion with the actor, because his family didn't go back beyond his grandfather) stroked a paw and scratched his head. "It's time we got up and went for a swim, old man. The sun's been saying so hours ago." He flung on an overcoat and went out.

The cottage where he lived was almost on the beach. Above it the town rose, a pile of red roofs and smoking chimneys, a misty cloud of pale blue smoke twisted and turned in the air. The world was full of delicious scents that the later day destroyed, and everything behaved as though it were seeing life for the first time; the blue smoke had never discovered the sky before, the waves had never discovered the sand before, the breeze had never discovered the trees before. Very soon they would lose that surprise and would find that they had done it all only yesterday, but, at first, it was all quite new.

Punch and Toby bathed; as they came out of the water they saw Morelli sitting on a rock. Punch sat down on the sand quite unconcernedly and watched the sea. He hadn't a towel, and so the sun must do instead. Toby, having barked once, sat down too.

"Good morning, Mr. Garrick," said Morelli.

Punch looked up for a moment. "A fine day," he said.

Morelli came over to him. He was dressed in a suit of some green stuff, so that against the background of green boughs that fringed the farther side of the little cove he seemed to disappear altogether.

"Good morning, Mr. Garrick," he said again. "A splendid day for a bathe. I'd have gone in myself only I know I should have repented it afterwards."

"Yes, sir," said Punch. "You can bathe 'ere all the year round. In point of fact, it's 'otter at Christmas than it is now. The sea takes a while to get warm."

"This fine weather," said Morelli, looking at the sea, "brings a lot of people to the place."

"Yes," said Punch, "the 'Man at Arms' is full and all the lodgings. It's a good season."

"I suppose it makes some difference to you, Mr. Garrick, whether there are people or no?"

"Oh yes," said Punch, "if there's no one 'ere I move. I'm staying this time."

"Do you find that the place changes?" said Morelli.

"No," said Punch, "it don't alter at all. Now there are places, Pendragon for one, that you wouldn't know for the difference. They've pulled down the Cove and built flats, and there are niggers and what not. It's better for the trade, of course, but I don't like the place."

"Oh yes, I remember Pendragon," said Morelli. "There was a house there, the Flutes—Trojan was the name of the people—a fine place."

"And 'e's a nice man that's there now," said Punch, "Sir 'Enry; what I call a man, but the place is rotten."

Toby looked in his master's face and knew that he was ill at ease. He knew his master so well that he recognised his sentiments about people without looking at him twice. His own feelings about other dogs were equally well defined; if he was suspicious of a dog he was on his guard, very polite of course, but sniffing inwardly; his master did the same.

"I can remember when there were only two or three houses in Pendragon," said Morelli; then suddenly, "You meet a great many people, Mr. Garrick. Everyone here seems to know you. Do you happen to have met a young fellow, Gale is his name? He is staying at the 'Man at Arms.'"

"Yes," said Punch. "I know Mr. Gale." Why did Morelli want to know?

"A nice boy," said Morelli. "I don't often take to the people who come here for the summer, they don't interest me as a rule. But this boy——"

He broke off and watched Toby. He began to whistle very softly, as though to himself. The dog pricked up his ears, moved as though he would go to him, and then looked up in his master's face.

"There's another man," continued Morelli, "that goes about with young Gale. An older man, Maradick his name is, I think. No relation, it seems, merely a friend."

Punch said nothing. It was no business of his. Morelli could find out what he wanted for himself. He got up. "Well," he said, wrapping his greatcoat about him, "I must be going back."

Morelli came close to him and laid a hand on his arm. "Mr. Garrick," he said, "you dislike me. Why?"

Punch turned round and faced him. "I do, sir," he said, "that's truth. I was comin' down the high road from Perrota one evenin' whistling to myself, the dog was at my heels. It was sunset and a broad red light over the sea. I came upon you suddenly sitting by the road, but you didn't see me in the dust. You were laughing and in your hands was a rabbit that you were strangling; it was dusk, but I 'eard the beast cry and I 'eard you laugh. I saw your eyes."

Morelli smiled. "There are worse things than killing a rabbit, Mr. Garrick," he said.

"It's the way you kill that counts," said Punch, and he went up the beach.

Meanwhile there is Janet Morelli.

Miss Minns was the very last person in the world fitted to give anyone a settled education; in her early days she had given young ladies lessons in French and music, but now the passing of years had reduced the one to three or four conversational terms and the other to some elementary tunes about which there was a mechanical precision that was anything but musical. Her lessons in deportment had, at one time, been considered quite the thing, but now they had grown a little out of date, and, like her music, lost freshness through much repetition.

Her ideas of life were confined to the three or four families with whom she had passed her days, and Janet had never discovered anything of interest in any of her predecessors; Alice Crate (her father was Canon Crate of Winchester Cathedral), Mary Devonshire (her father was a merchant in Liverpool), and Eleanor Simpson (her father was a stockbroker and lived in London). Besides, all these things had happened a long while ago; Miss Minns had been with Janet for the last twelve years, and fact had become reminiscence and reminiscence tradition within that time. Miss Minns of the moment with which we have to do was not a very lively person for a very young creature to be attached to; she was always on the quiver, from the peak of her little black bonnet to the tip of her tiny black shoes. When she did talk, her conversation suffered from much repetition and was thickly strewn with familiar proverbs, such as "All's well that ends well" and "Make hay while the sun shines." She served no purpose at all as far as Janet was concerned, save as an occasional audience of a very negative kind.

The only other person with whom Janet had been brought into contact, her father, was far more perplexing.

She had accepted him in her early years as somebody about whom there was no question. When he was amusing and played with her there was no one in the world so completely delightful. He had carried her sometimes into the woods and they had spent the whole day there. She remembered when he had whistled and sung and the animals had come creeping from all over the wood. The birds had climbed on to his shoulders and hands, rabbits and hares had let him take them in his hands and had shown no fear at all. She remembered once that a snake had crawled about his arm. He had played with her as though he had been a child like herself, and she had done what she pleased with him and he had told her wonderful stories. And then suddenly, for no reason that she could understand, that mood had left him and he had been suddenly angry, terribly, furiously angry. She had seen him once take a kitten that they had had in his hands and, whilst it purred in his face, he had twisted its neck and killed it. That had happened when she was very small, but she would never forget it. Then she had grown gradually accustomed to this rage and had fled away and hidden. But on two occasions he had beaten her, and then, afterwards, in a moment it had passed, and he had cried and kissed her and given her presents.

She had known no other man, and so she could not tell that they were not all like that. But, as the years had passed, she had begun to wonder. She had asked Miss Minns whether everybody could make animals come when they whistled, and Miss Minns had admitted that the gift was unusual, that, in fact, she didn't know anyone else who could do it. But Janet was growing old enough now to realise that Miss Minns' experience was limited and that she did not know everything. She herself had tried to attract the birds, but they had never come to her.

Her father's fury had seemed to her like the wind or rain; something that came to him suddenly, blowing from no certain place, and something, too, for which he was not responsible. She learnt to know that they only lasted a short time, and she used to hide herself until they were over.

With all this she did not love him. He gave her very little opportunity of doing so. His affection was as strangely fierce as his temper and frightened her almost as badly. She felt that that too was outside himself, that he had no love for her personally, but felt as he did about the animals, about anything young and wild. It was this last characteristic that was strangest of all to her. It was very difficult to put it into words, but she had seen that nothing made him so furious as the conventional people of the town. She was too young to recognise what it was about them that made him so angry, but she had seen him grow pale with rage at some insignificant thing that some one had said or done. On the other hand, he liked the wildest people of the place, the fishermen and tramps that haunted the lower quarters of the town. All this she grasped very vaguely, because she had no standard of comparison; she knew no one else. But fear had made love impossible; she was frightened when he was fond of her, she was frightened when he was angry with her. Miss Minns, too, was a difficult person to bestow love upon. She did not want it, and indeed resolutely flung it back with the remark that emotion was bad for growing girls and interfered with their education. When she lived at all she lived in the past, and Janet was only a very dim shadowy reflexion of the Misses Crate, Devonshire, and Simpson, who had glorified her earlier years.

Janet, therefore, had spent a very lonely and isolated childhood, and, as she had grown, the affection that was in her had grown too, and she had had no one to whom she might give it. At first it had been dolls, and ugly and misshapen though they were they had satisfied her. But the time came when their silence and immobility maddened her, she wanted something that would reply to her caresses and would share with her all her thoughts and ideas. Then Miss Minns came, and Janet devoted herself to her with an ardour that was quite new to the good lady; but Miss Minns distrusted enthusiasm and had learnt, whilst educating Miss Simpson, to repress all emotion, so she gave it all back to Janet again, carefully wrapped up in tissue paper. When Janet found that Miss Minns didn't want her, and that she was only using her as a means of livelihood, she devoted herself to animals, and in a puppy, a canary and a black kitten she found what she wanted. But then came the terrible day when her father killed the kitten, and she determined never to have another pet of any kind.

By this time she was about fifteen and she had read scarcely anything. Her father never talked to her about books, and Miss Minns considered most novels improper and confined herself to Mrs. Hemans and the "Fairchild Family." Janet's ideas of the world were, at this time, peculiar. Her father had talked to her sometimes strangely about places that he had seen, but they had never attracted her: mountain heights, vast unending seas, tangled forests, sun-scorched deserts; always things without people, silent, cold, relentless. She had asked him about cities and he had spoken sometimes about London, and this had thrilled her through and through. What she longed for was people; people all round her, friends who would love her, people whom she herself could help. And then suddenly, on an old bookshelf that had remained untouched for many years past, she had found "Kenilworth." There was a picture that attracted her and she had begun to read, and then a new world opened before her. There were several on the shelf: Lytton's "Rienzi" and "The Last of the Barons," George Eliot's "Middlemarch," Trollope's "Barchester Towers," and Miss Braddon's "Lady Audley's Secret." There were some other things; somebody's "History of England," a Geography of Europe, a torn volume of Shakespeare, and the "Pickwick Papers." Living, hitherto a drab and unsatisfactory affair, became a romantic thrilling business in which anything might happen, a tremendous bran pie into which one was continually plunging for plums. She had no doubt at all that there would be adventures for her in the future. Everyone, even the people in "Middlemarch," had adventures, and it was absurd to suppose that she wouldn't have them as well. She noticed, too, that all the adventures that these people had rose from the same source, namely love. She did not realise very thoroughly what this love was, except that it meant finding somebody for whom you cared more than anyone else in the world and staying with them for the rest of your life, and perhaps after. She did not admire all the people of whom the heroines were enamoured, but she realised that everyone thought differently about such things, and that there was apt to be trouble when two ladies cared for the same gentleman or *vice versa*.

Only you must, so to speak, have your chance, and that she seemed to be missing. It was all very well to watch romance from your high window and speculate on its possibilities as it passed down the street, but you ought to be down in the midst of it if you were going to do anything. It all seemed ridiculously simple and easy, and she waited for her knight to come with a quiet and assured certainty.

At first she had attacked Miss Minns on the question, but had got little response. Miss Minns was of the opinion that knights were absurd, and that it did not do to expect anything in this world, and that in any case young girls oughtn't to think about such things, and that it came of reading romances and stuff, with a final concession that it was "Love that made the world go round," and that "It was better to have loved and lost than never to have loved at all."

All this was to little purpose, but it was of trivial importance, because Janet was quite settled in her mind about the whole affair. She had no ideal knight; he was quite vague, hidden in a cloud of glory, and she did not want to see his face; but that he would come she was sure.

But, afterwards, she gave her knight kingdoms and palaces and a beautiful life in which she had some vague share, as of a worshipper before a misty shrine. And he, indeed, was long in coming. She met no one from one year's end to another, and wistful gazing from her window was of no use at all. She wished that she had other girls for company. She saw them pass, sometimes, through the town, arm in arm; fisher-girls, perhaps, or even ladies from the hotel, and she longed, with an aching longing, to join them and tell them all that she was thinking.

Her father never seemed to consider that she might be lonely. He never thought very much about her at all, and he was not on sufficiently good terms with the people of the place to ask them to his home; he would not have known what to do with them if he had had them there, and would have probably played practical jokes, to their extreme discomfiture.

And then Tony came. She did not see him with any surprise. She had known that it was only a matter of waiting, and she had no doubt at all that he was the knight in question. Her ignorance of the world prevented her from realising that there were a great many other young men dressed in the same way and with the same charming manners. From the first moment that she saw him she took it for granted that they would marry and would go away to some beautiful country, where they would live in the sunshine for ever. And with it all she was, in a way, practical. She knew that it would have to be a secret, that Miss Minns and her father must know nothing about it, and that there would have to be plots and, perhaps, an escape. That was all part of the game, and if there were no difficulties there would be no fun. She had no scruples about the morality of escaping from Miss Minns and her father. They neither of them loved her, or if they did, they had not succeeded in making her love them, and she did not think they would miss her very much.

She was also very thankful to Providence for having sent her so charming a knight. She loved every bit of him, from the crown of his head to the sole of his foot, his curly hair, his eyes, his smile, his mouth, his hands. Oh! he would fit into her background very handsomely. And charming though he was, it never entered her head for a moment that he was not in love with her. Of course he was! She had seen it in his eyes from the very first minute.

And so all the scruples, the maidenly modesty and the bashful surprise that surround the love affairs of most of her sex were entirely absent. It seemed to her like the singing of a lark in the sky or the murmur of waves across the sand; something inevitable and perfectly, easily natural. There might be difficulties and troubles, because there were people like Miss Minns in the world, but they would pass away in time, and it would be as though they had never existed.

The only thing that puzzled her a little was Maradick. She did not understand what he was doing there. Was he always coming whenever Tony came? He was old like her father, but she thought he looked pleasant. Certainly not a person to be afraid of, and perhaps even some one to whom one could tell things. She liked his size and his smile and his quiet way of talking. But still it was a nuisance his being there at all. There were quite enough complications already with Miss Minns and father without another elderly person. And why was Tony with him at all? He was an old man, one of those dull, elderly people who might be nice and kind but couldn't possibly be any use as a friend. She tried to get Miss Minns to solve the problem, but that lady murmured something about "Birds of a feather," and that it was always proper to pay calls in twos, which was no use at all.

So Janet gave up Maradick for the present with a sigh and a shake of the head. But she was most blissfully happy. That country that had remained so long without an inhabiter was solitary no longer, her dreams and pictures moved before her now with life and splendour. She went about her day with a light in her eyes, humming a little song, tender and sympathetic with Miss Minns because she, poor thing, could not know how glorious a thing it was, this love!

I do not know whether Miss Minns had her suspicions. She must have noticed Janet's pleasant temper and gaiety, but she said nothing. As to Morelli, there was no telling what he noticed.

He returned to the house after his conversation with Punch in no pleasant humour. Janet had been up since a very early hour; she never could sleep when the sun was bright, and she was very happy. She had a suspicion that Tony would come to-day. It was based on nothing very certain, but she had dreamt that he would; and it was the right kind of day for him to come on, when the sun was so bright and a butterfly had swept through the window like the petal of a white rose blown by the wind.

And so she met her father with a laugh when he came in and led the way gaily to breakfast. But in a moment she saw that something was wrong, and, at the thought that one of his rages was sweeping over him and that she would not be able to escape, her face grew very white and her lips began to tremble.

She knew the symptoms of it. He sat very quietly with his hands crumbling the bread at his side; he was frowning, but very slightly, and he spoke pleasantly about ordinary things. As a rule when he was like this she crept away up to her room and locked her door, but now there seemed no chance of escape.

But she talked gaily and laughed, although her heart was beating so loudly that she thought that he would hear it.

"Miss Minns and I are going to walk over to Tregotha Point this afternoon, father," she said; "there are flowers there and we shall take books. Only I shall be back for tea, and so we shall start early."

He said nothing, but looked at the tablecloth. She looked round the room as though for a means of escape. It was all so cheerful that it seemed to mock her, the red-tiled fireplace, the golden globe of the lamp, the shining strip of blue sky beyond the window.

"Tea, father?" The teapot trembled a little in her hand. She could not talk; when the storm was approaching some actual presence seemed to come from the clouds and place an iron grip upon her. It had been some while since the last time and she had begun to hope that it might not happen again, and now——She was afraid to speak lest her voice should shake. The smile on her lips froze.

"Well," he said, looking at her across the table, "talk to me." The look that she knew so well came into his face; there was a little smile at the corners of his mouth and his eyes stared straight in front of him as though he were looking past her into infinite distances.

"Well," he said again, "why don't you talk?"

"I—have nothing to say," she stammered, "we haven't done anything."

And then suddenly the storm broke. He gave a little scream like a wild animal, and, with one push of the hand, the table went over, crashing to the ground. The crockery lay in shattered pieces on the blue carpet. Janet crouched back against the wall, but he came slowly round the table towards her. His back was bent a little and his head stretched forward like an animal about to spring.

She was crying bitterly, with her hands pressed in front of her face.

"Please, father," she said, "I haven't done anything -I didn't know—I haven't done anything."

She said it again and again between her tears. Morelli came over to her. "There was a man," he said between his teeth, "a man whom I saw this morning, and he said things. Oh! if I had him here!" He laughed. "I would kill him, here, with my hands. But you see, you shall never speak to him again, you don't go near him." He spoke with passion.

She did not answer. He shook her shoulder. "Well, speak, can't you?" He took her arm and twisted it, and then, apparently maddened by her immobility and her tears, he struck her with his hand across the face.

He let her sink to the floor in a heap, then for a moment he looked down on her. There was absolute silence in the room, a shaft of light fell through the window, caught a gleaming broken saucer on the floor, lighted the red tiles and sparkled against the farther wall. Janet was sobbing very quietly, crouching on the floor with her head in her hands. He looked at her for a moment and then crept silently from the room.

The stillness and peace and the twittering of a bird at the window brought her to her senses. It had happened so often before that it did not take her long to recover. She got up from her knees and wiped her eyes; she pushed back her hair and put the pins in carefully. Then she felt her cheek where he had struck her. It always happened like that, suddenly, for no reason at all. She knew that it was due to no bitter feeling against herself. Anything that came in his way at the time would suffer, as Miss Minns had learnt. Doubtless she was up in her room now with her door locked.

But this occasion was different from all the others. When it had happened before, quite the worst part of it had been the loneliness. It had seemed such a terribly desolate world, and she had seen infinite, dreary years stretching before her in which she remained, defenceless and without a friend, at the mercy of his temper. But now that her knight had come she did not mind at all. It would not be long before she escaped altogether, and, in any case, he was there to be sorry for her and comfort her. She would, of course, tell him all about it, because she would tell him everything. She felt no anger against her father. He was like that; she knew what it felt like to be angry, she had screamed and stamped and bit when she was a little girl in just that kind of way. She was rather sorry for him, because she knew he was always sorry afterwards. And then it was such a relief that it was over. The worst part of it was that sickening terror at first, when she did not know what he might do.

She set up the table again, collected the pieces of crockery from the floor and carried them into the kitchen. She then wiped up the pool of tea that had dripped on to the carpet. After this she realised that she was hungry, that she had had nothing at all, and she sat down and made a picnicky meal. By the end of it she was humming to herself as though nothing had occurred.

Later, she took her work and sat in the window. Her thoughts, as indeed was always the case now, were with Tony. She made up stories for him, imagined what he was doing at the moment and what the people were like to whom he was talking. She still felt sure that he would come and see them that afternoon. Then the door opened, and she knew that her father had returned. She did not turn round, but sat with her back to the door, facing the window. She could see a corner of the street with its shining cobbles, a dark clump of houses, a strip of the sky. The noise of the market came distantly up to her, and some cart rattled round the corner very, very faintly; the sound of the mining-stamp swung like a hammer through the air.

She heard him step across the room and stand waiting behind her. She was not afraid of him now; she knew that he had come back to apologise. She hated that as much as the rage, it seemed to hurt just as badly. She bent her head a little lower over her work.

"Janet," he spoke imploringly behind her.

"Father!" She turned and smiled up at him.

He bent down and kissed her. "Janet! dear, I'm so sorry. I really can't think why I was angry. You know I do get impatient sometimes, and that man had made me angry by the things he said."

He stood away from her with his head hanging like a child who was waiting to be punished.

"No, father, please don't." She stood up and looked at him. "You know it is very naughty of you, and after you promised so faithfully last time that you wouldn't get angry like that again. It's no use promising if you never keep it, you know. And then think of all the china you've broken."

"Yes, I know." He shook his head dolefully. "I don't know what it is, my dear. I never seem to get any better. And I don't mean anything, you know. I really don't mean anything."

But she doubted that a little as she looked at him. She knew that, although his rage might pass, he did not forget. She had known him cherish things in his head long after they had passed from the other man's memory, and she had seen him take his revenge. Who was this man who had insulted him? A sudden fear seized her. Supposing . . .

"Father," she said, looking up at him, "who was it said things to you this morning that made you angry?"

"Ah, never mind that now, dear," he said, his lip curling a little. "We will forget. See, I am sorry; you have forgiven me?" He sat down and drew her to him. "Look! I am just like a child. I am angry, and then suddenly it all goes." He stroked her hair with his hand, and bent and kissed her neck. "Where was it that I hit her? Poor darling! There, on the cheek? Poor little cheek! But look! Hit me now hard with your fist. Here on the cheek. I am a brute, a beast."

"No, father," she laughed and pulled herself away from him, "It is nothing! I have forgotten it already. Only, dear me! all the broken china! Such expense!"

"Well, dear, never mind the expense. I have a plan, and we will have a lovely day. We will go into the wood with our lunch and will watch the sea, and I will tell you stories, and will play to you. What! now, won't that be good fun?"

His little yellow face was wreathed in smiles; he hummed a little tune and his feet danced on the floor. He passed his hand through his hair so that it all stood on end. "We'll have such a game," he said.

She smiled. "Yes, father dear, that will be lovely. Only, we will be back this afternoon, because perhaps — —"

"Oh! I know!" He laughed at her. "Callers! Why, yes, of course. We shall be here if they come." He chuckled to himself. "I am afraid, my dear, you have been lonely all these years. I ought to have thought of it, to give you companions." Then he added after a little pause, "But he is a nice young fellow, Mr. Gale."

She gave a little sigh of relief; then it was not he who had quarrelled with her father that morning. "That will be splendid. I'll go and get lunch at once." She bent down and kissed him, and then went singing out of the room.

He could, when he liked, be perfectly delightful, and he was going to like that afternoon, she knew. He was the best fun in the world. Poor thing! He would be hungry! He had no breakfast. And he sat in front of the window, smiling and humming a little tune to himself. The sun wrapped his body round with its heat, all the live things in the world were calling to him. He saw in front of him endless stretches of country, alive, shining in the sun. He stared in front of him.

It was market-day, and the market-place was crowded. Janet loved it, and her cheeks were flushed as she passed through the line of booths. As they crossed in front of the tower she saw that some one was leaning over the stall talking to the old fruit woman. Her heart began to beat furiously; he was wearing no cap, and she heard his laugh.

He turned round suddenly as though he knew who it was. The light suddenly flamed in his eyes, and he came forward:

"Good morning, Mr. Morelli," he said.

In all the crowded market-place she was the only thing that he saw. She was dressed in a white muslin with red roses on it, and over her arm was slung the basket with the lunch; her hair escaped in little golden curls from under her broad hat.

But she found that she didn't know what to say. This was a great surprise to her, because when she had thought about him in her room, alone, she had always had a great deal to say, and a great many questions to ask.

But now she stood in the sun and hung her head. Morelli watched them both.

Tony stammered. "Good-morning, Miss Morelli. I—I can't take off my cap because I haven't got one. Isn't it a ripping day?" He held out his hand and she took it, and then they both laughed. The old woman behind them in her red peaked hat screamed, "A-pples and O-ranges! Fine ripe grapes!"

"We're going out for a picnic, father and I," said Janet at last. "We've got lunch in this basket. It's a day that you can't be in doors, simply!"

"Oh! I know," he looked hungrily at the basket, as though he would have loved to have proposed coming as well. "Yes, it's a great day." Then he looked at her and started. She had been crying. She was smiling and laughing, but he could see that she had been crying. The mere thought of it made his blood boil; who had made her cry? He looked quickly at Morelli; was it he? Perhaps it was Miss Minns? or perhaps she wasn't well, but he must know if she were unhappy; he would find out.

"I was thinking of coming to call this afternoon, Mr. Morelli," he said, "Maradick and I . . . but if you are going to spend the day in the woods, another day——"

"Oh, no," said Morelli, smiling, "we shall be back again by four. We are only going to have lunch. We should be delighted to see you, and your friend." Then they said good-bye, and Tony watched them as they turned out of the market-place. They didn't talk very much as they passed through the town, they had, each of them, their own thoughts. Janet was very happy; he was coming to tea, and they would be able to talk. But how silly she was, she could suddenly think of a hundred things that she would like to have said to him. They turned off the hard white road that ran above the sea and passed along a narrow lane. It was deeply rutted with cart-tracks, and the trees hung so thickly over it that it was quite dark. It wound up the sides of a green hill and then dived suddenly into the heart of a wood. Here there were pine trees, and a broad avenue over which they passed crushing the needles under their feet. The trees met in a green tapestry of colours above their heads, and through it the sun twinkled in golden stars and broad splashes of light. The avenue dwindled into a narrow path, and then suddenly it ended in a round green knoll humped like the back of a camel. The grass was a soft velvety green, and the trees stood like sentinels on every side, but in front they parted and there was a wonderful view. The knoll was at the top of the hill, and you could see straight down, above and beyond the trees of the wood, the sea. To the right there was another clearing, and a little cove of white sand and brown rocks shone in the sun. There was perfect stillness, save for a little breeze that rocked the trees so that they stirred like the breathing of some sleeper.

Janet and her father always came to this place. Afterwards she was to see a great many cities and countries, but this green wood always remained to her the most perfect thing in the world. It was so still that you could, if you held your breath, hear the tiny whisper of the waves across the shingle and the murmur of the mining stamp. It was a wonderful place for whispers; the trees, the sea, the birds, even the flowers seemed to tell secrets, and Janet used to fancy that if she lay there, silently, long enough, she would, like the man in the fairy tale, hear what they were saying. She noticed that she always seemed to hear more when she was with her father. She had gone there sometimes with Miss Minns, and had wondered how she could be so fanciful. Nothing had whispered at all, and Miss Minns had had a headache. But to-day everything seemed to have a new meaning; her meeting with Tony had lent it a colour, an intensity that it had not had before. It was as though they all—the sea, the sky, the trees, the animals—knew that she had got a knight and would like to tell her how glad they were.

Morelli sat perched on the highest peak of the knoll with his legs crossed beneath him. He was at his very best; gay, laughing, throwing the pine needles like a child into the air, singing a little song.

"Come here, my dear, and talk to me." He made way for her beside him. "Everything is singing to-day. There is a bird in a tree above us who has just told me how happy he is. I hope you are happy, my dear."

"Yes, father, very." She gave a little sigh of satisfaction and lay back on the grass at his side.

"Well, don't be ashamed of showing it. Have your feelings and show them. Never mind what they are, but don't cover them as though you were afraid that they would catch cold. Don't mind feeling intensely, hurting intensely, loving intensely. It is a world of emotion, not of sham."

She never paid any very deep attention when he talked about rules of life. Existence seemed to her, at present, such an easy affair that rules weren't necessary; people made such a bother.

She lay back and stared straight into the heart of the sky. Two little clouds, like pillows, bulged against the blue; the hard sharp line of the pines cut into space, and they moved together slowly like the soft opening and closing of a fan.

"I knew a place once like this," said Morelli. "It was in Greece. A green hill overlooking the sea, and on it a white statue; they came to worship their god there."

"What is this talk of God?" she asked him, resting on one elbow and looking up at him. "You have never told me, father, but of course I have read and have heard people talk. Who is God?"

She asked it with only a very languid interest. She had never speculated at all about the future. The world was so wonderful, and there were such a number of things all around her to think about, that discussion about something that would affect her at the end of her life, when all the world was dark and she was old and helpless, seemed absurd. She would want the end to come then, when she was deaf and blind and cold; she would not spoil the young colour and intensity of her life by thinking about it. But with the sudden entrance of Tony the question came forward again. They would not live for ever; life seemed very long to her, but the time must come when they would die. And then? Who was this God? Would He see to it that she and Tony were together afterwards? If so, she would worship Him; she would bring Him flowers, and light candles as Miss Minns did. As she sat there and heard the woods and the sea she thought that the answer must be somewhere in them. He must have made this colour and sound, and, if that were so, He could not be unkind. She watched the two clouds; they had swollen into the shape of bowls, their colour was pale cream, and the sun struck their outer edges into a very faint gold.

"Who is God?" she said again.

Morelli looked at her. "There were gods once," he said. "People were faithful in those days, and they saw clearly. Now the world is gloomy, because of the sin that it thinks that it has committed, or because pleasure has been acid to the taste. Then they came with their songs and flowers to the hill, and, with the sky at their head and the sea at their feet, they praised the God whom they knew. Now — — " He stared fiercely in front of him. "Oh! these people!" he said.

She did not ask him any more. She could not understand what he had said, and she was afraid lest her questions should bring his fury back again. But the question was there; many new questions were there, and she was to spend her life in answering them.

So they had lunch whilst the two clouds divided into three and danced with white trailing garments across the sun; then again they were swans, and vanished with their necks proudly curved into space.

"Father," said Janet, with an abstracted air, as though she was thinking of some one else, "Do you think Mr. Gale handsome?"

"Yes, dear," he answered. "He's young, very young, and that is worth all the looks in the world."

"I think he is very handsome," she said, staring in front of him.

"Yes, dear, I know you do."

"You like him, father?"

"Of course." Morelli smiled. "I like to see you together."

"And Mr. Maradick, father? What do you think of him?"

"Poor Mr. Maradick!" Morelli laughed. "He is going to have a bad time; life comes late to some people."

"Yes, I like him," said Janet, thoughtfully, "I know he's kind, but he's old; he's older than you are, father."

"He'll be younger before he's left Treliss," said Morelli.

After lunch he took his flute from his pocket.

She lay motionless, with her arms behind her head; she became part of the landscape; her white dress lay about her like a cloud, her hair spread like sunlight over the grass, and her eyes stared, shining, into the sky. He sat, with his legs crossed under him, on the swelling grass, and stared at the tops of the trees and the sweep of the sea. No part of him moved except his fingers, which twinkled on the flute; the tune was a little gay dance that sparkled in the air and seemed to set all the trees in motion, even the three little clouds came back again and lay like monstrous white birds against the sky.

The two figures were absorbed into the surrounding country. His brown face and sharp nose seemed to belong to the ground on which he sat; the roses on her dress seemed to grow about her, and her hair lay around her like daffodils and primroses. The gay tune danced along, and the sun rose high above their heads; a mist rose from the sea like a veil and, shot with colour, blue and green, enveloped the woods.

Then there were stealthy movements about the two figures. Birds, thrushes, chaffinches, sparrows, hopped across the grass. A pigeon cooed softly above his head; two rabbits peeped out from the undergrowth. They grew bolder, and a sparrow, its head on one side, hopped on to Janet's dress.

More rabbits came, and the pigeon, with a soft whirr of its wings, swept down to Morelli's feet. The grass was soon dotted with birds, a squirrel ran down a tree-trunk and stayed, with its tail in the air, to listen. The birds grew bolder and hopped on to Morelli's knee; a sparrow stood for a moment on Morelli's head and then flew away.

Janet showed no astonishment at these things. She had often seen her father play to the animals before, and they had come. Suddenly he piped a shrill, discordant note, and with a whirr of their wings the birds had vanished and the rabbits disappeared.

He put his flute into his pocket.

"It's nearly four o'clock," he said.

"Father," she said as they went down the hill, "can other people do that? Make the birds and animals come?"

"No," he said.

"Why not? What is it that you do?"

"It's nothing that I do," he said. "It's what I am. Don't you worry your head about that, my dear. Only don't say that anything's impossible. 'There's more in Heaven and earth than is dreamed of in the philosophy' of those folks who think that they know such a lot. Don't ever disbelieve anything, my dear. Everything's true, and a great deal more as well."

Meanwhile Tony dragged a reluctant Maradick to tea. "They don't want me," he said, "you'll be making me hideously unpopular, Tony, if you keep dragging me there."

"I told them you were coming," said Tony resolutely. "And of course you are. There are simply heaps of reasons. The plot's thickening like anything, and it's absurd of you to pretend that you are not in it, because you are, right up to your neck. And now I'll give you my reasons. In the first place there's mother. At the picnic yesterday Alice spotted that there was some one else; of course she will speak to mother, probably has spoken already. As I have told you already, she has perfect confidence in you, and as long as you are there it's perfectly right, but if you leave me she'll begin to worry her head off. Then again, there's Janet herself. I want her to get to know you and trust you. She'll want some one older just as much as I do, probably more, because she's a girl and a frightful kid. Oh! rot! I'm no use at explaining, and the situation's jolly difficult; only how can she possibly trust you and the rest of it, if she never sees you? And last of all, there's me. I want you to see how the thing's going so that we can talk about it. There's something 'up,' I know, I could see this morning that she'd been crying. I believe Morelli's beastly to her or something. Anyhow, you're bound and pledged and everything, and you're a ripping old brick to be so decent about it," at the end of which Tony, breathless with argument and excitement seized Maradick by the arm and dragged him away.

But Maradick had a great deal to think about, and it was as much for this reason as for any real reluctance to visit the Morellis that he hesitated.

And the tea-party was a great success. Everyone was in the very best of humours, and the restraint that had been there a little on the first occasion had now quite passed away. The sun poured into the room, and shone so that everything burnt with colour. Maradick felt again how perfect a setting it made for the two who were its centre, the blue-tiled fireplace, the fantastic blue and white china on the walls, the deep blue of the carpet set the right note for a background. On the table the tea-things, the old silver teapot and milk jug, old red and white plates and an enormous bowl of flaming poppies, gave the colour. Then against the blue sky and dark brown roofs beyond the window was Janet, with her golden hair and the white dress with the pink roses. Miss Minns was the only dark figure in the room and she scarcely seemed to matter. The only words that she spoke were to Maradick, "In for a penny in for a pound," she suddenly flung at him à propos of some story of Epsom expenses, and then felt apparently that she had said too much and was quiet for the rest of the afternoon.

Morelli was at his pleasantest, and showed how agreeable a companion he could be. Maradick still felt the same distrust of him, but he was forced to confess that he had never before met anyone so entertaining. His knowledge of other countries seemed inexhaustible; he had been everywhere, and had a way of describing things and places that brought them straight with him into the room, so vivid were they.

His philosophy of life in general appeared, this afternoon pleasant and genial. He spoke of men who had failed with commiseration and a very wide charity; he seemed to extend his affection to everyone, and said with a smile that "It was only a question of knowing people; they were all good fellows at heart."

And yet, through it all, Maradick felt as though he were, in some unexplained way, playing at a game. The man was rather like a child playing at being grown-up and talking as he had heard his elders do. He had an impulse to say, "Look here, Morelli, it's boring you dreadfully talking like this, you're not a bit interested, really and truly, and we're only playing this game as a background for the other two."

And, in fact, that was what it all came to; that was Maradick's immediate problem that must be answered before any of the others. What was Morelli's idea about his daughter and Tony? Morelli knew, of course, perfectly well what was going on. You could see it in their eyes. And, apparently, as far as Maradick could see, he liked it and wanted it to continue. Why? Did he want them to marry? No, Maradick didn't think that he did. He watched them with a curious smile; what was it that he wanted?

And they, meanwhile, the incredible pair with their incredible youth, were silent. It was through no constraint, but rather, perhaps, because of their overflowing happiness. Tony smiled broadly at the whole world, and every now and again his eyes fastened on her face with a look of assured possession, in the glance with which she had greeted him he had seen all that he wanted to know.

Then she turned round to him. "Oh, Mr. Gale, you haven't seen the garden, our garden. You really must. It's small, but it's sweet. You will come, Mr. Maradick?"

Her father looked up at her with a smile. "You take Mr. Gale, dear. We'll follow in a moment." And so they went out together. He thought that he had never seen so sweet a place. The high walls were old red brick, the lawn stretched the whole length, and around it ran a brown gravelled path. In one corner was an enormous mulberry leaning heavily to one side, and supported by old wooden stakes and held together by bands of metal. Immediately beneath the wall, and around the length of the garden, was a flower bed filled with pansies and hollyhocks and nasturtiums; it was a blaze of colour against the old red of the wall and behind the green of the lawn.

Underneath the mulberry tree was a seat, and they sat down close enough to make Tony's heart beat very hard indeed.

"Oh, it's perfect!" he said with a sigh.

"Yes, it's very lovely, isn't it? I've never known any other garden, and now you don't know how nice it is to have some one to show it to. I've never had anyone to show it to before."

The old house looked lovely from the garden. Its walls bulged towards them in curious curves and angles, it seemed to hang over the lawn like a protecting deity. The light of the sun caught its windows and they flamed red and gold.

"You like having me to show it to?" he said.

"Of course," she answered.

They were both suddenly uncomfortable. Everything around and about them seemed charged with intensest meaning. They began, each of them, to be more uncertain about the other. Perhaps after all they had read the signs wrongly. Janet suddenly reflected that she had known no other young men, and, after all, they might all have that habit of smiling and looking pleasant. It might be merely politeness, and probably meant nothing at all. She had been much too hasty; she took a stolen glance at him and fancied that he looked as though he were a little bored.

"It's much nicer," she said a little coldly, "in the summer than the winter."

He looked at her for a moment, and then burst out laughing. "I say," he said, "don't let's start being polite to each other, we're friends. You know we made a compact the other day. We've got such a lot to talk about that we mustn't waste time."

"Oh! I'm so glad," she sighed with relief; "you see I know so few people that I didn't a bit know whether I was doing the right sort of thing. You looked a very little bit as though you were bored."

"By Jove!" he said. "I should think not. Do you know, it's the rippingest thing in the world coming and talking to you, and I'd been wondering ever since last time how soon it would be before I could come and talk to you again. And now, if you like my coming, it's simply splendid."

"Well, please come often," she said, smiling. "I haven't got many friends, and we seem to think the same about such lots of things."

"Well, I love this place and this garden and everything, and I expect that I shall come often."

"Oh! I think you're wonderful!" she said.

"No, please don't." He bent towards her and touched her hand. "That's only because you haven't seen other people much. I'm most awfully ordinary, quite a commonplace sort of chap. I'd be awfully sick with myself really if I had time to think about it, but there's such a lot going on that one simply can't bother. But you'll do me a lot of good if you'll let me come."

"I!" She opened her eyes wide. "How funny you are! I'm no use to anybody."

"We're both most fearfully modest," he said, smiling, "and when people say how rotten they are they generally mean just the opposite. But I don't, really. I mean it absolutely." Then he lowered his voice. "We're friends, aren't we?"

"Yes," she said, very softly.

"Always?"

"Yes, always."

His hand took hers very gently. At the touch of her fingers his heart began suddenly to pound his breast so that he could not hear, a quiver shook his body, he bent his head.

"I'm an awfully poor sort of fellow," he said in a whisper.

The mulberry tree, the lawn, the shining windows, the flowers caught the tone and for one moment fell like a burning cloud about the two, then the light died away.

In the green wood, on the knoll, a little breeze played with the tops of the trees; down, far below, the white beach shone in the sun and the waves curled in dancing rows across the blue.

Two rabbits fancied for a moment that they heard the tune that had charmed them earlier in the day. They crept out to look, but there was no one on the knoll.

CHAPTER X
IN WHICH EVERYONE FEELS THE AFTER EFFECT OF THE PICNIC

Meanwhile the picnic remained, for others besides Maradick, an interpretation. Lady Gale sat on the evening of the following day watching the sun sink behind the silver birch. She had dressed for dinner earlier than usual, and now it was a quarter to eight and she was still alone in the gradually darkening room.

Mrs. Lester came in. She was dressed in pale blue, and she moved with that sure confidence that a woman always has when she knows that she is dressed with perfect correctness.

"My dear," she said, bending down and kissing Lady Gale, "I'm perfectly lovely to-night, and it isn't the least use telling me that it's only vanity, because I know perfectly well I'm the real right thing, as Henry James would say if he saw me."

"I can't see, dear," said Lady Gale, "but from the glimpse I've got I like the dress."

"Oh, it's perfection! The only thing is that it seems such a waste down here! There's no one who cares in the least whether you're a fright or no."

"There's at any rate, Fred," said Lady Gale.

"Oh, Fred!" said Mrs. Lester scornfully. "He would never see if you stuck it right under his nose. He can dress his people in his novels, but he never has the remotest notion what his wife's got on."

"He knows more than you think," said Lady Gale.

"Oh, I know Fred pretty well; besides," Mrs. Lester added, smiling a little, "he doesn't deserve to have anything done for him just now. He's been very cross and nasty these few days."

She was sitting on a stool at Lady Gale's feet with her hands clasped round her knees, her head was flung back and her eyes shining; she looked rather like a cross, peevish child who had been refused something that it wanted.

Lady Gale sighed for a moment and looked out into the twilight; in the dark blue of the sky two stars sparkled. "Take care of it, dear," she said.

"Of what?" said Mrs. Lester, looking up.

"Love, when you've got it." Lady Gale put her hand out and touched Mrs. Lester's arm. "You know perfectly well that you've got Fred's. Don't play with it."

"Fred cares about his books," Mrs. Lester said slowly. "I don't think that he cares the very least about me."

"Oh, you know that's untrue. You're cross just now and so is he, and both of you imagine things. But down in your hearts you are absolutely sure of it."

Mrs. Lester shrugged her shoulders.

"I'm afraid that I may be tiresome," said Lady Gale gently, "but, my dear, I've lived such a long time and I know that it's sufficiently rare to get the right man. You've got him, and you're so certain that he's right that you think that you can play with it, and it's dangerous."

"I'm not a bit certain," said Mrs. Lester.

"Oh, you are, of course you are. You know that Fred's devoted to you and you're devoted to Fred. Only it's rather dull that everything should go along so soberly and steadily, and you think that you'll have some fun by quarrelling and worrying him. You're piqued sometimes because you don't think that he pays you enough attention and you imagine that other men will pay you more, and he is very patient."

"Oh, you don't know how annoying he can be sometimes," said Mrs. Lester, shaking her head. "When he shuts himself up in his stupid books and isn't aware that I'm there at all."

"Of course I know," said Lady Gale. "All men are annoying and so are all women. Anyone that we've got to live with is bound to be; that's the whole point of rubbing along. Marriage seems stupid enough and dull enough and annoying enough, but as a matter of fact it would be ever so much worse if the man wasn't there at all; yes, however wrong the man may be. We've got to learn to stick it; whether the *it* is a pimple on one's nose or a husband."

"Oh, it's so easy to talk." Mrs. Lester shook her shoulders impatiently. "One has theories and it's very nice to spread them out, but in practice it's quite different. Fred's been perfectly beastly these last few days."

"Well," said Lady Gale, "don't run a risk of losing him. I mean that quite seriously. One thinks that one's got a man so safely that one can play any game one likes, and then suddenly the man's gone; and then, my dear, you're sorry."

"You're dreadfully serious to-night. I wanted to be amused, and instead of that you speak as if I were on the verge of something dreadful. I'm not a bit. It's only Fred that's cross."

"Of course I don't think you're on the verge of anything dreadful." Lady Gale bent down and kissed her. "It's only that Treliss is a funny place. It has its effect—well, it's rather hard to say—but on our nerves, I suppose. We are all of us excited and would do things, perhaps, here that we shouldn't dream of doing anywhere else. Things look differently here." She paused a moment, then she added, "It's all rather worrying."

"Dear, I'm a pig," said Mrs. Lester, leaning over and kissing her. "Don't bother about me and my little things. But why are you worrying? Is it Tony?"

"Well, I suppose it is," said Lady Gale slowly; "it's quite silly of me, but we're all of us rather moving in the dark. Nobody knows what anyone else is doing. And then there's Alice."

"What exactly has she got to do with it?" asked Mrs. Lester.

"My dear, she has everything." Lady Gale sighed. You must have heard when you were in town that she was, more or less, 'allotted' to Tony. Of course it hadn't actually come to any exact words, but it was very generally understood. I myself hadn't any doubt about the matter. They were to come down here to fix it all up. As a matter of fact, coming down here has undone the whole thing."

"Yes, of course I'd heard something," said Mrs. Lester. "As a matter of fact I had been wondering rather. Of course I could see that it wasn't, so to speak, coming off."

"No. Something's happened to Tony since he came down, and to Alice too, for that matter. But at first I didn't worry; in fact, quite between ourselves, I was rather glad. In town they were neither of them very keen about it; it was considered a suitable thing and they were going to fall in with it, and they were quite nice enough, both of them, to have carried it on all right afterwards. But that wasn't the kind of marriage that I wanted for Tony. He's too splendid a fellow to be lost and submerged in that kind of thing; it's too ordinary, too drab. And so, when he came down here, I saw at once that something had happened, and I was glad."

"I understand," said Mrs. Lester, her eyes shining.

"But I asked him nothing. That has always been our plan, that he shall tell me if he wants to, but otherwise I leave it alone. And it has worked splendidly. He has always told me. But this time it is rather different. As soon as he told me anything I should have to act. If he told me who the girl was I should have to see her, and then you see, I must tell my husband. As soon as I know about it I become the family, and I *hate* the family."

Mrs. Lester could feel Lady Gale's hand quiver on her arm. "Oh, my dear, you don't know what it has always been. Before Tony came life was a lie, a lie from the very beginning. I was forced to eat, to sleep, to marry, to bear children, as the family required. Everything was to be done with one eye on the world and another on propriety. I was hot, impetuous in those days, now I am getting old and calm enough, God knows; I have learnt my lesson, but oh! it took some learning. Rupert was like the rest; I soon saw that there was no outlet there. But then Tony came, and there was something to live for. I swore that he should live his life as he was meant to live it, no square pegs in round holes for him, and so I have watched and waited and hoped. And now, at last, romance has come to him. I don't know who she is; but you've seen, we've all seen, the change in him, and he shall seize it and hold it with both hands, only, you see, I must not know. As soon as I know, the thing becomes official, and then there's trouble. Besides, I trust him. I know that he won't do anything rotten because he's Tony. I was just a little bit afraid that he might do something foolish, but I've put Mr. Maradick there as guard, and the thing's safe."

"Mr. Maradick?" asked Mrs. Lester.

"Yes. Tony's devoted to him, and he has just that stolid matter-of-fact mind that will prevent the boy from doing anything foolish. Besides, I like him. He's not nearly so stupid as he seems."

"I don't think he seems at all stupid," said Mrs. Lester, "I think he's delightful. But tell me, if they were neither of them very keen and the thing's off, why are you worried? Surely it is the very best thing that could possibly happen."

"Ah! that was before they came down." Lady Gale shook her head. "Something's happened to Alice. Since she's been down here she's fallen in love with Tony. Yes, wildly. I had been a little afraid of it last week, and then last night she came to me and spoke incoherently about going away and hating Treliss and all sorts of things jumbled up together and then, of course, I saw at once. It is really very strange in a girl like Alice. I used to think that I never knew anyone more self-contained and sensible, but now I'm afraid that she's in for a bad time."

"If one only knew," said Mrs. Lester, "what exactly it is that Tony *is* doing; we're all in the dark. Of course, Mr. Maradick could tell us." She paused for a moment, and then she said suddenly: "Have you thought at all of the effect it may be having on Mr. Maradick? All this business."

"Being with Tony, you mean?" said Lady Gale.

"Yes, the whole affair. He's middle-aged and solid, of course, but he seems to me to have—how can one put it?—well, considerable inclinations to be young again. You know one can't be with Tony without being influenced, and he *is* influenced, I think."

Lady Gale put her hand on the other's sleeve. "Millie," she said very earnestly, "look here. Leave him alone. I mean that seriously, dear. He's not a man to be played with, and it isn't really worth the candle. You love Fred and Fred loves you; just stick to that and don't worry about anything else."

Mrs. Lester laughed. "How perfectly absurd! As if I cared for Mr. Maradick in that kind of way! Why, I've only known him a few days, and, anyway, it's ridiculous!"

"I don't know," said Lady Gale, "this place seems to have been playing tricks with all of us. I'm almost afraid of it; I wish we were going away."

They said no more then, but the conversation had given Lady Gale something more to think about.

Rupert, his father and Alice came in together. It was half-past eight and quite time to go down. Sir Richard was, as usual, impatient of all delay, and so they went down without waiting for Tony and Mr. Lester. The room was not very full when they came in; most people had dined, but the Maradicks were there at their usual table by the window. The two little girls were sitting straight in their chairs with their eyes fixed on their plates.

Mrs. Lester thought that Alice Du Cane looked very calm and self-possessed, and wondered whether Lady Gale hadn't made a mistake. However, Tony would come in soon and then she would see.

"You can imagine what it's like at home," she said as she settled herself in her chair and looked round the room. "Thick, please" (this to the waiter). "Fred never knows when a meal ought to begin, never. He must always finish a page or a sentence or something, and the rest of the world goes hang. Alice, my dear" (she smiled at her across the table), "never marry an author."

Her blue dress was quite as beautiful as she thought it was, and it suited her extraordinarily well. Mrs. Lester's dresses always seemed perfectly natural and indeed inevitable, as though there could never, by any possible chance, have been anything at that particular moment that would have suited her better. She did not spend very much money on dress and often made the same thing do for a great many different occasions, but she was one of the best-dressed women in London.

Little Mr. Bannister, the landlord, rolled round the room and spoke to his guests. This was a function that he performed quite beautifully, with an air and a grace that was masterly in its combination of landlord and host.

He flattered Sir Richard, listened to complaints, speculated about the weather, and passed on.

"Oh, dear! it's so hot!" said Lady Gale, "let's hurry through and get outside. I shall stifle in here."

But Sir Richard was horrified at the idea of hurrying through. When your meals are the principal events of the day you don't intend to hurry through them for anybody.

Then Tony came in. He stopped for a moment at the Maradicks' table and said something to Maradick. As he came towards his people everyone noticed his expression. He always looked as though he found life a good thing, but to-night he seemed to be alive with happiness. They had seen Tony pleased before, but never anything like this.

"You look as if you'd found something," said Rupert.

"Sorry I'm late," said Tony. "No soup, thanks, much too hot for soup. What, father? Yes, I know, but I hurried like anything, only a stud burst and then I couldn't find a sock, and then—Oh! yes, by the way, Fred says he's awfully sorry, but he'll be down in a minute. He never noticed how late it was."

"He never does," said Mrs. Lester, moving impatiently.

"You can forgive a man anything if he writes 'To Paradise,'" said Tony. "Hullo, Alice, where on earth have you been all day? I looked for you this morning and you simply weren't to be found; skulking in your tent, I suppose. But why women should always miss the best part of the day by sticking in their rooms till lunch——"

"I overslept," she said, laughing. "It was after the picnic and the thunder and everything." She smiled across the table quite composedly at him, and Mrs. Lester wondered at her self-possession. She had watched her face when he came in, and she knew now beyond all possible doubt.

"Poor thing," she said to herself, "she is in for a bad time!"

The Maradicks had left the room, the Gales were almost alone; the silver moon played with the branches of the birch trees, the lights from the room flung pools and rivers of gold across the paths, the flowers slept. Sir Richard finished his "poire Melba" and grunted.

"Let's have our coffee outside," said Lady Gale. Outside in the old spot by the wall Tony found Maradick.

"I say," he whispered, "is it safe, do you suppose, to be so happy?"

"Take it while you can," said Maradick. "But it won't be all plain sailing, you mustn't expect that. And look here, Tony, things are going on very fast. I am in a way responsible. I want to know exactly what you intend to do."

"To do?" said Tony.

"Yes. I want it put down practically in so many words. I'm here to look after you. Lady Gale trusts me and is watching me. I *must* know!"

"Why! I'm going to marry her of course. You dear old thing, what on earth do you suppose? Of course I don't exactly know that she cares—in that sort of way, I mean. She didn't say anything in the garden this afternoon, in so many words. But I think that I understood, though of course a fellow may be wrong; but anyhow, if she doesn't care now she will in a very little time. But I say, I haven't told you the best of it all. I believe old Morelli's awfully keen about it. Anyhow, to-day when we were talking to Miss Minns he spoke to me and said that he was awfully glad that I came, that it was so good for Janet having a young friend, and that he hoped that I would come and see her as often as I could. And then he actually said that I might take her out one afternoon for a row, that she would like it and it would be good for her."

"I don't understand him," said Maradick, shaking his head. "I don't know what he wants."

"Oh, it's obvious enough," said Tony, "he thinks that it will be a good match. And I think he wants to get rid of her."

"I don't think it's quite as simple as that," said Maradick; "I wish I did. But to come back to the main question, what do you mean to do?"

"Well," said Tony, feeling in his pocket, "look here, I've written a letter. I didn't see why one should waste time. I'll read it to you." He stepped out of the shadow into the light from one of the windows and read it:—

DEAR MISS MORELLI,

Your father suggested this afternoon that you might come for a row one day. There's no time like the present, so could you possibly come to-morrow afternoon (Thursday)? I should suggest rather late, say four, because it's so frightfully hot earlier. I'll bring tea. If Miss Minns and your father cared to come too it would be awfully jolly.

Yours sincerely

ANTHONY GALE.

PS.—Will you be on the beach by Morna Pool about four?

"There," he said as he put it back, "I think that will do. Of course they won't come. It would be perfectly dreadful if they did. But they won't. I could see that in his face."

"Well, and then?"

"Oh, then! Well, I suppose, one day or other, I shall ask her."

"And after that?"

"Oh, then I shall ask Morelli."

"And if he says no."

"But he won't."

"I don't know. I should think it more than likely. You won't be able to say that your parents have consented."

"No. I shouldn't think he'd mind about that."

"Well, it's his only daughter." Maradick laid his hand on Tony's shoulder. "Look here, Tony, we've got to go straight. Let's look at the thing fair and square. If your people and her people consented there'd be no question about it. But they won't. Your people never will and Morelli's not likely to. Then you must either give the whole thing up or do it secretly. I say, give it up."

"Give it up?" said Tony.

"Yes, there'll be lots of trouble otherwise. Go away, leave for somewhere or other to-morrow. You can think of plenty of explanations. I believe it's this place as much as anything else that's responsible for the whole business. Once you're clear of this you'll see the whole thing quite plainly and thank God for your escape. But if, after knowing a girl a week, you marry her in defiance of everyone wiser and better than yourself, you'll rue the day, and be tied to some one for life, some one of whom you really know nothing."

"Poor old Maradick!" Tony laughed. "You've got to talk like that, I know; it's your duty so to do. But I never knew anyone say it so reluctantly; you're really as keen about it as I am, and you'd be most frightfully sick if I went off to-morrow. Besides, it's simply not to be thought of. I'd much rather marry her and find it was a ghastly mistake than go through life feeling that I'd missed something, missed the best thing there was to have. It's missing things, not doing them wrong, that matters in life."

"Then you'll go on anyhow?" said Maradick.

"Anyhow," said Tony, "I'm of age. I've got means of my own, and if she loves me then nothing shall stop me. If necessary, we'll elope."

"Dear me," said Maradick, shaking his head, "I really oughtn't to be in it at all. I told you so from the beginning. But as you'll go on whether I'm there or no, I suppose I must stay."

The night had influenced Mrs. Lester. She sat under the birches in the shadow with her blue dress like a cloud about her. She felt very romantic. The light in Tony's eyes at dinner had been very beautiful. Oh, dear! How lovely it would be to get some of that romance back again! During most of the year she was an exceedingly sane and level-headed person. The Lesters were spoken of in London as an ideal couple, as fond of each other as ever, but with none of that silly sentiment. And so for the larger part of the year it was; and then there came suddenly a moment when she hated the jog-trot monotony of it all, when she would give anything to regain that fire, that excitement, that fine beating of the heart. To do her justice, she didn't in the least mind about the man, indeed she would have greatly preferred that it should have been her husband; she was much more in love with Romance, Sentiment, Passion, fine abstract things with big capital letters, than any one person; only, whilst the mood was upon her, she must discover somebody. It was no use being romantic to the wind or the stars or the trees.

It really amounted to playing a game, and if Fred would consent to play it with her it would be the greatest fun; but then he wouldn't. He had the greatest horror of emotional scenes, and was always sternly practical with advice about hot-water bottles and not sitting in a draught. He did not, she told herself a hundred times a day, understand her moods in the least. He had never let her help him the least little bit in his work, he shut her out; she tossed her head at the stars, gathered her blue dress about her, and went up to bed.

The bedroom seemed enormous, and the shaded electric light left caverns and spaces of darkness; the enormous bed in the middle of the room seemed without end or boundary. She heard her husband in the dressing-room, and she sat down in front of her glass with a sigh.

"You can go, Ferris," she said to her maid, "I'll manage for myself to-night."

She began to brush her hair; she was angry with the things in the room, everything was so civilised and respectable. The silver on the dressing-table, a blue pincushion, the looking-glass; the blue dress, hanging over the back of a chair, seemed in its reflexion to trail endlessly along the floor. She brushed her hair furiously; it was very beautiful hair, and she wondered whether Fred had ever noticed how beautiful it was. Oh, yes! he'd noticed it in the early days; she remembered how he had stroked it and what nice things he had said. Ah! those early days had been worth having! How exciting they had been! Her heart beat now at the remembrance of them.

She heard the door of the dressing-room close, and Fred came in. He yawned; she glanced up. He was a little shrimp of a man certainly, but he looked rather nice in his blue pyjamas. He was brown, and his grey eyes were very attractive. Although she did not know it, she loved every inch of him from the top of his head to the sole of his foot, but, just now, she wanted something that he had decided, long ago, was bad for her. He had made what he would have called a complete study of her nervous system, treating her psychology as he would have treated the heroine of one of his own novels. He was quite used to her fits of sentiment and he knew that if he indulged her in the least the complaint was aggravated and she was, at once, highly strung and aggressively emotional. His own love for her was so profound and deep that this "billing and cooing" seemed a very unimportant and trivial affair, and he always put it down with a firm hand. They mustn't be children any longer; they'd got past that kind of thing. There were scenes, of course, but it only lasted for a very short time, and then she was quite all right again. He never imagined her flinging herself into anyone else because he would not give her what she wanted. He was too sure of her affection for him.

He had noticed that these attacks of "nerves," as he called them, were apt to come at Treliss, and he had therefore rather avoided the place, but he found that it did, in some curious way, affect him also, and especially his work. The chapters that he wrote at Treliss had a rich, decorated colour that he could not capture in any other part of the world. Perhaps it was the medieval "feeling" of the place, the gold and brown of the roofs and rocks, the purple and blue of the sea and sky; but it went, as he knew, deeper than that. That spirit that influenced and disturbed his wife influenced also his work.

They had been quarrelling for two days, and he saw with relief her smile as he came into the room. Their quarrels disturbed his work.

"Come here, Fred. Don't yawn; it's rude. I've forgiven you, although you have been perfectly hateful these last few days. I think it's ripping of me to have anything to do with you. But, as a matter of fact, you're not a bad old thing and you look rather sweet in blue pyjamas."

She laid her hand on his arm for a moment and then took his hand. He looked at her rather apprehensively; it might mean simply that it was the end of the quarrel, but it might mean that she had one of her moods again.

"I say, old girl," he said, smiling down at her, "I'm most awfully sleepy. I don't know what there is about this place, but I simply can't keep awake. It's partly the weather, I suppose. But anyhow, if you don't awfully mind I think I'll go off to sleep. I'm jolly glad you aren't angry any more. I know I was rather silly, but the book's a bit of a bother just now. . . ."

He yawned again.

"No, you *shan't* go to bed just yet, you sleepy old thing. I really don't feel as though I'd seen anything of you at all this week. And I want to hear all about everything, all about the book. You haven't told me a thing."

He moved his hand. "I say, my dear, you'll be getting the most frightful cold sitting in a draught like that. You'd much better come to bed and we'll talk to-morrow."

But she smiled at him. "No, Fred, I'm going to talk to you. I'm going to give you a sermon. You haven't been a bit nice to me all this time here. I know I've been horrid, but then that's woman's privilege; and you know a woman's only horrid because she wants a man to be nice, and I wanted you to be nice. This summer weather and everything makes it seem like those first days, the honeymoon at that sweet little place in Switzerland, you remember. That night . . ." She sighed and pressed his hand.

He patted her hand. "Yes, dear, of course I remember. Do you suppose I shall ever forget it? We'll go out to-morrow somewhere and have an afternoon together alone. Without these people hanging round. I ought to get the chapter finished to-morrow morning."

He moved back from the chair.

"What chapter, dear?" She leaned back over the chair, looking up in his face. "You know, I wish you'd let me share your work a little. I don't know how many years we haven't been married now, and you've always kept me outside it. A wife ought to know about it. Just at first you did tell me things a little and I was so frightfully interested. And I'm sure I could help you, dear. There are things a woman knows."

He smiled at the thought of the way that she would help him. He would never be able to show her the necessity of doing it all alone, both for him and for her. That part of his life he must keep to himself. He remembered that he had thought before their marriage that she would be able to help. She had seemed so ready to sympathise and understand. But he had speedily discovered the hopelessness of it. Not only was she of no assistance, but she even hindered him.

She took the feeble, the bad parts of the book and praised; she handled his beautiful delicacy, the so admirably balanced sentences, the little perfect expressions that had flown to him from some rich Paradise where they had waited during an eternity of years for some one to use them—she had taken these rare treasures of his and trampled on them, flung them to the winds, demanded their rejection.

She had never for a moment seen his work at all; the things that she had seen had not been there, the things that she had not seen were the only jewels that he possessed. The discovery had not pained him; he had not loved her for *that*, the grasping and sharing of his writing, but for the other things that were there for him, just as charmingly as before. But he could not bear to have his work touched by the fingers of those who did not understand. When people came and asked him about it and praised it just because it was the thing to do, he felt as though some one had flung some curtain aside and exposed his body, naked, to a grinning world.

And it was this, in a lesser degree, that she did. She was only asking, like the rest, because it was the thing to do, because she would be able to say to the world that she helped him; she did not care for the thing, its beauty and solemnity and grace, she did not even see that it *was* beautiful, solemn, or graceful.

"Never mind my work, dear," he said. "One wants to fling it off when one's out of it. You don't want to know about the book. Why, I don't believe you've ever read 'To Paradise' right through; now, have you?"

"Why, of course, I *loved* it, although there *were*, as a matter of fact, things that I could have told you about women. Your heroine, for instance——"

He interrupted hurriedly. "Well, dear, let's go to bed now. We'll talk to-morrow about anything you like." He moved across the room.

She looked angrily into the glass. She could feel that little choke in her throat and her eyes were burning. She tapped the table impatiently.

"I think it's a little hard," she said, "that one's husband should behave as if one were a complete stranger, or, worse still, an ordinary acquaintance. You might perhaps take more interest in a stranger. I don't think I want very much, a little sympathy and some sign of affection."

He was sitting on the bed. "That's all right, dear, only you must admit that you're a little hard to understand. Here during the last two days you've been as cross as it's possible for anyone to be about nothing at all, and then suddenly you want one to slobber. You go up and down so fast that it's simply impossible for an ordinary mortal to follow you."

"Isn't that charming?" she said, looking at the blue pincushion, "such a delightful way to speak to one's wife." Then suddenly she crossed over to him. "No, dear. I didn't mean that really, it was silly of me. Only I do need a little sympathy sometimes. Little things, you know, matter to us women; we remember and notice."

"That's all right." He put his arm round her neck and kissed her, then he jumped into bed. "We'll talk to-morrow." He nestled into the clothes with a little sigh of satisfaction; in a moment he was snoring.

She sat on the bed and stared in front of her. Her hair was down and she looked very young. Most of the room was in shadow, but her dressing-table glittered under the electric light; the silver things sparkled like jewels, the gleam fell on the blue dress and travelled past it to the wall.

She swung her feet angrily. How dare he go to sleep all in a moment in that ridiculous manner? His kiss had seemed a step towards sentiment, and now, in a moment, he was snoring. Oh! that showed how much he cared! Why had she ever married him?

At the thought of the splendid times that she might have been having with some one else, with some splendid strong man who could take her in his arms until she could scarcely breathe, some one who would understand her when she wanted to talk and not go fast off to sleep, some one, well, like Mr. Maradick, for instance, her eyes glittered.

She looked at the room, moved across the floor and switched off the lights. She crept into bed, moving as far away from her husband as possible. He didn't care—nobody cared—she belonged to nobody in the world. She began to sob, and then she thought, of the picnic; well, he had cared and understood. He would not have gone to sleep . . . soon she was dreaming.

And the other person upon whom the weather had had some effect was Mrs. Maradick. It could not be said that weather, as a rule, affected her at all, and perhaps even now things might be put down to the picnic; but the fact remains that for the first time in her selfish little life she was unhappy. She had been wounded in her most sensitive spot, her vanity. It did not need any very acute intelligence to see that she was not popular with the people in the hotel. The picnic had shown it to her quite conclusively, and she had returned in a furious passion. They had been quite nice to her, of course, but it did not need a very subtle woman to discover their real feelings. Fifteen years of Epsom's admiration had ill-prepared her for a harsh and unsympathetic world, and she had never felt so lonely in her life before.

She hated Lady Gale and Mrs. Lester bitterly from the bottom of her heart, but she would have given a very great deal, all her Epsom worshippers and more, for some genuine advance on their part.

She was waiting now in her room for her husband to come in. She was sitting up in bed looking very diminutive indeed, with her little sharp nose and her bright shining eyes piercing the shadows; she had turned out the lights, except the one by the bed. She did not know in the least what she was going to say to him, but she was angry and sore and lonely; she was savage with the world in general and with James in particular. She bit her lips and waited. He came in softly, as though he expected to find her asleep, and then when he saw her light he started. His bed was by the window and he moved towards it. Then he stopped and saw her sitting up in bed.

"Emmy! You still awake!"

He looked enormous in his pyjamas; he could see his muscles move beneath the jacket.

"Yes," she said, "I want to talk to you."

"Oh! must we? Now?" he said. "It seems very late."

"It's the only opportunity that one gets nowadays," she said, her eyes flaring, "you are so much engaged." It made her furious to see him looking so clean and comfortably sleepy.

"Engaged?" he said.

"Oh! we needn't go into that," she answered. "One doesn't really expect to see anything of one's husband in these modern times, it isn't the thing!"

He didn't remind her that during the last fifteen years she hadn't cared very much whether he were lonely or not. He looked at her gravely.

"Don't let's start that all over again now," he said. "I would have spent the whole time with you if you hadn't so obviously shown me that you didn't want me. You can hardly have forgotten already what you said the other day."

"Do you think that's quite true?" she said, looking up at him; she was gripping the bedclothes in her hands. "Don't you think that it's a little bit because there's some one else who did, or rather *does*, want you?"

"What do you mean?" he said, coming towards her bed. She was suddenly frightened. This was the man whom she had seen for the first time on that first evening at dinner, some one she had never known before.

"I mean what I say," she answered. "How long do you suppose that I intend to stand this sort of thing? You leave me deliberately alone; *I* don't know what you do with your days, *or* your evenings, neither does anyone else. I'm not going to be made a laughing-stock of in the hotel; all those beastly women . . ." She could scarcely speak for rage.

"There is nothing to talk about," he answered sternly. "It's only your own imagination. At any rate, we are not going to have a scene now, nor ever again, as far as that goes. I'm sick of them."

"Well," she answered furiously, "if you think I'm going to sit there and let myself be made a fool of and say nothing you're mightily mistaken; I've had enough of it."

"And so have I," he answered quietly. "If you're tired of this place we'll go away somewhere else, wherever you please; perhaps it would be a good thing. This place seems to have upset you altogether. Perhaps after all it would be the best thing. It would cut all the knots and end all these worries."

But she laughed scornfully. "Oh! no, thank you. I like the place well enough. Only you must be a little more careful. And if you think — —"

But he cut her short. "I don't think anything about it," he said. "I'm tired of talking. This place *has* made a difference, it's true. It's shown me some of the things that I've missed all these years; I've been going along like a cow . . . and now for the future it's going to be different."

"Oh! it's not only the place," she sneered. "Mrs. Lester — —"

But at the word he suddenly bent down and held her by the shoulders. His face was white; he was shaking with anger. He was so strong that she felt as though he was going to crush her into nothing.

"Look here," he whispered, "leave that alone. I won't have it, do you hear? I won't have it. You've been riding me too long, you and your nasty dirty little thoughts; now I'm going to have my own way. You've had yours long enough; leave me alone. Don't drive me too far. . . ."

He let her drop back on the pillows. She lay there without a word. He stole across the room on his naked feet and switched out the lights. She heard him climb into bed.

CHAPTER XI
OF LOVE—AND THEREFORE TO BE SKIPPED BY ALL THOSE WHO ARE TIRED OF THE SUBJECT

Above the knoll the afternoon sun hung in a golden mist. The heat veiled it, and the blue of the surrounding sky faded into golden shadows near its circle and swept in a vast arc to limitless distance. The knoll, humped like a camel's back, stood out a vivid green against the darker wall of trees behind it. Far below, the white sand of the cove caught the sun and shone like a pearl, and beyond it was the blue carpet of the sea.

Morelli sat, cross-legged, on the knoll. In his hands was his flute, but he was staring straight below him down on to the cove. He waited, the air was heavy with heat; a crimson butterfly hovered for a moment in front of him and then swept away, a golden bee buzzed about his head and then lumbered into the air. There was silence; the trees stood rigid in the heat.

Suddenly Morelli moved. Two black specks appeared against the white shadows of the beach; he began to play.

Punch was lying on the cliff asleep. To his right, curving towards the white sand, was a sea-pool slanting with green sea-weed down into dark purple depths. The sun beat upon the still surface of it and changed it into burning gold. Below this the sea-weed flung green shadows across the rock. It reflected through the gold the straight white lines of the road above it, and the brown stem, sharp like a sword, of a slender poplar. It seemed to pass through the depths of the pool into endless distance. Besides the green of the sea-weed and the gold of the sun there was the blue of the sky reflected, and all these lights and colours mingled and passed and then mingled again as in the curving circle of a pearl shell. Everything was metallic, with a hard outline like steel, under the blazing sun.

Tony turned the corner and came down the hill. He was in flannels and carried in one hand a large tea-basket. His body, long and white, was reflected in the green and blue of the pool. It spread in little ripples driven by a tiny wind in white shadows to the bank.

He was whistling, and then suddenly he saw Toby and Punch asleep in the grass. He stopped for a moment in the road and looked at them. Then he passed on.

The white sand gleamed and sparkled in the sun; the little wind had passed from the face of the pool, and there was no movement at all except the very soft and gentle breaking of tiny waves on the sand's edge. A white bird hanging for the moment motionless in the air, a tiny white cloud, the white edge of the breaking ripples, broke the blue.

Tony sat down. From where he was sitting he could see the town rising tier upon tier into a peak. It lay panting in the sun like a beast tired out.

The immediate problem was whether Morelli or Miss Minns would come. A tiny note in a tiny envelope had arrived at the "Man at Arms" that morning. It had said:

DEAR MR. GALE,

Thank you so very much. It is charming of you to ask us. We shall be delighted to come.

Yours sincerely

JANET MORELLI.

It wasn't like her, and short though it was he felt sure that somebody had watched her whilst she did it. And "we"? For whom did that stand? He had felt so sure in his heart of hearts that no one except Janet would come that he was, at first, bitterly disappointed. What a farce the whole thing would be if anyone else were there! He laughed sarcastically at the picture of Miss Minns perched horribly awry at the end of the boat, forcing, by her mere presence, the conversation into a miserable stern artificiality. And then suppose it were Morelli? But it wouldn't be, of that he was sure; Morelli had other things to do.

He glanced for a moment up to the cliff where Punch was. He didn't want the whole town to know what he was about. Punch could keep a secret, of course, he had kept a good many in his time, but it might slip out; not that there was anything to be ashamed of.

As a matter of fact, he had had some difficulty in getting away from the hotel; they had been about him like bees, wanting him to do things. He had noticed, too, that his mother was anxious. Since the day of the picnic she had watched him, followed him with her eyes, had evidently longed to ask him what he was going to do. That, he knew, was her code, that she should ask him nothing and should wait; but he felt that she was finding the waiting very difficult. He was quite sure in his own mind that Alice had spoken to her, and, although he would give everything in the world to be pleasant and easy, he found, in spite of himself, that he was, when he talked to her, awkward and strained. There was something new and strange in her attitude to him, so that the old cameraderie was quite hopelessly gone, and the most ordinary conventional remark about the weather became charged with intensest meaning. This all contrived to make things at the hotel very awkward, and everyone was in that state of tension which forced them to see hidden mysteries in everything that happened or was said. The Lesters had been barely on speaking terms at breakfast time and Maradick hadn't appeared at all.

Then, when the afternoon had come, his mother had asked him to come out with them. He had had to refuse, and had only been able to give the vaguest of reasons. They knew that he was not going with Mr. Maradick, because he had promised to walk with Mr. Lester. What was he going to do? He spoke of friends in the town and going for a row. It had all been very unpleasant. Life was, in fact, becoming immensely complicated, and if Miss Minns were to appear he would have all this worry and trouble for nothing.

He gazed furiously at the hard white road. The pool shone like a mirror; the road, the poplar, the sky were painted on its surface in hard vivid outline. Suddenly a figure was reflected in it. Some one in a white dress with a large white hat, her reflexion spread across the length of the pool. The water caught a mass of golden hair and held it for a moment, then it was gone.

Tony's eyes, straining towards the hill, suddenly saw her; she was alone. When he saw her his heart began to beat so furiously that for a moment he could not move. Then he sprang to his feet. He must not be too sure. Perhaps Miss Minns was late. He watched her turn down the path and come towards him. She was looking very cool and collected and smiling at him as she crossed the sand.

"Isn't it a lovely day?" she said, shaking hands. "I'm not late, am I?"

"No, I was rather early;" and then, suddenly, "Is Miss Minns coming?"

"Oh, no," Janet laughed, "it was far too hot. She is sleeping with all the curtains drawn and the doors and windows shut. Only I'm not to be late. Oh, dear! What fun! Where's the boat?"

The excitement of hearing that she really was alone was very nearly too much for Tony. He wanted to shout.

"Oh, I say, I'm so glad. No, I don't mean to be rude really; I think Miss Minns awfully decent, simply ripping" (this, I am afraid, due to general pleasure rather than strict veracity), "but it would have put a bit of a stopper on the talking, wouldn't it? and you know there are simply tons of things that I want to talk about. The boat's round here, round the corner over these rocks. I thought we'd row to Mullin's Cave, have tea, and come back."

They moved across the sand.

Punch had woke at the sound of voices and now was staring in front of him. He recognised both of them. "The couple of babies," he said, and he sighed.

And at that precise moment some one else came down the path. It was Alice du Cane. She carried a pink parasol. Her figure lay for a moment on the surface of the pool. She was looking very pretty, but she was very unhappy. They had asked her to go out with them, but she had refused and had pleaded a headache. And then she had hated the gloom and silence of her room. She knew what it was that she wanted, although she refused to admit it to herself. She pretended that she wanted the sea, the view, the air; and so she went out. She told herself a hundred times a day that she must go away, must leave the place and start afresh somewhere else. That was what she wanted; another place and she would soon forget. And then there would come fierce self-reproach and miserable contempt. She, Alice du Cane, who had prided herself on her self-control? The kind of girl who could quote Henley with satisfaction, "Captain of her soul?" At the turn of the road she saw Punch and Toby; then across the white sand of the cove two figures.

He said good-day, and she smiled at him. Then for a moment she stopped. It was Tony, she could hear his laugh; he gave the girl his hand to cross the rocks.

"A beautiful day, isn't it?" she said to Punch, and passed down the road.

They found the boat round the corner of the rocks lying with its clean white boards and blue paint. It lay with a self-conscious air on the sand, as though it knew at what ceremony it was to attend. It gurgled and chuckled with pleasure as it slipped into the water. Whilst he busied himself with the oars she stood silently, her hands folded in front of her, looking out to sea. "I've always wanted to know," she said, "what there is right out there on the other side. One used to fancy a country, like any child, with mountains and lakes, black sometimes and horrible when one was in a bad mood, and then, on other days, beautiful and full of sun. . . ."

They said very little as the boat moved out; the cove rapidly dwindled into a shining circle of silver sand; the rocks behind it assumed shapes, dragons and mandarins and laughing dogs, the town mounted like a pyramid into the sky and some of it glittered in the light of the sun like diamonds.

Janet tried to realise her sensations. In the first place she had never been out in a boat before; secondly, she had never been really alone with Tony before; thirdly, she had had no idea that she would have felt so silent as she did. There were hundreds of things that she wanted to say, and yet she sat there tongue-tied. She was almost afraid of breaking the silence, as though it were some precious vase and she was tempted to fling a stone.

Tony too felt as though he were in church. He rowed with his eyes fixed on the shore, and Janet. Now that the great moment had actually arrived he was frightened. Whatever happened, the afternoon would bring tremendous consequences with it. If she laughed at him, or was amazed at his loving her, then he felt that he could never face the long dreary stretches of life in front of him; and if she loved him, well, a good many things would have to happen. He realised, too, that a number of people were bound up with this affair of his; his mother, Alice, the Maradicks, even the Lesters.

"They didn't mind your coming alone?" he said at last.

"Oh, no, why should they?" she said, laughing. "Besides, father approves of you enormously, and I'm so glad! He's never approved of anyone as a companion before, and it makes such a difference."

"Is he kind to you?"

"Father! Why, of course!"

"Are you fond of him?"

"Why do you want to know?"

"I must know; I want to know all about it. We can't be real friends unless there's complete confidence. That's the best of being the ages we are. As things are, we can't have very much to hide, but later on people get all sorts of things that they have done and said that they keep locked up."

"No," said Janet, smiling, "I haven't got anything to hide. I'll try and tell you all you want to know. But it's very difficult, about father."

"Why?" said Tony.

"Well, you see, I haven't known other people's fathers at all, and up to quite lately I didn't think there was anything peculiar about mine, but just lately I've been wondering. You see there's never been any particular affection, there hasn't been any question of affection, and that's," she stopped for a moment, "that's what I've been wanting. I used to make advances when I was quite tiny, climb on his knee, and sometimes he would play, oh! beautifully! and then suddenly he would stop and push me aside, or behave, perhaps, as though I were not there at all."

"Brute!" said Tony between his teeth, driving the oar furiously through the water.

"And then I began to see gradually that he didn't care at all. It was easy enough even for a girl as young as I was to understand, and yet he would sometimes be so affectionate." She broke off. "I think," she said, looking steadily out to sea, "that he would have liked to have killed me sometimes. He is so furious at times that he doesn't in the least know what he's doing."

"What did you do when he was like that?" asked Tony in a very low voice.

"Oh, one waits," she said very quietly, "they don't last long."

She spoke dispassionately, as though she were outside the case altogether, but Tony felt that if he had Morelli there, in the boat with him, he would know what to do and say.

"You must get away," he said.

"There are other things about him," she went on, "that I've noticed that other people's fathers don't do. He's wonderful with animals, and yet he doesn't seem really to care about them, or, at least, he only cares whilst they are in certain moods. And although they come to him so readily I often think that they are really afraid as I am."

She began to think as she sat there. She had never spoken about it all to anyone before, and so it had never, as it were, materialised. She had never realised until now how badly she had wanted to talk to some one about it.

"Oh, you have been so fortunate," she said, a little wistfully, "to have done so many things and seen so many people. Tell me about other girls, are they all beautiful? Do they dress beautifully?"

"No," he said, looking at her. "They are very tiresome. I can't be serious with girls as a rule. That's why I like to be with you. You don't mind a fellow being serious. Girls seem to think a man isn't ever meant to drop his grin, and it gets jolly tiresome. Because, you know, life is awfully serious when you come to think about it. I've only realised," he hesitated a moment, "during this last fortnight how wonderful it is. That's, you know," he went on hurriedly, "why I really like to be with men better. Now a fellow like Maradick understands what one's feeling, he's been through it, he's older, and he knows. But then you understand too; it's jolly funny how well you understand a chap."

He dropped his oars for a moment and the boat drifted. They were rounding the point, and the little sandy beach for which they were making crept timidly into sight. There was perfect stillness; everything was as though it were carved from stone, the trees on the distant hill, the hanging curtain of sky, the blue mirror of the sea, the sharply pointed town. A flock of white sheep, tiny like a drifting baby cloud, passed for a moment against the horizon on the brow of the hill. There was a very faint sound of bells.

They were both very silent. The oars cut through the water, the boat gave a little sigh as it pushed along, there was no other sound.

They sat on the beach and made tea. Tony had thought of everything. There was a spirit lamp, and the kettle bubbled and hissed and spluttered. Tony busied himself about the tea because he didn't dare to speak. If he said the very simplest thing he knew that he would lose all self-control. She was sitting against a rock with her dress spread around her.

She looked up at him with big, wide-open eyes.

"Your name is Tony, isn't it?" she said.

"Yes," he answered.

"I suppose it is short for Anthony. I shall call you Tony. But see, there is something that I want to say. You will never now, after we have been such friends, let it go again, will you? Because it has been so wonderful meeting you, and has made such a difference to me that I couldn't bear it. If you went away, and you had other friends and — forgot."

"No, I won't forget."

He dropped a plate on to the sand and came towards her.

"Janet." He dropped on to his knees beside her. "I must tell you. I love you, I love you, Janet. I don't care whether you are angry or not, and if you don't feel like that then I will be an awfully decent friend and won't bother you about love. I'll never talk about it. And anyhow, I ought, I suppose, to give you time; a little because you haven't seen other fellows, and it's not quite fair."

He didn't touch her, but knelt on the sand, looking up into her face.

She looked down at him and laughed. "Why, how silly, Tony dear, I've loved you from the first moment that I saw you; why, of course, you must have known."

Their hands touched, and at that moment Tony realised the wonderful silence and beauty of the world. The sea spread before them like a carpet, but it was held with the rocks and sand and sky in breathless tension by

God for one immortal second. Nature waited for a moment to hear the story that it had heard so often before, then when the divine moment had passed the world went on its course once more. But in that moment things had happened. A new star had been born in the sky, the first evening star, and it sparkled and glittered above the town; in the minstrels' room at that moment the sun shone and danced on the faces of the lions, beneath the tower the apple-woman paused in her knitting and nodded her head solemnly at some secret pleasant thought, on the knoll the birds clustered in chattering excitement, far on the horizon a ship with gleaming sails rose against the sky.

"Janet, darling." He bent down and kissed her hand. Then he raised his face, hers bent down to his—they kissed.

Half an hour later they were in the boat again; she sat on the floor with her head against his knee. He rowed very slowly, which was natural, because it was difficult to move the oars.

The evening lights began to creep across the sky, and the sun sank towards the horizon; other stars had stolen into the pale blue sky; near the sea a pale orange glow, as of a distant fire, burned. The boat shone like a curved and shining pearl.

Tony had now a difficult business in front of him. The situation had to be made clear to her that his people must not be told. He was quite resolved within himself in what way he was going to carry the situation through, but he could not at all see that she would consider the matter in the same light. It would take time and considerable trouble to convey to her a true picture of the complicated politics of the Gale family.

"Janet, dear," he said, "we have now to be sternly practical. There are several things that have to be faced. In the first place, there is your father."

"Yes," she said, a little doubtfully.

"Well, how will he take it?"

"I don't know." She looked up at him and laid her hand very lightly upon his knee. The yellow light had crept up from the horizon, and was spreading in bands of colour over the sky; the sea caught the reflexion very faintly, but the red glow had touched the dark band of country behind them and the white road, the still black trees were beginning to burn as though with fire.

"Well," said Tony, "of course I shall tell him at once. What will he say?"

"I don't know. One never can tell with father. But, dear, must you? Couldn't we wait? It is not that I mind his knowing, but I am, in some way, afraid."

"But he likes me," said Tony; "you told me yourself."

"Yes, but his liking anybody never means very much. It's hard to explain; but it isn't you that he likes so much as something that you've got. It is always that with everybody. I've seen it heaps of times. He goes about and picks people up, and if they haven't got the thing he's looking for he drops them at once and forgets them as soon as he can. I don't know what it is that he looks for exactly, but, whatever it is, he finds it in the animals, and in the place even; that's why he lives at Treliss."

Janet was very young about the world in general, but about anything that she had herself immediately met she was wise beyond her years.

She looked at him a moment, and then added: "But of course you must speak to him; it is the only thing to do."

"And suppose," said Tony, "that he refuses to give his consent?"

"Oh, of course," Janet answered quietly, "then we must go away. I belong to you now. Father does not care for me in the least, and I don't care for anyone in the world except you."

Her calm acceptance of the idea that he himself had intended to submit to her very tentatively indeed frightened him. His responsibility seemed suddenly to increase ten-fold. Her suggesting an elopement so quietly, and even asserting it decisively as though there were no other possible alternative, showed that she didn't in the least realise what it would all mean.

"And then, of course," she went on quietly, "there are your people. What will they say?"

"That's it, dear. That's the dreadful difficulty. They mustn't be told at all. The only person in the family who really matters in the least is my mother, and she matters everything. The governor and my brother care for me only as the family, and they have to see that that isn't damaged."

"And they'd think that I'd damage it?" said Janet.

"Yes," said Tony, quietly, "they would. You see, dear, in our set in town the two things that matter in marriage are family and money. You've got to have either ancestors or coin. Your ancestors, I expect, are simply ripping, but they've got to be in Debrett, so that everyone can look them up when the engagement's announced. It isn't you they'd object to, but the idea."

"I see; well?"

"Well, if mother knew about it; if it was public she'd have to support the family, of course. But really in her heart of hearts what she wants is that I should be happy. She'd much rather have that than anything else; so that if we are married and it's too late for anyone to say anything, and she sees that we are happy, then it will be all right, but she mustn't know until afterwards."

Tony stopped, but Janet said nothing. Then he went on: "You see there was a sort of idea with people, before we came down here, that I should get engaged to some one. It was more or less an understood thing."

"Was there, is there anyone especially?" asked Janet.

"Yes; a Miss Du Cane. We'd been pals for a long time without thinking about marriage at all; and then people began to say it was time for me to settle down, and rot like that—and she seemed quite suitable, and so she was asked down here."

"Did you care about her?"

"Oh! like a friend, of course. She's a jolly good sort, and used to be lots of fun, but as soon as all this business came into it she altered and it became different. And then I saw you, and there was never more any question of anyone else in all the world."

Tony dropped the oars and let the boat drift. He caught her golden hair in his hands and twined it about his arm. He bent down and touched her lips. She leaned up towards him and they clung together. About them the sea was a golden flame, the sky was a fiery red, the country behind them was iron black. The boat danced like a petal out to sea.

Then, with her arm about his neck, Janet spoke again. "Your father would like you to marry this lady?" she asked.

"Yes. He thinks that I am going to."

"Ah! now I understand it all. You cannot tell them, of course; I see that. We must do it first and tell them afterwards. And father will never consent. I am sure of it. Oh, dear! what fun! we must go away secretly; it will be an elopement."

"What a ripping rag!" said Tony eagerly. "Oh! darling, I was so afraid that you would mind all those things, and I didn't want to tell you. But now that you take it like that! And then, you see, that's where Maradick comes in."

"Mr. Maradick?"

"Yes. He's really the foundation-stone of the whole affair. It's because mother trusts him so absolutely completely that she's feeling so safe. He knows all about it, and has known all about it all the time. Mother depends on him altogether; we all depend on him, and he'll help us."

The sun lay, like a tired warrior, on the breast of the sea; the clouds, pink and red and gold, gathered about him. The boat turned the creek and stole softly into the white shelter of the cove. Above the heads of the lovers the stars glittered, about them the land, purple and dark with its shadows, crept in on every side. Some bell rang from the town, there was the murmur of a train, the faint cry of some distant sheep.

Their voices came softly in the dusk:

"I love you."

"Janet!"

"Tony!"

The night fell.

CHAPTER XII
OUR MIDDLE-AGED HERO IS BURDENED BY RESPONSIBILITY BUT BOLDLY UNDERTAKES THE ADVENTURE

That same afternoon Maradick finished "To Paradise." He read it in the room of the minstrels with the sun beating through the panes in pools of gold on to the floor, the windows flung wide open, and a thousand scents and sounds flooding the air. The book had chimed in curiously with the things that were happening to him; perhaps at any other time, and certainly a year ago, he would have flung the book aside with irritation at its slow movement and attenuated action. Now it gave him the precisely correct sensation; it was the atmosphere that he had most effectually realised during these last weeks suddenly put for him clearly on to paper. Towards the end of the book there was this passage: "And indeed Nature sets her scene as carefully as any manager on our own tiny stage; we complain discordantly of fate, and curse our ill-luck when, in reality, it is because we have disregarded our setting that we have suffered. Passing lights, whether of sailing ships or huddled towns, murmuring streams heard through the dark but not seen, the bleating of countless sheep upon a dusky hill, are all, with a thousand other formless incoherent things, but sign-posts to show us our road. And let us, with pressing fingers, wilfully close our ears and blind our eyes, then must we suffer. Changes may come suddenly upon a man, and he will wonder; but let him look around him and he will see that he is subject to countless other laws and orders, and that he plays but a tiny rôle in a vast and moving scene."

He rose and stretched his arms. He had not for twenty years felt the blood race through his veins as it did to-day. Money? Office stools? London? No; Romance, Adventure. He would have his time now that it had come to him. He could not talk to his wife about it; she would not understand; but Mrs. Lester— —

The door opened suddenly. He turned round. No one had ever interrupted him there before; he had not known that anyone else had discovered the place, and then he saw that it was Lester himself. He came forward with that curious look that he often had of seeing far beyond his immediate surroundings. He stared now past the room into the blue and gold of the Cornish dusk; the vague misty leaves of some tree hung, a green cloud, against the sky, two tiny glittering stars shone in the sky above the leaves, as though the branches had been playing with them and had tossed them into the air.

Then he saw Maradick.

"Hullo! So you've discovered this place too?" He came towards him with that charming, rather timid little smile that he had. "I found it quite by chance yesterday, and have been absolutely in love with it— —"

"Yes," said Maradick, "I've known it a long time. Curiously enough, we were here last year and I never found it." Then he added: "I've just finished your book. May I tell you how very much I've enjoyed it? It's been quite a revelation to me; its beauty— —"

"Thank you," said Lester, smiling, "it does one a lot of good when one finds that some one has cared about one's work. I think that I have a special affection for this one, it had more of myself in it. But will you forgive my saying it, I had scarcely expected you, Maradick, to care about it."

"Why?" asked Maradick. Lester's voice was beautifully soft and musical, and it seemed to be in tune with the room, the scene, the hour.

"Well, we are, you know, in a way at the opposite ends of the pole. You are practical; a business man; it is your work, your place in life, to be practical. I am a dreamer through and through. I would have been practical if I could. I have made my ludicrous attempts, but I have long ago given it up. I have been cast for another rôle. The visions, the theories, the story of such a man as I am must seem stupidly, even weakly vague and insufficient to such a man as you. I should not have thought that 'To Paradise' could have seemed to you anything but a moonstruck fantasy. Perhaps that is what it really is."

He spoke a little sadly, looking out at the sky. "I am afraid that is what it is," he said.

"Is it not possible," said Maradick slowly, "that a man should, at different times in his life, have played both rôles? Can one not be practical and yet have one's dreams? Can one not have one's dreams and yet be practical?"

As he spoke he looked at the man and tried to see him from Mrs. Lester's point of view. He was little and brown and nervous; his eyes were soft and beautiful, but they were the eyes of a seer.

Mr. Lester shook his head. "I think it is possible to be practical and yet to have your dreams. I will not deny that you have yours; but the other thing—no, I shall never see the world as it is. And yet, you know," he went on, smiling a little, "the world will never let me alone. I think that at last I shall see that for which I have been searching, that at last I shall hear that for which I have been listening so long; and then suddenly the world breaks in upon it and shatters it, and it vanishes away. One has one's claims, one is not alone; but oh! if I had only an hour when there might be no interruption. But I'm really ashamed, Maradick; this must seem, to put it bluntly, so much rot to you, and indeed to anyone except myself."

"No," said Maradick. "I think I understand more than you would expect. A month ago it might have been different, but now——"

"Ah," said Lester, laughing, "the place has caught you, as it does everyone."

"No, not only the place," said Maradick slowly, "there is something else. I was here last year, but I did not feel, I did not see as I do now."

"Yes, it's Tony Gale as well."

"Tony?"

"Yes. Believe me, there's nothing that a boy like that cannot do with his happiness and youth. It goes out from him and spreads like a magic wand. If people only knew how much they owed to that kind of influence——"

"Well, perhaps it is Tony," said Maradick, laughing. "I am fonder of him than I can say; but, whatever the cause, the dreams are there."

Lester took out a book from under his arm. It was long and thin and bound in grey parchment.

"Here," he said, "is a book that perhaps you know. It is one of the most beautiful comedies in our language. This man was a dreamer too, and his dreams are amongst the most precious things that we have. I may write to the end of time, but I shall never reach that exquisite beauty."

Maradick took the book; it was Synge's "Play-boy of the Western World." He had never heard of the man or of the play. He turned its pages curiously.

"I am afraid," he said, "that I've never heard of it. It is Irish, I see. I think I do remember vaguely when the Dublin players were in London last year hearing something. The man has died, hasn't he?"

"Yes, and he didn't leave very much behind him, but what there is is of the purest gold. See, listen to this, one of the greatest love-scenes in our language. It is a boy and a girl in a lonely inn on an Irish moor."

He read:—

The Girl.—"What call have you to be that lonesome when there's poor girls walking Mayo in their thousands now?"

The Boy.—"It's well you know what call I have. It's well you know it's a lonesome thing to be passing small towns with the lights shining sideways when the night is down, or going in strange places with a dog noising before you and a dog noising behind, or drawn to the cities where you'd hear a voice kissing and talking deep love in every shadow of the ditch, and you passing on with an empty stomach failing from your heart."

Maradick listened to the beautiful words and his eyes glowed. The dusk was falling in the room, and half-lights of gold and purple hovered over the fireplace and the gallery. The leaves of the tree had changed from green to dark grey, and, above them, where there had been two stars there were now a million.

"And again," said Lester, "listen to this."

The Boy.—"When the airs is warming in four months or five, it's then yourself and me should be pacing Neifin in the dews of night, the time sweet smells do be rising, and you'd see a little shiny new moon, maybe, sinking on the hills."

The Girl. (playfully).—"And it's that kind of a poacher's love you'd make, Christy Mahon, on the sides of Neifin, when the night is down?"

The Boy.—"It's little you'll think if my love's a poacher's or an earl's itself, when you'll feel my two hands stretched around you, and I squeezing kisses on your puckered lips, till I'd feel a kind of pity for the Lord God in all ages sitting lonesome in his golden chair."

The Girl.—"That'll be right fun, Christy Mahon, and any girl would walk her heart out before she'd meet a young man was your like for eloquence or talk at all."

The Boy (encouraged).—"Let you wait, to hear me talking, till we're astray in Ennis, when Good Friday's by, drinking a sup from a well and making mighty kisses with our wetted mouths, or gaming in a gap of sunshine, with yourself stretched back unto your necklace, in the flowers of the earth."

The Girl (in a low voice moved by his tone).—"I'd be nice so, is it?"

The Boy (with rapture).—"If the mitred bishops seen you that time, they'd be the like of the holy prophets, I'm thinking, do be straining the bars of Paradise to lay eyes on the Lady Helen of Troy, and she abroad, pacing back and forward, with a nosegay in her golden shawl."

He stopped, and sat, silently, with the book in front of him. The half-light in the room spread into a circle of pale rose-colour immediately round the window; the night sky was of the deepest blue.

To Maradick it was as though the place itself had spoken. The colour of the day had taken voice and whispered to him.

"Thank you," he said. "That's very beautiful. Would you lend it to me some time?"

"Delighted," said Lester. "You can have it now if you like. Take it with you. The whole play won't keep you more than half an hour. I have his other things, if you care to look at them."

Maradick went off to dress with the book under his arm.

When he came down to the drawing-room he found Mrs. Lester there alone. Only one lamp was lit and the curtains were not drawn, so that the dusky sky glowed with all its colours, blue and gold and red, beyond the windows.

When he saw Mrs. Lester he stopped for a moment at the door. The lamplight fell on one cheek and some dark bands of her hair, the rest of her face was in shadow. She smiled when she saw him.

"Ah! I'm so glad that you've come down before the rest. I've been wanting to speak to you all day and there has been no opportunity."

"Your husband has been showing me a wonderful play by that Irishman, Synge," he said. "I hadn't heard of him. I had no idea——"

She laughed. "You've struck one of Fred's pet hobbies," she said; "start him on Synge and he'll never stop. It's nice for a time—at first, you know; but Synge for ever—well, it's like living on wafers."

She sighed and leaned back in her chair. She spoke in a low voice, and it gave a note of intimacy to their conversation. As she looked at him she thought again what a fine man he was. Evening dress suited him, and the way that he sat, leaning a little towards her with his head raised and the lamplight falling on his chin and throat, gave her a little thrill of pleasure. He was very big and strong, and she contrasted him with her husband. Maradick would probably be a bore to live with, whilst Fred, as a matter of fact, did very well. But for playing a game this was the very man, if, indeed, he knew that it was only a game; it would be a dreadful nuisance if he took it seriously.

"How long are you staying here?" she said. "We shall stop for another fortnight, I suppose, unless my husband suddenly takes it into his head to run away. Even then I shall probably stay. I love the place; let me see— to-day's the fourteenth—yes, we shall probably be here until the twenty-eighth."

"I must get back when the month is up," said Maradick.

"But I hate to think of going back. I'm enjoying every minute of it, but I don't think my wife will be sorry. The heat doesn't suit her."

"I hope," she bent forward a little and laid her hand on his chair, "that you didn't think it very impertinent of me to speak as I did at the picnic the other day. I thought afterwards that I had, perhaps, said too much. But then I felt that you were different from most men, that you would understand. I trust too much, I think, to intuition."

"No, please don't think that," he said eagerly. "We have only got another fortnight here. Why shouldn't we be friends? I'm beginning to think that I have wasted too much of my life by being afraid of going too far, of saying the wrong thing. I have begun to understand life differently since I have been here."

Whether he implied that it was since he had known her that he had begun to understand, she did not know; at any rate she would take it for that. "There are so many things that I could tell you," she said. "I think you are to be trusted. It is not often that a woman can feel that about anyone."

"Thank you for saying that," he said, looking her full in the face; "I will try and deserve it."

She touched his hand with hers and felt a delicious little thrill, then she heard steps and moved to the fireplace.

Lady Gale and Alice Du Cane came into the room, and it was evident at once that they were upset. Lady Gale talked to Maradick, but it was obvious that her mind was elsewhere.

"Has Tony been with you this afternoon?" she said. "Alice says she saw him about four o'clock, but no one has seen him since. He hasn't come back, apparently."

"No," Maradick said, "I haven't seen him since breakfast."

She looked at him for a moment, and he felt that her look had something of reproach in it. He suddenly was conscious that he was, in their eyes at any rate, responsible for anything that Tony might do. He ought to have stood guard. And, after all, where had the boy been? He should have been back by now.

"It is really too bad," Lady Gale said. "He knows that his father dislikes unpunctuality at meals above all things, and he has been late again and again just lately. I must speak to him. He's later than ever to-night. Where did you see him, Alice?"

"Down on the sand. But he didn't see *me*." She spoke uneasily, and Maradick saw at once that she was keeping something back.

"He's been going about with a Punch and Judy man recently," said Mrs. Lester. "I have nothing to say against Punch and Judy men personally. I always want to stop in the street and watch; but as a continual companion——"

"This particular one," said Maradick, "is especially nice, an awfully decent little fellow. I've talked to him several times. No, Lady Gale, I'm afraid my wife isn't well enough to come down to-night. She's had a bad headache all day. It's this heat, I think." He looked at her rather as a guilty schoolboy watches his master. He reproached himself for having left the boy alone during the whole day, and he began to be anxious on his own account. The situation was getting too much for his nerves. For the first time he considered Alice Du Cane. He had not thought of her as being very actively concerned in the business, but there was something in her face now that spoke of trouble. She was standing by the lamp nervously fingering some books at her side. The thought that she was in trouble touched him, and he began to feel the burden of the situation still more heavily upon him.

But he knew at once what it was that was troubling Lady Gale. It was Sir Richard. He had seen enough of that Gentleman to know that so long as superficial things were all right, so long as bells rang at the proper moment and everyone immediately concerned with him were respectful and decently dressed, he would ask no questions; but let him once begin to have suspicions that something was lacking in respect to himself and the family generally and nothing would hinder his irritable curiosity. He had probably begun already to ask questions about Tony. Here was a new element of danger.

The door opened and everyone turned eagerly towards it; it was Sir Richard and Rupert.

Rupert didn't appear to be more concerned than was usual with him, but Sir Richard was evidently annoyed. He advanced into the room with his customary before-dinner manner, that of one about to lead a cavalry regiment to the charge.

"It's late," he said; "late. Where's Tony?"

It was the question that everyone had been expecting, but no one answered it for a moment. Then Lady Gale got up from her chair.

"He'll be in in a minute, I expect," she said. "He's been kept. But it's no use waiting for dinner. I suppose Fred will be late, Millie? Never mind, we'll go down. You'll dine with us, Mr. Maradick, won't you?"

Sir Richard led the way with ominous silence.

The room was quite full, and for a breathless, agitated moment it seemed that their own table had been taken; but the alarm was false, and everyone could breathe again. Lady Gale's life was spent in the endeavour to prevent her husband from discovering a grievance. Let it once be discovered and a horrible time was before her, for Sir Richard petted it and nursed it until it grew, with a rapidity that was outside nature, into a horrible monster whose every movement caused the house to tremble.

She saw them, those grievances, come creeping round the corner and at once her hand was out and she held them, strangled, in her grip, and the danger was averted. Tony had often before been responsible for these agitations, but she had always caught them in time; now, she realised it as she crossed the dining-room, she was too late, and every moment of Tony's absence made matters worse. Sir Richard looked at the menu, and then complained about it in monosyllables for several minutes. Maradick watched the door with nervous eyes. This intrusion of Sir Richard into the business complicated things horribly. Let him once suspect that Tony was carrying on an affair with some girl in the town and the boy would at once be sent away; that, of course, would mean the end of everything, for him as well as for Tony. The Gales would go, the Lesters would go—everyone, everything. Tony himself would not allow it to be left at that, but, after all, what could he do?

Alice Du Cane was talking excitedly about nothing in particular, Mrs. Lester was very quiet, Rupert, as usual, was intent upon his food.

Alice chattered at Mrs. Lester, "Lucy Romanes was there; you know, that ridiculous girl with the scraped back hair and the pink complexion. Oh! too absurd for anything! You know Muriel Halliday said that she simply spends her days in following Captain Fawcett round. He rather likes it . . . the sort of man who would. I can't stand the girl."

Mrs. Lester smiled across the table. "It's old Mrs. Romanes's fault. She sends her round, she can't get rid of any of her girls anywhere . . . five of them, poor things; she'd sell any of them for twopence."

Sir Richard had finished his soup, and he leaned across the table towards his wife.

"What is the boy doing?" he said.

"Really, Richard, I don't know. He's been out sailing, I expect, and the wind or something has kept him."

"I won't have it"; he glowered at everyone. "He knows when meals are, he must be here. I must have obedience; and now I come to think of it"—he paused and looked round the table—"it has happened often lately. It hadn't occurred to me before, but I remember now; frequently—yes—late."

Then, after a pause during which no one said a word, "What has he been doing?"

This was so precisely the question that everyone else had been asking carefully and surreptitiously during the last few days that everyone looked guilty, as though they had been discovered in a crime. Then everyone turned to Maradick.

He smiled. "I've been about with him a good deal lately, Sir Richard. I really don't know what we've done very much beyond walking. But I think he was going to sail this afternoon."

Lady Gale looked anxiously at the waiter. If the food were all right the danger might be averted. But of course on this night of all nights everything was wrong: the potatoes were hard, the peas harder, the meat was overdone. Sir Richard glared at the waiter.

"Ask Mr. Bannister if he would spare me a minute," he said. Bannister appeared as spherical and red-cheeked as ever.

"Things are disgraceful to-night," Sir Richard said. "I must beg you, Mr. Bannister, to see to it."

Bannister was gently apologetic. The cook should be spoken to, it was abominable; meanwhile was there anything that he could get for Sir Richard? No? He was sorry. He bowed to the ladies and withdrew.

"It's abominable—this kind of thing. And Tony? Why, it's quarter to nine; what does he mean? It's always happening. Are these people he knows in the town?"

He looked at his wife.

"I really don't know, dear. I expect that he's met people down there; it's probable. But I shouldn't worry, dear. I'll speak to him." She looked across at Alice. "What were you saying about Mrs. Romanes, dear? I used to know her a long while ago; I don't suppose she would remember me now."

Maradick had a miserable feeling that she blamed him for all this. If he had only looked after Tony and stayed with him this would never have happened. But he couldn't be expected to stay with Tony always. After all, the boy was old enough to look after himself; it was absurd. Only, just now perhaps it would have been wiser. He saw that Mrs. Lester was smiling. She was probably amused at the whole affair.

Suddenly at the farther end of the room some one came in. It was Tony. Maradick held his breath.

He looked so perfectly charming as he stood there, recognising, with a kind of sure confidence, the "touch" that was necessary to carry the situation through. He could see, of course, that it *was* a situation, but whether he recognised the finer shades of everyone's feeling about it—the separate, individual way that they were all taking it, so that Alice's point of view and his mother's point of view and Maradick's point of view were all, really, at the opposite ends of the pole as far as seeing the thing went—that was really the important question. They all were needing the most delicate handling, and, in fact, from this moment onwards the "fat" was most hopelessly in the fire and the whole business was rolling "tub-wise" down ever so many sharp and precipitous hills.

But he stood there, looking down at them, most radiantly happy. His hair was still wet from his bath, and his tie was a little out of place because he had dressed in a hurry, and he smiled at them all, taking them, as it were, into his heart and scolding them for being so foolishly inquisitive, and, after it all, letting them no further into his confidence.

He knew, of course, exactly how to treat his father; his mother was more difficult, but he could leave her until afterwards.

To Sir Richard's indignant "Well?" he answered politely, but with a smile and a certain hurried breathlessness to show that he had taken trouble. "Really, I'm awfully sorry." He sat down and turned, with a smile, to the company. "I'm afraid I'm dreadfully late, but it was ever so much later than I'd thought. I was most awfully surprised when I saw the clock upstairs. I've smashed my own watch. You remember, mother, my dropping it when we were down in the town. Tuesday, wasn't it? Yes, I'll have soup, please. I say, I hope you people won't mind; I suppose you've about finished, but I'm going right through everything. I'm just as hungry as I can jolly well be. No, no sherry, thanks."

But Sir Richard's solemnity was imperturbable. "Where have you been?" he said coldly. "You know how strongly I dislike unpunctuality at meal-times, yes, unpunctuality. And this is not only unpunctuality, it is positively missing it altogether; I demand an explanation."

This public scolding before all the assembled company seemed to Maradick in very bad taste, and he shifted uneasily in his chair, but Tony did not seem to mind.

"I know," he said, looking up from his soup and smiling at his father, "I am most awfully careless. But it wasn't all that, as a matter of fact. I rowed round the Point to Boulter's Cove, and the tides are most awfully dicky and they played old Harry with us this evening, I simply couldn't get along at all. It was like rowing against a wall. I knew it was most beastly late, but I couldn't get any faster."

"Us?" said Sir Richard. "Who were your companions?"

There was a slight movement round the table.

"Oh," said Tony easily, "there are all sorts of old sailor Johnnies down there that one gets to know, and they're awfully good sorts. There's one fellow about eight foot and broad in proportion; the girls are simply mad about him, they — — "

But Lady Gale interrupted him. "You'd better be getting on with your meal, dear. It's late. I don't think we need wait. Shall we have coffee outside?"

"No, don't you people wait," said Tony, "I'll come along in a minute."

As Alice turned to go she stopped for a moment by his chair. "I saw you this afternoon," she said.

"Oh! *did* you?" he answered, looking up at her. For a moment he seemed disturbed, then he laughed.

"Where and when?" he asked.

"This afternoon, somewhere after four; you were on the beach." She looked at him for a moment, standing very straight and her head flung back. "I am glad you enjoyed your row," she said with a laugh.

"I must talk to Maradick about it," he said to himself. He was quite prepared for complications; of course, there were bound to be in such a situation. But at present the memory of the wonderful afternoon enwrapped him like a fire, so that he could not think of anything else, he could not see anything but her eyes and smile and golden hair. The empty room hung before his eyes, with the white cloths on innumerable tables gleaming like white pools in rows across the floor, and dark mysterious men, who might be perhaps, at more brightly lighted times, waiters, moved silently from place to place. But beyond, outside the room, there shone the white curve of the boat stealing like a ghost across the water, and behind it the dark band of hill, the green clump of trees, the dusky, trembling figures of the sheep. Oh! glorious hour!

A little waiter, with a waistcoat that was far too large for him and a tie that had crept towards his right ear, hung in the background. Tony pushed his plate away and looked round.

"I say," he said, "are you in love with anyone?"

The waiter, who hailed from Walham Green, and, in spite of his tender years, was burdened with five children and a sick wife, coughed apologetically.

"Well, sir," he said, "to be strictly truthful, I can't say as I am, not just at present. And perhaps it's just as well, seeing as how I've been a married man these fifteen years." He folded a table-cloth carefully and coughed again.

"Well, isn't it possible to be in love with your wife?" asked Tony.

The waiter's mind crept timidly back to a certain tea of shrimps and buns on the Margate sands many, very many years ago. He saw a red sun and a blue sky and some nigger minstrels, white and black; but that was another lifetime altogether, before there were children and doctor's bills.

"Well, sir," he said, "it gets kind o' casual after a time; not that it's anyone's fault exactly, only times 'is 'ard and there's the children and one thing and another, and there scarcely seems time for sentiment exactly."

He coughed his way apologetically back into the twilight at the farther end of the room.

"There scarcely seems time for sentiment exactly!" Tony laughed to himself at the absurdity of it and stepped out into the garden. He didn't want to see the family just at present. They would grate and jar. He could be alone; later, he would talk to Maradick.

And Lady Gale, for the first time in her life, avoided him. She did not feel that she could talk to him just yet; she must wait until she had thought out the new developments and decided on a course of action. The day had filled her with alarm, because suddenly two things had been shown to her. The first, that there was no one in the world for whom she really cared save Tony. There were other people whom she liked, friends, acquaintances; for her own husband and Rupert she had a protecting kindliness that was bound up intimately in her feeling for the family, but love!—no—it was Tony's alone.

She had never realised before how deeply, how horribly she cared. It was something almost wild and savage in her, so that she, an old lady with white hair and a benevolent manner, would have fought and killed and torn his enemies were he in danger. The wildness, the ferocity of it frightened her so that she sat there in the dark with trembling hands, watching the lights of the ships at sea and, blindly, blindly praying.

She had known, of course, before, that he was everything to her, that without him life would lose all its purpose and meaning and beauty, but there had been other things that counted as well; now it seemed that nothing else mattered in the least.

And the second thing that she saw, and it was this second revelation that had shown her the first, was that she was in danger of losing him. The relationship of perfect confidence that had, she fondly imagined, existed until now between them, had never been endangered, because there had been nothing to hide. He had not told her everything, of course; there must have been things at Oxford, and even before, that he had not told her, but she had felt no alarm because they had been, she was sure, things that did not matter. And then he had, so often, come and told her, told her with his charming smile and those open eyes of his, so that there could be no question of his keeping anything back.

She had studied the relationship of mother and son so perfectly that she had had precisely the right "touch" with him, never demanding what he was not ready to give, always receiving the confidences that he handed her. But now for the first time he was keeping things back, things that mattered. When she had spoken so bravely to Maradick a fortnight ago, on that day when she had first caught sight of the possible danger, she had thought that she was strong enough and wise enough to wait, patiently, with perfect trust. But it was not possible, it could not be done. She could not sit there, with her hands folded, whilst some strange woman down there in that dark, mysterious town caught her boy away from her. Every day her alarm had grown; she had noticed, too, that their relationship had changed. It had been so wonderful and beautiful, so delicate and tender, that any alteration in its colour was at once apparent to her. He had not been so frank, there had been even a little artificiality in his conversations with her. It was more than she could bear.

But, although the uncertainty of it might kill her, she must not know. She saw that as clearly, as inevitably as ever. Let her once know, from his own confession, that he loved some girl down there in the town, and she would be forced to stop it. The horizon would widen, and bigger, louder issues than their own personal feelings would be concerned. The family would be called into the issue, and she could not be false to its claims. She could not be untrue to her husband and all the traditions. And yet it was only Tony's happiness that she cared for; that must be considered above everything else. Maradick would know whether this girl were, so to speak, "all right." If she were impossible, then he assuredly would have stopped it by now. Maradick was, in fact, the only clue to the business that she had got.

But it was partly because she was losing her trust in him that she was unhappy now. His guard over Tony had, for to-day at any rate, been miserably inadequate. He might feel, perhaps, that he had no right to spend his time in hanging on to Tony's coat-tails, it wasn't fair on the boy, but he ought to have been with him more.

She was sitting now with Alice on the seat at the farther end of the garden overlooking the town. The place seemed hateful to her, as she stared down it acquired a personality of its own, a horrible menacing personality. It lay there with its dark curved back like some horrible animal, and the lights in the harbours were its eyes twinkling maliciously; she shuddered and leant back.

"Are you cold, dear?" It was the first time that Alice had spoken since they had come out. She herself was sitting straight with her head back, a slim white figure like a ghost.

"No, it's stiflingly warm, as a matter of fact. I was thinking, and that's about the only thing that an old woman can do."

"You are worried." Alice spoke almost sharply. "And I hate you to be worried. I've noticed during these last few days— —"

"Yes, I suppose I am a little," Lady Gale sighed. "But then you've been worried too, dear, for the matter of that. It hasn't been altogether a success, this place, this time. I don't know what's been wrong exactly, because the weather's been beautiful."

Alice put her hand on Lady Gale's. "You won't think me an utter pig, will you, dear, if I go up to Scotland at the end of the week? I think I had better, really. I'm not well down here, and it only makes it uncomfortable for the rest of you if I'm cross and absurd."

Lady Gale sighed. "If you really want to go, dear," she said, "of course you must. Do just what you like. Only, I shall miss you badly. You're a great help to me, you know. Of course there's Milly, but she's been funny lately. She always gets excited down here." Lady Gale put her arm round the girl. "Stay for a little, dear. I want you. We all want you."

Alice drew herself up for a moment as though she would repel the caress; then she tried to say something, but the words would not come. With a little cry she buried her face in the other's dress. For a few moments there was silence, then her shoulders heaved and she burst into passionate sobbing. Lady Gale said nothing—only, with her hand, she stroked her hair. The night was very still, so still that they could hear coming up from the town the distant chorus of some song.

At last Alice raised her head. "Please," she said, "don't worry about me." But she clutched Lady Gale's hand. "Oh! I'm ashamed of myself. I'm a fool to give way like this." She suddenly drew her hand fiercely away. But Lady Gale took it in hers.

"Why," she said, "I have been wanting you to speak to me all this time, and you wouldn't; of course I knew what the matter was, you can't keep that from his mother. We all seem to have been at cross-purposes, as it is in a play, when one word would put everything right, but everybody is afraid to say it. Why, I want to talk to you about it all. Do you suppose that I am not having a bad time too?"

Alice leaned towards her and kissed her. "I'm sorry," she said, "I've been so selfish lately. I haven't thought about anyone else. I hadn't realised what you must feel about it. I ought to have known."

She stopped for a moment, then she went on speaking in little gasps as though she had been running. "But I hadn't meant to speak at all anything about it. I hate myself for having given way. I, who had always prided myself on my restraint and self-possession, to cry like a child for the moon." She shrugged her shoulders and laughed bitterly. "I won't give way again," she said.

Lady Gale put her arm round her and drew her close. "Alice, dear, let me talk to you for a moment. You are going through a bad time, and it may be a crisis and alter your whole life. You are very young, my dear, and I am so old that I seem to have been through everything and to know it all from the beginning. So perhaps I can help you. I love you from the bottom of my heart, and this thing has drawn us together as nothing else in the world possibly could."

Alice pressed close against her. "Oh! I've been so lonely these last days, you can't know how bad it has been."

"Yes, dear, of course I know. I saw at once when we came down here that something was wrong. I wanted to talk to you, but it's no use forcing people's confidence. I knew that you'd speak to me if you wanted to. But we're together in this, we both love Tony."

"Oh! I'm ashamed." Alice spoke very low, it was almost a whisper. "And yet, do you know, in a way I'm glad. It showed me that I've got something that I was almost afraid wasn't in me at all. In spite of my pride I have been sometimes suddenly frightened, and wondered whether it were really in me to care for anyone at all. And then all in a moment this has come. I would die for Tony; I would let him trample on me, kill me, beat me. Sometimes, when we are sitting, all of us, so quietly there in the drawing-room or in the garden, and he talking, oh, I want to get up and fling myself at him and hold him there before them all. I have been afraid during these last few days that I shall suddenly lose control. I have wondered once or twice whether I am not going mad. Now you see why I must go."

She buried her face in her hands.

Lady Gale bent over her. "Alice dear, I understand, of course I understand. But let me try and show you, dear, why you must stay. Just for this next week or two. You can be of so much help to me and to Tony. I have been having rather a bad time too. It is like walking in the dark with things on every side of you that you cannot see. And I want you, dear."

Alice did not speak. The bells in the distant town struck ten, first one and then another and then five or six at once. Five lights of boats at sea gleamed in a row like stars that had fallen into the water, through the dark mist of the trees a curved moon sailed.

"You see, dear, things are so difficult now, and they seem to grow worse every day. And really it comes to this. You and I and Mr. Maradick all love Tony. The others don't count. Of course I'm not sure about Mr. Maradick, but I think he cares very much in his own way, and so we are, you see, a bodyguard for him. I mean to do as he wants to. Tony has always seen things perfectly clearly and has known what he wanted, but now there are other things that make it harder for him. I hoped when we came down here that he was going to marry you, dear, but perhaps after all it is better that he shouldn't. The only thing that matters in the least in this world is love, getting it and keeping it; and if a man or a woman have secured that, there is nothing else that is of any importance. And so I always determined that Tony should have his own choice, that he should go when he wished to."

She paused and took Alice's hand and stroked it. "This is the first time that he has ever really been in love. Of course I know—I knew at once by the light in his eyes—and I want him to have it and to keep it and, whatever happens, not to miss it. But of course I must not know about it, because then his father would have to be told. Sir Richard thinks a great deal of the family. It is the only thing that matters to him very much. And of course there would be terrible scenes and I should have to go with the family. So, whatever happens, I must not know about it."

"Yes," said Alice, "I see that."

"And so, you see, I put Mr. Maradick there as a guard. He is a worthy creature, a little dull, but very trustworthy, and I knew that he would do his best. But it is harder than I had thought it would be. Now Sir Richard is beginning to wonder where Tony goes, and I am afraid that in a day or two there will be some terrible scene and Tony will go, perhaps for ever. So I want you to be with me here. You can talk to Mr. Maradick, and if I see that you are satisfied then I shall know that it is all right. It will make all the difference in the world if I have you."

"You are asking rather a lot," Alice said. "I don't think you quite realise what it is to me. It is like some strange spell, and if I were fanciful or absurd I should imagine that the place had something to do with it. Of course it hasn't, but I feel as if I should be my normal self again if I could once get away."

"No. You'll never be quite the same person again. One never can get back. But look at it in this way, dear. Do you care enough for Tony to be of real help to him, to do something for him that no one else can possibly do?"

"Do I care for him?" Alice laughed. "I care for him as no one has ever cared for anyone before."

"Ah! That's what we all think, my dear. I thought that once about Sir Richard. But you can do everything for him now, if you will."

But Alice shrugged her shoulders. "As far as I understand it," she said, "you want me to spy on Mr. Maradick."

"No, not to spy, of course not. Only to behave to Tony as if nothing had happened, and to help me about Sir Richard. And then you can talk to Mr. Maradick, if you like; ask him right out about her."

"Oh, then he'll say, and quite rightly too, that it's none of my business."

"But it is. It's all our business. A thing like that can't happen to anybody without its interfering, like a stone and a pool, with everything around it. Of course it's your business, yours more than anybody's. And really, dear, I don't think you'll make things any better by going away. Things seem far worse when you've got to look over ever so many counties to see them at all. Stay here with Tony and live it down. It will pass, like the measles or anything else."

She paused. Then she suddenly put her arms round the girl and held her close. "I want you, I want you, dear. I am very miserable. I feel that I am losing Tony, perhaps for always. He will never be the same again, and I can't bear it. He has always been the centre of everything, always. I scarcely know how I could have faced some things if it hadn't been for him. And now I've got to face them alone; but if you are here with me I shan't be alone after all."

And Alice let her face rest in Lady Gale's dress and she promised. There was, as it happened, more in her promise than mere acquiescence. She had her own curiosity as to the way it was all going to turn out, and perhaps, deep in her heart, a hope that this girl down in the town would be nothing after all, and that Tony would return, when the two or three weeks were over, to his senses. But the real temptation that attacked her was terribly severe. It would be fatally easy to talk to Sir Richard, and, without saying anything either definite or circumstantial, to put him unmistakably on the track. The immediate issue would, of course, be instant marching orders for everybody, and that would be the last that Tony would see of his rustic. Her thoughts lingered around the girl. What was she like, she wondered? Coarse, with a face of beetroot red and flaxen hair; no, Tony had taste, he would know what to choose. She was probably pretty. Wild and uncouth, perhaps; that would be likely to catch him. And now she, Alice Du Cane, must stand quietly by and play the part of platonic friend. What fun life must be for the gods who had time to watch.

Meanwhile Tony had found Maradick in a deserted corner of the garden and had poured the afternoon's history into his ears. It was a complete manual on the way to make love, and it came out in a stream of uninterrupted eloquence, with much repetition and a continual impulse to hark back to the central incident of the story.

"And then, at last, I told her!" A small bird in a nest above their heads woke for a moment and felt a little thrill of sympathy. "By heaven, Maradick, old man, I had never lived until then. She and I were swept into Paradise together, and for a moment earth had gone, rolled away, vanished; I can't talk about it, I can't really. But there we were on the sand with the sea and the sky! Oh, my word! I can't make you feel it, only now I am hers always and she is mine. I am her slave, her knight. One always used to think, you know, that all the stuff men and women put about it in books was rot and dreadfully dull at that, but now it all seems different. Poetry, music, all the things that one loved, are different now. They are new, wonderful, divine! and there we were in the boat, you know, just drifting anywhere."

Maradick played audience to this enthusiasm with a somewhat melancholy patience. He had felt like that once about Mrs. Maradick. How absurd! He saw her as he had seen her last with the bed-clothes gathered about her in a scornful heap and her eyes half closed but flashing fire. She had refused to speak to him! And he had kissed her once and felt like Tony.

"No, but a fellow can't talk about it. Only, one thing, Maradick, that struck me as awfully funny, the way that she accepted everything. When I told her about my people, of course I expected her to be awfully disappointed. But she seemed to understand at once and accepted it as the natural thing. So that if it comes to running away she is quite prepared."

"If it comes to running away!" The words at once brought the whole situation to a point, and Maradick's responsibility hit him in the face like a sudden blow from the dark. For a moment fear caught him by the throat; he wanted, wildly, to fling off the whole thing, to catch the next train back to Epsom, to get away from this strange place that was dragging him, as it were, with a ghostly finger, into a whirlpool, a quagmire; anything was treacherous and dangerous and destructive. And then he knew, in the next instant, that though he might go back to Epsom and his office and all the drudgery of it, he would never be the same man again, he could never be the same man again. He knew now that the only thing in the world worth having was love—this town had shown him that—and that, for it, all the other things must go. This boy had found it and he must help him to keep it. He, Maradick, had found it; there were friends of his here—Tony, Mrs. Lester—and he couldn't go back to the loneliness of his old life with the memory of these weeks.

"Look here," he gripped Tony's arm, "I don't suppose I ought to have anything to do with it. Any man in his senses would tell your people, and there'd be an end of the whole thing; but I gave you my word before and I'll go on with it. Besides, I've seen the girl. I'd fall in love with her myself, Tony, if I were your age, and I don't want you to miss it all and make a damned muddle of your life just because you weren't brave enough or because there wasn't anyone to help you."

"By Jove, Maradick, you're a brick. I can't tell you how I feel about it, about her and you and everything, a chap hasn't got words; only, of course, it's going forward. You see, you couldn't tell my people after all that you've done—you wouldn't, you know; and as I'd go on whether you left me or no you may just as well help me. And then I'm awfully fond of you; I like you better than I've ever liked any man, you're such an understanding fellow."

Tony took breath a moment. Then he went on—

"The mater's really the only thing that matters, and if I wasn't so jolly sure that she'd like Janet awfully, and really would want me to carry the thing through, I wouldn't do it at all. But loving Janet as I do has made me know how much the mater is to me. You know, Maradick, it's jolly odd, but there are little things about one's mater that stick in one's mind far more than anything else. Little things . . . but she's always been just everything, and there are lots of blackguards, I know, feel just the same . . . and so it sort of hurts going on playing this game and not telling her about it. It's the first thing I've not told her . . . but it will be all right when it's over."

"There are other people," said Maradick; "your father ——"

"Oh, the governor! Yes, he's beginning to smell a rat, and he's tremendous once he's on the track, and that all means that it's got to be done jolly quickly. Besides, there's Alice Du Cane; she saw us, Janet and me, on the beach this afternoon, and there's no knowing how long she'll keep her tongue. No, I'll go and see Morelli to-morrow and ask him right off. I went back with her to-night, and he was most awfully friendly, although he must have had pretty shrewd suspicions. He likes me."

"Don't you be too sure about him," said Maradick; "I don't half like it. I don't trust him a yard. But see here, Tony, come and see me at once to-morrow after you've spoken to him, and then we'll know what to do."

Tony turned to him and put his hand on his shoulder. "I say. I don't know why you're such a brick to me. I'll never forget it"; and then suddenly he turned up the path and was gone.

Maradick climbed the dark stairs to his room. His wife was in bed, asleep. He undressed quietly; for an instant he looked at her with the candle in his hand. She looked very young with her hair lying in a cloud about the pillow; he half bent down as though he would kiss her. Then he checked himself and blew out the candle.

CHAPTER XIII
MORE OF THE ITINERANT OPTIMIST; ALICE DU CANE ASKS MARADICK A FAVOUR

Maradick awoke very early on the next morning. As he lay in his bed, his mind was still covered with the cobwebs of his dreams, and he saw the room in a fantastic, grotesque shape, so that he was not sure that it was his room at all, but he thought that it might be some sea with the tables and chairs for rocks, or some bare windy moor.

The curtain blew ever so slightly in the wind from the crevice of the door, and he watched it from his bed as it swelled and bulged and shrunk back as though it were longing to break away from the door altogether but had not quite courage enough. But although he was still confused and vague with the lazy bewilderment of sleep, he realised quite definitely in the back of his mind that there was some fact waiting for him until he should be clear-headed enough to recognise it. This certainty of something definite before him that had to be met and considered roused him. He did not, in the least, know what that something was that awaited him, but he tried to pull himself together. The sea receded, the beating of its waves was very faint in his ears, and the rocks resolved into the shining glass of the dressing-table and the solemn chairs with their backs set resolutely against the wall, and their expressions those of self-conscious virtue.

He sat up in bed and rubbed his eyes; he knew with absolute certainty that he should not sleep again. The light was trying to pierce the blind and little eyes of colour winked at him from the window, the silver things on the dressing-table stood out, pools of white, against the dark wood.

He got out of bed, and suddenly the fact stared him in the face: it was that he was committed, irrevocably committed, to help Tony. He had, in a way, been committed before, ever since Lady Gale asked him for his help; but there had always been a chance of escaping, the possibility, indeed, of the "thing" never coming off at all. But now it was coming off, and very soon, and he had to help it to come.

He had turned the whole situation over in his mind so very often, and looked at it from so very many points of view, with its absurdities and its tragedies and its moralities, that there was nothing more to be said about the actual thing at all; that was, in all conscience, concrete enough. He saw it, as he sat on the bed swinging his feet, there in front of him, as some actual personality with whom he had pledged himself in league. He had sworn to help two children to elope against everybody's wishes—he, Maradick, of all people the most law-abiding. What had come over him? However, there it was and there was nothing more to be said about it. It wasn't to be looked at again at all with any view of its possible difficulties and dangers, it had just to be carried through.

But he knew, as he thought about it, that the issue was really much larger than the actual elopement. It was the effect on him that really mattered, the fact that he could never return to Epsom again with any hope of being able to live the life there that he had lived before.

The whole circle of them would be changed by this; it was the most momentous event in all their lives.

Maradick looked again at the morning. The mists were rising higher in the air, and all the colours, the pale golden sand, the red roofs, the brown bend of the rocks, were gleaming in the sun. He would go and bathe and then search out Punch.

It was a quarter past five as he passed down the stairs; the house was in the most perfect stillness, and only the ticking of innumerable clocks broke the silence. Suddenly a bird called from the garden; a little breath of wind, bringing with it the scent of pinks and roses, trembled through the hall.

When he reached the cove the sea was like glass. He had never bathed early in the morning before, and a few weeks ago he would have laughed at the idea. A man of his age bathing at half-past five in the morning! The water would be terribly cold. But it wasn't. He thought that he had never known anything so warm and caressing as he lay back in it and looked up through the clear green. There was perfect silence. Things came into his mind, some operas that he had heard, rather reluctantly, that year in London. The opening of the third act of Puccini's "Tosca," with the bell-music and the light breaking over the city. He remembered that he had thought that rather fine at the time. The lovers in "Louise" on Montmartre watching the lights burst the flowers below them and saluting "Paris!" He had appreciated that too. A scene in "To Paradise," with a man somewhere alone in a strange city watching the people hurrying past him and counting the lamps that swung, a golden chain, down the street. Some picture in the Academy of that year, Sim's "Night Piece to Julia." He hadn't understood it or seen anything in it at the time. "One of those new fellows who just stick the paint on anyhow," he had remarked; but now he seemed to remember a wonderful blue dress and a white peacock in the background!

How funny it was, he thought, as he plunged, dripping, back on to the beach, that the things that a fellow scarcely noticed at all at the time should be just the things that came into his mind afterwards. And on the sand he saw Toby, the dog, gravely watching him. Toby came courteously towards him, sniffed delicately at his socks, and then, having decided apparently that they were the right kind of socks and couldn't really be improved on, sat down with his head against Maradick's leg.

Maradick tickled his head and decided that pugs weren't nearly so ugly as he had thought they were. But then there was a world of difference between Toby and the ordinary pug, the fat pug nestling in cushions on an old lady's lap, the aristocratic pug staring haughtily from the soft luxury of a lordly brougham, the town pug, over-fed, over-dressed, over-washed. But Toby knew the road, he had seen the world, he was a dog of the drama, a dog of romance; he was also a dog with a sense of humour.

He licked Maradick's bare leg with a very warm tongue and then put a paw on to his arm. They were friends. He ratified the contract by rolling over several times on the sand; he then lay on his back with his four paws suspended rigidly in the air, and then, catching sight of his master, turned rapidly over and went to meet him.

Punch expressed no surprise at finding Maradick there at that hour of the morning. It was the most natural thing in the world. People who came to Treliss were always doing things like that, and they generally spent the rest of their lives in trying to forget that they had done them.

"I've been wanting to see you, Mr. Maradick, sir," he said, "and I'm mighty glad to find you here when there's nothing to catch our words save the sea, and that never tells tales."

"Well, as a matter of fact, Garrick," said Maradick, "I came down after you. I meant to have gone up to your rooms after bathing, but as you are here it's all the better. I badly want to talk to you."

Punch sat down on the sand and looked quite absurdly like his dog.

"I want to talk to you about Morelli, Garrick." Maradick hesitated a moment. It was very difficult to put into words exactly what he wanted to say. "We have talked about the man before, and I shouldn't bother you about it again were it not that I'm very fond of young Tony Gale, and he, as you know, has fallen in love with Morelli's daughter. It's all a long story, but the main point is, that I want to know as much about the man as you can tell me. Nobody here seems to know very much about him except yourself."

Punch's brow had clouded at the mention of Morelli's name.

"I don't rightly know," he said, "as I can say anything very definite, and that being so perhaps one oughtn't to say anything at all; but if young Gale's going to take that girl away, then I'm glad. He's a good fellow, and she's on my mind."

"Why?" said Maradick.

"Well, perhaps after all it's best to tell what I know." Punch took out a pipe and slowly filled it. "Mind you, it's all damned uncertain, a lot of little things that don't mean anything when taken by themselves. I first met the man in '89, twenty years ago. I was a young chap, twenty-one or so. A kind of travelling blacksmith I used to be then, with Pendragon up the coast as a kind o' centre. It was at Pendragon I saw him. He used to live there then as he lives in Treliss now; it was a very different kind o' place then to what it is now—just a sleepy, dreamy little town, with bad lights, bad roads and the rest, and old tumbled down 'ouses. Old Sir Jeremy Trojan 'ad the run of it then, him that's father of the present Sir Henry, and you wouldn't have found a quieter place, or a wilder in some ways."

"Wild?" said Maradick. "It's anything but wild now."

"Yes, they've changed it with their trams and things, and they've pulled down the cove; but the fisher-folk were a fierce lot and they wouldn't stand anyone from outside. Morelli lived there with his wife and little girl. 'Is wife was only a young thing, but beautiful, with great eyes like the sea on a blue day and with some foreign blood in 'er, dark and pale.

"'E wasn't liked there any more than 'e is here. They told funny tales about him even then, and said 'e did things to his wife, they used to hear her crying. And they said that 'e'd always been there, years back, just the same, never looking any different, and it's true enough he looks just the same now as he did then. It isn't natural for a man never to grow any older."

"No," said Maradick, "it isn't."

"There were other things that the men down there didn't like about 'im, and the women hated 'im. But whenever you saw 'im he was charming— nice as 'e could be to me and all of 'em. And he was clever, could do things with his 'ands, and make birds and beasts do anything at all."

"That's strange," said Maradick. "Tony said something of the same sort the other day."

"Well, that ain't canny," said David, "more especially as I've seen other animals simply shake with fear when he comes near them. Well, I was telling you, they didn't like 'im down in the cove, and they'd say nothing to 'im and leave 'im alone. And then one night" — Punch's mouth grew set and hard — "they found Mrs. Morelli up on the moor lying by the Four Stones, dead."

"Dead!" said Maradick, startled.

"Yes; it was winter time and the snow blowing in great sheets across the moor and drifting about her dress, with the moon, like a yellow candle, hanging over 'er. But that weren't all. She'd been killed, murdered. There were marks on her face and hands, as though teeth had torn her. Poor creature!" Punch paused.

"Well," said Maradick excitedly, "what was the end of it all?"

"Oh! they never brought it 'ome to anyone. I 'ad my own thoughts, and the men about there kind o' talked about Morelli, but it was proved 'e was somewhere else when it 'appened and 'e cried like a child when 'e saw the body."

"Well," said Maradick, laughing, "so far it isn't very definite. That might have happened to any man." But it was, nevertheless, curiously in keeping with the picture that he had in his mind.

"Yes," said Punch, "I told you already that I 'adn't got anything very definite. I don't say as 'e did it or had anything to do with it, but it's all of a piece in a way. Thing got 'ot against 'im in Pendragon after that and 'e 'ad to go, and 'e came 'ere with 'is girl. But they say that 'e's been seen there since, and in other places too. And then I've seen 'im do other things. Kill rabbits and birds like a devil. 'E's cruel, and then again 'e's kind, just like a child will pull flies to bits. 'E is just like a child, and so 'e isn't to be trusted. 'E's wild, like Nature. 'E likes to have young things about 'im. That's why 'e's taken to young Gale, and 'e loves that girl in a way, although I know 'e's cruel — — "

"Cruel to her?" said Maradick.

"Yes, 'e beats her, I know. I've been watching a long way back; and then again 'e'll kiss 'er and give 'er things and play with 'er, and then one day 'e'll kill 'er."

Maradick started again. "Kill her?" he said.

"Yes. 'E'll do anything when 'e's mad. And a minute after 'e'll be sobbing and crying for sorrow over what 'e's hurt; and be like a drunkard when 'e's angry."

"Then what do you make of it all?" said Maradick.

"Make of it?" said Punch. "I don't know. There ain't another like 'im in the kingdom. There's more in the world than folk 'ave any idea of, especially those that keep to towns. But it's out on the road that you'll be seeing things, when the moon is up and the hedges purple in their shadows. And 'e belongs to all of that. 'E's like Nature in a way, cruel and kind and wild. 'E's not to be believed in by sober folks who laugh at spirits, but there's more in it than meets the eye."

And that was all that Maradick got from him; and after all it did not amount to very much except a vague warning. But there was this definite fact, that Janet was in danger where she was, and that was an added impulse, of course, for going on with the whole adventure. To the initial charm of helping a delightful boy was now added the romantic sensation of the release of a captive lady; Maradick, knight! Forty and married for a lifetime; oh! the absurd world.

Then Maradick went up for breakfast.

Mrs. Maradick's first thought in the morning was her hair, and then, at some considerable distance, the girls. It never happened that they were both "right" simultaneously, and she would indeed have been considerably surprised and felt a certain lack if there had been no cause for complaint on either score.

On the present morning everything was as it should be. Her hair "settled itself" as though by magic, the girls had given no possible cause of complaint; she came down to breakfast with an air of surprise and the kind of mind that is quite sure something unpleasant is going to happen simply because nothing unpleasant *has* "happened" so far. She presented, as she came down the hotel staircase, a delightful picture of neat compact charm; her girls, in precise and maidenly attendance behind her, accentuated her short stature by their own rather raw, long-legged size, but there was nothing loose or uncouth about her. In her colouring, in her light carnation silk waistband, in her high-heeled shiny shoes, she was neatness personified.

In the eyes of everyone except Mrs. Lawrence she had perhaps just a little too much the air of being "somebody," because really, of course, she was nothing at all, simply Mrs. Maradick of Epsom; but then when you were so small you had to do something to make up for it, and an "air" did help undoubtedly. Her husband, coming in from the garden, met her at the bottom of the stairs, and she treated him very graciously. He kissed the girls with a "Well, Lucy!" and "Well, Annie!" and then Mrs. Maradick, with a final feeling for her hair and a last pat to the carnation riband, led the way in to breakfast.

It appeared that she was inclined to treat him graciously, but in reality she was trying to make up her mind; she was not a clever woman, and she had never been so puzzled before.

She had, indeed, never been forced to puzzle about anything at all. In her orderly compact life things had always been presented to her with a decency and certainty that left no room for question or argument. She had been quiet and obedient at home, but she had always had her way; she had married the man that had been presented to her without any hesitation at all, it was a "good match," and it meant that, for the rest of her life, she would never be forced to ask any questions about anything or anybody. For a wild week or two, at first, she had felt strange undisciplined sensations that were undoubtedly dangerous; on their wedding night she had suddenly suspected that there was another woman there whose existence meant storm and disorder. But the morning had come with bills and calls and "finding a house," and that other Mrs. Maradick had died. From that day to this there had been no cause for alarm. James had soon been reduced to order and had become a kind of necessity, like the sideboard; he paid the bills. Child-birth had been alarming for a moment, but Mrs. Maradick had always been healthy and they had an excellent doctor, but, after Annie's appearance, she had decided that there should never be another. James presented no difficulties at all, and her only real worry in life was her "hair." There was not very much of it, and she spent her mornings and her temper in devising plans whereby it should be made to seem "a lot," but it never was satisfactory. Her "hair" became the centre of her life, her horizon. James fitted into it. If the "hair" were all right, he didn't seem so bad. Otherwise he was stupid, dull, an oaf.

And so she had come down to Treliss and life had suddenly changed. It had really changed from that first evening of their arrival when he had been so rude to her, although she had not realised it at the time. But the astonishing thing was that he had kept it up. He had never kept anything up before, and it was beginning to frighten her. At first it had seemed to her merely conceit. His head had been turned by these people, and when he got back to Epsom and found that he wasn't so wonderful after all, and that the people there didn't think of him at all except as her husband, then he would find his place again.

But now she wasn't so sure. She had not been asleep last night when he came to bed. She had seen him bend over with the candle in his hand, and the look in his eyes had frightened her, frightened her horribly, so that she had lain awake for hours afterwards, thinking, puzzling for the first time in her life. During all these twenty years of their married life he had been, she knew, absolutely faithful to her. She had laughed at it sometimes, because it had seemed so absolutely impossible that there should ever be anyone else. He did not attract people in Epsom in the least; he had never made any attempt to, and she had imagined him, poor fellow, sometimes trying, and the miserable mess that he would make of it.

And now she had got to face the certainty that there was some one else. She had seen it in his eyes last night, and she knew that he would never have had the strength to keep up the quarrel for nearly a fortnight unless some one else had been there. She saw now a thousand things that should have convinced her before, little things all culminating in that horrible picnic a few days ago. It was as though, she thought, he had come down to Treliss determined to find somebody. She remembered him in the train, how pleasant and agreeable he had been! He had arranged cushions for her, got things for her, but the moment they had arrived! Oh! this hateful town!

But now she had got to act. She had woke early that morning and had found that he was already gone. That alone was quite enough to stir all her suspicions.

Perhaps now he was down there in the town with some one! Why should he get up at an unearthly hour unless it were for something of the kind? He had always been a very sound sleeper. At Epsom he would never have thought of getting up before eight. Who was it?

She put aside, for a moment, her own feelings about him, the curious way in which she was beginning to look at him. The different side that he was presenting to her and the way that she looked at it must wait until she had discovered this woman, this woman! She clenched her little hands and her eyes flashed.

Oh! she would talk to her when she found her!

His early escape that morning seemed to her a sign that the "woman" was down in the town. She imagined an obvious assignation, but otherwise she might have suspected that it was Mrs. Lester. That, of course, she had suspected from the day of the picnic, but it seemed to her difficult to imagine that a woman of the world, as Mrs. Lester, to give her her due, most obviously was, could see anything in her hulk of a James; it would be much more probable if it were some uncouth fisherwoman who knew, poor thing, no better.

She looked at him now across the breakfast-table; his red cheeks, his great nostrils "like a horse's," his enormous hands, but it was not all hostility the look that she gave him. There was a kind of dawning wonder and surprise.

They had their table by the window, and the sun beat through on to the silver teapot and the ham and eggs. Annie had refused porridge. No, she wasn't hungry.

"You should have bathed, as I did, before breakfast," said Maradick.

So he'd bathed before breakfast, had he? She looked across at him smiling.

"You were up very early," she said.

"Yes, I slept badly." They were down again, those blinds! She saw him drop them down as though by magic. He was playing his game.

"Well, next time you must wake me and I'll come too," she said. His sense of humour was touched at the idea of her coming down at five in the morning, but he said nothing.

The knowledge, the increasing certainty that there was something in it all, was choking her so that she found it exceedingly difficult to eat. But that she should be baffled by James was so incredible an idea that she concealed her rising temper.

She nodded gaily at Mrs. Lawrence, who swam towards their table with outstretched hands and a blue scarf floating like wings behind her.

"My dear!"

"My dear!"

"But you generally have it upstairs, I thought . . ."

"Yes, I know; but *such* a day, one couldn't really . . ."

"Yes, I was awake ever so . . . But James has been bathing. No, Lucy, sit still, dear, until we've finished. Bathing before breakfast. I think I really must to-morrow."

Epsom closed about the table.

She was extremely nice to him throughout the meal, and even hinted at their doing something, spending the day, "and *such* a day." It was a shame not to take advantage of the weather "as a family." Quite a new idea, indeed, but he accepted it, and even began to suggest possible places. She was baffled again, and, as the terrible prospect of a whole day spent in James's company, quite alone except for the girls, pressed about her, became almost hysterical in her hurriedly discovered reasons why, after all, it would never do. But he smiled at her, and although he was quite ready to do anything that she might suggest, it was a different kind of agreeing from a week or two ago.

She retired from the breakfast-table baffled.

He had been watching the door of the breakfast-room eagerly, and when he went out down into the garden he was still looking for the same figure. There was no longer, there could be no longer any disguise about the person, it was Mrs. Lester beyond any possible question; but he *did* disguise the reason. He wanted to talk to her, he liked to talk to her, just as he liked to talk to any understanding person, quite irrespective of sex. She had, of course, her atmosphere; it had a great deal in common with the place and the weather and the amazing riot of colour that the weather had brought. He saw her always as she had been on that first day, primrose, golden, in that dark dim drawing-room; but that he should think of her in that way didn't show him, as it should have done, how the case was really beginning to lie.

He had the "Play-boy" on his knee and the light swung, as some great golden censor is swung before the High Altar, in waves of scent and colour backwards and forwards before him. He watched, looking eagerly down the sunlit path, but she did not come, and the morning passed in its golden silence and he was still alone.

It wasn't indeed until after lunch that things began to move again, and then Tony came to him. He was in a glow of pleasure and excitement; she had written to him.

"It was most awfully clever; she only wrote it after I left last night and she hadn't time to post it, of course, but she gave it to the old apple-woman — you know, down by the tower — and right under her father's nose, and he hadn't the least idea, and I've written back because I mayn't, perhaps, get a word with her this afternoon, and old Morelli will be there."

He sat on the edge of the stone wall, looking down at the town and swinging his legs. The town was in a blaze of sun, seen dimly through a haze of gold-dust. It hung like a lamp against the blue sky, because the mist gathered closely about its foundations, and only its roofs and pinnacles seemed to swing in the shifting dazzling sun before their eyes.

"The old apple-woman," said Tony, "is simply ripping, and I think she must have had an awfully sad life. I should like to do something for her." There were at least ten people a day for whom he wanted to do something. "I asked Bannister about her, but he wasn't very interested; but that's because his smallest baby's got whooping-cough. He told me yesterday he simply whooped all night, and Mrs. Bannister had to sit up with it, which pretty well rotted her temper next day." Tony paused with a consciousness that he was wandering from the point. "Anyhow, here's her letter, Janet's, I mean. I know she wouldn't mind you seeing it, because you are in it almost as much as I am." He held out the letter.

"Did Morelli see her give it to the apple-woman?" asked Maradick.

"Yes, she tells you in the letter. But he didn't spot anything. He's such a funny beggar; he seems so smart sometimes, and then other times he doesn't see anything. Anyhow, it doesn't matter much, because I'm going to see him now and tell him everything."

"Well; and then?" said Maradick.

"Oh! he'll agree, I know he will. And then I think we'll be married right at once; there's no use in waiting, you know, and there's a little church right over by Strater Cove, near the sea, a little tumbledown place with a parson who's an awful sportsman. He's got five children and two hundred a year, and—oh! where was I?—and then we'll just come back and tell them. They can't do anything then, you know, and father will get over it all right."

Tony was so serene about it, swinging his legs there in the sun, that Maradick could say nothing.

"And if Morelli doesn't take to the idea?" he ventured at last.

"Oh! he!" said Tony. "Oh, he's really most awfully keen. You noticed how we got on. I took to him from the first, there was something about him." But he swung round rather anxiously towards Maradick. "Why! do you think he won't?" he said.

"I'm not sure of him," Maradick answered. "I never have been. And then I was with Punch this morning and he told me things about him."

"Things! What sort of things?" asked Tony rather incredulously.

"Oh, about the way that he treated his wife." It was, after all, Maradick reflected, extremely vague, nothing very much that one could lay hands on. "I don't like the man, and I don't for a minute think that he's playing square with you."

But Tony smiled, a rather superior smile. After all, that was Maradick's way, to be pessimistic about things; it was to do with his age. Middle-aged people were always cautious and suspicious. For a moment he felt quite a distance from Maradick, and something akin to the same feeling made him stretch out his hand for Janet's letter.

"After all," he said rather awkwardly, "perhaps she would rather that I didn't show it to anyone, even you." He jumped down from the wall. "Well, I must be off. It's after three. I say, keep the family in the dark until I'm back. They're sure to ask. Now that Alice and father are both beginning to think about it we shall fairly have to begin the conspirator business." He laughed in his jolly way and stood in front of Maradick with a smile all over his face. Suddenly he leant forward and put his hands on the other man's shoulders and shook him gently.

"You silly old rotter, don't look so sad about it, you don't know what fun it will all be. And you are the biggest brick in the world, anyway. Janet and I will never forget you." He bent down lower. "I say, you're not sick with me, are you? Because, scold me like anything if I've done things. I always am doing things, you know." He turned round and faced the shining path and the sky like glass. "I say! Isn't it topping? But I must be off. I'll come at once and tell you when I get back. But I'll have to be in time for dinner to-night or the governor will keep me to my room on bread and water." He was gone.

Maradick, looking back on it all afterwards, always saw that moment as the beginning of the second act. The first act, of course, had begun with that vision of Janet on the stairs with the candle in her hand. That seemed a long while ago now. Then had come all the other things, the picnic, the swim, the talk with Mrs. Lester, Tony's proposal, his own talk with Punch that morning; all little things, but all leading the situation inevitably towards its climax. But they had all been in their way innocent, unoffending links in the chain. Now there was something more serious in it all, from that evening some other element mingled with the comedy.

He suddenly felt irritated with the sun and the colour and began to walk up and down the path. The uneasiness that he had felt all the afternoon increased; he began to wish that he had not allowed Tony to go down alone. Nothing, of course, could happen to the boy; it was absurd that he should imagine things, and probably it was due to the heat. Every now and again some sound came up from the town—a cry, a bell, the noisy rattle of a cart, and it seemed like an articulate voice; the town seemed to have a definite personality, some great animal basking there in the sun, and its face was the face of Morelli.

He sat down on one of the seats in the shadiest part of the garden; the trees hung over it in thick dark shadows, and at times a breeze pushed like a bird's wing through their branches.

All around him the path was dark, beyond it was a broad belt of light. He must have gone asleep, because almost immediately he seemed to be dreaming. The shadows on the path receded and advanced as a door opens and shuts; the branches of the trees bent lower and lower. It seemed in his dream that he recognised something menacing in their movement, and he rose and passed through the garden and in a moment he was in the town. Here too it was dark, and in the market-place the tower stood, a black mass against the grey sky behind it, and the streets twisted like snakes up and down about the hill.

And then suddenly he was at Morelli's house, he recognised the strange carving and the crooked, twisting shape of the windows. The door opened easily to his hand and he passed up the stairs. The house was quite dark; he had to grope to find his way. And then he was opposed by another door, something studded with nails—he could feel them with his hands— and heavily barred. He heard voices on the other side of the door, low, soft whispers, and then he recognised them, they were Tony and Morelli. He was driven by an impulse to beat the door and get at them; some fear clutched at his throat so that he felt that Tony was in terrible danger. In a minute he knew that he would be too late.

He knocked, at first softly and then furiously; for a moment the voices stopped, and then they began again. No one paid any attention to his knocking. He knew with absolute certainty that in a few minutes the door would open, but first something would happen. He began to beat on the door with his fists and to call out; the house was, for the rest, perfectly silent.

And then suddenly he heard Morelli's laugh. There was a moment's silence, and then Tony screamed, a terrified, trembling scream; the door began to open.

Maradick awoke to find himself on the garden seat with his head sunk on his breast and some one looking at him; in the hazy uncertainty of his waking his first thought was that it was Janet—he had scarcely recovered from his dream. He soon saw that it was not Janet, and, looking up confusedly, blushed on finding that it was Alice Du Cane. She was dressed in white, in something that clung about her and seemed to be made all in one piece. It looked to him very beautiful, and the great sweeping dark hat that she wore must have been delightfully shady, but it only had the effect of confusing him still more.

He knew Alice Du Cane very slightly, in fact he couldn't really be said to know her at all. They said "good morning" and "good evening," and it had occasionally happened that they had had to talk "just to keep the ball rolling" at some odd minute or other, but she had always given him the impression of being in quite "other worlds," from which she might occasionally look down and smile, but into which he could never possibly be admitted. He had quite acquiesced in all of this, although he had no feeling of the kind about the rest of the party; but she belonged, he felt, to that small, mysterious body of people who, in his mind at any rate, "were the very top." He was no snob about them, and he did not feel that they were any the better people for their high position, but he did feel that they were different. There were centuries of tradition behind them, that perhaps was really it, and there were the old houses with their lawns and picture galleries, and there were those wonderful ancestors who had ruled England from the beginning of time.

He had laughed sometimes when his wife had represented to him that certain people in Epsom, alluded to in a hushed voice and mysterious nods, were really "it." He knew so well that they were not; nothing to do with it at all. But he always recognised "it" at once when it was there. He did not recognise "it" in the Gales; there was a certain quality of rest arising from assurance of possession that they lacked, but Alice Du Cane had got "it," most assuredly she had got "it."

He liked to watch her. She moved with so beautiful a quiet and carried herself with so sure a dignity; he admired her enormously, but had been quite prepared to keep his distance.

And then suddenly he had seen that she was in love with Tony, and she was at once drawn into the vortex. She became something more than a person at whom one looked, whom one admired as a picture; she was part of the situation. He had been extremely sorry for her, and it had been her unhappiness more than anything else that had worried him about his part in the affair. But now, as he saw her there watching him with a smile and leaning ever so slightly on her parasol, of ever so delicate a pink, he was furiously embarrassed.

He had been sleeping, probably with his mouth open, and she had been watching him. He jumped to his feet.

"Oh, Miss Du Cane," he stammered, "I really — —"

But she broke in upon him, laughing.

"Oh! what a shame! Really, Mr. Maradick, I didn't mean to, but the gravel scrunched or something and it woke you. I've been doing the same thing, sleeping, I mean; it's impossible to do anything else with heat like this." Then her face grew grave. "All the same I'm not sure that I'm sorry, because I have wanted to talk to you very badly all day, and now, unless you *do* want to go to sleep again, it does seem to be a chance."

"Why, of course," he answered gravely, and he made way for her on the seat. He felt the sinister afternoon pressing upon him again. He was disturbed, worried, anxious; his nerves were all to pieces. And then she did most certainly embarrass him. The very way that she sat down, the careful slowness of her movement, and the grace with which she leant slightly forward so that the curve of her neck was like the curve of a pink shell against her white dress, embarrassed him. And he was tired, most undoubtedly tired; it was all beginning to be too much for him.

And then he suddenly caught a look in her eyes as she turned towards him; something melancholy and appealing in it touched his heart and his embarrassment left him.

"Mr. Maradick," she began hurriedly, with her face again turned away from him, "you are much older than I am, and so I expect you'll understand what I am trying to get at. And anyhow, you know all that's been going on this week, more than anyone else does, and so there's no need to beat about the bush. Besides, I always hate it. I always want to get straight at the thing, don't you?"

"Yes," he said. It was one of the true things about both of them.

"Well then, of course it's about Tony. We all want to know about Tony, and nobody does know except you, and everybody's afraid to ask you except myself, so there you are. You mustn't think me impertinent; I don't mean to be, but we *must* know—some of us, at any rate!"

"What *must* you know?" he said. He was suddenly on his mettle. He resented the note of command in her voice. About his general position in the world he was quite ready to yield place, but about Tony's affairs he would yield to no one; that was another matter.

"Why, of course," she said, looking at him, "what *I* want to know, what we all want to know, is what he is doing. Of course we have all, by this time, a pretty good idea. I saw him with that girl down on the beach, and it's been pretty obvious, by his being away so continually, what he is after. No, it isn't exactly so much what he is doing as whether it's all right."

"But then," said Maradick, facing her, "why exactly are you asking me? Why not ask Tony?"

"Oh! you know that would be no good," she said, shaking her head impatiently. "Tony would tell me nothing. If he wanted to tell us anything he would have told us. You can see how secret he's been keeping it all. And you're the only other person who knows. Besides, I don't want you to betray any secrets, it's only to tell us if it's all right. If you say it is then we shall know."

"And who exactly is 'we'?" Maradick asked.

Alice hesitated a moment. Then she said, "It's Lady Gale really who wants to know. She's suffering terribly all this time, but she's afraid to ask you herself because you might tell her too much, and then she couldn't be loyal to Sir Richard. But, you know, she spoke to you herself about it."

"Yes, she did," said Maradick slowly. "Then I suppose that this, her sending you, means that she doesn't quite trust me now. She said before that she would leave it in my hands."

"Yes. She trusts you just as much, of course. Only—well, you see, you haven't known Tony all his life as we have, you haven't cared for him quite as much as we have. And then I'm a woman, I should probably see a whole lot of things in it that you couldn't see. It's only that you should tell me a little about it, and then, if Lady Gale sees that we both think it's all right, she will be happier. Only, she's felt a little, just lately, that you weren't very comfortable about it."

"Is it only Lady Gale?" asked Maradick.

"Well, of course I want to know too. You see, I've known Tony since we were both babies, and of course I'm fond of him, and I should hate him to get in a mess"; she finished up rather breathlessly.

He had a strong feeling of the pathos of it all. He knew that she was proud and that she had probably found it very difficult to come to him as she had done.

He could see now that she was struggling to keep her old pride and reserve, but that she found it very hard.

His voice was very tender as he spoke to her.

"Miss Du Cane," he said, "I understand. I do indeed. I would have spoken to Lady Gale herself if she hadn't begged me to keep quiet about it. Besides, I wasn't sure, I'm not sure now, how things were really going, and I was afraid of alarming her."

"Then there *is* trouble?" Alice said; "you *are* anxious?"

"No, not really," Maradick hastened to assure her. "As far as the main thing goes—the girl herself, I mean—it's the best thing that could possibly happen to Tony. The girl is delightful; better than that, she is splendid. I won't tell you more, simply that it *is* all right."

"And Tony loves her?" Alice's voice trembled in spite of itself.

"Yes, heart and soul," said Maradick fervently; "and I think when you see her that you will agree about her. Only you must see the difficulties as well as I do; what we are doing is the only thing to do. I think that to take Tony away now would lead to dreadful disaster. He must go through with it. The whole thing has gone too far now for it possibly to be stopped."

"Then tell me," Alice said slowly, "was she, do you suppose, the girl that I saw down on the beach with Tony?"

"Yes," said Maradick, "she must have been."

The girl got up slowly from the seat and stood with her back to him, her slim white figure drawn to its full height; the sun played like fire about her dress and hair, but there was something very pathetic in the way that she let her arms with a slow hopeless gesture fall to her side, and stared, motionless, down the path.

Then she turned round to him.

"Thank you, Mr. Maradick," she said, "that's all I wanted to know. I am happier about it, and Lady Gale will be too. You're quite right about taking Tony away. It would only mean a hopeless break with Sir Richard, and then his mother would be caught into it too, and that must be averted at all costs. Besides, if she is as nice as you say, perhaps, after all, it is the best thing that could happen. And, at any rate," she went on after a little pause, "we are all most awfully grateful to you. I don't know what we should have done otherwise."

Some one was coming down the path. They both, at the same moment, saw that it was Mrs. Lester.

Alice turned. "I must go," she said. "Thank you again for what you told me."

He watched her walk down the path, very straight and tall, with a grace and ease that were delightful to him. The two women stopped for a moment and spoke; then Alice passed out of sight and Mrs. Lester came towards him.

Some clock in the distance struck six.

CHAPTER XIV
MARADICK IN A NEW RÔLE—HE AFTERWARDS SEES TONY'S FACE IN A MIRROR

He didn't precisely know what his feelings were; he was too hot, and the whole thing was too much of a surprise for him to think at all; the thing that he did most nearly resemble, if he had wanted similes, was some sharply contested citadel receiving a new attack on its crumbling walls before the last one was truly over.

But that again was not a simile that served with any accuracy, because he was so glad, so tumultuously and intensely glad, to see her. He wanted to keep that moment, that instant when she was coming down the path towards him, quite distinct from all the other moments of his life in its beauty and colours, and so he focussed in his mind the deep green of the trees and their purple shadows on the path, the noise that two birds made, and the deep rustle as of some moving water that her dress sent to him as she came.

He sat there, one hand on each knee, looking straight before him, motionless.

Mrs. Lester had that morning done her utmost to persuade her husband to "play a game." She was brimming over with sentiment, partly because of the weather, partly because Treliss always made her feel like that, partly because it was "in the air" in some vague way through Tony.

She did not understand it, but she knew that she had one of her "fits," a craving for excitement, for doing anything that could give one something of a fling.

But her talk with her husband had also partly arisen from her realisation of her feeling for Maradick. She was not a very serious woman, she took life very lightly, but she knew that her affection for her husband was by far the best and most important thing in her.

She knew this through all the passing and temporary moods that she might have, and she had learnt to dread those moods simply because she never knew how far she might go. But then Fred would be so provoking! As he was just now, for instance, paying no attention to her at all, wrapped in his stupid writing, talking about nerves and suggesting doctors.

But she had tried very hard that morning to awaken him to a sense of the kind of thing that was happening to her. She had even, with a sudden sense of panic, suggested leaving the place altogether, hinting that it didn't suit her. But he had laughed.

She had, in fact, during these last few days, been thinking of Maradick a great deal. For one thing, she hated Mrs. Maradick; she had never in her life before hated anyone so thoroughly. She took people easily as a rule and was charitable in her judgment, but Mrs. Maradick seemed to her to be everything that was bad. The little woman's assumption of a manner that quite obviously could never belong to her, her complacent patronage of everybody and everything, her appearance, everything seemed to Mrs. Lester the worst possible; she could scarcely bear to stay in the same room with her. She had, therefore, for Maradick a profound pity that had grown as the days advanced. He had seemed to her so patient under what must be a terrible affliction. And so "the game" had grown more serious than usual, serious enough to make her hesitate, and to run, rather as a frightened child runs to its nurse, to Fred for protection. But Fred wouldn't listen, or, what was worse, listened only to laugh. Well, on Fred's head be it then!

She had not, however, set out that afternoon with any intention of finding him; she was, indeed, surprised when she saw him there.

They both, at once, felt that there was something between them that had not been there before; they were both nervous, and she did not look at him as she sat down.

"How lazy we are!" she, said. "Why, during the last week we've been nothing at all but 'knitters in the sun!' I know that's a nice quotation out of somewhere, but I haven't the least idea where. But, as a matter of fact, it's only the irresponsible Tony who's been rushing about, and he's made up for most of us."

She was dressed in her favourite colour, blue, the very lightest and palest of blue. She had a large picture hat tied, in the fashion of a summer of a year or two before, with blue ribbon under her chin; at her belt was a bunch of deep crimson carnations. She took one of them out and twisted it round in her fingers.

She looked up at him and smiled.

"You're looking very cool and very cross," she said, "and both are irritating to people on a hot day. Oh! the heat!" She waved her carnation in the air. "You know, if I had my way I should like to be wheeled about in a chair carved out of ice and sprayed by cool negroes with iced rose water! There! Isn't that Théophile Gautier and Théodore de Banville and the rest? Oh dear! what rot I'm talking; I'm — —"

"I wish," he said, looking her all over very slowly, "that you'd be yourself, Mrs. Lester, just for a little. I hate all that stuff; you know you're not a bit like that really. I want you as you are, not a kind of afternoon-tea dummy!"

"But I am like that," she said, laughing lightly, but also a little nervously. "I'm always like that in hot weather and at Treliss. We're all like that just now, on the jump. There's Lady Gale and Sir Richard and Alice Du Cane, and Rupert too, if he wasn't too selfish, all worrying their eyes out about Tony, and there's Tony worrying his eyes out about some person or persons unknown, and there's my husband worrying his eyes out about his next masterpiece, and there's you worrying your eyes out about — —" She paused.

"Yes," said Maradick, "about?"

"Oh! I don't know — something. It was easy enough to see as one came along. I asked Alice Du Cane; she didn't know. What was she talking to you for?"

"Why shouldn't she?"

"Oh! I don't know; only she's on the jump like the rest of us and hasn't honoured anyone with her conversation very much lately. The place has got hold of you. That's what it is. What did I tell you? Treliss is full of witches and devils, you know, and they like playing tricks with people like yourself, incredulous people who like heaps of eggs and bacon for breakfast and put half a crown in the plate on Sundays. I know."

He didn't say anything, so she went on:

"But I suppose Alice wanted to know what Tony was doing. That's what they all want to know, and the cat will be out of the bag very soon. For my part, I think we'd all better go away and try somewhere else. This place has upset us." Suddenly her voice dropped and she leant forward and put her hand for a moment on his knee. "But please, Mr. Maradick — we're friends — we made a compact the other day, that, while we were here, you know, we'd be of use to each other; and now you must let me be of use, please."

That had never failed of its effect, that sudden passing from gay to grave, the little emotional quiver in the voice, the gentle touch of the hand; but now she was serious about it, it was, for once, uncalculated.

And it had its effect on him. A quiver passed through his body at her touch; he clenched his hands.

"Yes," he said in a low voice, "but I don't think you can help me just now, Mrs. Lester. Besides, I don't think that I want any help. As you say, we're all a little strained just now; the weather, I suppose." He paused and then went on: "Only, you don't know what it is to me to have you for a friend. I've thought a good deal about it these last few days. I've not been a man of very many friends, women especially little."

"Life," she said, "is so difficult." She liked to talk about life in the abstract; she was not a clever woman and she never pretended to keep pace with her husband in all his ideas, but, after all, it was something to be able to talk about life at all—if one said that it was "queer" or "difficult" or "odd" there was a kind of atmosphere.

She said it again; "Life is so difficult . . . one really doesn't know."

"I had never known," he answered, looking steadily in front of him, "until these last weeks how difficult it was. You've made it that, you know."

She broke in nervously, "Oh, surely, Mr. Maradick."

She was suddenly frightened of him. She thought she had never seen anyone so strong and fierce. She could see the veins stand out on the back of his hands and the great curve of his arm as he leant forward.

"Yes," he went on roughly, "I'm not fooling. I'd never seen what life was before. These last weeks, you and other things have shown me. I thought it was life just going on in an office, making money, dining at home, sleeping. Rot! That's not life. But now! now! I know. I was forty. I thought life was over. Rot! life's beginning. I don't care what happens, I'm going to take it. I'm not going to miss it again. Do you see? I'm not going to miss it again. A man's a fool if he misses it twice."

He was speaking like a drunken man. He stumbled over his words; he turned round and faced her. He saw the ribbon under her chin rise and fall with her breathing. She was looking frightened, staring at him like a startled animal. He saw her dress in a blue mist against the golden path and the green trees, and out of it her face rose white and pink and a little dark under the eyes and then shadows under the sweeping hat. He began to breathe like a man who has been running.

She put out her hand with a gesture as though she would defend herself, and gave a little cry as he suddenly seized and crushed it in his.

He bent towards her, bending his eyes upon her. "No, it's rot, missing it again. My wife never cared for me; she's never cared. Nobody's cared, and

I've been a fool not to step out and take things. It isn't any use just to wait, I see that now. And now we're here, you and I. Just you and I. Isn't it funny? I'm not going to make love to you. That's rot, there isn't time. But I've got you; I'm strong!"

She was terrified and shrunk back against the seat, but at the same time she had an overwhelming, overpowering realisation of his strength. He was strong. His hand crushed hers, she could see his whole body turning towards her as a great wave turns; she had never known anyone so strong before.

"Mr. Maradick! Please! Let me go!"

Her voice was thin and sharp like a child's. But he suddenly leaned forward and took her in his arms; he crushed her against him so that she could feel his heart beating against her like a great hammer. He turned her head roughly with his hand and bent down and kissed her. His mouth met hers as though it would never go.

She could not breathe, she was stifled—then suddenly he drew back; he almost let her fall back. She saw him bend down and pick up his hat, and he had turned the corner of the path and was gone.

He did not know how he left the garden. He did not see it or realise it, but suddenly he found himself in the stretch of cornfield that reached, a yellow band, from horizon to horizon. The field ran down the hill, and the little path along which he stumbled crept in and out across the top of the slope. Below the corn was the distant white road, and curving round to the left was the little heap of white cottages that stand, stupidly, almost timidly, at the water's edge. Then beyond that again was the wide blue belt of the sea. The corn was dark brown like burnt sugar at the top and a more golden yellow as it turned trembling to the ground. The scarlet poppies were still split in pools and lakes and rivers across its breast, and it seemed to have caught some of their colour in its darker gold.

Still not knowing what he was doing, he sat down heavily on a little green mound above the path and looked with stupid, half-closed eyes at the colour beneath him. He did not take it in, his heart was still beating furiously; every now and again his throat moved convulsively, his hands were white against his knee.

But, through his dazed feelings, he knew that he was glad for what he had done. Very glad! A kind of strange triumph at having really done it! There was something pounding, drumming through his veins that was new—a furious excitement that had never been there before.

He felt no shame or regret or even alarm at possible consequences. He did not think for an instant of Mrs. Maradick or the girls. His body, the muscles and the nerves, the thick arms, the bull neck, the chest like a rock — those were the parts of him that were glad, furiously glad. He was primeval, immense, sitting there on the little green hill with the corn and the sea and the world at his feet.

He did not see the world at all, but there passed before his eyes, like pictures on a shining screen, some earlier things that had happened to him and had given him that same sense of furious physical excitement. He saw himself, a tiny boy, in a hard tight suit of black on a Sunday afternoon in their old home at Rye. Church bells were ringing somewhere, and up the twisting, turning cobbles of the street grave couples were climbing. The room in which he was hung dark and gloomy about him, and he was trying to prevent himself from slipping off the shiny horsehair chair on which he sat, his little black-stockinged legs dangling in the air. In his throat was the heavy choking sensation of the fat from the midday dinner beef. On the stiff sideboard against the wall were ranged little silver dishes containing sugar biscuits and rather dusty little chocolates; on the opposite side of the room, in a heavy gilt frame, was the stern figure of his grandmother, with great white wristbands and a sharp pointed nose.

He was trying to learn his Sunday Collect, and he had been forbidden to speak until he had learnt it; his eyes were smarting and his head was swimming with weariness, and every now and again he would slip right forward on the shiny chair. The door opened and a gentleman entered, a beautiful, wonderful gentleman, with a black bushy beard and enormous limbs; the gentleman laughed and caught him up in his arms, the prayer-book fell with a clatter to the floor as he buried his curly head in the beard. He did not know now, looking back, who the gentleman had been, but that moment stood out from the rest of his life with all its details as something wonderful, magic. . . .

And then, later—perhaps he was about fifteen, a rather handsome, shy boy—and he was in an orchard. The trees were heavy with flowers, and the colours, white and pink, swung with the wind in misty clouds above his head. Over the top of the old red-brown wall a girl's face was peeping. He climbed an old gnarled tree that hung across the wall and bent down towards her; their lips met, and as he leaned towards her the movement of his body shook the branches and the petals fell about them in a shower. He had forgotten the name of the little girl, it did not matter, but the moment was there.

And then again, later still, was the moment when he had first seen Mrs. Maradick. It had been at some evening function or other, and she had stood with her shining shoulders under some burning brilliant lights that swung from the ceiling. Her dress had been blue, a very pale blue; and at the thought of the blue dress his head suddenly turned, the corn swam before him and came in waves to meet him, and then receded, back to the sky-line.

But it was another blue dress that he saw, not Mrs. Maradick's—the blue dress, the blue ribbon, the trees, the golden path. His hands closed slowly on his knees as though he were crushing something; his teeth were set.

Everything, except the one central incident, had passed from his mind, only that was before him. The minutes flew past him; in the town bells struck and the sun sank towards the sea.

He made a great effort and tried to think connectedly. This thing that had happened would make a great change in his life, it would always stand out as something that could never be altered. Anyone else who might possibly have had something to say about it—Mrs. Maradick, Mr. Lester— didn't count at all. It was simply between Mrs. Lester and himself.

A very faint rose-colour crept up across the sky. It lingered in little bands above the line of the sea, and in the air immediately above the corn tiny pink cushions lay in heaps together; the heads of the corn caught the faint red glow and held it in the heart of their dark gold.

The sheer physical triumph began to leave Maradick. His heart was beating less furiously and the blood was running less wildly through his veins.

He began to wonder what she, Mrs. Lester, was thinking about it. She, of course, was angry—yes, probably furiously angry. Perhaps she would not speak to him again; perhaps she would tell her husband. What had made him do it? What had come to him? He did not know; but even now, let the consequences be what they might, he was not sorry. He was right whatever happened.

A long time passed. He was sunk in a kind of lethargy. The pink cushions in the sky sent out fingers along the blue to other pink cushions, and ribbons of gold were drawn across and across until they met in a golden flame above the water. The sun was sinking and a little wind had stirred the sea, the waves were tipped with gold.

The breeze blew about his cheeks and he shivered. It must be late; the sun was setting, the field of corn was sinking into silver mist from out of which the poppies gleamed mysteriously. Suddenly he thought of Tony.

He had forgotten the boy. He had come back to the hotel probably by now; he remembered that he had said that he must be back in time for dinner. But Tony's affairs seemed very far away; he did not feel that he could talk about things to-night, or, indeed, that he could talk to anyone. He could not go back to the hotel just yet. The sun had touched the sea at last, and, from it, there sprung across the softly stirring water a band of gold that stretched spreading like a wing until it touched the little white houses now sinking into dusk. The sky was alive with colour and the white road ran in the distance, like a ribbon, below the corn.

The bells struck again from the town; he rose and stood, an enormous dark figure, against the flaming sky. There was perfect stillness save for the very gentle rustle of the corn. In the silence the stars came out one by one, the colours were drawn back like threads from the pale blue, and across the sea only the faintest gold remained; a tiny white moon hung above the white houses and the white road, the rest of the world was grey. The lights began to shine from the town.

He was cold and his limbs ached; the dim light, the mysterious hour began to press about him. He had a sudden wish, a sudden demand for company, people, lights, noise.

Not people to talk to, of course; no, he did not want anyone to talk to, but here, in this silence, with the mysterious rustling corn, he was nervous, uneasy. He did not want to think about anything, all that he wanted now was to forget. He could not think; his brain refused, and there was no reason why he should bother. To-morrow—to-morrow would do. He stumbled down the path through the field; he could not see very well, and he nearly fell several times over the small stones in his path; he cursed loudly. Then he found the hard white road and walked quickly down, past the little white houses, over the bridge that crossed the river, up into the town.

His need for company increased with every step that he took; the loneliness, the half light, the cold breeze were melancholy. He turned his head several times because he thought that some one was following him, but only the white road gleamed behind him, and the hedges, dark barriers, on either side.

The lights of the town came to him as a glad relief. They were not very brilliant; in the first streets of all the lamps were very wide apart, and in between their dim splashes of yellow were caverns of inky blackness.

These streets were almost deserted, and the few people that passed hurried as though they were eager to reach some more cheerful spot. Very few lamps burnt behind the windows, but Maradick felt as though the houses were so many eyes eagerly watching him. Everything seemed alive, and every now and again his ear caught, he fancied, the sound of a measured tread in his rear. He stopped, but there was perfect silence.

His exultation had absolutely left him. He felt miserably depressed and lonely. It seemed to him now that he had cut off his two friends with a sudden blow for no reason at all. Mrs. Lester would never speak to him again. Tony, on his return, would be furious with him for not being there according to his solemn promise. Lady Gale and Alice Du Cane would lose all their trust in him; his wife would never rest until she had found out where he had been that night, and would never believe it if she did find out. He now saw how foolish he had been not to go back to the hotel for dinner; he would go back now if it were not too late; but it was too late. They would have finished by the time that he was up the hill again.

He was hungry and tired and cold; he greeted the lights of the market-place with joy. It was apparently a night of high festival. The lamps on the Town Hall side showed crowds of swiftly moving figures, dark for a moment in the shadows of the corner houses and then suddenly flashing into light. The chief inn of the town, "The Green Feathers," standing flamboyantly to the right of the grey tower, shone in a blazing radiance of gas. Two waiters with white cloths over their arms stood on the top stair watching the crowd. Behind them, through the open door, was a glorious glimpse of the lighted hall.

The people who moved about in the market were fishermen and country folk. Their movement seemed aimless but pleasant; suddenly some one would break into song, and for a moment his voice would rise, as a fish leaps from the sea, and then would sink back again. There was a great deal of laughter and a tendency to grow noisier and more ill-disciplined.

Maradick, as he pushed his way through the crowd, was reminded of that first night when Tony and he had come down; the dance and the rest! What ages ago that seemed now! He was another man. He pushed his way furiously through the people. He was conscious now of tremendous appetite. He had not eaten anything since lunch, and then only very little. He was tired both mentally and physically; perhaps after a meal he would feel better.

He walked wearily up the steps of "The Green Feathers" and accosted one of the waiters. He must have food, a room alone, quiet. Maradick commanded respect; the waiter withdrew his eye reluctantly from the crowd and paid attention. "Yes—fish—a cutlet—a bottle of Burgundy—yes—perhaps the gentleman would like the room upstairs. It was a pleasant room. There was no one there just now; it overlooked the market, but, with the windows down, the noise— —"

The idea of overlooking the market was rather pleasant; the people and the lights would be there and, at the same time, there would be no need to talk to anyone. Yes, he would like that room. He walked upstairs.

There was much movement and bustle on the ground floor of the inn, chatter and laughter and the chinking of glasses, but above stairs there was perfect silence. The waiter lighted candles, two massive silver candlesticks of venerable age, and entered the long dining-room carrying them in front of him. He explained that they had not lighted this room with gas because candles were more in keeping. He hinted at the eighteenth century and powder and ruffles. He almost pirouetted as he held the candles and bent to put them on the table by the window. He was most certainly a waiter with a leg.

He did, beyond question, suit the room with its long gleaming walls and long gleaming table. The table at which he was to dine was drawn up close to the window, so that he could watch the antics of the square. The candle-light spread as far as the long table and then spread round in a circle, catching in its embrace a tall mirror that ran from the ceiling to the floor. This mirror was so placed that a corner of the square, with its lights and figures and tall dark houses, was reflected in it.

The room seemed close, and Maradick opened the window a little and voices came up to him. In places the people were bathed in light and he could see their faces, their eyes and their mouths, and then in other parts there was grey darkness, so that black figures moved and vanished mysteriously. The tower reminded him curiously of the tower in his dream; it rose black against the grey light behind it.

His dinner was excellent; the waiter was inclined to be conversational. "Yes, it was some kind o' feast day. No, he didn't know exactly. The place was full of superstitions—no, he, thank Gawd, was from London—yes, Clapham, where they did things like Christians—there were meringues, apple-tart, or custard—yes, meringues." He faded away.

Voices came up to the room. Vague figures of three people could be seen below the window. The quavering voice of an old man pierced the general murmurs of the square.

"Well, 'e'd seen the first wasp of the season, as early back as April; yus, 'e was minded to give 'im a clout, but 'e missed it." The wasp figured largely in the discussion. They were all three rapidly reaching that stage when excessive affection gives place to inimical distrust. The old man's voice quavered on. "If 'e called 'is woman names then 'e didn't see why 'e shouldn't call 'is woman names." This led to futile argument. But the old man was obstinate.

Stars burnt high over the roofs in a silver cluster, and then there trailed across the night blue a pale white path like silk that was made of other stars—myriads of stars, back in unlimited distance, and below them there hung a faint cloud of golden light, the reflexion from the lamps of the tower.

Maradick's dinner had done him good. He sat, with his chair tilted slightly forward, watching the square. The magnificent waiter had appeared suddenly, had caught the food in a moment with a magical net, as it were, and had disappeared. He had left whisky and soda and cigarettes at Maradicks side; the light of two candles caught the shining glass of the whisky decanter and it sparkled all across the table.

The question of Tony had come uppermost again; that seemed now the momentous thing. He ought to have been there when Tony came back. Whatever he had done to Mrs. Lester, or she to him—that matter could be looked at from two points of view at any rate—he ought to have gone back and seen Tony. The apprehension that he had felt during the afternoon about the boy returned now with redoubled force. His dream, for a time forgotten, came back with all its chill sense of warning. That man Morelli! Anything might have happened to the boy; they might be waiting for him now up at the hotel, waiting for both of them. He could see them all—Lady Gale, Alice Du Cane, Mrs. Lester, his wife. He had in a way deserted his post. They had all trusted him; it was on that condition that they had granted him their friendship, that they had so wonderfully and readily opened their arms to him. And now, perhaps the boy . . .

He drank a stiff whisky-and-soda, his hand trembling a little so that he chinked the glass against the decanter.

He felt reassured. After all, what reason had he for alarm? What had he, as far as Morelli was concerned, to go upon? Nothing at all; merely some vague words from Punch. The boy was perfectly all right. Besides, at any rate, he wasn't a fool. He knew what he was about, he could deal with Morelli, if it came to that.

He drank another whisky-and-soda and regarded the mirror. It was funny the way that it reflected that corner of the square, so that without looking at all out of the window you could see figures moving, black and grey, and then suddenly a white gleaming bit of pavement where the light fell. His head became undoubtedly confused, because he fancied that he saw other things in the mirror. He thought that the crowd in the square divided into lines. Some one appeared, dancing, a man with a peaked cap, dancing and playing a pipe; and the man—how odd it was!—the man was Morelli! And suddenly he turned and danced down the lines of the people, still piping, back the way that he had come, and all the people, dancing, followed him! They passed through the mirror, dancing, and he seemed to recognise people that he knew. Why, of course! There was Tony, and then Janet Morelli and Lady Gale, Mrs. Lester, Alice Du Cane; and how absurd they looked! There was himself and Mrs. Maradick! The scene faded. He pulled himself up with a jerk, to find that he was nodding, nearly asleep; the idea of the music had not been entirely a dream, however, for a band had gathered underneath the window. In the uncertain light they looked strangely fantastic, so that you saw a brass trumpet without a man behind it, and then again a man with his lips pressed blowing, but his trumpet fading into darkness.

The crowd had gathered round and there was a great deal of noise; but it was mostly inarticulate, and, to some extent, quarrelsome. Maradick caught the old man's voice somewhere in the darkness quavering "If 'e calls my old woman names then I'll call 'is old woman . . ." It trailed off, drowned in the strains of "Auld Lang Syne," with which the band, somewhat mistakenly, had commenced.

The time was erratic; the band too, it seemed, had been drinking, even now he could see that they had mugs at their sides and one or two of them were trying to combine drink and music.

One little man with an enormous trumpet danced, at times, a few steps, producing a long quivering note from his instrument.

The crowd had made a little clearing opposite the window, for an old man with a battered bowler very much on one side of his head was dancing solemnly with a weary, melancholy face, his old trembling legs bent double.

Maradick felt suddenly sick of it all. He turned back from the window and faced the mirror. He was unutterably tired, and miserable, wretchedly miserable. He had broken faith with everybody. He was no use to anyone; he had deceived his wife, Lady Gale, Tony, Mrs. Lester, everybody. A load of depression, like a black cloud, swung down upon him. He hated the band and the drunken crowd; he hated the place, because it seemed partly responsible for what had happened to him; but above all he hated himself for what he had done.

Then suddenly he looked up and saw a strange thing. He had pulled down the window, and the strains of the band came very faintly through; the room was strangely silent. The mirror shone very clearly, because the moon was hanging across the roofs on the opposite side of the square.

The corner of the street shone like glass. Nearly all the crowd had moved towards the band, so that that part of the square was deserted.

Only one man moved across it. He was coming with a curious movement; he ran for a few steps and then walked and then ran again. Maradick knew at once that it was Tony. He did not know why he was so certain, but as he saw him in the mirror he was quite sure. He felt no surprise. It was almost as though he had been expecting him. He got up at once from his chair and went down the stairs; something was the matter with Tony. He saw the waiter in the hall, and he told him that he was coming back; then he crossed the square.

Tony was coming with his head down, stumbling as though he were drunk. He almost fell into Maradick's arms. He looked up.

"You! Maradick! Thank God!"

He caught hold of his arm; his face was white and drawn. He looked twenty years older. His eyes were staring, wide open.

"I say—take me somewhere where I—can have a drink."

Maradick took him, without a word, back to the inn. He gulped down brandy.

Then he sighed and pulled himself together. "I say, let's get back!" He did not loosen his hold of Maradick's arm. "Thank God you were here; I couldn't have faced that hill alone . . . that devil . . ." Then he said under his breath, "My God!"

Maradick paid his bill and they left. They passed the crowd and the discordant band and began to climb the hill. Tony was more himself. "I say, you must think me a fool, but, my word, I've had a fright! I've never been so terrified in my life."

"Morelli!" said Maradick.

"Yes; only the silly thing is, nothing happened. At least nothing exactly. You see, I'd been there a deuce of a time; I wanted to speak to him alone, without Janet, but he wouldn't let her go. It was almost as if he'd meant it. He was most awfully decent all the afternoon. We fooled about like anything, he and all of us, and then I had to give up getting back to dinner and just risk the governor's being sick about it. We had a most ripping supper. He was topping, and then at last Janet left us, and I began. But, you know, it was just as if he knew what I was going to say and was keeping me off it. He kept changing the subject—pleasant all the time—but I couldn't get at it. And then at last my chance came and I asked him. He didn't say anything.

He was sitting on the other side of the table, smiling. And then suddenly, I don't know what it was, I can't describe it, but I began to be terrified, horribly frightened. I've never felt anything like it. His face changed. It was like a devil's. You could only see his eyes and his white cheeks and the tips of his ears, pointed. He was still laughing. I couldn't stir, I was shaking all over. And then he began to move, slowly, round the table, towards me. I pulled myself together; I was nearly fainting, but I rushed for the door. I got out just as he touched me, and then I ran for my life."

He was panting with terror at the recollection of it. They were on the top of the hill. He turned and caught Maradick's hand. "I say," he said, "what does it mean?"

CHAPTER XV
WHY IT IS TO BE THE TWENTY-SEVENTH, AND WHAT THE CONNEXION WAS BETWEEN JANET'S BEING FRIGHTENED AND TOBY'S JOINING THE GREAT MAJORITY

They all met at tea on the next afternoon, and for the gods who were watching the whole affair from the sacred heights of Olympus, it must have been a highly amusing sight.

Mrs. Lawrence was the only person who might really be said to be "right out of it," and she had, beyond question, "her suspicions"; she had *seen* things, she had noticed. She had always, from her childhood, been observant, and anyone could see, and so on, and so on; but nevertheless, she was really outside it all and was the only genuine spectator, as far as mere mortals went.

For the rest, things revolved round Sir Richard; it being everyone's hidden intention, for reasons strictly individual and peculiar, to keep everything from him for as long a period as possible. But everybody was convinced that he saw further into the matter than anyone else, and was equally determined to disguise his own peculiar cleverness from the rest of the company.

Tony was there, rather quiet and subdued. That was a fact remarked on by everybody. Something, of course, had happened last night; and here was the mystery, vague, indefinite, only to be blindly guessed at, although Maradick knew.

The fine shades of everybody's feelings about it all, the special individual way that it affected special individual persons, had to be temporarily put aside for the good of the general cause, namely, the hoodwinking and blinding of the suspicions of Sir Richard; such a business! Conversation, therefore, was concerned with aeroplanes, about which no one present had any knowledge at all, aeroplanes being very much in their infancy; but they did manage to cover a good deal of ground during the discussion, and everyone was so extraordinarily and feverishly interested that it would have been quite easy for an intelligent and unprejudiced observer to discover that no one was really interested at all.

Lady Gale was pouring out tea, and her composure was really admirable; when one considers all that she had to cover it was almost superhuman; but the central fact that was buzzing beyond all others whatever in her brain, whilst she smiled at Mrs. Lester and agreed that "it would be rather a nuisance one's acquaintances being able to fly over and see one so quickly from absolutely anywhere," was that her husband had, as yet, said nothing whatever to Tony about his last night's absence. That was so ominous that she simply could not face it at all; it meant, it meant, well, it meant the tumble, the ruin, the absolute débâcle of the house; a "house of cards," if you like, but nevertheless a house that her admirable tact, her careful management, her years of active and unceasing diplomacy, had supported. What it had all been, what it had all meant to her since Tony had been anything of a boy, only she could know. She had realised, when he had been, perhaps, about ten years old, two things, suddenly and sharply. She had seen in the first place that Tony was to be, for her, the centre of her life, of her very existence, and that, secondly, Tony's way through life would, in every respect, be opposed to his father's.

It would, she saw, be a question of choice, and from the instant of that clear vision her life was spent in the search for compromise, something that would enable her to be loyal to Tony and to all that his life must mean to him, and something that should veil that life from his father. She was, with all her might, "keeping the house together," and it was no easy business; but it was not until the present crisis that it seemed an impossible one.

She had always known that the moment when love came would be the moment of most extreme danger.

She had vowed to her gods, when she saw what her own marriage had made of her life, that her son should absolutely have his way; he should choose, and she would be the very last person in the world to stop him. She had hoped, she had even prayed, that the woman whom he should choose would be some one whom her husband would admit as possible. Then the strength of the house would be inviolate and the terrible moment would be averted. That was, perhaps, the reason that she had so readily and enthusiastically welcomed Alice Du Cane. The girl would "do" from Sir Richard's point of view, and Lady Gale herself liked her, almost loved her. If Tony cared, why then . . . and at first Tony had seemed to care.

But even while she had tried to convince herself, she knew that it was not, for him at any rate, the "real thing." One did not receive it like that, with that calmness, and even familiar jocularity, when the "real thing" came. But she had persuaded herself eagerly, because it would, in nearly every way, be so suitable.

And then suddenly the "real thing" had come, come with its shining eyes and beautiful colour; Tony had found it. She had no hesitation after that. Tony must go on with it, must go through with it, and she must prevent Sir Richard from seeing anything until it was all over. As to that, she had done her best, heaven knew, she had done her best. But circumstances had been too strong for her; she saw it, with frightened eyes and trembling hands, slipping from her grasp. Why had Tony been so foolish? Why had he stayed out again like that and missed dinner? Why was he so disturbed now? It was all threatening to fall about her ears; she saw the quarrel; she saw Tony, arrogant, indignant, furious. He had left them, never to return. She saw herself sitting with her husband, old, ill, lonely, by some desolate fireside in an empty house, and Tony would never return.

But she continued to discuss aeroplanes; she knew another thing about her husband. She knew that if Tony was once married Sir Richard might storm and rage but would eventually make the best of it. The house must be carried on, that was one of his fixed principles of life; Tony single, and every nerve should be strained to make his marriage a fitting one, but Tony married! Why then, curse the young fool, what did he do it for? . . . but let us nevertheless have a boy, and quick about it!

Provided the girl were possible—the girl *must* be possible; but she had Maradick's word for that. He had told Alice that she was "splendid!" Yes, let the marriage only take place and things might be all right, but Sir Richard must not know.

And so she continued to discuss aeroplanes. "Yes, there was that clever man the other day. He flew all round the Crystal Palace; what was his name? Porkins or Dawkins or Walker; she knew it was something like Walker because she remembered at the time wondering whether he had anything to do with the Walkers of Coming Bridge—yes, such nice people—she used to be a Miss Temple—yes, the *Daily Mail* had offered a prize."

At the same time, Tony's face terrified her. He was standing by the window talking to Alice. She had never seen him look like that before, so white and grave and stern—years older. What had he been doing last night?

She gave Mrs. Lawrence her third cup of tea. "Yes, but they are such tiny cups—oh! there's nothing. No, I've never been up in a balloon—not yet—yes, I'm too old, I think; it doesn't do, you know, for me at my age."

Supposing it were all "off." Perhaps it might be better; but she knew that she would be disappointed, that she would be sorry. One didn't get the "real thing" so often in life that one could afford to miss it. No, he mustn't miss it—oh, he *mustn't* miss it. The older she grew, the whiter her hair, the stiffer her stupid bones, the more eagerly, enthusiastically, she longed that every young thing—not only Tony, although he, of course, mattered most—should make the most of its time. They didn't know, dear people, how quickly the years and the stiffness and the thinning of the blood would come upon them. She wanted them all, all the world under thirty, to romp and live and laugh and even be wicked if they liked! but, only, they must not miss it, they *must* not miss the wonderful years!

Sir Richard was perfectly silent. He never said more than a word or two, but his immobility seemed to freeze the room. His hands, his head, his eyes never moved; his gaze was fixed on Tony. He was sitting back in his chair, his body inert, limp, but his head raised; it reminded the terrified Mrs. Lawrence of a snake ready to strike.

Mrs. Lawrence found the situation beyond her. She found a good many situations beyond her, because she was the kind of person whom people continually found it convenient to leave out.

Her attempts to force a way in—her weapons were unresting and tangled volubility—always ended in failure; but she was never discouraged, she was not clever enough to see that she had failed.

She was sitting next to Sir Richard, and leant across him to talk to Lady Gale. Mrs. Maradick and Mrs. Lester were sitting on the other side of the table, Maradick talking spasmodically to Lester in the background; Alice and Tony were together at the window.

Maradick had not spoken to Mrs. Lester since their parting on the day before. He was waiting now until her eyes should meet his; he would know then whether he were forgiven. He had spent the morning on the beach with his girls. He had come up to lunch feeling as he usually did after a few hours spent in their company, that they didn't belong to him at all, that they were somebody else's; they were polite to him, courteous and stiffly deferential, as they would be to any stranger about whom their mother had spoken to them. Oh! the dreariness of it!

But it amused him, when he thought of it, that they, too, poor innocent creatures, should be playing their unconscious part in the whole game. They were playing it because they helped so decisively to fill in the Epsom atmosphere, or rather the way that he himself was thinking of Epsom—the particular greyness and sordidness and shabbiness of the place and the girls.

He had come up to lunch, therefore, washing his hands of the family. He had other things to think of. The immediate affair, of course, was Tony, but he had had as yet no talk with the boy. There wasn't very much to say. It had been precisely as he, Maradick, had expected.

Morelli had refused to hear of it and Tony had probably imagined the rest. In the calm light of day things that had looked fantastic and ominous in the dark were clear and straightforward.

After all, Tony was very young and over-confident. Maradick must see the man himself. And so that matter, too, was put aside.

"Yes," Lester was saying, "we are obviously pushing back to Greek simplicity, and, if it isn't too bold a thing to say, Greek morals. The more complicated and material modern life becomes the more surely will all thinking men and lovers of beauty return to that marvellous simplicity. And then the rest will have to follow, you know, one day."

"Oh yes," said Maradick absently. His eyes were fixed on the opposite wall, but, out of the corners of them, he was watching for the moment when Mrs. Lester should look up. Now he could regard yesterday afternoon with perfect equanimity; it was only an inevitable move in the situation. He wondered at himself now for having been so agitated about it; all that mattered was how she took it. The dogged, almost stupid mood had returned. His eyes were heavy, his great shoulders drooped a little as he bent to listen to Lester. There was no kindness nor charity in his face as he looked across the floor. He was waiting; in a moment she would look up. Then he would know; afterwards he would see Morelli.

"And so, you see," said Lester, "Plato still has the last word in the matter."

"Yes," said Maradick.

Mrs. Lawrence was being entirely tiresome at the tea-table. The strain of the situation was telling upon her. She had said several things to Sir Richard and he had made no answer at all.

He continued to look with unflinching gaze upon Tony. She saw from Lady Gale's and Mrs. Lester's curious artificiality of manner that they were extremely uneasy, and she was piqued at their keeping her, so resolutely, outside intimacy.

When she was ill at ease she had an irritating habit of eagerly repeating other people's remarks with the words a little changed. She did this now, and Lady Gale felt that very shortly she'd be forced to scream.

"It will be such a nuisance," said Mrs. Lester, still continuing the "flying" conversation, "about clothes. One will never know what to put on, because the temperature will always be so very different when one gets up."

"Yes," said Mrs. Lawrence eagerly, "nobody will have the slightest idea what clothes to wear because it may be hot or cold. It all depends— —"

"Some one," said Lady Gale, laughing, "will have to shout down and tell us."

"Yes," said Mrs. Lawrence, "there'll have to be a man who can call out and let us know."

Tony felt his father's eyes upon him. He had wondered why he had said nothing to him about his last night's absence, but it had not really made him uneasy. After all, that was very unimportant, what his father or any of the rest of them did or thought, compared with what Morelli was doing. He was curiously tired, tired in body and tired in mind, and he couldn't think very clearly about anything. But he saw Morelli continually before him. Morelli coming round the table towards him, smiling—Morelli . . . What was he doing to Janet?

He wanted to speak to Maradick, but it was so hard to get to him when there were all these other people in the room. The gaiety had gone out of his eyes, the laughter from his lips. Maradick was everything now; it all depended on Maradick.

"You're looking tired," Alice said. She had been watching him, and she knew at once that he was in trouble. Of course anyone could see that he wasn't himself, but she, who had known him all his life, could see that there was more in it than that. Indeed, she could never remember to have seen him like that before. Oh! if he would only let her help him!

She had not been having a particularly good time herself just lately, but she meant there to be nothing selfish about her unhappiness. There are certain people who are proud of unrequited affection and pass those whom they love with heads raised and a kind of "See what I'm suffering for you!" air. They are incomparable nuisances!

Alice had been rather inclined at first to treat Tony in the same sort of way, but now the one thought that she had was to help him if only he would let her! Perhaps, after all, it was nothing. Probably he'd had a row with the girl last night, or he was worried, perhaps, by Sir Richard.

"Tony," she said, putting her hand for a moment on his arm, "we are pals, aren't we?"

"Why, of course," pulling himself suddenly away from Janet and her possible danger and trying to realise the girl at his side.

"Because," she went on, looking out of the window, "I've been a bit of a nuisance lately—not much of a companion, I'm afraid—out of sorts and grumpy. But now I want you to let me help if there's anything I can do. There might be something, perhaps. You know"—she stopped a moment—"that I saw her down on the beach the other day. If there was anything——"

She stopped awkwardly.

"Look here," he began eagerly; "if you're trying to find out——" Then he stopped. "No, I know, of course you're not. I trust you all right, old girl. But if you only knew what a devil of a lot of things are happening——" He looked at her doubtfully. Then he smiled. "You're a good sort, Alice," he said, "I know you are. I'm damned grateful. Yes, I'm not quite the thing. There are a whole lot of worries." He hesitated again, then he went on: "I tell you what you *can* do—keep the family quiet, you know. Keep them off it, especially the governor. They trust you, all of them, and you can just let them know it's all right. Will you do that?"

He looked at her eagerly.

She smiled back at him. "Yes, old boy, of course. I think I can manage Sir Richard, for a little time at any rate. And in any case, it isn't for very long, because we're all going away in about a week; twenty-seventh or twenty-eighth, I think Lady Gale said."

Tony started. "Did she?" he said. "Are you sure of that, Alice? Because it's important."

"Yes. I heard Lady Gale discussing it with Sir Richard last night."

"By Jove. I'm glad to know that. Well, anyhow, Alice, I'll never forget it if you help us. We want it, by Jove."

She noticed the "we." "Oh, that's all right," she said, smiling back at him. "Count on me, Tony."

At that moment a general move was made. The meal, to everyone's infinite relief, was over. Mrs. Lester got up slowly from her chair, she turned round towards Maradick. For an instant her eyes met his; the corners of her mouth were raised ever so slightly—she smiled at him, then she turned back to his wife.

"Mrs. Maradick," she said, "do come over and sit by the window. There'll be a little air there. The sun's turned the corner now."

But Mrs. Maradick had seen the smile. Suddenly, in a moment, all her suspicions were confirmed. She knew; there could be no doubt. Mrs. Lester, Mrs. Lester and her husband—her husband, James. Dear, how funny! She could have laughed. It was quite a joke. At the same time, she couldn't be well, because the room was turning round, things were swimming; that absurd carpet was rising and flapping at her.

She put her hand on the tea-table and steadied herself; then she smiled back at Mrs. Lester.

"Yes, I'll bring my work over," she said.

The rest of the company seemed suddenly to have disappeared; Maradick and Tony had gone out together, Lady Gale and Alice, followed by Sir Richard and Lester, had vanished through another door; only Mrs. Lawrence remained, working rather dismally at a small square piece of silk that was on some distant occasion to be christened a table-centre.

Mrs. Maradick sometimes walked on her heels to increase her height; she did so now, but her knees were trembling and she had a curious feeling that the smile on her face was fixed there and that it would never come off, she would smile like that always.

As she came towards the table where Mrs. Lester was another strange sensation came to her. It was that she would like to strangle Mrs. Lester.

As she smiled at her across the table her hands were, in imagination, stretching with long twisting fingers and encircling Mrs. Lester's neck. She saw the exact spot; she could see the little blue marks that her fingers would leave. She could see Mrs. Lester's head twisted to one side and hanging in a stupid, silly way over her shoulder. She would draw her fingers very slowly away, because they would be reluctant to let go. Of course it was a very stupid, primitive feeling, because ladies that lived in Epsom didn't strangle other ladies, and there were the girls to be thought of, and it wouldn't really do at all. And so Mrs. Maradick sat down.

"It is quite cool," she said as she brought out her work, "and after such a hot day, too."

Mrs. Lester enjoyed the situation very much. She knew quite well that Maradick had been watching her anxiously all the afternoon. She knew that he was waiting to see what she was going to do about yesterday. She had not been quite sure herself at first. In fact, directly after he had left her she had been furiously angry; and then she had been frightened and had gone to find Fred, and then had cried in her bedroom for half an hour. And then she had dried her eyes and had put on her prettiest dress and had come down to dinner intending to be very stiff and stately towards him. But he had not been there; no one had known where he was. Mrs. Maradick had more or less conveyed that Mrs. Lester could say if she wanted to, but of course she wouldn't.

However, she really didn't know. The evening was stupid, tiresome, and very long. As the hours passed memories grew stronger. No one had ever held her like that before. She had never known such strength. She was crushed, gasping. There was a man! And after all, it didn't matter; there was nothing *wrong* in *that*. Of course he oughtn't to have done it. It was very presumptuous and violent; but then that was just like the man.

It was the kind of thing that he did, the kind of thing, after all, that he was meant to do! In the Middle Ages, of course, would have been his time. She pictured him with some beautiful maiden swung across the crupper, and the husband, fist in air but impotent—that was the kind of man.

And so she had smiled at him, to show him that, after all, she wasn't very angry. Of course, she couldn't be always having it; she didn't even mean that she'd altogether forgiven him, but the whole situation was given an extra piquancy by the presence of Mrs. Maradick. She didn't mean any harm to the poor little spectacle of a woman, but to carry him off from under her very nose! Well! it was only human nature to enjoy it!

"You must come and see us, dear Mrs. Maradick, both of you, when you're back in town. We shall so like to see more of you. Fred has taken enormously to your husband, and it's so seldom that he really makes a friend of anyone."

"Thank you so much," said Mrs. Maradick, smiling, "we'll be sure to look you up. And you must come out to Epsom one day. People call it a suburb, but really, you know, it's quite country. As I often say, it has all the advantages of the town and country with none of their disadvantages. A motor-van comes down from Harrods' every day."

"That must be delightful," said Mrs. Lester.

"And Lord Roseberry living so near makes it so pleasant. He's often to be seen driving; he takes great interest in the school, you know—Epsom College for doctors' sons—and often watches their football!"

"Oh yes," said Mrs. Lester.

Mrs. Maradick paused and looked out of the window. What was she going to do? What was she going to do? The great black elms outside the window swept the blue sky like an arch. A corner of the lawn shone in the sun a brilliant green, and directly opposite a great bed of sweet-peas fluttered like a swarm of coloured butterflies with the little breeze. What was she to do?

She was feeling now, suddenly, for the first time in her selfish, self-centred life utterly at a loss. She had never been so alone before. There had always been somebody. At Epsom there had been heaps of people; and, after all, if the worst came to the worst, there had always been James. She had never, in all these years, very actively realised that he was there, because she had never happened to want him; there had always been so many other people.

Now suddenly all these people had gone. Epsom was very, very far away, and, behold, James wasn't there either!

She realised, too, that if it had been some one down in the town, a common woman as she had at first imagined it, it would not have hurt so horribly. But that some one like Mrs. Lester should care for James, should really think him worth while, seemed at one blow to disturb, indeed to destroy all the theories of life in general and of James in particular that had governed her last twenty years.

What could she see? What could any one of them see in him? she asked herself again and again.

Meanwhile, of course, it must all be stopped somehow. They must go away at once. Or perhaps it would be better to be quiet for a day or two and see. They would all be gone in a week or so. And then Epsom again, and everything as it had been and none of this—she called it "intrigue."

"I'm so glad," said Mrs. Lester, smiling, "that Tony Gale has taken so strong a liking to your husband. It's so good for a boy of that age to have some one older. . . . He's a charming boy, of course, but they always need some one at that age just to prevent them from doing anything foolish."

This was fishing, Mrs. Maradick at once felt. She couldn't see exactly what Mrs. Lester wanted, but she *did* want something, and she wasn't going to get it. She had a sudden desire to prove to Mrs. Lester that she was a great deal more to her husband than appeared on the surface. A great deal more, of course, than any of the others were. For the first time in their married life she spoke of him with enthusiasm.

"Ah! James," she said, "is splendid with young men. Only I could really tell the world what he has been to some of them. They take to him like anything. There's something so strong and manly about him—and yet he's sympathetic. Oh! I could tell you——" She nodded her head sagaciously.

"Yes," said Mrs. Lester; "I can't tell you how I admire him, how we all do, in fact. He must be very popular in Epsom."

"Well, as a matter of fact he rather keeps himself to himself there. They all like him enormously, of course; but he doesn't want anything really except just the family—myself and the girls, you know. He's a very domestic man, he always has been."

"Yes, one can see that," said Mrs. Lester, smiling. "It's delightful when one sees that nowadays. It so seldom happens, I am afraid. You must be very proud of him."

"I am," said Mrs. Maradick.

The impulse to lean over and take Mrs. Lester's head and slowly bend it back until the bones cracked was almost too strong to be resisted.

Mrs. Maradick pricked her finger and stopped the blood with her handkerchief. Both ladies were silent. The last rays of the sun as it left the corner of the lawn fell in a golden shower upon the sweet-peas.

Mrs. Lawrence could be heard counting her stitches.

Meanwhile Mrs. Lester's smile had had its effect upon Maradick. He had waited, tortured, for the smile to come, but now it was all right. They were still friends. He could not see it any farther than that. After all, why should he trouble to look at it any more deeply? They were friends. He would be able to talk to her again; he would see her smile again. If she did not want him to behave like that, if she did not want him to hold her hand, he was ready to obey in anything. But they were still friends. She was not angry with him.

His depression took wings and fled. He put his arm on Tony's shoulder as they went down the stairs. "Well, old chap," he said, "I'm off to see Morelli now. You can bet that it will be all right. Things looked a bit funny last night. They always do when one's tired and it's dark. Last night, you see, you imagined things."

But Tony looked up at him quietly with grave eyes.

"No," he said, "there was nothing to imagine. It was just as I told you. Nothing happened. But I know now that there's something in what the chaps in the town said. I believe in devils now. But my God, Maradick"—he clutched the other's arm—"Janet's down there. It isn't for myself I care. He can do what he likes to me. But it's *her*, we must get her away or there's no knowing. . . . I didn't sleep a wink last night, thinking what he might be doing to her. He may carry her away somewhere, where one can't get at her; or he may do—God knows. But that's what he said last night, just that!

that she wasn't for me or for anyone, that she was *never* for anyone—that he would keep her." Tony broke off.

"I'm silly with it all, I think," he said, "it's swung me off my balance a bit. One can't think; but it would be the most enormous help if you'd go and see. It's the uncertainty that's so awful. If I could just know that it's all right . . . and meanwhile I'm thinking out plans. It's all got to happen jolly soon now. I'll talk when you come back. It's most awfully decent of you. . . ."

Maradick left him pacing the paths with his head down and his hands clenched behind his back.

He found Morelli sitting quietly with Janet and Miss Minns in the garden. They had had tea out there, and the tea-things glittered and sparkled in the sun. It would have been difficult to imagine anything more peaceful. The high dark red brick of the garden walls gave soft velvet shadows to the lawn; the huge tree in the corner flung a vast shade over the beds and paths; rooks swung slowly above their heads through the blue spacious silence of the summer evening; the air was heavy with the scent of the flowers.

Morelli came forward and greeted Maradick almost eagerly. "What! Have you had tea? Sure! We can easily have some more made, you know. Come and sit down. Have a cigar—a pipe? Right. I wondered when you were going to honour us again. But we had young Gale in yesterday evening for quite a long time."

Janet, with a smile of apology, went indoors. Miss Minns was knitting at a distance. This was obviously the right moment to begin, but the words would not come. It all seemed so absurd in this delicious garden with the silence and the peace, and, for want of a better word, the sanity of it all; all the things that Maradick had been thinking, Tony's story and the fantastic scene in the market-place last night, that and the ideas that had sprung from it, were all so out of line now. People weren't melodramatic like that, only one had at times a kind of mood that induced one to think things, absurd things.

But Morelli seemed to be waiting for Maradick to speak. He sat gravely back in his chair watching him. It was almost, Maradick thought, as though he knew what he had come there for. It was natural enough that Morelli should expect him, but he had not imagined precisely that kind of quiet waiting for him. He had to clear all the other ideas that he had had, all the kind of picture that he had come with, out of his head. It was a different kind of thing, this sheltered, softly coloured garden with its deep shadows and high reds and browns against the blue of the sky. It was not, most emphatically it was not, melodrama.

The uncomfortable thought that the quiet eyes and grave mouth had guessed all this precipitated Maradick suddenly into speech. The peace and silence of the garden seemed to mark his words with a kind of indecency. He hurried and stumbled over his sentences.

"Yes, you know," he said. "I thought I'd just come in and see you—well, about young Gale. He told me—I met him—he gave me to understand— that he was here last night." Maradick felt almost ashamed.

"Yes," said Morelli, smiling a little, "we had some considerable talk."

"Well, he told me, that he had said something to you about your daughter. You must forgive me if you think that I'm intrusive at all."

Morelli waved a deprecating hand.

"But of course I'm a friend of the boy's, very fond of him. He tells me that he spoke about your daughter. He loves Miss Morelli."

Maradick stopped abruptly.

"Yes," said Morelli gently, "he did speak to me about Janet. But of course you must look on it as I do; two such children. Mind you, I like the boy, I liked him from the first. He's the sort of young Englishman that we can't have too much of, you know. My girl wouldn't be likely to find a better, and I think she likes him. But of course they're too young, both of them. You must feel as I do."

Could this be the mysterious terror who had frightened Tony out of his wits? This gentle, smiling, brown-faced little man lying back there so placidly in his chair with his eyes half closed? It was impossible on the face of it. Absurd! And perhaps, after all, who knew whether it wouldn't be better to wait? If Morelli really felt like that about it and was prepared eventually to encourage the idea; and then after all Janet might be introduced gradually to the family. They would see, even Sir Richard must see at last, what a really fine girl she was, fine in every way. He saw her as she had stood up to meet him as he stepped across the lawn, slim, straight, her throat rising like a white stem of some splendid flower, her clear dark eyes pools of light.

Oh! they must see if you gave them time. And, after all, this was rather carrying the matter with a high hand, this eloping and the rest!

The garden had a soothing, restful effect upon him, so that he began to be sleepy. The high red walls rose about him on every side, the great tree flung its shadow like a cloud across, and the pleasant little man smiled at him with gentle eyes.

"Oh yes, of course, they are very young."

"And then there's another thing," went on Morelli. "I don't know, of course, but I should say that young Gale's parents have something else in view for him in the way of marriage. They're not likely to take some one of whom they really know nothing at all. . . . They'll want, naturally enough, I admit, something more." He paused for a moment, then he smiled. "But perhaps you could tell me," he said.

Maradick had again the sensation that the man knew perfectly well about the whole affair, about the Gales and Alice and Tony, and even perhaps about himself. He also felt that whatever he could say would be of no use at all; that Morelli was merely playing with him, as a cat plays with a mouse.

Meanwhile he had nothing to say.

"Well, you see," he began awkwardly, "as a matter of fact, they haven't had the opportunity—the chance, so to speak, of knowing—of meeting Miss Morelli yet. When they do— —"

"They've been here," broke in Morelli quietly, "some weeks now. Lady Gale could have called, I suppose, if she had been interested. But I gather that Gale hasn't told her; hasn't, indeed, told any of them. You see," he added almost apologetically, "she is my only child; she has no mother; and I must, in a way, see to these things."

Maradick agreed. There was really nothing to be said. It was perfectly true that the Gales didn't want Janet, wouldn't, in fact, hear of her. The whole affair seemed to lose a great deal of its immediate urgency in this quiet and restful place, and the fact that Morelli was himself so quiet and restful was another motive for waiting. The girl was in no danger; and, strangely enough, Maradick seemed to have lost for the first time since he had known Morelli the sense of uneasy distrust that he had had for the man; he was even rather ashamed of himself for having had it at all.

"Well," he said slowly, "you don't object to things being as they are for a time. I'm sure Tony will see it sensibly, and perhaps Miss Morelli might meet Lady Gale. It would be a pity, don't you think, to put a stop altogether to the acquaintance?"

"Ah yes," said Morelli, "certainly. We'll say no more about it for the present. It was very pleasant as it was. As I told you, I like young Gale; and who knows?—perhaps one day— —"

Maradick sat back in his chair and looked up lazily at the sky. It was all very pleasant and comfortable here in this delicious old garden; let the matter rest.

And then Morelli proved himself a most delightful companion. He seemed to have been everywhere and to have seen everything. And it was not only knowledge. He put things so charmingly; he had a thousand ways of looking at things, a thousand ways of showing them off, so that you saw them from new points of view, and the world was an amusing, entertaining treasure-house of wonders.

The minutes slipped by; the sun went down the sky, the shadow of the tree spread farther and farther across the lawn, the pinks and roses lay in bunches of red and pink and yellow against the dark background of the wall.

Maradick got up to go and Morelli walked with him, his hat set back, his hands in his pockets. As they entered the house he said, "Ah, by the way, there was that Spanish sword that I promised to show you. It's a fine thing and of some value; I'll bring it down."

He disappeared up the stairs.

Suddenly Janet was at Maradick's elbow. He had not seen her coming, but she looked round with quick, startled eyes. Her white dress shone against the dark corners of the hall. He saw, too, that her face was very white and there were dark lines under her eyes; to his surprise she put her hand on his arm, she spoke in a whisper.

"Mr. Maradick, please," she said, "I must speak to you. There is only a minute. Please listen, it's dreadfully important. Tony says you want to help us. There isn't anyone else;" she spoke in little gasps and her hand was at her throat as though she found it difficult to breathe. "I must get away somehow, at once, I don't know what will happen if I don't. You don't know father, and I can't explain now, but I'm terribly frightened; and he will suddenly—I can see it coming." She was nearly hysterical; he could feel her whole body trembling. "Tony said something yesterday that made father dreadfully angry. Tony ought not to have come; anything might happen when father's like that. If you can't help me I will run away; but you *must* help."

She grew calmer but still spoke very rapidly, still throwing frightened glances at the stairs. "Listen; on the twenty-seventh—that's Thursday—father's going away. He's going to Pendragon for the whole day; it was arranged long ago. He was to have taken me, but he has decided not to; I heard him tell Miss Minns—I——"

But suddenly she was gone again, as quietly as she had come. He saw now that there had been a door behind her leading to some room. He looked up and saw that Morelli was coming downstairs carrying the sword. Five minutes afterwards he had left the house.

It had all happened so suddenly, so fantastically, that it was some minutes before he could straighten it out. First he had the impression of her, very young, very frightened, very beautiful. But there was no question of the reality of her terror. All the feelings of danger that he had had with Tony last night came crowding back now. It was true then? It hadn't only been Tony's imagination. After all, Janet must know. She hadn't lived with her father all those years without knowing more about it than he, Maradick, possibly could. She wouldn't have been likely to have taken the risk of seeing him like that if there was nothing in it, if there was only the mere ordinary domestic quarrel in it. But above all, there was the terror in her eyes; that he had seen.

He could not, he must not, leave her then. There was danger threatening her somewhere. The whole business had entirely changed from his original conception of it. It had been, at first, merely the love affair of a boy and girl, and he, from a pleasant sense of romance and a comfortable conviction that it was all good for his middle-aged solidity, had had his share in it. But now it had become suddenly a serious and most urgent affair, perhaps even a matter of life and of death.

He turned, as he had turned before, to Punch. There was no time to lose, and he was the man to see about it; he must find him at once.

The lights were coming out in the town as he passed through the streets; there were not many people about, and the twilight was lingering in the air so that all the colours of the sky and the houses and the white stretches of pavement had a faint pure light. The sky was the very tenderest blue, and the last gleam from the setting sun still lingered about the dark peaks and pinnacles of the houses.

He was soon on the outskirts of the town, and at last he trod the white high road. At the farther turn were Punch's lodgings. There was a full round globe of a moon, and below him he could hear the distant beating of the sea.

Some one was walking rapidly behind him; he turned round, and to his astonishment saw, as the man came up to him, that it was the very person for whom he was looking.

"Ah! that's splendid, Garrick," he said, "I was just coming for you. I'm a bit worried and I want your advice."

"I'm a bit worried too, sir, as a matter of fact," said Punch, "but if there's anything I can do——"

Maradick saw now that the man was very different from his usual cheerful self. He was looking anxious, and his eyes were staring down the road as though he were expecting to see something.

"What's the matter?" said Maradick.

"Well, it's the dog," said Punch, "Toby, you know. He's missing, been gone all the afternoon. Not that there's very much in that in the ordinary way. He often goes off by 'imself. 'E knows the neighbourhood as well as I do; besides, the people round 'ere know him and know his mind. But I'm uneasy this time. It's foolish, perhaps, but when a man's got only one thing in the world——" He stopped.

"But why should you be uneasy?" said Maradick. The loss of a dog seemed a very small thing compared with his own affairs.

"Well, as a matter of fact, it's Morelli." The lines of Punch's mouth grew hard. "'E's owed me a grudge ever since I spoke to 'im plain about them animals. And 'e knows that I know a good bit, too. He passed me in the market-place two days back, and stopped for an instant and looked at the dog. To them that don't know Morelli that's nothing; but for them that do—'e'd think nothing of having his bit of revenge. And it's late now, and the dog's not home." The little man looked at Maradick almost piteously, as though he wanted to be reassured.

"Oh, I expect it's all right," said Maradick. "Anyhow, I'll come along with you and we can talk as we go."

In a few words he explained what had happened that afternoon.

Punch stopped for a moment in the road and stared into Maradick's face.

"Get 'er awāy, sir," he said, "whatever you do, get 'er away. I know the girl; she wouldn't have spoken to you like that unless there was something very much the matter. And I know the man; there's nothing 'e'd stop at when 'e's roused."

"But why," said Maradick, "if he feels like this about it did he let them go about together? He helped them in every way. He seemed to love to have Tony there. I can't understand it."

"Ah, sir, if you take Morelli as an ordinary man you won't understand 'im. But 'e's a kind of survival. 'E loves to be cruel, as they did in the beginning of things when they didn't know any better. It's true. I've seen it once or twice in my life. It's a lust like any other lust, so that your body quivers with the pleasure of it. But there's more in it than that. You see 'e wants to have young things about 'im. 'E's always been like that; will play with kittens and birds and puppies, and then p'r'aps, on a sudden, kill them. That's why he took to young Gale, because of 'is youth. And 'e liked to watch them together; but now, when young Gale comes and talks of marriage, why, that means that they both leave 'im and 'e can't play with them any more, so 'e'll kill them instead. Take 'er away, sir, take 'er away."

They were out now upon the moor that ran between the woods and the sea; the world was perfectly still save for the distant bleating of some sheep and the monotonous tramp of the waves on the shore far below them. There was no sign of any other human being; the moon flung a white unnatural light about the place.

Punch walked with his eyes darting from side to side; every now and again he whistled, but there was no answering bark.

"It may seem a bit absurd to you, sir," Punch said almost apologetically, "to be fussing this way about a dog, but 'e's more to me than I could ever explain. If I hadn't got 'im to talk to and have about at nights and kind o' smile at when you're wanting company the world would be another kind of place."

Maradick tried to fix his mind on Punch's words, but the ghostliness of the place and the hour seemed to hang round him so that he could not think of anything, but only wanted to get back to lights and company. Every now and again he turned round because he fancied that he heard steps. Their feet sank into the soft soil and then stumbled over tufts of grass. Faint mists swept up from the sea and shadowed the moon.

Behind them the lights of the town twinkled like the watching eye of some mysterious enemy. A bird rose in front of them with shrill protesting cries, and whirled, screaming, into the skies.

Punch seemed to be talking to himself. "Toby, boy, where are you? Toby, old dog. You know your master and you wouldn't hide from your master. It's time to be getting home, Toby. Time for bed, old boy. Damn the dog, why don't 'e come? Toby, old boy!"

Every few minutes he started as though he saw it, and he would run forward a few paces and then stop. And indeed, in the gathering and shifting mist that went and came and took form and shape, there might have been a thousand white dogs wandering, an army of dogs, passing silently, mysteriously across the moor.

"Toby, old boy, it's time to be getting back. 'E was that used to the place you couldn't imagine 'is being lost anywhere round about. 'E was that cunning . . ."

But the army of dogs passed silently by, curving with their silent feet in and out of the mists. One new dog had joined their ranks. He fell in at the rear and went by with the others; but his master did not see them.

Suddenly the mists broke and the moon shone out across the moor like a flame. The moon leapt into the light. A little to the right on a raised piece of ground lay something white.

The army of dogs had vanished. The woods, the moor, the sea, were bathed in white colour.

Punch ran forward with a cry; he was down on his knees and his arms were round the dog's body.

He bent down, and for a moment there was perfect silence, only, in a far distant field, some sheep was crying. Then he looked up.

The tears were rolling down his face; he lifted his hand and brushed them back. "It's Toby. My dog! 'E's been killed. Something's torn 'im. . . ."

He bent down and picked it up and held it in his arms. "Toby, old dog, it's time to go back. It's all right; 'e hasn't hurt you, old boy. It's all right." He broke off. "Curse him," he said, "curse him! 'E did it—I know his marks—I'll kill 'im for it." His hands fell down to his side. "Toby, old dog! Toby. . . ."

The moon crept back again behind the mist. In the shadow the man sat nursing the dog in his arms.

Far below him sounded the sea.

PART III
THE TOWER

CHAPTER XVI
MRS. LESTER, TOO, WOULD LIKE IT
TO BE THE TWENTY-SEVENTH BUT
MARADICK IS AFRAID OF THE DEVIL

On Monday the 24th the weather broke. Cold winds swept up from the sea, mists twisted and turned about the hotel, the rain beat in torrents against the panes. In all the rooms there were fires, and it seemed impossible that, only the day before, there should have been a burning, dazzling sun.

It was after lunch, and Lady Gale and Tony were sitting over the fire in the drawing-room. Tony had been obviously not himself during these last few days, and his mother felt that her silence could last a very little time longer. However, matters were at length approaching a crisis. Things must decide themselves one way or the other in a day or two, for Sir Richard had, at lunch, announced his intention of departing on Saturday the 29th; that is, they had the inside of a week, and then Treliss, thank Heaven, would be left behind. Surely nothing very much could happen in a week.

Her earlier feeling, that above all she did not want Tony to miss this girl if she were the right one for him, had yielded now to a kind of panic. All that she could think of now was to get him away. There was a look in his eyes that she had never seen in his face before. It was a look that aged him, that robbed him altogether of that delightful youth and vitality that had been his surprising, his charming gift! But there was more than a look of weariness and distress, there was positive fright there!

She watched him when he was in the room with her, and she had seen him suddenly start and tremble, fling back his head as though he expected to find some one behind him. He, her boy Tony, who had never been afraid of anyone or anything. And then, too, she had seen a new look of determination in his mouth and eyes during these last days. His mind was made up to something, but to what she was too afraid to think!

She must get him away, and she had heard her husband's decision about Saturday with tremendous relief. She had watched Tony's face at the announcement. But it had not changed at all; only, for a moment he had looked quickly across at Maradick; it had apparently not startled him.

His indifference frightened her. If he was taking it so calmly then he must have decided on something that this date could not affect, on something probably before the date? But what could he do before Saturday? She seemed to miss altogether the obvious thing that he could do.

But it had been seldom enough that she had had him to herself during these last weeks, and now she snatched eagerly at her opportunity. She sat on one side of the fire, one hand up to shield her face, her rings glittering in the firelight; her brown dress stood out against the white tiles of the fireplace and her beautiful snow-white hair crowned her head gloriously.

Tony sat at her feet, one hand in hers. He stared straight before him into the fire. She had noticed during these last three days a delightful tenderness towards her. His attitude to her had always been charming, courteous, affectionate and yet companionable; but now he seemed to want to do everything that he could to show her that he loved her. And yet though she valued and treasured this it also frightened her. It was a little as though he were preparing for some departure, at any rate some change, that might hurt her.

Well, they were going at the end of the week, only a few more days.

He took her fingers and stroked them. His hand stopped at the wedding ring and he passed his thumb across it.

"I say, mother," he looked up in her face with a little laugh, "I suppose you'd say that you'd rather lose anything in the world than that."

"Yes, dear, it's very precious;" but she sighed.

"I suppose it is. It must be ripping having something that is just yours and nobody else's, that you simply don't share with anyone. It must be ripping having somebody that belongs to you and that you belong to; just you two."

"Yes, But that ring means more to me than that. It means you and Rupert as well as your father. It means all those hours when you screamed and kicked, and the day when you began to talk, and the first adventurous hours when you tried to cross the nursery floor. And yes, a thousand things besides."

"Dear old mater," he said softly. "It's been just ripping having you. You've always understood so splendidly. Some chaps' mothers I've seen, and they don't know their sons in the very least. They do all the things that are most likely to drive them wild, and they never seem to be able to give them a bit what they want."

"Yes, but it works both ways," she answered. "A son's got to try and understand his mother too. It's no use their leaving it all to her, you know."

"No, of course not." Then he turned his body round and looked her in the face. "But you do understand so splendidly. You always have understood. You see, you trust a fellow." Then he added quickly, "You're trusting me now, aren't you?"

"Yes," she answered, looking at him steadily, "perfectly. Only, just these last few days, perhaps I've been a little tiny bit worried. You haven't been looking happy, and then I'm always worried; it's so seldom that you're not all right."

"But you'd rather not know—what's going on, I mean. It's all right, perfectly right, and if it wasn't—if it wasn't right for you, I mean, as well as for me—I wouldn't go on with it for a moment. Only it's dreadfully important."

"Yes, dear, I know. And if Mr. Maradick knows about it——"

"He's a brick, isn't he?" Tony interrupted eagerly. "You know, so few middle-aged men can understand the point of view of a chap who's only about twenty-five. They are either fatherly and patronising or schoolmasterly and bossing, or kind of wise and beneficent; but Maradick's most awfully young really, and yet he's wise too. He's a ripper."

He stopped. They neither of them spoke for some minutes. "It will be quite all right, mother," he said, "very soon. Just now things are a little difficult, but we'll pull through."

He got up and stood looking down at her. "You are a brick to trust me and not to ask," he said. "It would make things so awfully difficult if you asked." He bent down and kissed her. "It's a bit of luck having you," he said.

But as soon as he had left the room his face was serious again. He passed Mrs. Lester on the stairs and smiled and hurried on. It was all very well; she was there, of course, real enough and all that sort of thing, but she simply didn't count for him at that moment, she didn't exist, really, any more than the hotel or the garden did. Nothing existed except that house in the town with Janet somewhere in it waiting for him to set her free.

That was the one point on which his eyes were now fixed. In his earlier days it had, perhaps, been one of his failings—that he had run rather too eagerly after too many interests, finding in everything so immediate an excitement that he forgot the purpose of yesterday in the purpose of to-day. It had always been the matter with him that he had too many irons in the fire. Life was so full and such fun!—that had been the excuse. *Now* it was deadly earnest.

But it was the first time that the world had so resolved into one single point for him. He was already years older; these last days had made him that, the uncertainties, the indecisions, the fluctuating enthusiasms, the passing from wonder to wonder. All these had solidified into one thing, and one thing only—Janet, how to get her out, how to marry her, how to have her for always; the rest of the world was in shadow.

To-day was Monday; Tuesday, Wednesday, and then Thursday, Thursday the 27th. That was the day on which everything must be done. He was thinking it all out, they had got that one chance. If they missed it Morelli would be back, and for ever. They must not miss it.

But he was perfectly calm about it. His agitation seemed curiously to have left him. He was cold and stern and absolutely collected. He and Maradick were going to pull it through.

He could not find Maradick. He searched for him in the dining-room, the passages, the billiard-room.

No. The servants hadn't seen him. Mrs. Maradick was with Mrs. Lawrence in one of the drawing-rooms; no, they hadn't see him, he had disappeared after lunch.

Mrs. Maradick smiled. "Find Mrs. Lester" was the advice that she would have given him. She went back to her novel with tightly closed mouth and refused to talk to Mrs. Lawrence.

And then Tony suddenly remembered. Of course, he would be up in that old room where he so often went, the room with the gallery. Tony found him there.

The rain was beating furiously against the panes, and there was a very dismal light that struggled across the floor and lost itself hopelessly in the dark corners under the gallery. Maradick was sitting close up against the window, reading in the rather feeble light. He looked up when he saw Tony and put his book down.

"Ah, Tony, I was coming down to find you; Sir Richard's decision at lunch pretty well settles things, doesn't it? We must move at once."

He looked up at the boy and saw the age in his face.

"Don't worry," he said. "We're going to pull it through all right."

"Oh, I'm not worrying," Tony answered shortly. "It's too damned serious, and besides, there's no time." He paused as though he were collecting his thoughts, and then he went on. "Look here, I've thought it all out. I've been able to write to Janet and have had several letters from her. She's plucky, my word, you can't think! Anyhow, that beast's all right for the moment, it seems, only he keeps looking at her as though he was meaning to do something, and she's terribly frightened, poor little girl. But he's going on Thursday all right, and that's when we've got to do the trick."

"Yes," said Maradick. "I'm absolutely at your service." Their positions had changed. Tony was taking the lead.

"Yes," said Tony, very solemnly and speaking rather quickly. "It's all got to be Thursday. I want you to go off this afternoon, if you don't very much mind, to that parson I was telling you of—the parson at Tremnan. He knows me and he's a real sportsman. He must do the trick. You can tell him, 1.30 Thursday. Then there's the licence to be got. I'll see to that. I've been here three weeks now, so that's all right. Then it only remains to think about that, I'm going to get 'em—the family, I mean—to go for an expedition on Thursday. Mother will understand if I ask her, and that will get them out of the way. Then we just take a cab, you and I and Janet and Miss Minns."

"Miss Minns?" broke in Maradick.

"Yes," said Tony, still very seriously. "The poor woman's frightened out of her life, and Janet's taken her into her confidence. We're going to take her away with us. She's going to live with us. That'll be all right. She's got more sense than you think. Well, we four drive out to the church and there the thing's done. Then we get back and catch the three o'clock up to town. Then off to Paris that same night; and there you are!"

He stopped and looked at Maradick for a moment.

"The only thing," he said, "is about you."

"About me?" Maradick looked up, smiling.

"Yes. What are we going to do about you? Of course you can come off with us, too, if you like, but then there's your wife and the girls. You couldn't do that very well, I suppose?"

"No," said Maradick, "I couldn't."

"Well, but, you know, if you're left, why then, everybody's got you, so to speak—Morelli, my people, everybody. There's only you to turn on;

you'll have a pretty rotten time. It isn't fair. And even now, you know, if you'd rather get out of it I expect I'll manage."

Maradick said nothing.

"I hadn't really seen how damned selfish it all was until just now. I asked you to come and didn't see it really a bit, what it would all lead to, I mean, and especially for you."

Maradick looked up, laughing.

"My dear boy, do you suppose I, at any rate, haven't seen? Why, from the beginning, from that first night of all when we talked about it, I was responsible; responsible to your mother at any rate, and she's the only person who really matters. As to Morelli, he can do nothing. When I see a girl look as Janet looked the other night, why, then it was time some steps were taken by somebody to get her away."

He put his hand on Tony's arm. "And besides, whatever happened to me, do you suppose that I could ever cease to be grateful for all that you've done for me, your being with me, your showing me a new kind of life altogether? I'd be a bit of a cur if I wasn't ready to help you after that. Nothing that I can do can quite repay you."

"That's all right, then," said Tony. He was a little impatient, just then, of Maradick's approach to sentiment. It was off the mark; it hadn't anything at all to do with Janet, and besides, it was all rot, anyway, to talk about all that he'd done. He'd done nothing. But he didn't, in the least, want to be ungracious. "But that's most awfully good of you, really, and I don't suppose, as a matter of fact, they'll do very much. They can't, anyhow. I'm over age, and I shan't have to go to the governor for money. Besides, it will be all right in a week or two. The governor's like that; I know him, and once the thing's over he'll get over it, because he loathes things being uncomfortable; besides, mother will manage him. Anyhow, are you sure you don't mind going off to the parson? I'd come, too, but I think it would be safer for me on the whole to hang round here this afternoon."

No, Maradick didn't mind. Maradick would like to go; Maradick would do anything. And, as a matter of fact, he wanted to get out and away—away from the house and the people in it, where he could think undisturbed.

He left Tony and started down to the town. His brain was still on fire with his meeting with Mrs. Lester on the evening before. During these last three days they had had very few opportunities of meeting, but the affair had nevertheless advanced with extraordinary rapidity. Then, last night, he had been alone with her, after dinner, in the garden. It had been terribly hot and oppressive, a prelude to the storm that came a few hours later.

There was not a breath of wind; the world might have been of carved stone, so motionless was it. He had had her in his arms; her hands had crept round his neck and had pulled his head down until it rested on her breast. He had been on fire—the world had been on fire—and he had poured into her ear, in fierce hurried words, passion such as it seemed to him no man had ever known before. He had told her the old, old arguments; things that seemed to him absolutely new and fresh. Their marriages had been, both of them, absurd. They had been joined, each of them, to persons who did not understand them, people who did not even care to understand them. After all, what were marriage vows? A few words spoken hurriedly when they could not possibly tell whether there was even a chance of their being able to keep them.

They were not meant to keep them. They had made their mistake, and now they must pay for it; but it was better to break with those bonds now, to have done with them once and for all, than to go on for ever in hypercritical mockery, pretending what they could not feel, acting a lie before God and man.

But now, if they could escape now, away from this stupid country with its stupid conventions, away to some place where they would be happy together for ever until death . . . and so on, and so on; and the leaves and the paths and the dark sky were held together, motionless, by the iron hand of God.

And then some one had in a moment interrupted them; some fool from the hotel. Maradick's fingers itched to be about his throat. "What a close night! Yes, a storm must be coming up. They'd heard very distant thunder; how solemn the sea sounded . . ." and so they had gone into the hotel.

The rain had ceased. The streets stretched in dreary wet lines before him, the skies were leaden grey; from some room the discordant jingle of a piano came down to him, a cart bumped past him through the mud and dirt.

And then suddenly the tower in the market-place sprung upon him. It was literally that, a definite springing out from all the depths of greyness and squalor behind it to meet him. On shining days, when the sky was very blue and the new smart hotel opposite glittered in all its splendour, the tower put on its most sombre cloak of grey and hid itself.

That was no time or place for it when other things could look so brilliant, but now, in the absolutely deserted market-place, when the cobbles glittered in the wet and the windows, like so many stupid eyes, gave back the dead colour of the sky, it took its rightful place.

It seemed to be the one thing that mattered, with its square and sturdy strength, its solidity that bid defiance to all the winds and rains of the world. Puddles lay about its feet and grey windy clouds tugged at its head, but it stood confidently resolute, while the red hotel opposite shrunk back, with its tawdry glitter damped and torn and dishevelled.

So Maradick stood alone in the market-place and looked at it, and suddenly realised it as a symbol. He might have his room from which he looked out and saw the world, and he held it to be good; Tony had shown him that. He might have his freedom, so that he might step out and take the wonderful things that he had seen; Punch had shown him that. But he must also have—oh! he saw it so clearly—his strength, the character to deal with it all, the resolution to carve his own actions rather than to let his actions carve him; and the tower had shown him that!

As he looked at it, he almost bowed his head before it. Foolish to make so much of an old thing like that! Sentimental and emotional with no atom of common-sense in it, but it had come out to meet him just when he wanted it most. It needed all his resolution to persuade himself that it had not a life of its own, that it did not know, like some old, sober, experienced friend, what danger he was running.

He passed out into the country. Although the rain had ceased and the grass was scenting the air with the new fragrance that the storm had given it, the sky was dark and overcast, grey clouds like Valkyries rushed furiously before the wind, and the sea, through the mist, broke into armies of white horses. As far as the eye could reach they kept charging into the grey dun-coloured air and fell back to give way to other furious riders.

The mist crept forward like live things, twisting and turning, forming into pillars and clouds, and then rent by the screaming wind into a thousand tatters.

The road was at a high level, and he could see the coast for some miles bending round until it reached the headland; a line of white foam stretched, with hard and clear outline, from point to point. This was a new Cornwall to him, this grey mysterious thing, hinting at so much, with a force and power almost terrible in its ominous disregard of human individuality. He had thought that the right light for Cornwall was on a day of gold and blue, now he knew that he had not seen half the wonder and fascination; it was here, with this crawling foam, the sharp rocks, the screaming wind and the turning, twisting mist, that she was rightly to be seen.

The wind tore at his coat and beat him about the face. It was incredible that only yesterday there should have been heat and silence and dazzling colour. He pressed forward.

His thought now was that he was glad Mrs. Maradick did not know. Until this morning he had not considered her at all. After all, she had given him a bad twenty years of it, and she had no right to complain. Other men did it with far less excuse.

But there had been something when she had met him at breakfast this morning that he had not understood. She had been almost submissive. She had spoken to him at breakfast as she had never spoken to him in their married life before. She had been gentle, had told Annie not to jingle her teaspoon because it worried father, and had inquired almost timidly what were his plans for the day.

He had felt yesterday that he rather wanted her to see that Mrs. Lester was fond of him; she had driven it into him so often that he was only accepted by people as her husband, that he had no value in himself at all except as a payer of bills. She had even chaffed him about certain ladies of whom she had ironically suggested that he was enamoured. And so it had seemed in its way something of a triumph to show her that he wasn't merely a figurehead, a person of no importance; that there was somebody who found him attractive, several people, indeed. But now he was ashamed. He had scarcely known how to answer her when she had spoken to him so gently. Was she too under influence of the place?

In fact, he did not know what he was going to do. He was tired, worn out; he would not think of it at all. He would see how things turned out.

The character of the day had changed. The mists were still on the sea, but behind them now was the shining of the sun, only as a faint light vaguely discerned, but the water seemed to heave gently as though some giant had felt the coming of the sun and was hurrying to meet it.

The light was held back by a wall of mist, but in places it seemed to be about to break through, and the floor of the sea shone with all the colours of mother of pearl.

The little church stood back from the cliff; it stood as though it had faced a thousand years of storm and rain, as an animal stands with its feet planted wide and its ears well back ready for attack. Its little tower was square and its stone was of weather-beaten grey, only the little windows with deep blue glass caught the haze from the sea and shone like eyes through the stone and across the grass.

The little rectory stood on the other side of the road. It also was minute and absolutely exposed to the elements; here lived the Rev. Mark Anstey, aged eighty-two, quite alone except for the company of five dogs, six cats, three pigeons, a parrot, two tame rabbits, a hedgehog and a great many frogs, these last in a pond near by.

When Maradick came up the road he saw the old man standing in his garden watching the sea. The mist had been drawn back, as a veil is drawn back by a mysterious hand, until it lay only on the horizon. The sea was still grey, but it hinted, as it were, at wonderful colours. You fancied that you could see blue and gold and purple, and yet when you looked again it was still grey. It was as though a sheet of grey gauze had been stretched over a wonderful glittering floor and the colours shone through.

The old man was a magnificent figure of enormous height. He had a great white beard that fell almost to his waist and his snow-white hair had no covering. Three of his dogs were at his side and the five cats sat in a row on his doorstep. He was standing with his hands behind his back and his head up as though to catch the wind.

Maradick introduced himself and stated his errand. The old man shook him warmly by the hand.

"Ah, yes; come in, won't you? Very pleased to meet you, Mr. Maradick. Come into my study and I'll just take down details."

His voice was as clear as a bell, and his eyes, blue as the sea, looked him through and through.

"Here, this is my room. Bit of a mess, isn't it? But a bachelor can't help that, you know; besides, I like a mess, always did."

Whatever it was, it was the right kind of mess. The fireplace was of bright blue tiles; there were books, mostly, it seemed, theological, fishing tackle cumbered one corner, guns another, a writing-desk took up a good deal of the room. The old man filled the place. He really was enormous, and he had a habit of snapping his fingers with a sharp, clicking noise like the report of a pistol. Two deerhounds were lying by the fireplace, and these came to meet him, putting their noses into his hands.

"Ah, ha! Hum—where are we? Oh! yes! Sit down, Mr. Maradick, won't you? Oh, clear those things off the chair—yes—let me see! Anthony Gale— Janet Morelli—what? Morelli? How do you spell it? What? M-o-r-e—oh! yes, thanks! Thursday—1.30. Yes, I know the boy; going to be married, is he? Well, that's a good thing—can't start breeding too young—improves the race—fill the country with children. Married yourself, Mr. Maradick? Ah! that's good."

Maradick wondered whether the name, Morelli, would seem familiar to him, but he had obviously never heard it before. "We don't have many weddings up in this church here, nowadays. They don't come this way much. Just the people down at the cove, you know. . . . Have some tea—oh, yes! you must have some tea."

He rang the bell and a small boy with a very old face came and received orders. "Remarkable thing, you know," said Mr. Anstey when the boy had gone out again. "That boy's twenty-three. You wouldn't think it, now, would you? But it's true. Stopped growing, but he's a good boy; rings the bell in the church, and digs in the garden and all the rest of it. We'll have tea outside. It's warm enough and it's going to be fine, I think. Besides, I always must have my eyes on the sea if it's possible."

They had tea in the little porch over the door; the honeysuckle was still in flower and there were still roses in the beds, a mass of red hollyhocks at the farther end of the garden stood out against the sky. The old man talked of Tony.

"Yes, I've met him several times; a splendid boy, a friend of Garrick's who's brought him up here. Ah, you know Garrick?"

Yes, Maradick knew Garrick.

"Well, there's a man! God made that man all right, even though he isn't often inside a church. He worships in his own kind way, you know, as most of us do, if you only look into it. God's more tolerant than most of us parsons, I can tell you, and understands people a lot better, too. Not that we parsons aren't a pretty good lot on the whole, but we're a bit apt to have our eyes fixed on our little differences and our creeds and our little quarrels when we ought to be having our eyes on the sky. Ah, if I could get a few of those gentlemen who are quarrelling there up in London and just set them here in this garden in rows with that to look at!" He waved his hand at the sea.

The hill bent at the end of the garden and disappeared, and beyond the bend there was nothing but the sea. The blue was beginning to steal into it in little lakes and rivers of colour.

"That's God's work, you know; take your atheist and show him that."

He talked about Tony.

"A nice boy, if ever there was one. But what's this about marriage? Well, I suppose I mustn't ask questions. You're a friend of his and you're looking after him. But that's a boy who'll never go wrong; I'd trust any woman to him."

Soon Maradick got up to go. This man had impressed him strangely; he had got that thing that Tony and Punch had got, but he had used it in the right way. There was not only the sentiment, the emotion of the view, there was the strength of the tower as well.

Maradick left him standing gazing at the sea. His figure seemed to fill the sky.

On his way back the sky grew clearer, and although the sun was never actually to be seen its light was felt in the air and over the sea. There was a freshness about everything around him. The sheaves on the hills, the grass waving on the moor, the sheep clustered in their pens, the hard white clean lines of the road surrounded him with new life. He felt suddenly as though he had been standing during these last days in a dark, close room with the walls pressing about him and no air.

And yet he knew, as he neared the town, that the fascination, the temptation was beginning to steal about him again. As the door of the hotel closed round him, the tower, the clear colours of the land and sky, the man standing gazing at the sea—these things were already fading away from him.

He had nearly finished dressing when his wife came into his room. She talked a little, but had obviously nothing very much to say. He was suddenly conscious that he avoided looking at her. He busied himself over his tie, his shirt; it was not, he told himself angrily, that he was ashamed of facing her. After all, why should he be? All that he had done was to kiss another woman, and most men had done that in their time. He was no saint and, for that matter, neither was she. Nobody was a saint; but he was uncomfortable, most certainly uncomfortable. Looking into the glass as he brushed his hair, he caught sight of her staring at him in a strange way, as though she were trying to make up her mind about something.

Puzzled—puzzled—puzzled about what? Perhaps it was just possible that she too was just discovering that she had missed something in all these years. Perhaps she too was suddenly wondering whether she had got everything from life that she wanted; perhaps her mind was groping back to days when there did seem to be other things, when there were, most obviously, other people who had found something that she had never even searched for.

The thought touched him strangely. After all, what if there was a chance of starting again? Lord! what a fool he was to talk like that! Didn't he know that in another two hours' time he would be with the other woman, his pulses beating to a riotous tune that she, his wife, could never teach him; you couldn't cure the faults, the mistakes, the omissions of twenty years in three weeks.

Dinner that night was of the pleasantest. Tony was at his very best. He seemed to have recovered all his lost spirits. That white, tense look had left his face, the strain had gone out of his eyes; even the waiters could not keep back their smiles at his laughter.

They discussed the hour of departure and Tony did not turn a hair. Mrs. Lester glanced for an instant at Maradick, but that was all.

"I'm afraid I shall have to go up on Thursday night," said Lester. "One's publishers, you know, need continual looking after, and if I don't see them on Friday morning it may be some time before I get a chance again. But I'll leave my wife in your hands, Lady Gale. I know she'll be safe enough."

"Oh! we'll look after her, Lester," said Tony, laughing; "won't we, Milly? We'll look after you all the time. I'll constitute myself your special knight-errant, Milly. You shall want for nothing so long as I am there."

"Thank you, Tony," said Mrs. Lester.

It was a fine enough night for them all to go into the garden, and very soon Maradick and Mrs. Lester were alone. It was all about him once again, the perfume that she used, the rustle of her dress, the way that her hair brushed his cheek. But behind it, in spite of himself, he saw his wife's face in the mirror, he saw Tony, he saw the tower, and he felt the wind about his body.

She bent over him and put her arms about his neck; but he put them back.

"No," he said almost roughly, "we've got to talk; this kind of thing must be settled one way or the other."

"Please, don't be cross." Her voice was very gentle; he could feel her breath on his cheek. "Ah, if you knew what I'd been suffering all day, waiting for you, looking forward, aching for these minutes; no, you mustn't be cruel to me now."

But he stared in front of him, looking into the black depths of the trees that surrounded them on every side.

"No, there's more in it than I thought. What are we going to do? What's going to happen afterwards? Don't you see, we must be sensible about it?"

"No," she said, holding his hand. "There is no time for that. We can be sensible afterwards. Didn't you hear at dinner? Fred is going away on Thursday night; we have that, at any rate."

"No," he said, roughly breaking away from her, "we must not."

But she pressed up against him. Her arm passed slowly round his neck and her fingers touched, for a moment, his cheek. "No; listen. Don't you see what will happen if we don't take it? All our lives we'll know that we've missed it. There's something that we might have had—some life, some experience. At any rate we had lived once, out of our stuffy lives, our stupid, dull humdrum. Oh! I tell you, you mustn't miss it! You'll always regret, you'll always regret!"

Her whole body was pressed against his. He tried to push her away with his hand. For a moment he thought that he saw Tony watching him and then turning away, sadly, scornfully. And then it swept over him like a wave. He crushed her in his arms; for some minutes the world had stopped. Then again he let her go.

"Ah!" she said, smiling and touching her dress with her fingers. "You are dreadfully strong. I did not know how strong. But I like it. And now Thursday night will be ours; glorious, wonderful, never to be forgotten. I must go. They'll be wondering. You'd better not come back with me. Good-night, darling!" She bent down, kissed him and disappeared.

But he sat there, his hands gripping his knees.

What sort of scum was he? He, a man?

This then was the fine new thing that Tony and Punch had shown him. *This* the kind of world! *This* the great experience. Life!

No. With all his soul he knew that it was not; with all his soul he knew that the devil and all his angels were pressing about his path—laughing, laughing.

And the moon rose behind the trees and the stars danced between the branches.

CHAPTER XVII
MORNING AND AFTERNOON OF THE TWENTY-SEVENTH—TONY, MARADICK, JANET, AND MISS MINNS HAVE A RIDE AFTER THE WEDDING

But Mrs. Lester had not the courage of her convictions. Those convictions were based very largely on an audacious standing up against Providence, although she herself would never have seen it in that light. In each of her "affairs" she went breathlessly forward, as it were on tiptoe, with eyes staring and heart beating; wondering what would be the dangers, gasping at possibly startling adventures.

But the real thing had never met her before. The two or three men who had been concerned in her other experiences had understood quite as well as she did that it was only a game, *pour passer le temps*, and a very pleasant way of passing it too. But this man was taking it very differently. It was no game at all to him; he did not look as though he could play a game if he wanted to. But it was not Maradick who frightened her; it was herself. She had never gone so far as this before, and now as she undressed she was suddenly terribly frightened.

Her face seemed white and ghostly in the mirror, and in a sudden panic, she turned on all the lights. Then the blaze frightened her and she turned them all out again, all save the one over the mirror.

She sat gazing into it, and all the dark corners of the room seemed to gather round her like living things; only her white face stared out of the glass. If Fred hadn't been so horribly humdrum, if she hadn't known so thoroughly every inch of him, every little trick that he had, every kind of point of view that he ever had about anything, then this never would have happened. Because, really, he had been a very good husband to her, and she was really fond of him; when one came to think of it, he had been much better than a good many husbands she had known. She leaned back in her chair and looked at herself.

It had once been more than mere fondness, it had been quite exciting; she smiled, reminiscences crowded about her . . . dear old Fred!

But she pulled herself up with a jerk. That, after all, wasn't the point; the point, the thing that mattered, was Thursday night. Out there in the garden, when he had held her like that, a great lawlessness had come upon her. It was almost as though some new spirit had entered into her and was showing her things, was teaching her emotions that she had never been shown or learnt before. And, at that moment, it had seemed to her the one thing worth having.

She had never lived before. Life was to be counted by moments, those few golden moments that the good gods gave to one, and if one didn't take them, then and there, when they were offered, why then, one had never lived at all, one might as well never have been born.

But now, as she sat there alone in her room, she was realising another thing—that those moments had their consequences. What were they going to do afterwards? What would Maradick do? What, above all, would her own attitude to Fred be? She began, very slowly, to realise the truth, that the great laws are above creeds and all dogmas because they are made from man's necessities, not from his superstitions. What was she going to do?

She knew quite well what she would do if she were left there alone on Thursday night, and at the sudden thought of it she switched off the light and plunged the room into darkness. She lay in bed waiting for Fred to come up. She felt suddenly very unprotected. She would ask him to take her with him on Thursday, she would make some excuse; he would probably be glad.

She heard him undressing in the next room. He was whistling softly to himself; he stumbled over something and said "Damn." She heard him gargle as he brushed his teeth. He hummed a song of the moment, "I wouldn't go home in the dark"; and then she heard him stepping across the carpet towards the bed, softly lest he should wake her. He got into bed and grunted with satisfaction as he curled up into the sheets; his toe touched her foot and she shivered suddenly because it was cold.

"Hullo, old girl," he said, "still awake?"

She didn't answer. Then she turned slowly round towards him.

"Fred," she said, "I think I'll come away with you on Thursday after all." But, as she said it to him, she was suddenly afraid of his suspecting something. He would want to know the reason. "It's not," she added hurriedly, "that I'm not perfectly happy here. I'm enjoying it awfully, it's delightful; but, after all, there isn't very much point in my staying here. I don't want to after you're gone."

But he was sleepy. He yawned.

"I'm awfully tired, dear. We'll talk about it to-morrow. But anyhow, I don't quite see the point. You won't want to be pottering about London with me. I'm only up there for business — these beastly publishers," he yawned again. "You'd be bored, you know; much better stay here with Lady Gale. Besides, it's all arranged." His voice died off into a sleepy murmur.

But the terror seemed to gather about her in the darkness. She saw with amazing vision. She did not want to be left; she must not be left.

She put her hand on his arm.

"Fred, please — it's important; I don't want to stay."

And then she was suddenly frightened. She had said too much. He would want to know why she didn't want to stay. But he lay there silently. She was afraid that he would go to sleep. She knew that when the morning came things would seem different. She knew that she would persuade herself that there was no immediate hurry. She would leave things to settle themselves; and then. Oh! well! there would be no question as to how things would go! She saw, with absolute clearness that this was the moment that was granted her. If she could only persuade him to take her now, then she would have that at any rate afterwards to hold herself back. She would not want to go back on her word again. Her only feeling now was that Fred was so safe. The thought of the evening, the garden, Maradick, filled her now with unreasoning terror; she was in a panic lest this minute, this opportunity, should leave her.

She turned towards him and shook his arm.

"Fred, just keep awake for a minute; really it's important. Really, I want to go away with you, on Thursday, not to stay on. I don't like the place. I shan't a bit mind being in London, it will be rather fun; there are lots of people I want to see. Besides, it's only a day or two after all."

But he laughed sleepily.

"What's all the fuss, old girl? I'm simply damned tired; I am, really. We'll talk about it to-morrow. But anyhow, you'd better stay; it's all arranged, and Lady Gale will think it rather funny."

His voice trailed off. For a moment there was silence and she heard his breathing. He was asleep.

She listened furiously. Oh, well, if he didn't care more than that! If he couldn't keep awake longer than that! She dug her nails into her hand. There it was; he could go to sleep when she was in torture. He didn't care; the other man! Her mind flew back to the evening again. Ah! he would not have gone off to sleep! He would have listened—listened.

But she lay for hours staring into the darkness, listening to the man's even breathing.

But there had been another example of "any wife to any husband," that must, for a moment, have its record.

Maradick feared, on coming into his room, that his wife was not yet in bed. She was sitting in front of her glass brushing her hair. She must have seen him in the mirror, but she did not move. She looked very young, almost like a little doll; as she sat there he had again the curious feeling of pathos that he had known at breakfast. Absurd! Emmy Maradick was the last person about whom anyone need be pathetic, but nevertheless the feeling was there. He got into bed without a word. She went on silently combing her hair. It got on his nerves; he couldn't take his eyes off her. He turned his eyes away towards the wall, but slowly they turned back again, back to the silent white figure in the centre of the room by the shining glass.

He suddenly wanted to scream, to shout something at her like "Speak, you devil!" or "don't go on saying nothing, you mummy, sitting still like that."

At last he did speak.

"You're late, Emmy," he said, "I thought you'd have been in bed." His voice was very gentle. If only she would stop moving that brush up and down with its almost mechanical precision! She put the brush slowly down on the table and turned towards him.

"Yes," she said, "I was waiting for you, really, until you came up."

He was suddenly convinced that she knew; she had probably known all about it from the first. She was such a clever little woman, there were very few things that she didn't know. He waited stupidly, dully. He wondered what she was going to say, what she was going to propose that they should do.

But having got so far, she seemed to have nothing more to say. She stared at the glass with wide, fixed eyes; her cheeks were flushed, and her fingers played nervously with the things on the dressing-table.

"Well," he said at last, "what is it?"

Then, to his intense surprise, she got up and came slowly towards him; she sat on the edge of the bed whilst he watched her, wondering, amazed. He had never seen her like that before, and his intense curiosity at her condition killed, for a moment, the eagerness with which he would discover how much she knew. But her manner of taking it was surely very strange.

Temper, fury, passion, even hate, that he could understand, and that, knowing her, he would have expected, but this strange dreamy quiet frightened him. He caught the bed-clothes in his hands and twisted them; then he asked again: "Well, what is it?" But when she did at last speak she did not look at him, but stared in front of her. It was the strangest thing in the world to see her sitting there, speaking like that; and he had a feeling, not to be explained, that she wasn't there at all really, that it was some one else, even, possibly, some strange thing that his actions of these last few days had suddenly called forth—called forth, that was, to punish him. He shrunk back on to his pillows.

"Well," her voice just went on, "it isn't that I've really anything to say; you'll think me silly, and I'm sure I don't want to keep you when you want to go to sleep. But it isn't often that we have anything very much to say to one another; it isn't, at any rate, very often here. We've hardly, you know, talked at all since we've been here.

"But these last few days I've been thinking, realising perhaps, that it's been my fault all these years that things haven't been happier. . . . I don't think I'd thought about anyone except myself. . . . In some sort of way I hadn't considered you at all; I don't quite know why."

She paused as though she expected him to say something, but he made no sound.

Then she went on: "I suppose you'll think it foolish of me, but I feel as though everything has been different from the moment that we came here, from the moment that we came to Treliss; you have been quite different, and I am sorry if I have been so disagreeable, and I'm going to try, going to try to be pleasanter."

She brought it out with a jerk, as though she were speaking under impulse, as though something was making her speak.

And he didn't know what to say; he could say nothing—his only emotion that he was angry with her, almost furious, because she had spoken like that. It was too bad of her, just then, after all these years. There had, at any rate, been some justification before, or, at least, he had tried to persuade himself that there was, in his relations with Mrs. Lester. He had been driven by neglect, lack of sympathy, and all the rest of it; and now, suddenly, that had been taken away from under his feet. Oh! it was too bad.

And then his suspicions were aroused again. It was so unlike her to behave like that. Perhaps she was only behaving like this in order to find out, to sound him, as it were. Oh, yes! it was a clever move; but he couldn't say anything to her, the words refused to come.

She waited, a little pathetically, there on the bed, for him to speak; and then as nothing came, still without looking at him, she said quietly "Good-night," and stepped softly across the room.

He heard her switch the light off, the bed-clothes rustled for a moment, and then there was silence.

And these next two days were torture to him, the most horrible days that he had ever known. Partly they were horrible because of the general consciousness that something was going to happen. Lady Gale, in obedience to Tony, had arranged a picnic for Thursday, but "for ladies only. You see, Mr. Lester is leaving in the afternoon, and my husband and Rupert talk of going with him as far as Truro; my husband has some relations there. And really, I know you and Tony would rather go off on your own, Mr. Maradick. It would be too boring for you. We're only going to sit in the sun, you know, and talk!"

It was understood that Mr. Maradick had, as a matter of fact, fixed up something. Yes, he had promised his day to Tony, it being one of the last that they would have together. They would probably go for a sail. He would like to have come. He enjoyed the last, &c., &c.

But this was quite enough to "do" the trick. What a picnic! Imagine! With everyone acutely conscious that there was something "going on" just over the hill, something that, for Lady Gale, at any rate, meant almost life and death. Thursday began to loom very large indeed. What would everyone be doing and thinking on Friday? Still more vital a question, *where* would everyone be on Friday?

But at any rate he could picture them: the ladies—Lady Gale, Alice Du Cane, Mrs. Lester, his wife, even poor Mrs. Lawrence—sitting there, on the edge of the hill, silent, alert, listening.

What a picnic!

But their alertness, or rather their terrible eagerness to avoid seeming alert, horrified him. They seemed to pursue him, all five of them, during those two dreadful days with questioning glances; only his wife, by her curious patient intentness, as though she were waiting for the crisis to come, frightened him most of all. The more he thought of her strange behaviour the less he understood her. It was all so utterly unlike her. And it was not as though she had altered at all in other ways. He had heard her talking to other people, he had watched her scolding the girls, and it was the same sharp, shrill voice, the same fierce assumption that the person she was with must necessarily be trying to "get" at her; no, she was the same Emmy Maradick as far as the rest of the world was concerned. But, with him, she was some one altogether new, some one he had never seen before; and always, through it all, that strange look of wonder and surprise. He often knew that her eyes were upon him when he was talking to some one else; when he talked to her himself her eyes avoided him.

And then Mrs. Lester, too, was so strange. During the whole of Tuesday she avoided him altogether. He had a few minutes with her at teatime, but there were other people there, and she seemed anxious to get away from him, to put the room between them. And seeing her like this, his passion grew. He felt that whatever happened, whatever the disaster, he must have her, once at least, in his arms again. The memories of their other meetings lashed him like whips. He pictured it again, the darkness, the movement of the trees, the touch of her cheek against his hand; and then he would feel that his wife was looking at him from somewhere across the room. He could feel her eyes, like little gimlets, twisting, turning into his back. And then other moods would come, and the blackest despair. He was this kind of man, this sort of scoundrel; he remembered once that there had been a man at Epsom who had run away with a married woman, a man who had been rather a friend of his. He remembered what he had said to him, the kind of way that he had looked at him, poor, rotten creature; and now what was he?

But he could not go; he could not move. He was under a spell. When he thought of Mrs. Lester his blood would begin to race again. He told himself that it was the sign of his freedom, the natural consequences of the new life that had come to him; and then suddenly he would see that moment when his wife, sitting forlornly on his bed, had spoken to him.

And then on Wednesday there was a moment when Mrs. Lester was herself again. It was only a moment, an instant after dinner. Their lips met; he spoke of Thursday and she smiled at him, then the others had come upon them. For an hour or two he was on fire, then he crept miserably, like a thief, to the room of the minstrels and sat wretchedly, hour after hour, looking at the stars.

The day would soon dawn! Thursday! The crisis, as it seemed to him, of the whole of his life. He saw the morn draw faint shadows across the earth, he saw all the black trees move like a falling wall against the stars, he felt the wind with the odour of earth and sea brush his cheek, as he waited for the day to come.

He knew now that it was to be no light thing; it was to be a battle, the fiercest that he had ever waged. Two forces were fighting over him, and one of them, before the next night had passed, would win the day. No Good and Evil? No God and Devil? No Heaven and Hell? Why, there they were before his very eyes; the two camps and the field between! And so Thursday dawned!

But it came with grey mists and driving rain. The sea was hidden; only the tops of the trees in the garden stood disconsolately dripping above the fog.

Everyone came down shivering to breakfast, and disappointments that seemed unjust on ordinary days were now perfectly unbearable. If there were no letters, one was left out in the cold, if there were a lot, they were sure to be bills. It was certain to be smoked haddock when that was the one thing above all others that you loathed; and, of course, there were numbers of little draughts that crept like mice about your feet and wandered like spiders about your hair.

But one thing was perfectly obvious, and that was, that of course there could be no picnic. To have five ladies sitting desolately alone on the top of the hill, bursting with curiosity, was melancholy enough; but to have them sitting there in driving rain was utterly impossible.

Nevertheless some people intended to venture out. Sir Richard and Rupert—mainly, it seemed, to show their contempt of so plebeian a thing as rain—were still determined on Truro.

Tony also was going to tramp it with Maradick.

"Where are you going?" This from Sir Richard, who had just decided that his third egg was as bad as the two that he had already eaten.

"Oh! I don't know!" said Tony lazily, "over the hills and far away, I expect. That's the whole fun of the thing—not knowing. Isn't it, Maradick?"

"It is," said Maradick.

He showed no signs of a bad night. He was eating a very hearty breakfast.

"But you must have some idea where you are going," persisted Sir Richard, gloomily sniffing at his egg.

"Well, I expect we'll start out towards that old church," said Tony. "You know, the one on the cliff; then we'll strike inland, I expect. Don't you think so, Maradick?"

"Yes," said Maradick.

There was no doubt at all that the five ladies were extremely glad that there was to be no picnic. Mrs. Lawrence meant to have a really cosy day reading by the fire one of those most delightful stories of Miss Braddon. She was enormously interested in the literature of the early eighties; anything later than that rather frightened her.

"We can have a really cosy day," said Mrs. Lester.

"Yes, we shall have quite a comfortable time," said Mrs. Lawrence.

"It is so nice having an excuse for a fire," said Lady Gale.

"I do love it when one can have a fire without being ashamed, don't you?" said Mrs. Lawrence.

Mrs. Maradick gathered her two girls about her and they disappeared.

Slowly the clock stole towards half-past eleven, when the first move was to be made. Mr. Lester had left quite early. He said good-bye to Maradick with great cordiality.

"Mind you come and see us, often. It's been delightful meeting you. There's still plenty to talk about."

He said good-bye to his wife with his usual rather casual geniality.

"Good-bye, old girl. Send me a line. Hope this weather clears off" —and he was gone.

She had been standing by the hall door. As the trap moved down the drive she suddenly made a step forward as though she would go out into the rain after him and call him back. Then she stopped. She was standing on the first step in front of the door; the mist swept about her.

Lady Gale called from the hall: "Come in, dear, you'll get soaking wet."

She turned and came back.

To Tony, as he watched the hands of the clock creep round, it seemed perfectly incredible that the whole adventure should simply consist in quietly walking out of the door. It ought to begin, at any rate, with something finer than that, with an escape, something that needed secrecy and mystery. It was so strange that he was simply going to walk down and take Janet; it was, after all, a very ordinary affair.

At quarter-past eleven he found his mother alone in her room.

He came up to her and kissed her. "I'm going off with Maradick now," he said.

"Yes," she answered, looking him in the eyes.

"You know I'm in for an adventure, mother?"

"Yes, dear."

"You trust me, don't you?"

"Of course, dear, perfectly."

"You shall know all about it to-morrow."

"When you like, dear," she answered. She placed her arms on his shoulders, and held him back and looked him in the face. Then she touched his head with her hands and said softly—

"You mustn't let anything or anyone come between us, Tony?"

"Never, mother," he answered. Then suddenly he came very close to her, put his arms round her and kissed her again and again.

"God bless you, old boy," she said, and let him go.

When he had closed the door behind him she began to cry, but when Mrs. Lester found her quarter of an hour later there were no signs of tears.

Maradick and Tony, as half-past eleven struck from the clock at the top of the stairs, went down the steps of the hotel.

As they came out into the garden the mists and rain swam all about them and closed them in. The wind beat their faces, caught their coats and lashed them against their legs, and went scrambling away round the corners of the hill.

"My word! what a day!"[7] shouted Tony. "Here's a day for a wedding!" He was tremendously excited. He even thought that he liked this wind and rain, it helped on the adventure; and then, too, there would be less people about, but it would be a stormy drive to the church.

They secured a cab in the market-place. But such a cab; was there ever another like it? It stood, for no especial reason it seemed, there in front of the tower, with the rain whirling round it, the wind beating at the horse's legs and playing fantastic tricks with the driver's cape, which flew about his head up and down like an angry bird. He was the very oldest aged man Time had ever seen; his beard, a speckly grey, fell raggedly down on to his chest, his eyes were bleared and nearly closed, his nose, swollen to double its natural size, was purple in colour, and when he opened his mouth there was visible an enormous tooth, but one only.

His hands trembled with ague as he clutched the reins and addressed his miserable beast. The horse was a pitiful scarecrow; its ribs, like a bent towel-rack, almost pierced the skin; its eye was melancholy but patient. The cab itself moved as though at any moment it would fall to pieces. The sides of the carriage were dusty, and the wheels were thick with mud; at every movement the windows screamed and rattled and shook with age—the cabman, the four-wheeler and the horse lurched together from side to side.

However, there was really nothing else. Time was precious, and it certainly couldn't be wasted in going round to the cab-stand at the other end of the town. On a fine day there would have been a whole row of them in the market-place, but in weather like this they sought better shelter.

The wind whistled across the cobbles; the rain fell with such force that it hit the stones and leaped up again. The aged man was murmuring to himself the same words again and again. "Eh! Lor! how the rain comes down; it's terrible bad for the beasts." The tower frowned down on them all.

Tony jumped in, there was nothing else to be done; it rattled across the square.

Tony was laughing. It all seemed to him to add to the excitement. "Do you know," he said, "James Stephens's poem? It hits it off exactly;" and he quoted:

> "The driver rubbed at his nettly chin,
> With a huge, loose forefinger, crooked and black,
> And his wobbly violent lips sucked in,
> And puffed out again and hung down slack:
> One fang shone through his lop-sided smile,
> In his little pouched eye flickered years of guile.
>
> And the horse, poor beast, it was ribbed and forked,
> And its ears hung down, and its eyes were old,
> And its knees were knuckly, and as we talked
> It swung the stiff neck that could scarcely hold
> Its big, skinny head up—then I stepped in
> And the driver climbed to his seat with a grin.

Only this old boy couldn't climb if he were paid for it. I wonder how he gets up to his box in the morning. I expect they lift him, you know; his old wife and the children and the grandchildren—a kind of ceremony."

They were being flung about all this time like peas in a bladder, and Tony had to talk at the top of his voice to make himself heard. "Anyhow he'll get us there all right, I expect. My word, what rain! I say, you know, I can't in the very least realise it. It seems most frightfully exciting, but it's all so easy, in a kind of way. You see I haven't even had to have a bag or anything, because there'll be heaps of time to stop in town and get things. And to-morrow morning to see the sun rise over Paris, with Janet!"

His eyes were on fire with excitement. But to Maradick this weather, this cab, seemed horrible, almost ominous. He was flung against the side of the window, then against Tony, then back again. He had lost his breath.

But he had realised something else suddenly; he wondered how he could have been so foolish as not to have seen it before, and that was, that this would be probably, indeed almost certainly, the last time that he would have Tony to himself. The things that the boy had been to him during these weeks beat in his head like bells, reminding him. Why, the boy had been everything to him! And now he saw suddenly that he had, in reality, been nothing at all to the boy. Tony's eyes were set on the adventure—the great adventure of life. Maradick, and others like him, might be amusing on the way; were of course, "good sorts," but they could be left, they must be left if one were to get on, and there were others, plenty of others.

And so, in that bumping cab, Maradick suddenly realised his age. To be "at forty" as the years go was nothing, years did not count, but to be "at forty" in the way that he now saw it was the great dividing line in life. He now saw that it wasn't for him any more to join with those who were "making life," that was for the young, and they would have neither time nor patience to wait for his slower steps; he must be content to play his part in other people's adventures, to act the observer, the onlooker. Those young people might tell him that they cared, that they wanted him, but they would soon forget, they would soon pass on until they too were "at forty," and, reluctantly, unwillingly, must move over to the other camp.

He turned to Tony.

"I say, boy," he said almost roughly, "this is the last bit that we shall have together; alone, I mean. I say, don't forget me altogether afterwards. I want to come and see you."

"Forget you!" Tony laughed. "Why never! I!"

But then suddenly the aged man and his coach bumped them together and then flung them apart and then bumped them again so that no more words were possible. The cab had turned the corner. The house, with its crooked door, was before them.

In the hall there were lights; underneath the stairs there was a lamp and against the wall opposite the door there were candles. In the middle of the hall Janet was standing waiting; she was dressed in some dark blue stuff and a little round dark blue hat, beneath it her hair shone gloriously. She held a bag in her hand and a small cloak over her arm. Tony came forward with a stride and she stepped a little way to meet him. Then he caught her in his arms, and her head went back a little so that the light of the lamp caught her hair and flung a halo around it. Miss Minns was in the background in a state of quite natural agitation. It was all very quiet and restrained. There seemed to Maradick to fall a very beautiful silence for a moment about them. The light, the colour, everything centred round those two, and the world stood still. Then Tony let go and she came forward to Maradick.

She held out her hand and he took it in his, and he, suddenly, moved by some strange impulse, bent down and kissed it. She let it lie there for a moment and then drew it back, smiling.

"It's splendid of you, Mr. Maradick," she said; "without you I don't know what we'd have done, Tony and I."

And then she turned round to Tony and kissed him again. There was another pause, and indeed the two children seemed perfectly ready to stand like that for the rest of the day. Something practical must be done.

"I think we ought to be making a move," said Maradick. "The cab's waiting outside and the train has to be caught, you know."

"Why, of course." Janet broke away from Tony. "How silly we are! I'm so sorry, Miss Minns, have you got the bag with the toothbrush? It's all we've got, you know, because we can buy things in Paris. Oh! Paris!"

She drew a breath and stood there, her eyes staring, her hands on her hips, her head flung back. It really was amazing the way that she was taking it. There was no doubt or alarm at the possible consequences of so daring a step. It must be, Maradick thought, her ignorance of all that life must mean to her now, all the difference that it would have once this day was over, that saved her from fear.

And yet there was knowledge as well as courage in her eyes, she was not altogether ignorant.

Miss Minns came forward, Miss Minns in an amazing bonnet. It was such an amazing bonnet that Miss Minns must positively have made it herself; it was shaped like a square loaf and little jet beads rang little bells on it as she moved. She was in a perfect tremble of excitement, and the whole affair sent her mind back to the one other romantic incident in her life—the one and only love affair. But the really amazing discovery was that romance wasn't over for her yet, that she was permitted to take part in a real "affair," to see it through from start to finish. She was quivering with excitement.

They all got into the cab.

It was a very silent drive to the church. The rain had almost stopped. It only beat every now and again, a little doubtfully, against the window and then went, with a little whirl of wind, streaming away.

The cab went slowly, and, although it lurched from side to side and every now and again pitched forward, as though it would fall on its head, they were not shaken about very badly. Janet leaned back against Tony, and he had his arm round her. They neither of them spoke at all, but his fingers moved very lightly over her hand and then to her cheek, and then back to her hand again.

As they got on to the top of the hill and started along the white road to the church the wind from the sea met them and swept about them. Great dark clouds, humped like camels, raced across the sky; the trees by the roadside, gnarled and knotted, waved scraggy arms like so many witches.

Miss Minns's only remark as they neared the church was, "I must say I should have liked a little bit of orange-blossom."

"We'll get that in Paris," said Tony.

The aged man was told to wait with his coach until they all came out of church again. He seemed to be quite prepared to wait until the day of doom if necessary. He stared drearily in front of him at the sea. To his mind, it was all a very bad business.

Soon they were all in the church, the clergyman with the flowing beard, his elderly boy, acting as a kind of verger and general factotum, Miss Minns, Maradick, and there, by the altar rails, Tony and Janet.

It was a very tiny church indeed, and most of the room was taken up by an enormous box-like pew that had once been used by "The Family"; now it was a mass of cobwebs. Two candles had been lighted by the altar and they flung a fitful, uncertain glow about the place and long twisting shadows on the wall. On the altar itself was a large bowl of white chrysanthemums, and always for the rest of his life the sight of chrysanthemums brought back that scene to Maradick's memory: the blazing candles, the priest with his great white beard, the tiny, dusty church, Miss Minns and her bonnet, Tony splendidly erect, a smile in his eyes, and Janet with her hair and her blue serge dress and her glance every now and again at Tony to see whether he were still there.

And so, there, and in a few minutes, they were married.

For an instant some little wind blew along the floor, stirred the dust and caught the candles. They flared into a blaze, and out of the shadows there leapt the dazzling white of the chrysanthemums, the gold of Janet's hair, and the blue of the little stained-glass windows. The rain had begun again and was beating furiously at the panes; they could hear it running in little streams and rivers down the hill past the church.

Maradick hid his head in his hands for an instant before he turned away. He did not exactly want to pray, he had not got anyone to pray to, but he felt again now, as he had felt before in the room of the minstrels, that there was something there, with him in the place—touching him, Good and Evil? God and the Devil? Yes, they were there, and he did not dare to raise his eyes.

Then at last he looked up again and in the shock of the sudden light the candles seemed to swing like golden lamps before him and the altar was a throne, and, before it, the boy and girl.

And then, again, they were all in the old man's study, amongst his fishing-rods and dogs and books.

He laid both his hands on Tony's shoulders before he said good-bye. Tony looked up into his face and smiled.

And the old man said: "I think that you will be very happy, both of you. But take one word of advice from some one who has lived in the world a very long time and knows something of it, even though he has dwelt in only an obscure corner of it. My dear, keep your Charity. That is all that I would say to you. You have it now; keep it as your dearest possession. Judge no one; you do not know what trouble has been theirs, what temptation, and there will be flowers even in the dreariest piece of ground if only we sow the seed. And remember that there are many very lonely people in the world. Give them some of your vitality and happiness and you will do well."

Miss Minns, who had been sniffing through the most of the service, very nearly broke down altogether at this point. And then suddenly some one remembered the time.

It was Tony. "My word, it's half-past two. And the train's quarter-past three. Everything's up if we miss it. We must be off; we'll only just do it as it is."

They found the aged man sitting in a pool of water on the box. Water dripped from the legs of the trembling horse. The raindrops, as though possessed of a devil, leaped off the roof of the cab like peas from a catapult.

Tony tried to impress the driver with the fact that there was no time to lose, but he only shook his head dolefully. They moved slowly round the corner.

Then there began the most wonderful drive that man or horse had ever known.

At first they moved slowly. The road was, by this time, thick with mud, and there were little trenches of water on both sides. They bumped along this for a little way. And then suddenly the aged man became seized, as it were, by a devil. They were on the top of the hill; the wind blew right across him, the rain lashed him to the skin. Suddenly he lifted up his voice and sang. It was the sailor's chanty that Maradick had heard on the first day of his coming to Treliss; but now, through the closed windows of the cab, it seemed to reach them in a shrill scream, like some gull above their heads in the storm.

Wild exultation entered into the heart of the ancient man. He seemed to be seized by the Furies. He lashed his horse wildly, the beast with all its cranky legs and heaving ribs, darted madly forward, and the rain came down in torrents.

The ancient man might have seemed, had there been a watcher to note, the very spirit of the moor. His eyes were staring, his arms were raised aloft; and so they went, bumping, jolting, tumbling along the white road.

Inside the cab there was confusion. At the first movement Miss Minns had been flung violently into Maradick's lap. At first he clutched her wildly. The bugles on her bonnet hit him sharply in the eyes, the nose, the chin. She pinched his arm in the excitement of the moment. Then she recovered herself.

"Oh! Mr. Maradick!" she began, "I— —" but, in a second, she was seized again and hurled against the door, so that Tony had to clutch her by the skirt lest the boards should give and she should be hurled out into the road. But the pace of the cab grew faster and faster. They were now all four of them hurled violently from one side of the vehicle to the other. First forward, then backwards, then on both sides at once, then all in a tangled heap together in the middle; and the ancient man on the top of the box, the water dripping from his hat in a torrent, screamed his song.

Then terror suddenly entered into them all. It seemed to strike them all at the same moment that there was danger. Maradick suddenly was afraid. He was bruised, his collar was torn, he ached in every limb. He had a curious impulse to seize Miss Minns and tear her to pieces, he was wild with rage that she should be allowed to hit and strike him like that. He began to mutter furiously. And the others felt it too. Janet was nearly in tears; she clung to Tony and murmured, "Oh! stop him! stop him!"

And Tony, too. He cried, "We must get out of this! We must get out of this!" and he dragged furiously at the windows, but they would not move; and then his hand broke through the pane, and it began to bleed, there was blood on the floor of the carriage.

And they did not know that it was the place that was casting them out. They were going back to their cities, to their disciplined places, to their streets and solemn houses, their inventions, their rails and lines and ordered lives; and so the place would cast them out. It would have its last wild game with them. The ancient man gave a last shrill scream and was silent. The horse relapsed into a shamble; they were in the dark, solemn streets. They climbed the hill to the station.

They began to straighten themselves, and already to forget that it had been, in the least, terrible.

"After all," said Tony, "it was probably a good thing that we came at that pace. We might have missed the train."

He helped Janet to tidy herself. Miss Minns was profuse in her apologies: "Really, Mr. Maradick, I don't know what you can have thought of me. Really, it was most immodest; and I am afraid that I bumped you rather awkwardly. It was most——"

But he stopped her and assured her that it was all right. He was thinking, as they climbed the hill, that in another quarter of an hour they would both be gone, gone out of his life altogether probably. There would be nothing left for him beyond his explanations; his clearing up of the bits, as it were, and Mrs. Lester. But he would not think of her now; he put her resolutely from him for the moment. The thought of her seemed desecration when these two children were with him—something as pure and beautiful as anything that the world could show. He would think of her afterwards, when they had gone.

But as he looked at them a great pang of envy cut him like a knife. Ah! that was what life meant! To have some one to whom you were the chief thing in the world, some one who was also the chief thing to you!

And he? Here, at forty, he had got nothing but a cheque book and a decent tailor.

They got out of the cab.

It was ten minutes before the train left. It was there, waiting. Tony went to get the tickets.

Janet suddenly put her hand on Maradick's arm and looked up into his face:

"Mr. Maradick," she said, "I haven't been able, I haven't had a chance to say very much to you about all that Tony and I owe you. But I feel it; indeed, indeed I do. And I will never, never forget it. Wherever Tony and I are there will always be a place for you if you want one. You won't forget that, will you?"

"No, indeed," said Maradick, and he took her hand for a moment and pressed it. Then suddenly his heart stopped beating. The station seemed for a moment to be pressed together, so that the platform and the roof met and the bookstall and the people dotted about disappeared altogether.

Sir Richard and Rupert were walking slowly towards them down the platform. There was no question about it at all. They had obviously just arrived from Truro and Rupert was staring in his usual aimless fashion in front of him. There was simply no time to lose. They were threatened with disaster, for Tony had not come back from the ticket-office and might tumble upon his father at any moment.

Maradick seized Janet by the arm and dragged her back into the refreshment room. "Quick," he said, "there isn't a moment to lose—Tony's father. You and Miss Minns must get in by yourselves; trust to luck!" In a moment she had grasped the situation. Her cheeks were a little flushed, but she gave him a hurried smile and then joined Miss Minns. Together they walked quietly down the platform and took their seats in a first-class carriage at the other end of the train. Janet was perfectly self-possessed as she passed Sir Richard. There was no question that this distinguished-looking gentleman must be Tony's father, and she must have felt a very natural curiosity to see what he looked like; she gave him one sharp glance and then bent down in what was apparently an earnest conversation with Miss Minns.

Then Rupert saw Maradick. "Hullo! there's Maradick!" He came forward slowly; but he smiled a little in a rather weary manner. He liked Maradick. "What a day! Yes, Truro had been awful! All sorts of dreadful people dripping wet!"

Yes, Maradick had been a tramp in the rain with Tony. Tony was just asking for a parcel that he was expecting; yes, they'd got very wet and were quite ready for tea! Ah! there was Tony.

Maradick gazed at him in agony as he came out of the ticket office. Would he give a start and flush with surprise when he saw them? Would he look round vaguely and wildly for Janet? Would he turn tail and flee?

But he did none of these things. He walked towards them as though the one thing that he had really expected to see, there on the platform, was his father. There was a little smile at the corners of his mouth and his eyes were shining especially brightly, but he sauntered quite casually down the platform, as though he hadn't the least idea that the train was going off in another five minutes, and that Janet was close at hand somewhere and might appear at any moment.

"Hullo, governor! Rupert! Who'd have thought of seeing you here? I suppose the weather sent you back. Maradick and I have been getting pretty soaked out there on the hill. But one thing is that it sends you in to a fire with some relish. I'm after a rotten old parcel that Briggs was sending me— some books. He says it ought to have come, but I can't get any news of it here. We'll follow you up to the hotel to tea in a minute."

But Rupert seemed inclined to stay and chat. "Oh! we'll come on with you; we're in no particular hurry, are we, governor? I say, that was a damned pretty girl that passed just now; girl in blue. Did you see her, Maradick?"

No, Maradick hadn't seen her. In blue? No, he hadn't noticed. The situation was beginning to get on his nerves. He was far more agitated than Tony. What were they to do? The guard was passing down the platform looking at tickets. Doors were beginning to be banged. A great many people were hurriedly giving a great many messages that had already been given a great many times before. What was to be done? To his excited fancy it almost seemed as though Sir Richard was perfectly aware of the whole business. He thought his silence saturnine; surely there was a malicious twinkle.

"Yes," Rupert was saying, "there she was walking down Lemon Street, dontcher know, with her waterproof thing flapping behind her in the most *absurd*——" The doors were all banged; the guard looked down the line.

Suddenly Sir Richard moved. "I'm damned cold; wet things." He nodded curtly to Maradick. "See you later, Mr. Maradick."

They moved slowly away; they turned the corner and at the same instant the train began to move. Tony snatched at Maradick's hand and then made a wild leap across the platform. The train was moving quite fast now; he made a clutch at one of the carriages. Two porters rushed forward shouting, but he had the handle of the door. He flung it open; for a sickening instant he stood swaying on the board; it seemed as though he would be swept back. Then some one pulled him in. He lurched forward and disappeared; the door was closed.

A lot of little papers rose in a little cloud of dust into the air. They whirled to and fro. A little wind passed along the platform.

Maradick turned round and walked slowly away.

CHAPTER XVIII
AFTERNOON AND EVENING OF THE TWENTY-SEVENTH—MARADICK GOES TO CHURCH AND AFTERWARDS PAYS A VISIT TO MORELLI

As he came out of the station and looked at the little road that ran down the hill, at the grey banks of cloud, at the white and grey valley of the sea, he felt curiously, uncannily alone. It was as though he had suddenly, through some unknown, mysterious agency been transported into a new land, a country that no one ever found before. He walked the hill with the cautious adventurous sense of surprise that some explorer might have had; he was alone in the world of ghosts.

When he came to the bottom of the road he stopped and tried to collect his thoughts. Where was he? What was he going to do? What were the thoughts that were hovering, like birds of prey, about his head, waiting for the moment of descent to come? He stood there quite stupidly, as though his brain had been suddenly swept clear of all thought; it was an empty, desolate room. Everything was empty, desolate. Two plane trees waved mournfully; there were little puddles of rain-water at his feet reflecting the dismal grey of the sky; a very old bent woman in a black cloak hobbled slowly up the hill. Then suddenly his brain was alive again, suddenly he knew. Tony was gone. Tony was gone and he must see people and explain.

The thought of the explanations troubled him very little; none of those other people really mattered. They couldn't do very much; they could only say things. No, they didn't matter. He didn't mind about them, or indeed about anyone else in the world except Tony. He saw now a thousand little things that Tony had done, ways that Tony had stood, things that Tony had said, little tricks that he had; and now he had gone away.

Things could never be quite the same again. Tony had got some one else now. Everyone had got some one else, some one who especially belonged to them; he saw the world as a place where everyone—murderer, priest, king, prostitute—had his companion, and only he, Maradick, was alone. He had been rather proud of being alone before; he had rather liked to feel that he was quite independent, that it didn't matter if people died or forgot, because he could get on as well by himself! What a fool he had been! Why, that was simply the only thing worth having, relationships with other people, intimacy, affection, giving anything that you had to some one else, taking something in return from them. Oh! he saw that now!

He had been walking vaguely, without thought or purpose. Now he saw that his feet had led him back into the town and that he was in the market-place, facing once more the town. He was determined not to go back to the hotel until he had seen Morelli, and that he could not do before the evening; but that would be the next thing. Meanwhile he would walk—no matter where—but he would get on to the road, into the air, and try and straighten out all the tangled state of things that his mind was in.

For a moment he stood and looked at the tower. It gave him again that sense of strength and comfort. He was, after all, not quite alone, whilst the world was the place that it was. Stocks and stones had more of a voice, more of a personal vital activity than most people knew. But he knew! He had known ever since he came to this strange town, this place where every tree and house and hill seemed to be alive.

And then, with the thought of the place, Mrs. Lester came back to him. He had forgotten her when he was thinking of Tony. But now that Tony was gone, now that that was, in a way, over, the other question suddenly stepped forward. Mrs. Lester with her smile, her arms, the curve of her neck, the scent that she used, the way that her eyes climbed, as it were, slowly up to his just before she kissed him. . . . Mrs. Lester . . . and it must be decided before to-night.

He started walking furiously, and soon he was out on the high road that ran above the sea. The rain had stopped; the sun was not actually shining, but there was a light through the heavy clouds as though it were not very far away, and the glints of blue and gold, not actually seen, but, as it were, trembling on the edge of visible appearance, seemed to strike the air. Everything shone and glittered with the rain. The green of trees and fields was so bright against the grey of sea and sky that it was almost dazzling; its brightness was unnatural, even a little cruel. And now he was caught up in the very heat of conflict. The battle seemed suddenly to have burst upon him, as though there were in reality two visible forces fighting for the possession of his soul. At one moment he seemed calm, resolute; Tony, Janet, his wife (and this was curious, because a few days before she would not have mattered at all), Punch, the tower, all kinds of queer bits of things, impressions, thoughts, and above all, a consciousness of some outside power fighting for him—all these things determined him. He would see Mrs. Lester to-night and would tell her that there must be nothing more; they should be friends, good friends, but there must be no more of that dangerous sentiment, one never knew where it might go. And after all, laws were meant to be kept. A man wasn't a man at all if he could injure a woman in that sort of way. And then he had been Lester's friend. How could he dishonour his wife?

And then suddenly it came from the other side, fierce, hot, wild, so that his heart began to beat furiously, his eyes were dim. He only saw her, all the rest of the world was swept away. They should have this one adventure, they *must* have their one adventure. After all they were no longer children. They had neither of them known what life was before; let them live it now, their great experience. If they missed it now they would regret it all their lives. They would look back on the things that they might have done, the things that they might have known, and see that they had passed it all simply because they had not been brave enough, because they had been afraid of convention, of old musty laws that had been made thousands of years ago for other people, people far less civilised, people who needed rules. And then the thought of her grew upon him—details, the sense of holding her, keeping her; and then, for an instant, he was primitive, wild, so that he would have done anything to seize her in the face of all the world.

But it passed; the spirit left him, and again he was miserable, wretched, penitent. He was that sort of man, a traitor to his wife, to his friends, to everything that was decent. He was walking furiously, his hair was blown by the wind, his eyes stared in front of him, and the early dusk of a grey day began to creep about his feet.

It all came to this. Was there one ethical code for the world, or must individuals make each their law for their individual case?

There were certain obvious things, such as doing harm to your neighbours, lying, cruelty, that was bad for the community and so must be forbidden to the individual; but take an instance of something in which you harmed no one, did indeed harm yourself by denying it, was that a sin even if the general law forbade it? What were a man's instincts for? Why was he placed so carefully in the midst of his wonderful adventurous life if he were forbidden to know anything of it? Why these mists? This line of marble foam far below him? This hard black edge of the rocks against the sky? It was all strong, remorseless, inevitable; and he by this namby-pamby kind of virtue was going contrary to nature.

He let the wind beat about his face as he watched the mists in great waves and with encircling arms sweep about the cove. There came to him as he watched, suddenly, some lines from end of "To Paradise." He could not remember them exactly, but they had been something like this:

> To Tressiter, as to every other human being, there had come suddenly his time of revelation, his moment in which he was to see without any assistance from tradition, without any reference to things or persons of the past. He beheld suddenly with the vision of some one new-born, and through his brain and body into the locked recesses of his soul there passed the elemental passions and movements of the world that had swayed creation from the beginning. The great volume of the winds, the tireless beating of waves upon countless shores, the silent waters of innumerable rivers, the shining flanks of a thousand cattle upon moorlands that stretch without horizon to the end of time—it was these things rather than any little acts of civilisation that some few hundred years had seen that chimed now with the new life that was his. He had never seen before, he had never known before. He saw now with unprejudiced eyes, he knew now with a knowledge that discounted all man-made laws and went, like a child, back to Mother Earth. . . . But with this new knowledge came also its dangers. Because some laws seemed now of none effect it did not mean that there must be no laws at all. That way was shipwreck. Only, out of this new strength, this new clarity of vision, he must make his strength, his restraint, his discipline for himself, and so pass, a new man, down the other side of the hill. . . . This is the "middle-age" that comes to every man. It has nothing to do with years, but it is the great Rubicon of life. . . .

And so Lester. Fine talk and big words, and a little ludicrous, perhaps, if one knew what Lester was, but there was something in it. Oh! yes! there was something in it!

And now this time, this "middle-age," had come upon him.

He found that his steps had led him back again to the little church where he had been already that day. He thought that it might be a good place to sit and think things out, quiet and retired and in shelter, if the rain came on again.

The dusk was creeping down the little lane, so that the depths of it were hidden and black; but above the dark clumps of trees the sky had begun to break into the faintest, palest blue. Some bird rejoiced at this return of colour and was singing in the heart of the lane; from the earth rose the sweet clean smell that the rain leaves. From behind the little blue windows of the church shone a pale yellow light, of the same pallor as the faint blue of the sky, seeming in some intimate, friendly way, to re-echo it. The body of the church stood out grey-white against the surrounding mists. It seemed to Maradick (and this showed the way that he now credited everything with vitality) to be bending forward a little and listening to the very distant beating of the sea; its windows were golden eyes.

The lights seemed to prophesy company, and so he was surprised, on pushing the door softly back and entering, to find that there was no one there. But there were two large candles on the altar, and they waved towards him a little with the draught from the door as though to greet him. The church seemed larger now in the half light. The great box-like family pew was lost in the dark corners by the walls; it seemed to stretch away into infinite space. The other seats had an air of conscious waiting for some ceremony. On one of them was still an open prayer-book, open at the marriage service, that had been left there that afternoon. And at the sight of it the memories of Tony and Janet came back to him with a rush, so that they seemed to be there with him. Already it seemed a very, very long time since they had gone, another lifetime almost. And now, as he thought of it, perhaps, after all, it was better that they had gone like that.

He thought over the whole affair from the beginning. The first evening in Treliss, that first night when he had quarrelled with her, and then there had been Tony. That dated the change in him. But he could not remember when he had first noticed anything in her. There had been the picnic, the evening in their room when he had nearly lost control of himself and shaken her. . . . Yes, it was after that. That placed it. Well, then, it was only, after all, because he had shown himself firm, because, for once, he had made her afraid of him. Because, too, no doubt, she had noticed that people paid him attention. For the first time in their married life he had become "somebody," and that perhaps had opened her eyes. But then there had been that curious moment the other night when she had spoken to him. That had been extraordinarily unpleasant. He could feel again his uncomfortable sensation of helplessness, of not in the least knowing how to deal with her. That was the new Mrs. Maradick. He had therefore some one quite new to reckon with.

And then he saw suddenly, there in the church, the right thing to do. It was to go back. To go back to Epsom, to go back to his wife, to go back to the girls. He saw that she, Mrs. Maradick, in her own way, had been touched by the Admonitus Locorum—not that he put it that way; he called it the "rum place" or "the absurd town." She was going to try (she had herself told him so) to be better, more obliging. He could see her now, sitting there on the end of the bed, looking at him so pathetically.

The shadows gathered about the church, creeping along the floor and blotting out the blue light from the windows, and only there was a glow by the altar where the candles seemed to increase in size, and their light, like a feathery golden mist, hung in circles until it lost itself in the dusky roof.

But he stared in front of him, seeing simply the two women, one on each side of him. He had forgotten everything else. They stood there waiting for him to make his choice. It was the parting of the ways.

And then suddenly he fell asleep. He did not know that his eyes closed; he seemed to be still stupidly staring at the two candles and the rings that they made, and the way that the altar seemed to slope down in front of him like the dim grey side of a hill. And it was a hill. He could see it stretch in front of him, up into the air, until the heights of it were lost. At the foot of the hill ran a stream, blue in the half-light, and in front of the stream a green plain stretching to his feet. Along the stream were great banks of rushes, green and brown, and away to the right and left were brown cliffs running sheer down into the sea.

And then in his dream he suddenly realised that he had seen the place before. He knew that beyond the plain there should be a high white road leading to a town, that below the cliffs there was a cove with a white sandy bay; he knew the place.

And people approached. He could not see their faces, and they seemed in that half light in which the blue hills and the blue river mingled in the grey of the dusk to be shadows such as a light casts on a screen. They were singing very softly and moving slowly across the plain. Then they passed away and there was silence again, only a little wind went rustling down the hill and the rushes all quivered for an instant. Then the rushes were parted, and a face looked out from between them and looked at Maradick and smiled. And Maradick recognised the smile. He had seen it for the first time in a public-house, thick with smoke, noisy with drinking and laughter. He could see it all again; the little man in brown suddenly at his table, and then that delightful charming laugh unlike anything else in the world—Morelli.

But this figure was naked, his feet were goats' feet and on his head were horns; his body was brown and hairy and in his hand was a pipe. He began to play and slowly the shadowy figures came back again and gathered about him. They began to dance to his playing moving slowly in the half-light so that at times they seemed only mist; and a little moon like a golden eye came out and watched them and touched the tops of the blue hills with flame.

Maradick woke. His head had slipped forward on to the seat in front of him. He suddenly felt dreadfully tired; every limb in his body seemed to ache, but he was cold and the seat was very hard.

Then he was suddenly aware that there was some one else in the church. Over by the altar some one was kneeling, and very faintly there came to him the words of a prayer. "Our Father, which art in heaven, Hallowed be Thy name. . . . Thy will be done, . . . as it is in Heaven. . . . lead us not into temptation; But deliver us from evil. . . ." It was the old clergyman, the old clergyman with the white beard.

Maradick sat motionless in his seat. He made no movement, but he was praying, praying furiously. He was praying to no God that had a name, but to the powers of all honour, of all charity, of all goodness.

Love was the ultimate test, the test of everything. He knew now, with a clearness that seemed to dismiss all the shadows that had lingered for days about him, that he had never loved Mrs. Lester. It was the cry of sensuality, the call of the beast; it was lust.

"Deliver us from evil." He said it again and again, his hands clenched, his eyes staring, gazing at the altar. The powers of evil seemed to be all about him; he felt that if he did not cling with all his strength to that prayer, he was lost. The vision of Mrs. Lester returned to him. She seemed to get between him and the old man at the altar. He tried to look beyond her, but she was there, appealing, holding out her arms to him. Then she was nearer to him, quite close, he could feel her breath on his cheek; and then again, with all the moral force that was in him, he pushed her away.

Then he seemed to lie for a long time in a strange lassitude. He was still sitting forward with his hands pressed tightly together, his eyes fixed on the altar, but his brain seemed to have ceased to work. He had that sensation of suddenly standing outside and above himself. He saw Maradick sitting there, he saw the dusky church and the dim gold light over the altar, and outside the sweep of the plain and the dark plunging sea; and he was above and beyond it all. He wondered a little that that man could be so troubled about so small an affair. He wondered and then pitied him. What a perspective he must have, poor thing, to fancy that his struggles were of so vast an importance.

He saw him as a baby, a boy, a man—stolid, stupid self-centred, ignorant. Oh! so dull a soul! such a lump of clay, just filling space as a wall fills it; but no use, with no share at all in the music that was on every side of him.

And then, because for an instant the flame has descended upon him and his eyes have been opened, he rushes at once to take refuge in his body. He is afraid of his soul, the light of it hurts him, he cowers in his dark corner groping for his food, wanting his sensuality to be satisfied; and the little spark that has been kindled is nearly out, in a moment it will be gone, because he did not know what to do with it, and the last state of that man is worse than the first.

And slowly he came back to himself. The candles had been extinguished. The church was quite dark. Only a star shone through the little window and some late bird was singing. He gathered himself together. It must be late and he must see Morelli. He stumbled out of the church.

He knew as he faced the wind and the night air that in some obscure way, as yet only very vaguely realised, he had won the moral victory over himself. He had no doubt about what he must do; he had no doubt at all about the kind of life that he must lead afterwards. He saw that he had been given something very precious to keep—his *vie sacré*, as it were—and he knew that everyone had this *vie sacré* somewhere, that it was something that they never talked about, something that they kept very closely hidden, and that it was when they had soiled it, or hurt it, or even perhaps for a time lost it, that they were unhappy and saw life miserably and distrusted their fellow beings. He had never had it before; but he had got it now, his precious golden box, and it would make all life a new thing.

But there was still his body. He had never felt so strong in his life before; the blood raced through his veins, he felt as though he would like to strip himself naked and fight and battle with anything furious and strong.

His sense of weariness had left him; he felt that he must have some vent for his strength immediately or he would commit some crime. For a few minutes he stood there and let the wind blow about his forehead. The storm had passed away. The sky was a very dark blue, and the stars had a wind-blown, misty look, as they often have after a storm. Their gold light was a little watery, as though they had all been dipped in some mysterious lake somewhere in the hills of heaven before they were out in the sky. In spite of the wind there was a great silence, and the bird on some dark wind-bent tree continued to sing. The trees on either side of the lane rose, dark walls, against the sky. Then in the distance there were cries, at first vague and incoherent, almost uncanny, and then, coming down the lane, he heard the bleating of innumerable sheep. They passed him, their bodies mysteriously white against the dark hedges; they pressed upon each other and their cries came curiously to him, hitting the silence as a ball hits a board; there were very many of them and their feet pattered away into distance. They seemed to him like all the confused and dark thoughts that had surrounded him all these weeks, but that he had now driven away. His head was extraordinarily clear; he felt as though he had come out of a long sleep.

The lights were beginning to come out in the town as he entered it. It must be, he thought, about eight o'clock, and Morelli had probably returned from Truro. It had not occurred to him until now to think of what he was going to say to Morelli. After all, there wasn't really very much to say, simply that his daughter was gone and that she would never come back again, and that he, Maradick, had helped her to go. It hadn't occurred to him until now to consider how Morelli would probably take his share in it. He wouldn't like it, of course; there would probably be some unpleasantness.

And then Morelli was undoubtedly a queer person. Tony was a very healthy normal boy, not at all given to unnecessary terror, but he had been frightened by Morelli. And then there were a host of little things, none of them amounting to anything in themselves, but taken together—oh yes! the man was queer.

The street was quite empty; the lamplighter had not yet reached that part of the town and the top of the hill was lost in darkness. Maradick found the bell and rang it, and even as he did so a curious feeling of uneasiness began to creep over him. He, suddenly and quite unconsciously, wanted to run away. He began to imagine that there was something waiting for him on the other side of the door, and when it actually opened and showed him only Lucy, the little maid-of-all-work, he almost started with surprise.

"No, sir; they're all out. I don't know when Miss Janet will be back, I'm sure. I'm expecting the master any moment, sir." She seemed, Maradick thought, a little frightened. "I don't know, I'm sure, sir, about Miss Janet; she said nothing about dinner, sir. I've been alone." She stopped and twisted her apron in her hands.

Maradick looked down the street, then he turned back and looked past her into the hall. "Mr. Morelli told me that he would be back about now," he said; "I promised to wait."

She stood aside to let him enter the hall. She was obviously relieved that there was some one else in the house. She was even inclined to be a little confidential. "That kitchen," she said and stopped.

"Yes?" he said, standing in the hall and looking at her.

"Well, it fairly gives you the creeps. Being alone all day down in the basement too. . . ." There was a little choke in her voice and her face was very white in the darkness. She was quite a child and not very tidy; pathetic, Maradick thought.

"Well," he said, "your master will be back in a minute."

"Yes, sir, and it's all dark, sir. I'll light the lamp upstairs."

She led the way with a candle. He followed her up the stairs, and his uneasiness seemed to increase with every step that he took. He had a strange consciousness that Morelli had really returned and that he was waiting for him somewhere in the darkness. The stairs curved, and he could see the very faint light of the higher landing above him; the candle that the girl carried flung their two heads on to the wall, gigantic, absurd. His hair seemed to stand up in the shadow like a forest and his nose was hooked like an elephant's trunk.

She lit the lamp in the sitting-room and then stood with the candle by the door.

"I suppose you couldn't tell me, sir," she said timidly, "when Miss Janet is likely—what time she'll be in?"

"Your master will probably be able to tell you," said Maradick.

Lucy was inclined for conversation. "It's funny, sir," she said, "what difference Miss Janet makes about the house, comin' in and goin' out. You couldn't want a better mistress; but if it weren't for 'er . . . I must be seein' to things downstairs." She hurried away.

The room was quiet save for the ticking of the clock. The little blue tiles of the fireplace shone under the lamp, the china plates round the wall made eyes at him.

He was sitting straight up in his chair listening. The uneasiness that he had felt at first would soon, if he did not keep it in check, grow into terror. There was no reason, no cause that he could in the least define, but he felt as though things were happening outside the door. He didn't know what sort of things, but he fancied that by listening very hard he could hear soft footsteps, whispers, and a noise like the rustling of carpets. The ticking of the clock grew louder and louder, and to forget it he flung up the window so that he could hear the noises of the town. But there weren't any noises; only, very far away, some cat was howling. The night was now very dark; the stars seemed to have disappeared; the wind made the lamp flare. He closed the window.

At the same moment the door opened and he saw Morelli standing there smiling at him. It was the same charming smile, the trusting, confiding laugh of a child; the merry twinkle in the eyes, taking the whole world as a delightful, delicious joke.

"Why, Maradick!" He seemed surprised, and came forward holding out his hand. "I'm delighted! I hope you haven't been waiting long. But why is Janet not entertaining you? She's only upstairs, I expect. I'll call her." He moved back towards the door.

"Miss Morelli isn't in," Maradick said slowly. He was standing up and resting one hand on the table.

"Not in?"

"No. Your servant told me so."

He wanted to say more. He wanted to give his message at once and go, but his tongue seemed tied. He sat down, leaning both his arms on the table.

Morelli laughed. "Oh well, I expect she's out with Minns somewhere—walking, I suppose. They're often late; but we'll wait supper a little if you don't mind. We'll give them ten minutes. Well, how's young Gale?"

Seeing him like this, it was almost impossible to reconcile him with all the absurdly uncouth ideas that Maradick had had of him. But the uncanny feeling of there being some one outside the door was still with him; he had a foolish impulse to ask Morelli to open it.

Then he leant across the table and looked Morelli in the face.

"That's what I came to tell you. Young Gale has gone."

"Gone? What, with his people? I'm sorry. I liked him."

"No. Not with his people. He was married to your daughter at two o'clock this afternoon. They have gone to London."

There was absolute silence. Morelli didn't move. He was sitting now on the opposite side of the table facing Maradick.

"My daughter has gone to London with Gale?" he said very slowly. The smile had died away from his face and his eyes were filled with tears.

"Yes. They were married to-day. They have gone to London."

"Janet!" He called her name softly as though she were in the next room. "Janet!" He waited as though he expected an answer, and then suddenly he burst into tears. His head fell forward between his arms on to the table; his shoulders shook.

Maradick watched him. It was the most desolate thing in the world; he felt the most utter cad. If it had been possible he would have, at that moment, brought Janet and Tony back by main force.

"I say," he muttered, "I'm awfully sorry." He stopped. There was nothing to say.

Then suddenly Morelli looked up. The tears seemed to have vanished, but his eyes were shining with extraordinary brilliance. His hands, with their long white fingers, were bending over the table; his upper lip seemed to have curled back like the mouth of a dog.

He looked at Maradick very intently.

"You saw them married?"

"Yes."

"You saw them leave for London?"

"Yes."

"You have helped them all this time?"

"Yes."

"Why?"

"I thought that they ought to marry; I was fond of both of them. I wanted them to marry."

"And now I will kill you."

He said it without moving; his face seemed to grow more like a beast's at every moment. His hands stretched across the table; the long fingers were like snakes.

"I must go." Maradick got up. Panic was about him again. He felt that he ought to make some kind of defence of what he had done, but the words would not come.

"You will see, afterwards, that what I did was best. It was really the best. We will talk again about it, when you feel calmer."

He moved towards the door; but Morelli was coming towards him with his head thrust forward, his back a little bent, his hands hanging, curved, in mid-air, and he was smiling.

"I am going to kill you, here and now," he said. "It is not a very terrible affair. It will not be very long. You can't escape; but it is not because you have done this or that, it is not for anything that you have done. It is only because you are so stupid, so dreadfully stupid. There are others like you, and I hate you all, you fools. You do not understand anything—what I am or who I am, or the world—nothing."

Maradick said nothing. The terror that had once seized Tony was about him now like a cloud; the thing that was approaching him was not a man, but something impure, unclean. It was exactly as though he were being slowly let down into a dungeon full of creeping snakes.

His breath was coming with difficulty. He felt stifled.

"You must let me out," he gasped.

"Oh no, I will throw you out, later. Now, you are here. That boy understood a little, and that girl too. They were young, they were alive, they were part of me; I loved to have them about me. Do you suppose that I care whether they are married; what is that to me? But they are gone. You with your blundering, you fat fool, you have done that; and now I will play with you."

Maradick, suddenly feeling that if he did not move soon he would be unable to move at all, stumbled for the door. In an instant Morelli was upon him. His hand hung for an instant above Maradick like a whip in the air, then it fastened on his arm. It passed up to Maradick's neck; his other hand was round his waist, his head was flung back.

Then curiously, with the touch of the other man's hand Maradick's strength returned. He was himself again; his muscles grew taut and firm. He knew at once that it was a case of life and death. The other man's fingers seemed to grip his neck like steel; already they were pressing into the flesh. He shot out his arm and caught Morelli's neck, but it was like gripping iron, his hand seemed to slip away. Then Morelli's hand suddenly dug into Maradick's shoulder-bone. It turned about there like a gimlet. Suddenly something seemed to give, and a hot burning pain twisted inside his flesh as an animal twists in its burrow. They swayed backwards and forwards in the middle of the room. Maradick pushed the other body slowly back and, with a crash, it met the table. The thing fell, and the lamp flamed for an instant to the ceiling and then was on the floor in a thousand pieces.

When the lamp fell the darkness seemed to leap like a wall out of the ground. It fell all about them; it pressed upon them, and the floor heaved to and fro.

They had turned round and round, so that Maradick was confused and could not remember where the door was. Then the other man's hand was pressing on his throat so that he was already beginning to be stifled; then he felt that he was dizzy. He was swimming on a sea, lights flashed in and out of the darkness; the window made a grey square, and through this there seemed to creep innumerable green lizards—small with burning eyes; they crawled over the floor towards him. He began to whimper, "No, Morelli, please . . . my God . . . my God!" His shoulder burnt like fire; his brain began to reel so that he fancied that there were many people there crushing him. Then he knew that Morelli was slowly pressing him back. One hand was about his neck, but the other had crept in through his shirt and had touched the skin. Maradick felt the fingers pressing over his chest. Then the fingers began to pinch. They caught the flesh and seemed to tear it; it was like knives. All his body was on fire. Then the fingers seemed to be all over his limbs. They crept down to his hip, his thigh. They bit into his flesh, and then he knew that Morelli was pressing some nerve in his hip and pushing it from the socket. At that moment he himself became aware, for the first time, of Morelli's body. He pressed against his chest and his fingers had torn the man's clothes away. Morelli's chest was hairy like an animal's and cold as marble. He was sweating in every pore, but Morelli was icy cold. He dug his nails into the flesh, but they seemed to slip away. His arm was right round Morelli's body; the cold flesh slipped and shrunk beneath his touch. His mouth was against Morelli's neck. He had a sudden wild impulse to bite. He was becoming a wild beast. . . .

Then Morelli seemed to encircle the whole of him. Every part of his body was touched by those horrible fingers—his arms, his neck; it was as though he were being bitten to death. Then he felt in his neck teeth; something was biting him. . . .

He screamed again and again, but only a hoarse murmur seemed to come from his lips. He was still struggling, but he was going; the room seemed full of animals. They were biting him, tearing him; and then again he could feel the soft fingers stealing about his body.

A curious feeling of sleepiness stole over him. The pain in his shoulder and his arm was so terrible that he wanted to die; his body twitched with a fresh spasm of pain. Things—he did not know what they were—were creeping up his legs; soon they would be at his chest.

He knew that they were both naked to the waist. He could feel the blood trickling down his face and his arms. . . .

Tony was in the room! Yes, Tony. How was he there? Never mind! He would help him! "Tony! Tony! They're doing for me!" Tony was all over the room. He pulled himself together, and suddenly fell against the knob of the door. They fell against it together. He hit at the other's naked body, hit at it again and again. Strength seemed to pour back into his body in a flood. He had been nearly on his knees, but now he was pressing up again.

He snatched at the hand about his neck and tore it away. Again they were surging about the room. His hand was upon the door. Morelli's hands were about his and tried to drag it away, but he clung. For an age they seemed to hang there, panting, heaving, clutching.

Then he had turned it. The door flew open and his foot lunged out behind him. He kicked with all his force, but he touched nothing. There was nothing there.

He looked back. The door was open. There was a grey light over the room. Something was muttering, making a noise like a dog over a bone. He could hear the ticking of the clock through the open door; it struck nine. There was perfect stillness; no one was near him.

Then silently, trembling in every limb, he crept down the stairs. In a moment he was in the street.

CHAPTER XIX
NIGHT OF THE TWENTY-SEVENTH—
MARADICK AND MRS. LESTER

But the gods had not yet done with his night.

As the sharp night air met him he realised that his clothes were torn apart and that his chest was bare. He pulled his shirt about him again, stupidly made movements with his hand as though he would brush back the hair from his eyes, and then found that it was blood that was trickling from a wound in his forehead.

That seemed to touch something in him, so that he suddenly leaned against the wall and, with his head in his arm, began to cry. There was no reason really why he should cry; in fact, he didn't want to cry—it was like a woman to cry. He repeated it stupidly to himself, "like a woman, like a woman. . . ."

Then he began slowly to fling himself together, as it were; to pick up the bits and to feel that he, Maradick, still existed as a personal identity. He pulled his clothes about him and looked at the dark house. It was absolutely silent; there were no lights anywhere. What had happened? Was Morelli looking at him now from some dark corner, watching him from behind some black window?

And then, as his head grew cooler under the influence of the night air, another thought came to him. What was the little parlour-maid doing? What would happen to her, shut up all night in that house alone with that . . .? Ought he to go back? He could see her cowering, down in the basement somewhere, having heard probably the noise of the crashing lamp, terrified, waiting for Morelli to find her. Yes, he ought to go back. Then he knew that nothing, nothing in the world—no duty and no claim, no person, no power—could drive him back into that house again. He looked back on it afterwards as one of the most shameful things in his life, that he had not gone back to see what had happened to the girl; but he could not go, nothing would make him. It was not anything physical that he might have to face. If it had been ordinary normal odds—a "scrap," as he would call it—then he would have faced it without hesitation. But there was something about that struggle upstairs that made him sick; it was something unreal, unclean, indecent. It had been abnormal, and all that there had been in it had not been the actual struggle, the blows and wounds, but something about it that must be undefined, unnamed: the "air," the "atmosphere" of the thing, the sudden throwing down of the decent curtain that veils this world from others.

But he couldn't analyse it like that now. He only felt horribly sick at the thought of it, and his one urgent idea was to get away, far, far away, from the house and all that it contained.

The night was very dark; no one would see him. He must get back to the hotel and slip up to his room and try and make himself decent. He turned slowly up the hill.

Then, as his thoughts became clearer, he was conscious of a kind of exultation at its being over. So much more than the actual struggle seemed to be over; it swept away all the hazy moral fog that he had been in during the last weeks. In casting off Morelli, in flinging him from him physically as well as morally, he seemed to have flung away all that belonged to him— the wildness, the hot blood, the unrest that had come to him! He wondered whether after all Morelli had not had a great deal to do with it. There were more things in it all than he could ever hope to understand.

And then, on top of it all, came an overwhelming sensation of weariness. He went tottering up the hill with his eyes almost closed. Tired! He had never felt so tired in his life before. He was already indifferent to everything that had happened. If only he might just lie down for a minute and close his eyes; if only he hadn't got this horrible hill to climb! It would be easier to lie down there in the hedge somewhere and go to sleep. He considered the advisability of doing so. He really did not care what happened to him. And then the thought came to him that Morelli was coming up the hill after him; Morelli was waiting probably until he *did* fall asleep, and then he would be upon him. Those fingers would steal about his body again, there would be that biting pain. He struggled along. No, he must not stop.

At last he was in the hotel garden. He could hear voices and laughter from behind closed doors, but there seemed to be no one in the hall. He stumbled up the stairs to his room and met no one on the way. His bath seemed to him the most wonderful thing that he had ever had. It was steaming hot, and he lay absolutely motionless with his eyes closed letting his brain very slowly settle itself. It was like a coloured puzzle that had been shaken to pieces and scattered; now, of their own initiative, all the little squares and corners seemed to come together again. He was able to think sanely and soberly once more, and, above all, that terrible sensation of having about him something unreal was leaving him. He began to smile now at the things that he had imagined about Morelli. The man had been angry at his helping Janet to run away—that was natural enough; he was, of course, hot-tempered—that was the foreign blood in him. Thank God, the world wasn't an odd place really. One fancied things, of course, when one was run down or excited, but those silly ideas didn't last long if a man was sensible.

He found that the damage wasn't very serious. There were bruises, of course, and nasty scratches, but it didn't amount to very much. As he climbed out of the bath, and stretched his limbs and felt the muscles of his arms, he was conscious of an enormous relief. It was all over; he was right again once more. And then suddenly in a flash he remembered Mrs. Lester.

Well, that was over, of course. But to-night was Thursday. He had promised to see her. He must have one last talk, just to tell her that there must be nothing more of the kind. As he slowly dressed, delighting in the cool of clean linen, he tried to imagine what he would say; but he was tired, so dreadfully tired! He couldn't think; he really couldn't see her to-night. Besides, it was most absolutely over, all of it. He had gone through it all in the church that afternoon. He belonged to his wife now, altogether; he was going to show her what he could be now that he understood everything so much better; and she was going to try too, she had promised him in that funny way the other night.

But he was so tired; he couldn't think connectedly. They all got mixed up, Morelli and Mrs. Lester, Tony and his wife. He stood, trying with trembling fingers to fasten his collar. The damned stud! how it twisted about! When he had got its silly head one way and was slipping the collar over it, then suddenly it slipped round the other way and left his fingers aching.

Oh! he supposed he must see her. After all, it was better to have it out now and settle it, settle it once and for ever. These women—beastly nuisance. Damn the stud!

He had considered the question of telling the family and had decided to leave it until the morning. He was much too tired to face them all now with their questions and anger and expostulation. Oh! he'd had enough of that, poor man!

Besides, there wouldn't be any anxiety until the morning. Tony was so often late, and although Sir Richard would probably fume and scold at his cutting dinner again, still, he'd done it so often. No, Lady Gale was really the question. If she worried, if she were going to spend an anxious night thinking about it, then he ought to go and tell her at once. But she probably had a pretty good idea about the way things had gone. She would not be any more anxious now than she had been during all these last weeks, and he really felt, just now, physically incapable of telling her. No, he wouldn't see any of them yet. He would go up to the room of the minstrels and think what he was to do. He always seemed to be able to think better up there.

But Mrs. Lester! What was he to do about her? He felt now simply antagonism. He hated her, the very thought of her! What was he doing with that kind of thing? Why couldn't he have left her alone?

A kind of fury seized him at the thought of her! He shook his fist at the ceiling and scowled at the looking-glass; then he went wearily to the room. But it was dark, and he was frightened now by the dark. He stood on the threshold scarcely daring to enter. Then with trembling fingers he felt for the matches and lit the two candles. But even then the light that they cast was so uncertain, they left so many corners dark, and then there were such strange grey lights under the gallery that he wasn't at all happy. Lord! what a state his nerves were in!

He was afraid lest he should go to sleep, and then anything might happen. He faced the grey square of the window with shrinking eyes; it was through there that the green lizards . . .

He would have liked to have crossed the room to prevent the window from rattling if he'd had the courage, but the sound of his steps on the floor frightened him. He remembered his early enthusiasm about the room. Well, that was a long, long time ago. Not long in hours, he knew, but in experience! It was another lifetime!

It was the tower that he wanted. He could see it now, in the market-place, so strong and quiet and grey! That was the kind of thing for him to have in his mind: rest and strength. Drowsing away in his chair—the candles flinging lions and tigers on the wall, the old brown of the gallery sparkling and shining under the uneven light—the tower seemed to come to him through all the black intervening space of night. It grew and grew, until it stood beyond the window, great grey and white stone, towering to the sky, filling the world; that and the sea alone in all creation.

He was nearly asleep, his head forward on his chest, his arms hanging loosely over the sides of the chair, when he heard the door creak.

He started up in sudden alarm. The candles did not fling their circle of light as far as the door—*that* was in darkness, a black square darker than the rest of the world; and then as his eyes stared at it he saw that there was a figure outlined against it, a grey, shadowy figure.

In a whisper he stammered, "Who is that?"

Then she came forward into the circle of the candles—Mrs. Lester! Mrs. Lester in her blue silk dress cut very low, Mrs. Lester with diamonds in her hair and a very bright red in her cheeks, Mrs. Lester looking at him timidly, almost terrified, bending a little forward to stare at him.

"Ah! it's you!" He could hear her breath of relief. "I didn't know, I thought it might be!" She stood staring at him, a little smile hovering on her lips, uncertainly, as though it were not sure whether it ought to be there.

"Ah! it's you!"

He stood up and faced her, leaning heavily with one hand on the chair.

He wanted to tell her to go away; that he was tired and wasn't really up to talking—the morning would be better. But he couldn't speak. He could do nothing but stand there and stare at her stupidly.

Then at last, in a voice that did not seem his own at all, he said, "Won't you sit down?" She laughed, leaning forward a little with both hands on the green baize table, looking at him.

"You don't mind, do you? If you do, I'll go at once. But it's our last evening. We may not see much of each other again, and I'd like you to understand me." Then she sat down in a chair by the table, her dress rustling like a sea about her. The candle light fell on it and her, and behind her the room was dark.

But Maradick sat with his head hidden by his hand. He did not want to look at her, he did not want to speak to her. Already the fascination of her presence was beginning to steal over him again. It had been easy enough whilst she had been away to say that he did not care. But now the scent, violets, that she used came very delicately across the floor to him. He seemed to catch the blue of her dress with the corner of his eye even though he was not looking at her. She filled the room; the vision that he had had of the tower slipped back into the night, giving place to the new one. He tapped his foot impatiently on the floor. Why could she not have left him alone? He didn't want any more struggles. He simply wasn't up to it, he was so horribly tired. Anything was better than a struggle.

He spoke in a low voice without raising his eyes. "Wasn't it—isn't it— rather risky to come here—like this, now?" After all, how absurd it was! What heaps of plays he had seen with their third act just like this. It was all shadowy, fantastic—the woman, the place. He wanted to sleep.

She laughed. "Risky? Why, no. Fred's in London. Nobody else is likely to bother. But Jim, what's the matter? What's happened? Why are you suddenly like this? Don't you think it's a little unkind on our last evening, the last chance that we shall get of talking? I don't want to be a nuisance or a worry——" She paused with a pathetic little catch in her voice, and she let her hand fall sharply on to the silk of her dress.

He tried to pull himself together, to realise the place and the woman and the whole situation. After all, it was his fault that she was there, and he couldn't behave like a cad after arranging to meet her; and she had been awfully nice during these weeks.

"No, please." He raised his eyes at last and looked at her. "I'm tired, beastly tired; or I was until you came. Don't think me rude, but I've had an awfully exhausting day, really awfully exhausting. But of course I want to talk."

She was looking so charmingly pretty. Her colour, her beautiful shoulders, the way that her dress rose and fell with her breathing—a little hurriedly, but so evenly, like the rise and fall of some very gentle music.

He smiled at her and she smiled back. "There, I knew that you wouldn't be cross, really; and it is our last time, isn't it? And I have got a whole lot of things that I want to say to you."

"Yes," he said, and he leaned back in his chair again, but he did not take his eyes off her face.

"Well, you know, for a long time I wondered whether I would come or not; I couldn't make up my mind. You see, I'd seen nothing of you at all during these last days, nothing at all. Perhaps it was just as well. Anyhow, you had other things to do; and that is, I suppose, the difference between us. With women, sentiment, romance, call it what you like, is everything. It is life; but with you men it is only a little bit, one amongst a lot of other things. Oh! I know. I found that out long ago without waiting for anyone to tell me. But now, perhaps, you've brought it home to me in a way that I hadn't realised before."

He was going to interrupt her, but she stopped him.

"No, don't think that I'm complaining about it. It's perfectly natural. I know—other men are like that. It's only that I had thought that you were a little different, not quite like the rest; that you had seen it as something precious, valuable. . . ."

And so he had, of course he had. Why, it had made all the difference in his life. It was all very well his thinking, as he had that afternoon, that it was Tony or the place or Punch, one odd thing or another that had made him think like that, but, as a matter of fact, it was Mrs. Lester, and no one else. She had shown him all of it.

"No, you mustn't think that of me," he said; "I have taken it very seriously indeed." He wanted to say more, but his head was so heavy that he couldn't think, and he stopped.

Meanwhile she was wondering at her own position. She had come to him that evening in a state of pique. All day she had determined that she would not go. That was to be the end of an amusing little episode. And after all, he was only a great stupid hulk of a thing. He could crush her in his arms, but then so could any coalheaver. And she had got such a nice letter from Fred, the dear, that morning. He had missed her even during the day that he had been away. Oh yes! she wouldn't see any more of Mr. Maradick!

But she would like to have just a word alone with him. She expected to see him at teatime. But no; Sir Richard and Rupert had seen him at the station and he had said that he was following them back. But no; well, then, at dinner. Neither Tony nor he were at dinner.

Oh well! he couldn't care very much about her if he could stay away during the whole of their last day together! She was well out of it all. She read Fred's letter a great many times and kissed it. Then directly after dinner—they were *so* dull downstairs, everyone seemed to have the acutest depression and kept on wondering where Tony was—she went to her room and started writing a long, long letter to her "little pet of a Fredikins"; at least it was going to be a long, long letter, and then somehow it would not go on.

Mr. Maradick was a beast. If he thought that he could just play fast and loose with women like that, do just what he liked with them, he was mightily mistaken. She flung down her pen. The room was stifling! She went to her window and opened it; she leaned out. Ah! how cool and refreshing the night air was. There was somebody in the distance playing something. It sounded like a flute or a pipe. How nice and romantic! She closed the window. After all, where was he? He must be somewhere all this time. She must speak to him just once before she went away. She must, even though it were only to tell him . . . Then she remembered that dusty, empty room upstairs. He had told her that he often went up there.

And so she came. That was the whole history of it. She hadn't, when she came into the room, the very least idea of anything that she was going to do or say. Only that it was romantic, and that she had an extraordinarily urgent desire to be crushed once more in those very strong arms.

"I have taken it very seriously indeed." He wondered, as he said it to her, what it was, exactly, that he had taken seriously. The "it" was very much more than simply Mrs. Lester; he saw that very clearly. She was only the expression of a kind of mood that he had been in during these last weeks, a kind of genuine atmosphere that she stood for, just as some quite simple and commonplace thing—a chair, a picture, a vase of flowers—sometimes stands for a great experience or emotion. And then—his head was clearer now; that led him to see further still.

He suddenly grasped that she wasn't really for him a woman at all, that, indeed, she never had been. He hadn't thought of her as the woman, the personal character and identity that he wanted, but simply as a sort of emotional climax to the experiences that he had been having; any other woman, he now suddenly saw, would have done just as well. And then, the crisis being over, the emotional situation being changed, the woman would remain; that would be the hell of it!

And that led him—all this in the swift interval before she answered him—to wonder whether she, too, had been wanting him also, not as a man, not as James Maradick, but simply as a cap to fit the mood that she was in: any man would fit as well. If that were the case with her as well as with him what a future they were spared by his suddenly seeing as clearly as he did. If that were not so, then the whole thing bristled with difficulties; but that was what he must set himself to find out, now, at once.

Then, in her next speech, he saw two things quite clearly—that she was determined, come what might, to have her way about to-night at any rate, and to go to any lengths to obtain it. She might not have been determined when she came into the room, but she was determined now.

She leant forward in her chair towards him, her cheeks were a little redder, her breath was coming a little faster.

"Jim, I know you meant it seriously. I know you mean it seriously now. But there isn't much time; and after all, there isn't much to say. We've arranged it all before. We were to have this night, weren't we, and then, afterwards, we'd arrange to go abroad or something. Here we are, two modern people, you and I, looking at the thing squarely. All our lives we've lived stupidly, dully, comfortably. There's never been anything in the very least to disturb us. And now suddenly this romance has come. Are we, just because of stupid laws that stupid people made hundreds of years ago, to miss the chance of our lives? Jim!"

She put one hand across towards him and touched his knee.

But he, looking her steadily in the face, spoke without moving.

"Wait," he said. "Stop. I want to ask you a question. Do you love me—really, I mean? So that you would go with me to-morrow to Timbuctoo, anywhere?"

For an instant she lowered her eyes, then she said vehemently, eagerly, "Of course, of course I do. You know—Jim, how can you ask? Haven't I shown it by coming here?"

But that was exactly what she hadn't done. Her coming there showed the opposite, if anything; and indeed, at once, in a way that she had answered him, he had seen the truth. She might think, at that moment, quite honestly that she loved him, but really what she wanted was not the man at all, but the expression, the emotion, call it what you will.

And he saw, too, exactly what the after-results would be. They would both of them in the morning postpone immediate action. They would wait a few weeks. She would return to her husband; for a little, perhaps, they would write. And then gradually they would forget. She would begin to look on it as an incident, a "romantic hour"; she would probably sigh with relief at the thought of all the ennui and boredom that she had avoided by not running away with him. He, too, would begin to regard it lightly, would put it down to that queer place, to anything and everything, even perhaps to Morelli; and then—well, it's no use in crying over spilt milk, and there's no harm done after all—and so on, until at last it would be forgotten altogether. And so "the unforgiveable sin" would have been committed, "the unforgiveable sin," not because they had broken social laws and conventions, but because they had acted without love—the unforgiveable sin of lust of the flesh for the sake of the flesh alone.

After her answer to his question she paused for a moment, and he said nothing; then she went on again: "Of course, you know I care, with all my heart and soul." She said the last three words with a little gasp, and both her hands pressed tightly together. She had moved her chair closer to his, and now both her hands were on his knee and her face was raised to his.

"Then you would go away with me to-morrow anywhere?"

"Yes, of course," she answered, now without any hesitation.

"You know that you would lose your good name, your life at home, your friends, most of them? Everything that has made life worth living to you?"

"Yes—I love you."

"And then there is your husband. He has been very good to you. He has never given you the least cause of complaint. He's been awfully decent to you."

"Oh! he doesn't care. It's you, Jim; I love you heart and soul."

But he knew through it all that she didn't: the very repetition of the phrase showed that. She was trying, he knew, to persuade herself that she did because of the immediate pleasure that it would bring her. She wasn't consciously insincere, but he shrank back in his chair from her touch, because he was not sure what he would do if he let her remain there.

He put her hands aside firmly. "No, you mustn't. Look here, I've something to tell you. I know you'll think me an awful cad, but I must be straight with you. I've found out something. I've been thinking all these days, and, you know, I don't love you as I thought I did. Not in the fine way that I imagined; I don't even love you as I love my wife. It is only sensual, all of it. It's your body that I want, not you. That sounds horrible, doesn't it? I know, I'm ashamed, but it's true."

His voice sank into a whisper. He expected her to turn on him with scorn, loathing, hatred. Perhaps she would even make a scene. Well, that was better, at any rate, than going on with it. He might just save his soul and hers in time. But he did not dare to look at her. He was ashamed to raise his eyes. And then, to his amazement, he felt her hand on his knee again. Her face was very close to his and she was speaking very softly.

"Well—perhaps—dear, that other kind of love will come. That's really only one part of it. That other love cannot come at once."

He turned his eyes to her. She was looking at him, smiling.

"But you don't understand, you can't?"

"Yes, I understand."

Then something savage in him began to stir. He caught her hands in his fiercely, roughly.

"No, you can't. I tell you I don't love you at all. Not as a decent man loves a decent woman. A few weeks ago I thought that I had found my soul. I saw things differently; it was a new world, and I thought that you had shown it me. But it was not really you at all. It isn't I that you care for, it's your husband, and we are both being led by the devil—here—now!"

"Ah!" she said, drawing back a little. "I thought you were braver than that. You do care for all the old conventional things after all, 'the sanctity of the marriage tie,' and all the rest of it. I thought that we had settled all that."

"No," he answered her. "It isn't the conventions that I care for, but it's our souls, yours and mine. If we loved each other it would be a different thing; but I've found out there's something more than thrilling at another person's touch—that isn't enough. I don't love you; we must end it."

"No!" She had knelt down by his chair and had suddenly taken both his hands in hers, and was kissing them again and again. "No, Jim, we must have to-night. Never mind about the rest. I want you—now. Take me."

Her arms were about him. Her head was on his chest. Her fascination began to steal about him again. His blood began to riot. After all, what were all these casuistries, this talk about the soul? Anyone could talk, it was living that mattered. He began to press her hands; his head was swimming.

Then suddenly a curious thing happened. The room seemed to disappear. Mrs. Maradick was sitting on the edge of her bed looking at him. He could see the pathetic bend of her head as she looked at him. He felt once again, as he had felt in Morelli's room, as though there were devils about him.

He was tired again, dog-tired; in a moment he was going to yield. Both women were with him again. Beyond the window was the night, the dark hedges, the white road, the tower, grey and cold with the shadow lying at its feet and moving with the moon as the waves move on the shore.

For a moment the fire seized him. He felt nothing but her body—the pressure, the warmth of it. His fingers grated a little on the silk of her dress.

There was perfect silence, and he thought that he could hear, beyond the beating of their hearts, the sounds of the night—the rustle of the trees, the monotonous drip of water, the mysterious distant playing of the flute that he had heard before. His hands were crushing her. In another moment he would have bent and covered her face, her body, with kisses; then, like the coming of a breeze after a parching stillness, the time was past.

He got up and gently put her hands away. He walked across the room and looked out at the stars, the moon, the light on the misty trees.

He had won his victory.

His voice was quite quiet when he spoke to her.

"You had better, we had both better go to bed. It must never happen, to either of us, because it isn't good enough. I'm not the sort of man, you're not the sort of woman, that that does for; you know that you don't really love me."

She had risen too, and now stood by the door, her head hanging a little, her hands limply by her side. Then she gave a hard little laugh.

"I've rather given myself away," she said harshly. "Only, don't you think it would have been kinder, honester, to have said this a week ago?"

"I don't try to excuse myself," he said quietly. "I've been pretty rotten, but that's no reason — —" He stopped abruptly.

She clenched her hands, and then suddenly flung up her head and looked at him across the room furiously.

"Good night, Mr. Maradick," she said, and was gone.

CHAPTER XX
MARADICK TELLS THE FAMILY, HAS BREAKFAST WITH HIS WIFE, AND SAYS GOOD-BYE TO SOME FRIENDS

But he did not sleep.

Perhaps it was because his fatigue lay upon him like a heavy burden, so that to close his eyes was as though he allowed a great weight to fall upon him and crush him. His fatigue hung above him like a dark ominous cloud; it seemed indeed so ominous that he was afraid of it. At the moment when sleep seemed to come to him he would pull himself back with a jerk, he was afraid of his dreams.

Towards about four o'clock in the morning he fell into confused slumber. Shapes, people—Tony, Morelli, Mrs. Lester, his wife, Epsom, London—it was all vague, misty, and, in some incoherent way, terrifying. He wanted to wake, he tried to force himself to wake, but his eyes refused to open, they seemed to be glued together. The main impression that he got was of saying farewell to some one, or rather to a great many people. It was as though he were going away to a distant land, somewhere from which he felt that he would never return. But when he approached these figures to say good-bye they would disappear or melt into some one else.

About half-past six he awoke and lay tranquilly watching the light fill the windows and creep slowly, mysteriously, across the floor. His dreams had left him, but in spite of his weariness when he had gone to bed and the poor sleep that he had had he was not tired. He had a sensation of relief, of having completed something and, which was of more importance, of having got rid of it. A definite period in his life seemed to be ended, marked off. He had something of the feeling that Christian had when his pack left him. All the emotions, the struggles, the confusions of the last weeks were over, finished. He didn't regret them; he welcomed them because of the things that they had taught him, but he did not want them back again. It was almost like coming through an illness.

He knew that it was going to be a difficult day. There were all sorts of explanations, all kinds of "settling up." But he regarded it all very peacefully. It did not really matter; the questions had all been answered, the difficulties all resolved.

At half-past seven he got up quietly, had his bath and dressed. When he came back into the bedroom he found that his wife was still asleep. He watched her, with her head resting on her hand and her hair lying in a dark cloud on the pillow. As he stood above her a great feeling of tenderness swept over him. That was quite new; he had never thought of her tenderly before. Emmy Maradick wasn't the sort of person that you did think of tenderly. Probably no one had ever thought of her in that way before.

But now—things had all changed so in these last weeks. There were two Emmy Maradicks. That was his great discovery, just of course as there were two James Maradicks.

He hadn't any illusion about it. He didn't in the least expect that the old Emmy Maradick would suddenly disappear and never come out again. That, of course, was absurd, things didn't happen so quickly. But now that he knew that the other one, the recent mysterious one that he had seen the shadow of ever so faintly, was there, everything would be different. And it would grow, it would grow, just as this new soul of his own was going to grow.

Whilst he looked at her she awoke, looked at him for a moment without realisation, and then gave a little cry: "Oh! Is it late?"

"No, dear, just eight. I'll be back for breakfast at quarter to nine."

In her eyes was again that wondering pathetic little question. As an answer he bent down and kissed her tenderly. He had not kissed her like that for hundreds of years. As he bent down to her her hands suddenly closed furiously about him. For a moment she held him, then she let him go. As he left the room his heart was beating tumultuously.

And so he went downstairs to face the music, as he told himself.

He knocked on the Gales' sitting-room door and some one said "Come in." He drew a deep breath of relief when he saw that Lady Gale was in there alone.

"Ah! that's good!"

She was sitting by the window with her head towards him. She seemed to him—it was partly the grey silk dress that she wore and partly her wonderful crown of white hair—unsubstantial, as though she might fade away out of the window at any moment.

He had even a feeling that he ought to clutch at her, hold her, to prevent her from disappearing. Then he saw the dark lines under her eyes and her lack of colour; she was looking terribly tired.

"Ah, I am ashamed; I ought to have told you last night."

She gave him her hand and smiled.

"No, it's all right; it's probably better as it is. I won't deny that I was anxious, of course, that was natural. But I was hoping that you would come in now, before my husband comes in. I nearly sent a note up to you to ask you to come down."

Her charming kindness to him moved him strangely. Oh! she was a wonderful person.

"Dear Lady," he said, "that's like you. Not to be furious with me, I mean. But of course that's what I'm here for now, to face things. I expect it and I deserve it; I was left for that."

"Left?" she said, looking at him. He saw that her hand moved ever so quickly across her lap and then back again.

"Yes. Of course Tony's gone. He was married yesterday afternoon at two o'clock at the little church out on the hill. The girl's name is Janet Morelli. She is nineteen. They are now in Paris; but he gave me this letter for you."

He handed her the letter that Tony had given to him on the way up to the station.

She did not say anything to him, but took the letter quickly and tore it open. She read it twice and then handed it to him and waited for him to read it. It ran:—

DEAREST AND MOST WONDERFUL OF MOTHERS,

By the time that you get this I shall be in Paris and Janet will be my wife. Janet Morelli is her name, and you will simply love her when you see her. Do you remember telling me once that whatever happened I was to marry the right person? Well, suddenly I saw her one night like Juliet looking out of a window, and there was never any question again; isn't it wonderful? But, of course, you know if I had told you the governor would have had to know, and then there would simply have been the dickens of a rumpus and I'd have got kicked out or something, and no one would have been a bit the better and it would have been most awfully difficult for you. And so I kept it dark and told Maradick to. Of course the governor will be sick at first, but as you didn't know anything about it he can't say anything to you, and that's all that matters. Because, of course, Maradick can look after himself, and doesn't, as a matter of fact, ever mind in the least what anyone says to him. We'll go to Paris directly afterwards, and then come back and live in Chelsea, I expect. I'm going to write like anything; but in any case, you know, it won't matter, because I've got that four hundred a year and we can manage easily on that. The governor will soon get over it, and I know that he'll simply love Janet really. Nobody could help it.

And oh! mother dear, I'm so happy. I didn't know one could be so happy; and that's what you wanted, didn't you? And I love you all the more because of it, you and Janet. Send me just a line to the Hôtel Lincoln, Rue de Montagne, Paris, to say that you forgive me. Janet sends her love. Please send her yours.

Ever your loving son,
Tony.

PS.—Maradick has been simply ripping. He's the most splendid man that ever lived. I simply don't know what we'd have done without him.

There was silence for a minute or two. Then she said softly, "Dear old Tony. Tell me about the girl."

"She's splendid. There's no question at all about her being the right thing. I've seen a lot of her, and there's really no question at all. She's seen nothing of the world and has lived down here all her life. She's simply devoted to Tony."

"And her people?"

"There is only her father. He's a queer man. She's well away from him. I don't think he cares a bit about her, really. They're a good old family, I believe. Italians originally, of course. The father has a good deal of the foreigner in him, but the girl's absolutely English."

There was another pause, and then she looked up and took his hand.

"I can't thank you enough. You've done absolutely the right thing. There was nothing else but to carry it through with a boy of Tony's temperament. I'm glad, gladder than I can tell you. But of course my husband will take it rather unpleasantly at first. He had ideas about Tony's marrying, and he would have done anything he could to have prevented its happening like this. But now that it has happened, now that there's nothing to be done but to accept it, I think it will soon be all right. But perhaps you had better tell him now at once, and get it over. He will be here in a minute."

At that instant they came in—Sir Richard, Rupert, Alice Du Cane, and Mrs. Lester.

It was obvious at once that Sir Richard was angry. Rupert was amused and a little bored. Alice was excited, and Mrs. Lester tired and white under the eyes.

"What's this?" said Sir Richard, coming forward. "They tell me that Tony hasn't been in all night. That he's gone or something."

Then he caught sight of Maradick.

"Ha! Maradick—Morning! Do you happen to know where the boy is?"

Maradick thought that he could discern through the old man's anger a very real anxiety, but it was a difficult moment.

Lady Gale spoke. "Mr. Maradick has just been telling me——" she began.

"Perhaps Alice and I——" said Mrs. Lester, and moved back to the door. Then Maradick took hold of things.

"No, please don't go. There's nothing that anyone needn't know, nothing. I have just been telling Lady Gale, Sir Richard, that your son was married yesterday at two o'clock at the little church outside the town, to a Miss Janet Morelli. They are now in Paris."

There was silence. No one spoke or moved. The situation hung entirely between Sir Richard and Maradick. Lady Gale's eyes were all for her husband; the way that he took it would make a difference to the rest of their married lives.

Sir Richard breathed heavily. His face went suddenly very white. Then in a low voice he said—

"Married? Yesterday?" He seemed to be collecting his thoughts, trying to keep down the ungovernable passion that in a moment would overwhelm him. For a moment he swallowed it. Holding himself very straight he looked Maradick in the face.

"And why has my dutiful son left the burden of this message to you?"

"Because I have, from the beginning, been concerned in the affair. I have known about it from the first. I was witness of their marriage yesterday, and I saw them off at the station."

Sir Richard began to breathe heavily. The colour came back in a flood to his cheeks. His eyes were red. He stepped forward with his fist uplifted, but Rupert put a hand on his arm and his fist fell to his side. He could not speak coherently.

"You—you—you"; and then "You dared? What the devil have you to do with my boy? With us? With our affairs? What the devil is it to do with you? You—you—damn you, sir—my boy—married to anybody, and because a——"

Rupert again put his hand on his father's arm and his words lingered in mid-air.

Then he turned to his wife.

"You—did you know about this—did you know that this was going on?"

Then Maradick saw how wise she had been in her decision to keep the whole affair away from her. It was a turning-point.

If she had been privy to it, Maradick saw, Sir Richard would never forgive her. It would have remained always as a hopeless, impassable barrier between them. It would have hit at the man's tenderest, softest place, his conceit. He might forgive her anything but that.

And so it was a tremendous clearing of the air when she raised her eyes to her husband's and said, without hesitation, "No, Richard. Of course not. I knew nothing until just now when Mr. Maradick told me."

Sir Richard turned back from her to Maradick.

"And so, sir, you see fit, do you, sir, to interfere in matters in which you have no concern. You come between son and father, do you? You——"

But again he stopped. Maradick said nothing. There was nothing at all to say. It was obvious that the actual affair, Tony's elopement, had not, as yet, penetrated to Sir Richard's brain. The only thing that he could grasp at present was that some one—anyone—had dared to step in and meddle with the Gales. Some one had had the dastardly impertinence to think that he was on a level with the Gales, some one had dared to put his plebeian and rude fingers into a Gale pie. Such a thing had never happened before.

Words couldn't deal with it.

He looked as though in another moment he would have a fit. He was trembling, quivering in every limb. Then, in a voice that could scarcely be heard, he said, "My God, I'll have the law of you for this."

He turned round and, without looking at anyone, left the room.

There was silence.

Rupert said "My word!" and whistled. No one else said anything.

And, in this interval of silence, Maradick almost, to his own rather curious surprise, entirely outside the whole affair, was amused rather than bothered by the way they all took it, although "they," as a matter of strict accuracy, almost immediately resolved itself down to Mrs. Lester. Lady Gale had shown him, long ago, her point of view; Sir Richard and Rupert could have only, with their limited conventions, one possible opinion; Alice Du Cane would probably be glad for Tony's sake and so be indirectly grateful; but Mrs. Lester! why, it would be, he saw in a flash, the most splendid bolstering up of the way that she was already beginning to look on last night's affair. He could see her, in a day or two, making his interference with the "Gale pie" on all fours with his own brutal attack on her immaculate virtues. It would be all of a piece in a short time, with the perverted imagination that she would set to play on their own "little" situation. It would be a kind of rose-coloured veil that she might fling over the whole proceeding. "The man who can behave in that kind of way to the Gales is just the kind of man who would, so horribly and brutally, insult a defenceless woman."

He saw in her eyes already the beginning of the picture. In a few days the painting would be complete. But this was all as a side issue. His business, as far as these people were concerned, was over.

Without looking at anyone, he too left the room.

It had been difficult, but after he had had Lady Gale's assurance the rest didn't matter. Of course the old man was bound to take it like that, but he would probably soon see it differently. And at any rate, as far as he, Maradick, was concerned, that—Sir Richard's attitude to him personally— didn't matter in the very least.

But all that affair seemed, indeed, now of secondary importance. The first and only vital matter now was his relations with his wife. Everything must turn to that. Her clasp of his hand had touched him infinitely, profoundly. For the first time in their married lives she wanted him. Sir Richard, Mrs. Lester, even Tony, seemed small, insignificant in comparison with that.

But he must tell her everything—he saw that. All about Mrs. Lester, everything—otherwise they would never start clear.

She was just finishing her dressing when he came into her room. She turned quickly from her dressing-table towards him.

"I'm just ready," she said.

"Wait a minute," he answered her. "Before we go in to the girls there's something, several things, that I want to say."

His great clumsy body moved across the floor, and he sat down hastily in a chair by the dressing-table.

She watched him anxiously with her sharp little eyes. "Yes," she said, "only hurry up. I'm hungry."

"Well, there are two things really," he answered slowly. "Things you've got to know."

She noticed one point, that he didn't apologise in advance as he would have done three weeks ago. There were no apologies now, only a stolid determination to get through with it.

"First, it's about young Tony Gale. I've just been telling his family. He married a girl yesterday and ran off to Paris with her. You can bet the family are pleased."

Mrs. Maradick was excited. "Not really! Really eloped? That Gale boy! How splendid! A real elopement! Of course one could see that something was up. His being out so much, and so on; I knew. But just fancy! Really doing it! Won't old Sir Richard ——!"

Her eyes were sparkling. The romance of it had obviously touched her, it was very nearly as though one had eloped oneself, knowing the boy and everything!

Then he added, "I had to tell them. You see, I've known about it all the time, been in it, so to speak. Helped them to arrange it and so on, and Sir Richard had a word or two to say to me just now about it."

"So *that's* what you've been doing all this time. *That's* your secret!" She was just as pleased as she could be. "That's what's changed you. Of course! One might have guessed!"

But behind her excitement and pleasure he detected also, he thought, a note of disappointment that puzzled him. What had she thought that he had been doing?

"I have just been telling them—the Gales. Sir Richard was considerably annoyed."

"Of course—hateful old man—of course he'd mind; hurt his pride." Mrs. Maradick had clasped her hands round her knees and was swinging a little foot. "But you stood up to them. I wish I'd seen you."

But he hurried on. That was, after all, quite unimportant compared with the main thing that he had to say to her. He wondered how she would take it. The new idea that he had of her, the new way that he saw her, was beginning to be so precious to him, that he couldn't bear to think that he might, after all, suddenly lose it. He could see her, after his telling her, return to the old, sharp, biting satire. There would be the old wrangles, the old furious quarrels; for a moment at the thought of it he hesitated. Perhaps, after all, it were better not to tell her. The episode was ended. There would never be a recrudescence of it, and there was no reason why she should know. But something hurried him on; he must tell her, it was the decent thing to do.

"But there's another thing that I must tell you, that I ought to tell you. I don't know even that I'm ashamed of it. I believe that I would go through it all again if I could learn as much. But it's all over, absolutely over. I've fancied for the last fortnight that I was in love with Mrs. Lester. I've kissed her and she's kissed me. You needn't be afraid. That's all that happened, and I'll never kiss her again. But there it is!"

He flung it at her for her to take it or leave it. He hadn't the remotest idea what she would say or do. Judging by his past knowledge of her, he expected her to storm. But it was a test of the new Mrs. Maradick as to whether, indeed, it had been all his imagination about there being any new Mrs. Maradick at all.

There was silence. He didn't look at her; and then, suddenly, to his utter amazement she broke into peals of laughter. He couldn't believe his ears. Laughing! Well, women were simply incomprehensible! He stared at her.

"Why, my dear!" she said at last, "of course I've seen it all the time. Of course I have, or nearly all the time. You don't suppose that I go about with my eyes shut, do you? Because I don't, I can tell you. Of course I hated it at the time. I was jealous, jealous as anything. First time I've been jealous of you since we were married; I hated that Mrs. Lester anyhow. Cat! But it was an eye-opener, I can tell you. But there've been lots of things happening since we've been here, and that's only one of them. And I'm jolly glad. I like women to like you. I've liked the people down here making up to you, and then you've been different too."

Then she crossed over to his chair and suddenly put her arm around his neck. Her voice lowered. "I've fallen in love with you while we've been down here, for the first time since we've been married. I don't know why, quite. It started with your being so beastly and keeping it up. You always used to give way before whenever I said anything to you, but you've kept your end up like anything since you've been here. And then it was the people liking you better than they liked me. And then it was Mrs. Lester, my being jealous of her. And it was even more than those things—something in the air. I don't know, but I'm seeing things differently. I've been a poor sort of wife most of the time, I expect; I didn't see it before, but I'm going to be different. I could kiss your Mrs. Lester, although I do hate her."

Then when he kissed her she thought how big he was. She hadn't sat with her arms round him and his great muscles round her since the honeymoon, and even then she had been thinking about her trousseau.

And breakfast was quite an extraordinary meal. The girls were amazed. They had never seen their father in this kind of mood before. They had always rather cautiously disliked him, as far as they'd had any feeling for him at all, but their attitude had in the main been negative. But now, here he was joking, telling funny stories, and mother laughing. Cutting the tops off their eggs too, and paying them quite a lot of attention.

He found the meal delightful, too, although he realised that there was still a good deal of the old Mrs. Maradick left. Her voice was as shrill as ever; she was just as cross with Annie for spreading her butter with an eye to self-indulgence rather than economy. She was still as crude and vulgar in her opinion of things and people.

But he didn't see it any longer in the same way. The knowledge that there was really the other Mrs. Maradick there all the time waiting for him to develop, encourage her, made the things that had grated on him at one time so harshly now a matter of very small moment. He was even tender about them. It was a good thing that they'd both got their faults, a very fortunate thing.

"Now, Annie, there you go, slopping your tea into your saucer like that, and now it'll drop all over your dress. Why *can't* you be more careful?"

"Yes, but mother, it was so full."

"I say," this from Maradick, "what do you think of our all having this afternoon down on the beach or somewhere? Tea and things; just ourselves. After all, it's our last day, and it's quite fine and warm. No more rain."

Everyone thought it splendid. Annie, under this glorious new state of things, even found time and courage to show her father her last French exercise with only three mistakes. The scene was domestic for the next half-hour.

Then he left them. He wanted to go and make his farewell to the place; this would be the last opportunity that he would have.

He didn't expect to see the Gales again. After all, there was nothing more for him to say. They had Tony's address. It only remained for Sir Richard to get over it as quickly as he could. Lady Gale would probably manage that. He would like to have spoken to her once more, but really it was as well that he shouldn't. He would write to her.

He discovered before he left the house that another part of the affair was over altogether. As he reached the bottom of the stairs Mrs. Lester crossed the hall, and, for a moment, they faced each other. She looked through him, past him, as though she had never seen him before. Her eyes were hard as steel and as cold. They passed each other silently.

He was not surprised; he had thought that that was the way that she would probably take it. Probably with the morning had come fierce resentment at his attitude and fiery shame at her own. How she could! That would be her immediate thought, and then, very soon after that, it would be that she hadn't at all. He had led her on. And then in a week's time it would probably be virtuous resistance against the persuasions of an odious sensualist. Of course she would never forgive him.

He passed out into the air.

As he went down the hill to the town it struck him that the strange emotional atmosphere that had been about them during these weeks seemed to have gone with the going of Tony. It might be only coincidence, of course, but undoubtedly the boy's presence had had something to do with it all. And then his imagination carried him still further. It was fantastic, of course, but his struggle with Morelli seemed to have put an end to the sort of influence that the man had been having. Because he had had an influence undoubtedly. And now to-day Morelli didn't seem to go for anything at all.

And then it might be, too, that they had all at last got used to the place; it was no longer a fresh thing, but something that they had taken into their brains, their blood. Anyhow, that theory of Lester's about places and people in conjunction having such influence, such power, was interesting. But, evolve what theories he might, of one thing he was certain. There had been a struggle, a tremendous straggle. They had all been concerned in it a little, but it had been his immediate affair.

He turned down the high road towards the town. The day was a "china" day; everything was of the faintest, palest colours, delicate with the delicacy of thin silk, of gossamer lace washed by the rain, as it were, until it was all a symphony of grey and white and a very tender blue. It was a day of hard outlines. The white bulging clouds that lay against the sky were clouds of porcelain; the dark black row of trees that bordered the road stood out from the background as though they had been carved in iron; the ridge of back-lying hills ran like the edge of a sheet of grey paper against the blue; the sea itself seemed to fling marble waves upon a marble shore.

He thought, as he paused before he passed into the town, that he had never seen the sea as it was to-day. Although it was so still and seemed to make no sound at all, every kind of light, like colours caught struggling in a net, seemed to be in it. Mother of pearl was the nearest approach to the beauty of it, but that was very far away. There was gold and pink and grey, and the faintest creamy yellow, and the most delicate greens, and sometimes even a dark edge of black; but it never could be said that this or that colour were there, because it changed as soon as one looked at it and melted into something else; and far away beyond the curving beach the black rocks plunged into the blue, and seemed to plant their feet there and then to raise them a little as the sea retreated.

He passed through the market-place and saluted the tower for the last time. There were very few people about and he could make his adieux in privacy. He would never forget it, its grey and white stone, its immovable strength and superiority to all the rest of its surroundings. He fancied that it smiled farewell to him as he stood there. It seemed to say: "You can forget me if you like; but don't forget what I've taught you—that there's a spirit and a courage and a meaning in us all if you'll look for it. Good-bye; try and be more sensible and see a little farther than most of your silly fellow-creatures." Oh yes! there was contempt in it too, as it stood there with its white shoulders raised so proudly against the sky.

He tenderly passed his hand over some of the rough grey stones in a lingering farewell. Probably he'd been worth something to the tower in an obscure sort of way. He believed enough in its real existence to think it not fantastic that it should recognise his appreciation of it and be glad.

His next farewell was to Punch.

He climbed the little man's dark stairs with some misgiving. He ought to have been in there more just lately, especially after the poor man losing his dog. He owed a great deal to Punch; some people might have found his continual philosophising tiresome, but to Maradick its sincerity and the very wide and unusual experience behind it gave the words a value and authority.

He found Punch sitting on his bed trying to teach the new dog some of the things that it had to learn. He jumped up when he saw Maradick, and his face was all smiles.

"Why, I'm that glad to see you," he said, "I'd been hopin' you'd come in before you were off altogether. Yes, this is the new dog. It ain't much of a beast, only a mongrel, but I didn't want too fine a dog after Toby; it looks like comparison, in a way, and I'm thinkin' it might 'urt 'im, wherever 'e is, if 'e knew that there was this new one takin' 'is place altogether."

The new one certainly wasn't very much of a beast, but it seemed to have an enormous affection for its master and a quite pathetic eagerness to learn.

"But come and sit down, sir. Never mind them shirts, I'll chuck 'em on the floor. No, my boy, we've had enough teachin' for the moment. 'E's got an astonishin' appetite for learnin', that dog, but only a limited intelligence.'"

Maradick could see that Punch didn't want to say any more about Toby, so he asked no questions, but he could see that he felt the loss terribly.

"Well, Garrick," he said, "I've come to say good-bye. We all go back to-morrow, and, on the whole, I don't know that I'm sorry. Things have happened here a bit too fast for my liking, and I'm glad to get out of it with my life, so to speak."

Punch, looked at him a moment, and then he said: "What's happened about young Gale, sir? There are all sorts of stories afloat this morning."

Maradick told him everything.

"Well, that's all for the best. I'm damned glad of it. That girl's well away, and they'll make the prettiest married couple for many a mile. They'll be happy enough. And now, you see for yourself that I wasn't so far out about Morelli after all."

Maradick thought for a moment and then he said: "But look here, Garrick, if Morelli's what you say, if, after all, there's something supernatural about him, he must have known that those two were going to run away; well, if he knew and minded so much, why didn't he stop them?"

"I'm not saying that he did know," said Punch slowly, "and I'm not saying that he wanted to stop them. Morelli's not a man, nor anything real at all. 'E's just a kind of vessel through which emotions pass, if you understand me. The reason, in a way, that 'e expresses Nature is because nothing stays with him. 'E's cruel, 'e's loving, 'e's sad, 'e's happy, just like Nature, because the wind blows, or the rivers run, or the rains fall. 'E's got influence over everything human because 'e isn't 'uman 'imself. 'E isn't a person at all, 'e's just an influence, a current of atmosphere in a man's form.

"There are things, believe me, sir, all about this world that take shape one day like this and another day like that, but they have no soul, no personal identity, that is, because they have no beginning or end, no destiny or conclusion, any more than the winds or the sea. And you look out for yourself when that's near you—it's mighty dangerous."

Maradick said nothing. Punch went on—

"You can't see these things in cities, or in places where you're for ever doing things. You've got to have your mind like an empty room and your eyes must be blind and your ears must be closed, and then, slowly, you'll begin to hear and see."

Maradick shook his head. "No, I don't understand," he said. "And when I get back to my regular work again I shall begin to think it's all bunkum. But I do know that I've been near something that I've never touched before. There's something in the place that's changed us all for a moment. We'll all go back and be all the same again; but things can't ever be quite the same again for me, thank God."

Punch knocked out his pipe against the heel of his boot.

"Man," he said suddenly, "if you'd just come with me and walk the lanes and the hills I'd show you things. You'd begin to understand." He gripped Maradick's arm. "Come with me," he said, "leave all your stupid life; let me show you the real things. It's not worth dying with your eyes shut."

For a moment something in Maradick responded. For a wild instant he thought that he would say yes. Then he shook his head.

"No, David, my friend," he answered. "That's not my life. There's my wife, and there are others. That's my line. But it will all be different now. I shan't forget."

Punch smiled. "Well, perhaps you're right. You've got your duty. But just remember that it isn't only children we men and women are begetting. We're creating all the time. Every time that you laugh at a thought, every time that you're glad, every time that you're seeing beauty and saying so, every time that you think it's better to be decent than not, better to be merry than sad, you're creating. You're increasing the happy population of the world. Young Gale was that, and now you've found it too. That's religion; it's obvious enough. Plenty of other folks have said the same, but precious few have done it."

Then, as they said good-bye, he said—

"And remember that I'm there if you want me. I'll always come. I'm always ready. All winter I'm in London. You'll find me in the corner by the National Gallery, almost opposite the Garrick Theatre, with my show, most nights; I'm your friend always."

And Maradick knew as he went down the dark stairs that that would not be the last that he would see of him.

He climbed, for the last time, up the hill that ran above the sea. Its hard white line ran below him to the town, and above him across the moor through the little green wood that fringed the hill. For a moment his figure, black and tiny, was outlined against the sky. There was a wind up here and it swept around his feet.

Far below him the sea lay like a blue stone, hard and sharply chiselled. Behind him the white road curved like a ribbon above him, and around him was the delicate bending hollow of the sky.

For a moment he stood there, a tiny doll of a man.

The wind whistled past him laughing. Three white clouds sailed majestically above his head. The hard black body of the wood watched him tolerantly.

He passed again down the white road.

CHAPTER XXI
SIX LETTERS

The Elms, Epsom.
October 17.

MY DEAREST LOUIE,

I've been meaning to write all this week, but so many things have accumulated since we've been away that there's simply not been a minute to write a decent letter. No, Treliss wasn't very nice this time. You know, dear, the delightful people that were there last year? Well, there were none of them this year at all except that Mrs. Lawrence, who really got on my nerves to such an extent!

There were some people called Gale we saw something of—Lady and Sir Richard Gale. I must say I thought them rather bad form, but Jim liked them; and then their boy eloped with a girl from the town, which made it rather thrilling, especially as Sir Richard was simply furious with Jim because he thought that he'd had something to do with it. And you can't imagine how improved dear old Jim is with it all, really quite another man, and so amusing when he likes; and people quite ran after him there, you wouldn't have believed it. There was a horrid woman, a Mrs. Lester, who would have gone to any lengths, I really believe, only, of course, Jim wasn't having any. I always said that he could be awfully amusing if he liked and really nice, and he's been going out quite a lot since we've been back and everybody's noticed the difference.

And what do you think? We may be leaving Epsom! I know it'll be simply hateful leaving you, dear, but it'll only be London, you know, and you can come up whenever you like and stay just as long as you please, and we'll be awfully glad. But Epsom is a little slow, and what Jim says is quite true—why not be either town or country? It's what

I've always said, you know, and perhaps we'll have a little cottage somewhere as well.

By the way, dear, as you are in town I wish you'd just look in at Harrod's and see about those patterns. Two and elevenpence is much too much, and if the ones at two and sixpence aren't good enough you might ask for another sort!

Do come and see us soon. I might come up for a matinée some day soon. Write and let me know.

Your loving

EMMY.

To Anthony Gale, Esq.,
     20 Tryon Square,
          Chelsea, S.W.

MY DEAR BOY,

I was very glad to get your letter this morning. You've been amazingly quick about settling in, but then I expect that Janet's an excellent manager. I'll be delighted to come to dinner next Wednesday night, and shall look forward enormously to seeing you both and the kind of home that you have. I can't tell you what a relief it is to me to hear that you are both so happy. Of course I knew that you would be and always, I hope, will be, but the responsibility on my part was rather great and I wanted to hear that it was all right. I'm so glad that your mother likes Janet so much. I knew that they would get on, and I hope that very soon your father will come as well and make everything all right in that direction. We're all quite settled down here again now; well, not quite. Treliss has left its mark on both of us, and we're even thinking—don't jump out of your chair with excitement—of coming up to London to live. A little wider life will suit both of us better now, I think. Nothing is settled yet, but I'm going to look about for a house.

Treliss did rather a lot for all of us, didn't it? It all seems a little incredible, really; but you've got Janet to show you that it's real enough, and I've got, well, quite a lot of things, so that it can't have been all a dream.

Well until Wednesday. Then I'll hear all the news.

My affection to Janet.

Your friend,
JAMES MARADICK.

To James Maradick,
The Elms, Epsom.

20 Tryon Square,
Chelsea, S.W.
October 25, 1909.

MY DEAR MARADICK,

Hurray! I'm so glad that you can come on Wednesday, but I'm just wild with joy that you are really coming to live in London. Hurray again! Only you must, you positively must come to live in Chelsea. It's the only possible place. Everybody who is worth knowing lives here, including a nice intelligent young couple called Anthony and Janet Gale. The house—our house—is simply ripping. All white and distempered by your humble servant; and Janet's been simply wonderful. There's nothing she can't do, and everybody all over the place loves her. We haven't had a word from her father, so I don't suppose that he's going to take any more trouble in that direction, but I heard from Garrick the other day—you remember Punch—and he says that he saw him not long ago sitting on the shore and piping to the waves with a happy smile on his face. Isn't he rum?

The Minns is here and enjoying herself like anything. She's bought a new bonnet and looks no end—my eye! And what do you think? Who should turn up this morning but the governor! Looking awfully cross at first, but he couldn't stand against Janet; and he went away as pleased as anything, and says we must have a better sideboard in the dining-room, and he's going to give us one. Isn't that ripping? The writing's getting on. I met a fellow at tea the other day, Randall, he's editor of the *New Monthly*; he was a bit slick up, but quite decent, and now he's taken one of my things, and I've had quite a lot of reviewing.

Well, good-bye, old chap. You know that Janet and I would rather have you here than anyone else in the world, except the mater, of course. We owe you everything. Buck up and come here to live. Love from Janet.

Your affect.
TONY.

To LADY GALE,

12 Park Lane, W.

Rossholm,
Nr. Dartford, Kent,
October 25.

MY DEAR,

This is only a hurried little scrawl to say that Fred and I are going to be up in town for a night next week and should awfully like to see you if it's possible. Fred's dining that night with some silly old writer, so if I might just come in and have a crumb with you I'd be awfully glad. Fred and I have both decided that we didn't like Treliss a bit this year and we're never going there again. If it hadn't been for you I simply don't know what we'd have done. There's something about the place.

Fred felt it too, only he thought it was indigestion. And then the people! I know you rather liked those Maradick people. But I thought the man perfectly awful. Of course one had to be polite, but, my dear, I really don't think he's very nice, not quite the sort of man—oh well! you know! Not that I'd say anything against him for the world, but there's really no knowing how far one can go with a man of that kind. But of course I scarcely saw anything of them.

How is Tony? I hear that they've settled in Chelsea. Is Sir Richard reconciled? You must tell me everything when we meet. Fred—he is such a pet just now—sends regards.

Ever
Your loving
MILLY.

To JAMES MARADICK, ESQ.,
The Elms, Epsom.

12 Park Lane, W.
October 21.

DEAR MR. MARADICK,

I've been wanting to write to you for some days, but so many things crowd about one in London, and even now I've only got a moment. But I thought that you would like to know that both my husband and myself have been to see Tony in Chelsea and that we think Janet perfectly charming. My husband was conquered by her at once; one simply cannot help loving her. She is no fool either. She is managing that house splendidly, and has got a good deal more common-sense than Tony has.

Of course now you'll say that we ought to have shown her to Sir Richard at once if he's got to like her so much. But that isn't so. I'm quite sure that he would never have allowed the marriage if there'd been a chance of it's being prevented. But now he's making the best of it, and it's easy enough when it's Janet.

I think he feels still sore at your having "interfered," as he calls it, but that will soon wear off and then you must come and see us. Alice Du Cane is staying with us. She has been so much improved lately, much more human; she's really a charming girl.

And meanwhile, how can I thank you enough for all that you have I done? I feel as though I owed you everything. It won't bear talking or writing about, but I am more grateful than I can ever say.

But keep an eye on Tony. He is devoted to you. He is still very young, and you can do such a lot for him.

Please remember me to your wife.

I am,

Yours very sincerely,

Lucy Gale.

To James Maradick, Esq.,
  The Elms, Epsom.

On the road to Ashbourne,

Derbyshire.

11 a.m.

I'm sitting under a hedge with this bit of paper on my knee; dirty you'll be thinking it, but I find that waiting for paper means no letter at all, and so it's got to be written when the moment's there. I'm tramping north—amongst the lakes I'm making for. It's fine weather and a hard white road, and the show's been going strong these last days. There's a purple line of hills behind me, and a sky that'll take a lot of poet's talking to glorify it, and a little pond at the turn of the road that's bluer than blue-bells.

The new dog's none so stupid as I thought him; not that he's Toby, but he's got a sense of humour on him that's more than a basketful of intelligence. Last night I was in a fine inn with a merry company. I wish that you could have heard the talking, but you'll have been dining with your napkin on your knee and a soft carpet at your feet. There was a fine fellow last night that had seen the devil last week walking on the high ridge that goes towards Raddlestone. Maybe it was Morelli; like enough. He's often round that way. I'm thinking of you often, and I'll be back in London, November. I'd like to have you out here, with stars instead of chimney pots and a red light where the sun's setting.

I'll write again from the North.

Yours very faithfully,

DAVID GARRICK.

CHAPTER XXII
THE PLACE

It is twilight. The cove is sinking with its colours into the evening mists. The sea is creeping very gently over the sand, that shines a little with the wet marks that the retreating tide has left.

The rocks, the hills, the town, rise behind the grey mysterious floor that stretches without limit into infinite distance in black walls sharply outlined against the night blue of the sky.

There is only one star. Some sheep are crying in a fold.

A cold wind passes like a thief over the sand. The sea creeps back relentlessly, ominously . . . eternally.